Wild Rose

www.coteaubooks.com

Wild Rose

SHARON BUTALA

COTEAU BOOKS

Edited by Dave Margoshes
Book designed by Tania Craan
Cover image by Lee, Russell, 1903-1986, Library of Congress LC-USF33-012666-M2
Typeset by Susan Buck
Printed and bound in Canada at Friesens

Library and Archives Canada Cataloguing in Publication

Butala, Sharon, 1940-, author
Wild rose / Sharon Butala.

Issued in print and electronic formats.
ISBN 978-1-55050-636-5 (pbk.).--ISBN 978-1-55050-643-3 (pdf).--
ISBN 978-1-55050-868-0 (epub).--ISBN 978-1-55050-875-8 (mobi

I. Title.

PS8553.U6967W55 2015 C813'.54 C2015-902954-6

C2015-902955-4

2517 Victoria Avenue
Regina, Saskatchewan
Canada S4P 0T2
www.coteaubooks.com

Available in Canada from:
Publishers Group Canada
2440 Viking Way
Richmond, British Columbia
Canada V6V 1N2

10 9 8 7 6 5 4

Coteau Books gratefully acknowledges the financial support of its publishing program by: the Saskatchewan Arts Board, The Canada Council for the Arts, the Government of Saskatchewan through Creative Saskatchewan, the City of Regina. We further acknowledge the [financial] support of the Government of Canada. Nous reconnaissons l'appui [financier] du gouvernement du Canada.

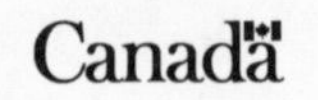

This book is dedicated to the women
who settled western Canada
and
especially to my aunts
Cécile (now in her nineties)
and Germaine (in her eighties)
both née Le Blanc

contents

CHAPTER ONE • Wind 1

CHAPTER TWO • Spiritus Sanctus 16

CHAPTER THREE • La région sauvage 22

CHAPTER FOUR • Sanctuary 48

CHAPTER FIVE • Introibo ad Altare Dei I 76

CHAPTER SIX • Angels 106

CHAPTER SEVEN • Beginning 120

CHAPTER EIGHT • Bone Pile 150

CHAPTER NINE • Introibo ad Altare Dei II 182

CHAPTER TEN • Night Music 206

CHAPTER ELEVEN • Saecula Saeculorum 239

CHAPTER TWELVE • Work 259

CHAPTER THIRTEEN • Fire 292

CHAPTER FOURTEEN • Winter 322

CHAPTER FIFTEEN • Return 342

CHAPTER SIXTEEN • Le village 365

CHAPTER ONE

Wind

THE FIRST NIGHT she hardly noticed he was gone, and even though she had expected him back before the moon rose, she slept soundly. Probably, she thought, he has stopped overnight at the Beausoleil's so he and Napoléon can have a good chin wag and a glass of brandy together. He will surely be back by ten tomorrow morning. Charles asked, *"Papa?"* more than once, but a crust of bread, a sip of milk, a song complete with nose-touching and hand-patting, soon made him forget his father's absence. The second night, though, the slightest sound disturbed her, twice she rose from her bed, carefully, so as not to wake her son, and peered out their cabin's one window onto the moonlit prairie, but there was no one to be seen, not even a wild animal. Not that there was anything to fear – grizzlies were rarely seen anymore, indeed they had never seen one, only their droppings. The cabin walls kept out any wolves or rare mountain lion, and the Indians, subdued since the rebellion, posed no threat to settlers, if they ever had. And yet, all night she felt uneasy, lying for long periods awake, changing positions in the bed cautiously and, if Charles moved, holding still until he lapsed back into sleep.

Toward dawn, drowsing, she came awake with a start to a low moan in the distance – ceaseless, growing louder as it advanced toward the cabin, until, arriving, it pushed against the cabin walls, the furred body of a great animal blundering determinedly by, the force of its desire set always on something further on, at the far edge of the prairie, while she lay, already tense, listening over the wind's noise for the sound of hoofbeats, or the creak of the wagon's approach.

Again, she fell asleep and this time slept deeply, opening her eyes to stained canvas walls that swelled, then collapsed inward with gusts of wind. Pierre lay snoring beside her, and she tried once more to orient herself. A tent. She was back in the canvas tent they had set up on the prairie while they built their small house. The sloping ceiling had turned from greyish white to a burning golden-yellow, meaning the sun was up and they had overslept, both of them, exhausted as they were from the hammering and lifting, from the dragging and the sorting. Around their cots the sacks of their perishable goods – flour, sugar – leaned against each other waiting for the sod roof to be finished on the house. Wind caught the closed tent-flap door and snapped it noisily, as if to say *rise, there is work to be done*. Then she was working in her garden, pulling weeds. The soil, usually thin and a pale brown, now rich and dark as the garden of her grandparents' house back in Québec and she worked doggedly, pulling and digging, checking the tiny plants, saying a prayer to them to grow. Then she was standing alone in the endless sweep of strange prairie grasses and small flowering plants, the wind tearing at her skirt and apron, her face turned upward to the sun, and all around her a music rose that seemed to be made of rippling grass, birdsong, a throaty murmuring from the earth itself, and a high-pitched keening from the sky that rose and fell with the music of the wind. She saw all of it would sweep her away; she wasn't afraid, lifted her arms in preparation, pulled the fastenings from her hair and loosening the buttons at her throat, then her bodice, until she had bared her breasts to the elements and the music.

She woke then, still feeling the heat of the sun on her bosom and throat, and lay stunned, trying to come awake to the day, and the cabin, and the fact of Pierre's continuing absence. But she couldn't catch her breath, and her heart fluttered and tripped against her skin, each hair on her head bristling with its own life. She pulled herself to a sitting position and gazed into the shadows of the room where everything sat as it always had, rough and shabby, waiting for her to begin work. Her breath slowed to normal, her heart retreated into its cage and resumed its steady beat; even the hair on her head lay subdued. Such a dream! She lifted herself from the bed and padded to the pail of water where she filled the dipper and drank thirstily from it. Morning, and still no Pierre. Now the dream dwindled fully and vanished. Both elated and frightened by it, not daring to pursue it, she let it go, for there was exigency this morning to which she must attend. Where was Pierre?

But this was not the first time he had failed to return home when he said he would. Once, it had been a deluge of rain that turned the trail to gumbo, forcing him to camp until it dried enough for the team and wagon to get through. Another time, when a wheel had broken on a rock he had failed to notice on the trail, he'd stayed at the Beausoleil's while he and Napoléon repaired it. This past winter he stayed two nights with l'anglais, Harry Adamson, whose shack was at the edge of the village by the trail that led into the wilderness and home. Night was falling, Adamson had seen Pierre trying to get his horses to face into the growing blizzard sweeping up from across the American border. Pierre wasn't good with horses, a more serious weakness in a settler – although one never to be mentioned – than Sophie would have guessed. His horses knew better than Pierre. In the spring, to the west, the bodies of two unnamed travellers were found huddled by the trail.

"Adamson, he didn't even put a coat on," Pierre had told her in his dramatic way – the flash of light in his black eyes, the quick lift of chin, his black hair tossed from his forehead, his smile. "He came rushing out in the wind and the snow – he caught Belle by the bridle and shouted to me, *"Venez–vous a moi! Chez moi!* I could barely understand his French! But –" his shrug, wide-handed, his mouth comically pursed, his eyes full of merriment, so that, imagining that excellent, overly-large bachelor in his crudely mended trousers, she had laughed too.

She hadn't the energy in this too-early morning, in this late summer of unending dryness and oven-like heat, the fourth of their sojourn here, and now, in his worrisome absence, to feel anything at the memory of that gesture. Once, that movement had brought heat to her face and chest, so that after he had left, as she walked in her grandparents' garden in the Québec village where she'd been raised, she would fan herself, and ponder in wonder, dismay, and some half-denied delight, the deep-seated sensation by which she'd been overcome whenever he fixed those dark eyes on hers, smiled, and tossed back that lock of hair. She hadn't understood then that what she felt wasn't so much love, as she had thought, as physical desire. But no, she thought, remembering again how overcome she was when at last she was freely able to put her fingers in his hair, her palm against his cheek, her mouth against his. She had been in love with him since the first kiss by her great-uncle Henri's graveside – no, sooner, since she was a child and with grandfather, visiting the Hippolyte farm. Surely, she corrected herself, there is no separating love from such desire.

On the third morning since his departure, the stillness came as it always did, the only sound, the piping of small birds in the buff-coloured grass, the occasional call from a single coyote somewhere toward the west where the land rose, hazy and mauve, into a line of low hills. It was her favourite time of day, strolling to the barn with Charles walking at her side as the sun climbed slowly above the horizon sending its first gold, then yellow rays across the grass, the light rising higher, soon blotting out the stars. And the heat, even so early, beginning.

At the barn she pumped the trough full of water, then opened the corral gate so that their five cows could move out to spend the day grazing on the prairie, while she kept a constant eye on them to see that they didn't venture near the crop or her garden so parched in the heat. She turned Fleurette, her milk cow, into the pole corral, gave her hay, and milked her while the cow munched contentedly. Charles wandered, chirping to himself, picking up an insect and bringing it to her to admire, whether crushed to a bloody pulp on his palm or crawling up his arm. *Papa?* he thought to ask, but not waiting for an answer, toddled off to whatever new matter had caught his attention: a yellow wildflower quivering under the weight of a bee, a tiny green snake slithering into the grass. All the while the warm milk hissing into the wooden pail, and birds singing their morning song in the still, clear air, and the sun rising higher, a bath of lemon and gold light lifting the night-dull prairie into the blaze of day. Then she and Charles let the chickens out of their shed, and gathered whatever eggs they could find. Last, she led Tonerre, Pierre's saddle horse, and Fleurette, one by one out onto the prairie, pounded tethering pins into the ground, tied them, and left them to graze. One day soon there would be fences, but for now, not being able to risk losing either animal, tethering pins would have to do.

Later, Charles leaned his sturdy little body against her knee as she stood looking out the open cabin door across the unending expanse of grass. So intense was the heat that at the far horizon the earth lifted, shivered, melted slowly downward to rise again, so that sometimes she could see the land on the far side of the upward tilt of the plain floating, the palest aqua, low in the sky. She gazed, sweeping the quivering horizon, searching for the first sign of someone approaching, a darker spot in the wavering heat, tiny, growing bigger by infinitesimal degrees, until she could decide if she saw a wild thing, or horse or cow, or human.

She could feel through her skirt how hot Charles was, and she bent and lifted him into her arms. He settled his head into the crook of her shoulder and she kissed his cheek, patting his damp back at the same time. He lifted his head and said into her ear, *"Maman?"* And then, letting his head return to that curve of neck and shoulder where it fitted perfectly, *"Où est Papa?"* Such a bright child, she thought, only three and speaking so well. Already she was worrying about where he would go to school. Would she have to send him away? And where would she find the money to do that? She had been no scholar herself, nor was she much good at the skills the nuns and her grandmother had insisted on, her fingers still prickling at the thought of all the embroidery. Even her devil-may-care Pierre complained when the socks she had darned for him raised blisters. But for her little Charles all would be different. She would find a school where the teachers would cherish her bright boy and teach him well.

She said in English, "Soon papa will come 'ome." Then, correcting herself, "Home," aspirating the "h" carefully and adding, *"Bientôt."* She wanted Charles to speak both languages and spoke to him in her own imperfect English, never hesitating, on the few occasions she was with the English–speaking settlers' wives, or the few women in town, to enquire how one said this or that, finding them only too eager to help as if she, a heathen and an *idiote*, had at last come to her senses. Then she would practice on the way home, irritating Pierre with her efforts.

"We are Québécois," he would insist to her. "We are French."

"Can't you see?" she would say. "Already settlers come from other places – they all learn English. Everyone who is important here is English. If we are to survive, we must learn English too." But Pierre merely grimaced, and if she insisted, he would shout. She had faltered only during the rebellion, especially after they hung Riel, and wondered for a while if it was a mistake to throw in their lot with les anglais.

Then their perfect peace, or so she thought of it, had been disturbed by the fear running through all the settlers, men riding from one tiny, isolated farmstead to the next to ask of news, to try to think of plans for the safety of their wives and children should the Indians rise up too, and kill them all. Or the mad Métis.

"We are French," she had argued. "They will not harm us."

"Oh, so now we are French," Pierre had bellowed at her, and in front of Napoléon Beausoleil. Exasperated and embarrassed, glaring at him, she had snapped back, "We cannot be anything else, of course. But we must be practical, Pierre," a pleading note entering her voice. She knew Beausoleil thought her mad: To be French was to be French, that was all there was to it. One didn't argue about it, or mitigate it; one was, and would always be. She gritted her teeth, holding back her argument, that one could be French privately and among other French people, while in the larger community working to fit in. In her mind it was simple, and not one whit treasonous, as the men clearly thought.

And were not the Beausoleils their only neighbours for miles in any direction on this never-ending, boundless plain? Somewhere far to the east there were swamps and bogs and near-impenetrable forests of pine and spruce that went on forever before one reached Toronto and then Montréal. Below them lay the United States of America, much-longer settled than the newcomers they knew themselves to be, where, if one went far enough, the winding trails made by wagons and mule trains or teams of oxen had become real roads. Where there were schools and churches and governments elected by the local people, unlike them who, despite the Territorial Council, were truly still governed from the East. To the West, equally impenetrable, the Rocky Mountains, snow-covered at their summits all the year round she had heard, and then the rainforest and the ocean. Above them, the north, everyone said fit only for the Indians and the Eskimos. Legion upon legion of trees, then tundra, then unimaginable millions of acres of ice and snow leading to a frozen bluish-white sea. No, Beausoleil had ridden half a day to see them. For half a day he had ridden his plow horse across the undulating sun-cured grasses of this blessed golden plain, seeing not another soul, and if he rode on, as he said he might, it would be more than another half day before he again found a settler's flimsy shack rising grey and shabby, a miniscule dot above the lie of land and beneath the endless dome of sky. She had said, then, "Dear Monsieur Beausoleil, do share our meal before you go on. We will say a rosary to speed you on your way." She had felt Pierre relaxing.

Now she asked, "Are you hungry, Charles?"

"*Oui*, Maman," he replied, and she said, automatically, "Yes, Mother," but he was intent on a lock of her hair that had come untucked.

She went back inside, closing the door behind her to keep out mosquitoes and flies – a hopeless task, that one – and set her son down, waiting for her eyes to adjust to the interior gloom. They could afford only one window, so as long as the weather allowed, they spent most of their waking hours outside. If she were cooking, though, she hurried inside every few minutes to make sure the chimney hadn't overheated. In their first year, there had been a prairie fire to the north, flames leaping more than a hundred feet in the air, devastating the grassland for many miles killing everything in its path from wildlife to cattle and horses, and burning out every settler's shack in its way. All that long night they had waited, watching, falling asleep to wake with a start, the wagon loaded, the horses in harness, ready to run should the wind shift. She would never forget how terrifying it was as the horizon blazed against the black sky and the wind blew eastward in howling gales.

Charles's eyes seemed to need no time to adjust. As soon as she put him down he was attracted by an ant struggling across the rough wooden floor, and toddled toward it, his fat little hand outstretched, murmuring to it. What quick eyes he has, she thought, and would have laughed at herself except that how could any child be quicker or more curious than Charles? And where was Pierre?

What if he has had a runaway and was thrown from the wagon and lay, all his bones broken, somewhere on the prairie? Four years ago when she and Pierre had begun to search for the quarter of land they had filed on in Swift Current, the entire area was nearly empty of other people. But since then, more of them crisscrossed the prairie on their way here and there. Some stopping to ask Pierre for advice in finding a section or quarter-section stake, miles away from Sophie and Pierre's cabin, so that she thought they stopped more out of fear, and to hear a human voice not their own. And now, the newcomers, too, those who stayed, stood in their cabin doors as she did, gazing out across the stiff pale grass, and spotted every rock, every animal, and if they could not at first tell a rock from a cow, it did not take long for them to educate themselves: horses as black strokes against the tawny landscape, cows black dots. She did not believe Pierre was lying half-dead on the prairie. He followed trails; someone would have seen him as a still black spot where one had not been before. Someone would have found him.

Yet she could see no reason why his trip to the blacksmith in town to repair a broken part from his binder in such perfect travelling weather should take so long. He drank yes, what man did not enjoy a glass of wine, or a brandy now and then, but he was not a drunkard as so many of the men in the West seemed to be, no doubt because they had no women to remind them of a normal way of life. What else to expect when no single woman could even apply for free land?

She thought back to the morning Pierre had left. He came to the house, the horses already hitched, the broken part, she assumed, tossed into the wagon-box. He had seemed angry, in a hurry, ignoring Charles who had called, "*Papa, papa*," so she hadn't questioned him, didn't even ask him to get her this or that, not even if she might go with him. A sheen of sweat lay on his forehead, a line of it trickled down his neck, but then, he'd been cutting wheat since not long past dawn, and the morning was such that heat came up off the prairie in billows, as if it was the earth itself churning it up. He hadn't once looked into her face, and that had also troubled her.

Charles climbed into his seat at the table, and she picked his bowl from the shelf and at the stove spooned a little of the porridge she had made the evening before when the prairie cooled and it was possible to make a fire in the stove without fainting from its heat, then carried it to the table where she set it in front of him. Guillaume and Claire had sent the bowl for Charles when he was born, and the shiny silver spoon too, in which he could see his own face upside down, and that, no matter how many ways he turned it, to his eternal mystification, remained upside down. She poured a little of the pitcher of cream she had separated earlier in the morning onto the porridge.

"Careful, *c'est chaud!*" She said to Charles, as she always said to him, sitting down beside him, and taking the spoon from his hand to demonstrate yet again, "It's hot, very hot. Blow, blow very hard." She gave the spoon back to him and Charles blew, sending porridge in all directions, grinning happily into her face.

She rose and went to the door again, opened it and stared once more out over the prairie to the southeast where the village of Bone Pile sat some ten miles away, then she turned to look out to where Pierre had left the binder against the last row of cut wheat, at the other end of the field from where she stood. He had made a few stooks, but they ended far back from where the binder sat. He wouldn't allow her to stook for him, having some prejudice about what a woman of her sort could and could not be asked to do that he refused to relax even in the face of their need. Hadn't she helped build their house? Hadn't she carried sods to him? Hadn't she delivered Charles with only Madame Beausoleil to help? Didn't she dig the soil of her garden herself, waiting for a spring rain to soften the ground, and planting seeds his mother saved and sent West with her? She could be stooking behind the binder, speeding up the harvest. This, their best crop yet: the first year, only five acres plowed, there were so many other things needing doing: the second year twenty, the third year nearly double that, and now, sixty acres seeded to crop, and where was he? She was terrified a storm might come and they would lose it all, even thought of getting on the binder herself and cutting more crop, or stooking what hadn't been done yet, even though he would be angry. And what to do with Charles if she did? Tie him beside her to the binder seat? What was it Pierre wanted from her, besides a child, besides a home, besides her unbounded love for him? She watched the sky, cloudless and distant, and the land, flattened now by the high, clear light, without seeing them.

She was thinking of her first summer here. She had been fearless, riding Tonerre by herself to search for berry patches – had picked pails of Saskatoons and chokecherries, once near the creek a mile to the north where Saskatoon bushes grew abundantly on the banks among the wild roses and wolf willow, beside a group of native women, not even knowing they were there, until they came through the bushes to pick side by side with her. Sophie, unsure what to do, until one of them reached silently in front of her, pulled down a fruit-laden branch she couldn't reach, and held it for her as Sophie stripped its fruit.

"*Merci,*" she had said, smiling, but the Indian woman did not speak or smile, and slipped away through the bushes. Sometimes she thought that perhaps she had dreamt that strange, silent encounter, for it was rare these days to see even one lone Indian, much less a group of them. Bees buzzing by, flies whispering around them, the air rich with the scent of the roses and grasses, the sun bronzing all their skins with its relentless heat, the sky pale and far away. Why was she then so unafraid? Her first taste of freedom, her soul free at last and spreading out as far as the plains allowed – forever – there being no end to them. Or, it might have been the wind; sometimes she was sure it was the wind, what it carried, heat from the sun, glinting particles of sun-matter, scents she had never before smelled, the very distance the wind had covered to reach her.

She thought of the plagues of mosquitoes, the never-ending swarms of flies, of the thunder and lightning storms followed by rains so heavy and intense that it would be days before they could leave the homestead, even this blazing heat, and in winter its opposite, so cold sometimes that they had had to wear all their clothes in bed to keep warm. This past one had been the very worst of all their winters here, with snow several feet deep on the level, except when a hurricane force wind blew it into ten foot drifts, and bitterly cold day following bitterly cold day, and day after day Pierre shovelling the snow down from the roof and away from the door. She and Pierre had survived only because they had a good supply of food and fuel. But it was a life of their own, a thing they could never have had in the comfortable, God-loving village from which they had come. It was *la grande aventure*; it had shown her what it meant to be alive.

Behind her, Charles murmured to himself and struck his spoon against his bowl gently to listen to the sound the glass made. Still no trace of anything moving far out over the prairie, only a pair of hunting hawks circling above, their shrieks reaching faintly down through layers of blue to where she stood alone in the cabin doorway, puzzling over her husband's absence. Two nights now, and soon three days.

She knew before she knew; maybe she had always known it, the sudden weight of her knowing buckling her knees, so that she slumped against the door frame, clinging to it so as not to fall, terror at what would become of her and her child seizing her before a single clear image of perils ahead emerged. She made her way, staggering, to the wooden table in front of the stove where her babe played with his porridge and sang to himself, fell into the first chair, the one in which Pierre always sat. A roaring was in her ears; her breath came quickly: *Pierre wasn't coming back. Pierre had left them.*

The room's shadows had taken on a strange, bruise-like colour. She held the tabletop with both hands as if the cabin were a ship at sea tilting to the left and to the right; bile rose into her throat and she swallowed, forcing herself to breathe evenly through her nose until her stomach quieted and the room stopped its crazed pitching. Charles was carefully putting a fingertip into his porridge, lifting a tiny dollop, then placing it on the table top, pausing to consider it, then reaching for another and placing it beside the first. She watched the care with which he did this, even in her fear and shock marvelling at the precision a three-year-old could muster.

Tears sprang into her eyes. She wept copiously for less than a minute before fear returned, lifting her to her feet so abruptly she knocked over the chair and Charles looked up and would have wept had she not leaned over him quickly, kissing his dark hair, briefly caressing his face.

Back to the door, opening it again, this time with hands that shook. He hated the hard labour of plowing virgin soil from sunrise to sundown; it troubled him deeply to see what the sun and constant wind were doing to his handsome face, how his hands were thickened and scarred. *Voyez!* he had shouted at her, lifting them to her face. She had gazed silently at her own, pleading, "It is honest labour. Soon we will have a crop." He had turned away, pushed open the door and gone out onto the prairie. She should have known then that they would be leaving their homestead, for town, she supposed, where there were people, real houses, a community, where he would find some sort of work to do. Or perhaps he'd been planning to return to Québec. But if so, wouldn't he have taken them? How could he make such a decision and never once ask her? When they had vowed to be one, to think as one, to work together as one? Was he not the only possible man for her life?

Wherever he had gone, it was not back to Québec where he would be shamed and worse if she and Charles weren't with him. Where then? North to the Métis communities near Prince Albert? Farther West to the French villages near Fort Edmonton? No, that would only be more of the same. More likely he had gone south to cross the border into the United States. The border had barely been established there, there were no guards nearby; crossing it would be easy. Or – he could have had trouble getting his broken part fixed. Maybe he had to go on to Swift Current or even to Garden City where – but no. Even if he had gone on, he would have been back by now. He would have sent a messenger. Wouldn't he have?

Wait! Why did he take the wagon and team if he knew he was leaving forever? Why didn't he just saddle the horse he loved so much and gallop away across the prairie as he had done more than once before? But she had been washing clothes the day he left and had noticed nothing missing from his meagre wardrobe. He hadn't loaded the wagon with any of his belongings, so why did he not take Tonerre?

Charles had grown tired of his porridge game, climbed down from the table and was once again pursuing an ant. She said aloud, "Pierre has left with a woman." Charles looked up from where he squatted in his pursuit and asked, *"Maman?"*

"He has taken a woman with him." Her child came clumsily toward her, one hand out as if to offer comfort. That is why he took the team and wagon and not his beloved saddle horse. How long has he been seeing a woman? Who is she? But he has no money – how could he – unless she has money – but, wait, I have no money, I have only this farm, this half-done harvest, this one horse and few cows he has left me, an aging milk cow. He has left our child!

She clutched her head to stop her brain's skittering, then released it, began to pace, fists clenched, feet thudding on the rough wooden floor. Back and forth she went until she noticed that Charles, laughing uncertainly, had begun to toddle after her. This halted her and she lifted him again, burying her face in his silky hair – Pierre's hair – clutching him tightly to her. *I am abandoned!*

A wave of shame engulfed her, melding before she could stop it into longing: His smooth skin, golden beside her whiteness, his black hair, blacker even than hers, and gleaming black eyes, his muscled torso, arms, and thighs – for a second, she couldn't breathe. But – he loves me so! She could feel by the weight of her child, his warm body molded to hers, that he had fallen asleep. He would sleep an hour, two hours, and she would think. She would find out what to do. She carried him into the bedroom and carefully placed him on the bed, pushing a chair against its edge so that he wouldn't roll off onto the floor. She returned to the kitchen and began to clean the porridge from the table, and then to sweep the floor. She worked slowly, with extreme care, missing not a particle of food or dirt, as if important guests were coming.

The crop! She paused in her careful sweeping. She couldn't farm without him. Would she have to sell the farm to get money to buy train tickets to return to Québec? She faltered, because returning to Québec struck no chord of joy, the opposite, rather, and fear and disgust, all that she had escaped coming back to her as well as the fact that she could never return, tail between her legs, and no one to take her in. Then the image appeared involuntarily behind her eyelids of the plain spreading endlessly in every direction, glowing as if with its own light.

She thought of the few French women in town – the pretty ones –

there was only Madame Clothilde Le Fèbvre, but wait, hadn't they moved on? Or…the unmarried daughter of those newcomers, Marguerite – she could not recall the family name. Or – maybe the woman had left behind an angry husband. Maybe *he* would go after them and bring them both back. Or the father. And the loss of her own poor dead father, of whom she hadn't thought much for years, loomed before her now, and she felt she would weep forever over him even though he had been dead since her early childhood, as had her mother, and – if only my brothers were here! Guillaume would go after Pierre, or Hector. Even in her turmoil she turned her mind from Hector as quickly as she thought of him.

Stop such foolishness, she told herself, because her brothers wouldn't come running to save her. They might not even send money so she could go home, Guillaume angry already, Hector uncaring. Banished. He was banished too, but the faceless woman with whom Pierre had run away blotted out random thoughts of her brothers. She imagined the slender curving line that ran from the woman's girlish bosom to the swell of her hip, the waist as narrow as hers had been before Charles, bent and retched, tasting the bile of her husband's hatred of her that she had never even seen. But he hid it from me – he knew he was wrong! Yet, he left anyway. She despised him, she told herself, but she didn't, she yearned for him; she even dared to hope this was all her own foolish mistake, that he would come across the plains with the new part for his machine, he would laugh at her terror, he would hold her…

She went to the door one last time to stare out across the prairie. Far in the distance, shimmering through the waves of heat rising off the land, someone approached. She waited, her hands pressed against her chest. The black spot drew closer, it was a team of horses – no, a single horse pulling – what? She waited again, saw that it was a buggy, not a wagon, that another horse was tied to the back of the buggy. Not Pierre then, but maybe – yes, it would be news of him.

CHAPTER TWO

Spiritus Sanctus

It was a morning like all the others she could remember, although it did not occur to her to try to remember; at six years old every morning was an astonishment, every quicksilver birdsong heard through her bedroom window the first. She lay, her eyes open, watching the play of tree-shadows on the ceiling, hearing the creak and clink of a wagon, the muted hoof-falls of a horse drawing it down the street past the house. The starched white curtains billowed into the space near her head and were sucked back with a slap, as if Antoinette were angry at the wall and slapping it hard with her flattened palm. Soon she would come swiftly through the door, her skirts whispering their morning melody as she hurried to Sophie's bedside. Up would go the window, or down, whichever it was not, for sometimes her *grand-mère* or her brother Hector would come in while Sophie was sleeping and change it.

Watching with interest and something that might be a touch of fear how briskly the maid attended to the window, she had once asked Antoinette why up or why down every single morning. She was still far too young to know that duty, honour, thoughtlessness required many things of people that they could not explain had it occurred to them that perhaps explanation was required. She was a maid, Sophie was in her care, therefore, she opened or closed Sophie's window to establish her authority, to insist on her very presence. One day Sophie would remember this and think how all her life she loathed in women such mindless bustling, as if to say, without me this world would collapse.

Her bladder pressed; she climbed from her bed, pulled out the chamber pot, sat, then, finished, her feet freezing on the cold floor, climbed back into the high bed, pulled up the feather quilt, and waited, patiently, with interest, to see what the morning would bring. No one, not Antoinette, not *grand-mère* would let her out of bed until they said she could get out of it. Except for the need of her bladder to be emptied. Sometimes, as she lay on her back singing softly to herself a made-up song she wondered if her mother were not in heaven, would she let Sophie up when she wanted to be up? It was a question for which she had no answer. Mothers were gifts from God, were they not? Maybe they did not have to answer to God every single day as Sophie did.

As she waited she wondered if the rhythmic thudding on the hard-packed dirt road had been, perhaps, the bishop arriving. This amazing thought drove her up to a sitting position; forgetting the stricture, she was throwing back the quilt so as to run to the window, just as the door opened and Antoinette entered.

"Is it the bishop?" Sophie cried, as Antoinette, pushing down the window in its sash, said "Up already, little one? My, my, my!" They stopped talking simultaneously, looked at each other, Antoinette, shrewdly, into the little girl's eyes, Sophie holding her breath, her eyes open so wide she could feel cold air on their surface and had to blink. The maid laughed; Sophie plunked herself in her flannel nightgown onto the edge of the bed letting her bare feet dangle, and rubbed her closed eyes with both hands.

"No bishop, Sophie. Only *le curé* Deschambeault. Are you ready for today?"

"I'm thirsty," Sophie said, petulant suddenly, remembering... something, but what?

"No water," Antoinette said. "If you drink, you cannot take Communion. You will have to wait another year. Your *grand-mère et grand-père* would be so angry." Sophie considered, a reckoning that soared backward and downward where space opened waiting for her to connect to...what?... Something. How grave and enormous, tingling with minuscule points of light that place. Must she be hungry, thirsty? No, in the face of such enormity she felt only awe.

Already Antoinette had produced a jug of hot water, was pouring it into the basin, the welcome sound of it splashing as it met the bottom of the china basin with its sprays of mauve flowers up the sides, the noise causing Sophie to click back to the morning and the chilly room, to Antoinette finished pouring, now readying the bar of soap, the Turkish towelling. Demurely, pensively, her hands lying loose on her lap, she waited for the scrubbing, while outside, their neighbour, Monsieur Allemande's fierce black dog that all the children were frightened of began to bark, the sound moving as he ran. The dog was loose!

"Antoinette!" she cried, pulling away from the cloth as it scrubbed at her face as though she had overnight dipped it in tar when she had only been sleeping. *"Le chien –"* Before Antoinette could reply an angry male voice could be heard shouting as fiercely as the dog barked, but not so piercingly, so that Sophie couldn't make out the words. The barking subsided.

"No breakfast today," Antoinette sang, pulling Sophie's nightgown off over her head, then beginning to scrub her. "Today great things will happen. Today you will receive the Host for the first time. Such a holy day." On and on she went, while Sophie stood, beginning to shiver although the window was closed. *Grand-mère* had said it was May, no more fires in her room. Now a heavy towel was draped around her and she grasped it where it fell on each side of her thighs and pulled it tight across her legs and then her shoulders. To her surprise, Antoinette kissed her on the top of her head, she felt it as an airy glance that stirred her night-loose hair, then the hairbrush tugging, the pulling, setting her scalp tingling, and finally, the lovely long silky *shshsh* of the brush through its thickness, and the coiling and tight pinning. Finished, the maid stood back, gazing down at Sophie, her eyes wide, her mouth held in an 'O' waiting for Sophie to fill in what came next.

"My dress!" Sophie remembered, and would have rushed to the wardrobe to look at it again, but the door to her room opened and grand-mère stepped inside, her black taffeta skirt swishing crisply back into place as she halted. She stared grimly down at her abruptly subdued granddaughter, then to the similarly cowed maid.

"Vite," she said to Sophie – *grand-mère* did not raise her voice – or smile, *"Dépêche-toi!"* To Antoinette she said, "We must go shortly. I will put on the veil when we are about to leave. Bring it downstairs." She went out, closing the door smartly behind her, she did not slam doors either, a glitter of jet beads at the shoulder as she vanished into the hall. Already Antoinette was sliding on Sophie's stockings, pulling up her frilly white drawers, patting her tummy as she buttoned all in place, reaching for vest and then the petticoat and then – at last! The dress!

Antoinette opened the wardrobe's door with a flourish, reached in to grasp the mass of white silk and tulle, it expanding as she brought it forward, Sophie's eyes fixed on it, her heart tripping quickly. The maid held it up to herself for a second as though she remembered when she had first donned her own white dress so many years ago. But no, Antoinette had already told Sophie she had not had so pretty a dress. "You are a rich little girl," Antoinette had admonished. "For you, the best; for me, a farmer's daughter, a handed-down dress." But she didn't seem angry, although when Sophie asked her *grand-mère* if she was a rich little girl, *grand-mère* had washed out her mouth with soap. But when, at dinner, *grand-mère* told *grand-père*, he laughed, and the next day took her away to his store, the clerks nodding and smiling down at her, so that she might see that they were *très satisfait* but never *riche*. And Antoinette had cried.

She swooped, Sophie was lost in the whistle of silk as it slid down her body, the rustle, the whisper, oh, the lightness of it! How her body disappeared inside it, as if now her legs, her *derrière* had become silk and tulle, and were filled now with nothing but air; might she now fly?

Then, her long veil firmly pinned to her scalp, her new white boots pinching her toes so that she wiggled them – grandmother wouldn't be able to see that – they were seated in their buggy in the line of buggies all going to the church, riding together with her two nearly grown brothers, Guillaume and Hector – she did not like Hector although she couldn't remember why not–and her grandfather in his high black hat brushed and brushed until it gleamed, to the magnificent occasion of Sophie's First Communion.

THE LONG DOUBLE LINE of communicants was ushered in by the priest wearing a gold chasuble over his black soutane and white alb, his servers following in starched white with perfect lace edges resting on ruby gowns. Wide beams of coloured light moved aslant, serenely through the stained glass of the high windows, dust riding on them, all the way down to pool on the white-clad children as they walked slowly, in step, girls on one side, boys on the other, down the main aisle to the pews saved for them. One by one they bent a knee and the head and slid to the left or the right, tiny white people in the heavy, dark oak pews, packed in, the girls' long veils poofing out satisfyingly, their hair, dark mostly, but a few blondes, one redhead, muted by the white tulle. The sopranos reached up to the domed ceiling, the basses vibrating in Sophie's eardrums and chest, the brand new organ's thunder swelling and softening as Brother Fleury pulled stops, pushed against the pedals, his torso twisting as his fingers moving rapidly across the keyboards, and his legs pumped or stretched to reach this pedal or that. The vault of the church pulsed with sound that invaded and set every particle of Sophie's being to quivering.

The communicants waited, not moving or speaking, trying to see the altar over the ladies' hats, or around their husbands' stiff fabric shoulders. Sophie's heart fluttered, her breath was short; but wait, the incense! Sanctifying as it filled the new stone church of which the parishioners were so proud, it being far nicer than the one the parishioners of the nearby village of Ste Anne had just finished, it drifted from the altar down the rows of dark pews where the people rose or sat, the headiest, most unusual odour Sophie had ever smelled and she breathed hard not to miss any of it. And listened to the chink of the censer as the priest swung it rhythmically back against its chain.

Then, no time having passed, no signal having been given, the children were once again lining up in the wide aisle, walking slowly, palms pressed together and held chest-high, their new rosaries dangling from between their palms. Sophie's was silver and white, her grandmother had given it to her, already blessed, after she had set Sophie's long veil on her head and fastened it with pins that dug into her scalp. How precious, her very own rosary, the white beads glowing softly as if within they made their own light, the polished silver links and joining medallions gleaming so that the Virgin's face engraved on the biggest one flashed light. It had seemed too precious to hold, but *grand-mère* scolded, pushing her hands together hard, to show how she must place it, and so she did. They knelt one by one at the altar, hands tucked beneath the starched cloth so white it was hard to look at, that covered the rail in front of them, and the priest came by to set, for the first time ever, the Host on each of their tongues.

Do not chew! Sister Mary Magdalene had exhorted in her most fierce manner, although admittedly this was her usual expression: *Let it rest on your tongue; let it melt away. It is the body of the Holy Christ* – Sophie hadn't heard the rest, terrified as she was but no, she would never chew as Rose had claimed she had seen Monsieur Robitaille do on his way back down the aisle only the Sunday past. Sister Mary Magdalene had slapped her face for that. No, Sophie would not chew.

Now however, as its cool smoothness rested on her tongue and she rose and genuflected and turned to find her place in line to go to her pew, her mouth closing at the same time, she thought of none of that. It was all gone. In its place, as she walked the long way back down the aisle, the adults still clad in bulky winter blacks and dark blues nodding and smiling on each side as the rows of white-clad children passed at bridesmaid pace in this vast gilt and blue interior, she felt herself lifted out of the darkness of her own solid being while, slowly, wondrously, her small chest expanded as it filled with a cloud of pure white light.

CHAPTER THREE

La région sauvage

THE HORSES WERE HITCHED to the loaded wagon and waiting in the yard in the front of the farmhouse, Pierre already in the driver's seat holding the reins, his younger brother Herménègilde mounting on the other side, he to bring back the horses and wagon once their goods were safely loaded on the train, Sophie between them, the older brothers Alexandre and Marcel, watching silently, hands on hips, lips pursed in either disapproval or concern, Sophie wasn't sure which and didn't care. M. Hippolyte paced beside the load, Mme Hippolyte, alternately sobbing and praying below them, Pierre's sisters, Lucie and Cécile, trying to comfort her although in tears themselves. Neighbours and relatives were gathering from every direction to say *au revoir* and *bon voyage*, calling advice, weeping, laughing, admonishing, Sophie so eager to be off that she had to force herself to smile and nod whether she heard what was said or not. Tucked safely between her breasts was a small packet, something handed to her not by grandmother, but by Antoinette, immediately after her marriage. She had been puzzled, but only for a second. They were the diamond earrings that had been her mother's, promised to be hers on the day she married.

A tiny pressure there, for one infinitely small part of a second causing her to remember she was leaving behind the graves of her parents, and the long, usually unacknowledged childhood dream that they would someday return to her. She wavered, before she remembered Pierre beside her, and the promise of freedom, and thousands of acres of their own gleaming wheat rippling in the prairie breeze. And a triumphant return someday, before too long. What a thought! She would not return, Sophie thought, and turned her face away toward Sherbrooke and the future.

But the young *abbé* Chabot had rushed his buggy past the people, leaving it by the barn and was hurrying across the yard toward the gathering crowd, and the horses and wagon containing the newlyweds, his cassock swaying, beads rattling rhythmically, heavy wooden cross slapping against his skirted thighs, chickens flapping indignantly, squawking, out of his way. Sophie had expected no priest and was annoyed. There was no stopping him: First he addressed the small crowd that had gathered about this foolish venture of theirs, leaving behind *la patrie* – yes, foolish even now as they were about to drive away – then asked all of them to pray for their safety in *la région sauvage*, then that they would never forget their blessed and providential church, and the great language of their birth, *la langue française*. And their people–he went on at some length about their people until he had more of the crowd weeping. The courageous few who had come from France nearly two hundred years earlier, had made friends, finally, with the Indians too, after Père Brébeuf and Père Lalemant and so many other martyrs were created, and let us never forget Adam Dollard, Sieur des Ormeaux, and *les coureurs-de-bois*, who had cut down trees and plowed the land and made homes in the new world, and had many children and would have many more, all for the greater glory of God and their church, and... Here he suddenly wound down, as if he had perhaps just remembered another engagement, made a flattening gesture with his palm held high above his head which the crowd interpreted without difficulty and knelt as if one in the dirt, whereupon he murmured a long prayer over Mme Hippolyte's sobs before standing again, so that all the others could stand too.

Then Pierre called to the horses, flicked the reins, and they were off, Sophie, blinking back something that might have been unwanted tears that warred with a schoolgirl's strong desire to stand, throw her arms in the air, and scream with joy, Herménègilde taking off his hat to wave it to everybody, although he was only going as far as

Sherbrooke, and Pierre, frowning and too busy with the reins, his jaw set as if he were angry, or, she suddenly thought, holding back his tears, not even acknowledging the good-bye waves until they had gone a way down the road when he thrust out one hand backwards, widely, glancing over his shoulder one last time at the crowd. But Sophie did not wave again, nor did she look back.

THEIR GOODS LOADED INTO one of the cars reserved for settlers' effects, Herménègilde already having driven the team and empty wagon away toward home, Sophie and Pierre were taking one last look at Québec before they would mount the steps into the passenger car.

Pierre was being particularly solicitous to her, so that Sophie, unused from earliest childhood to being closely attended to with love rather than disapproval, was touched and thrilled until, glancing up to his face while he was looking away, it occurred to her, seeing again the reappearance of the odd set to his mouth, that he was anxious, maybe even afraid, and his solicitousness to her was to quiet his own unease. Still, puzzling as she found it, she loved him more for it, his sudden apprehension making her want to soothe and reassure him. But she would not; fearing shaming him, she would never even let him know what she had seen.

But there, coming down the platform toward them, past the noisy train, puffs of steam issuing from around its iron wheels, clanking noises mixed with long, steaming sighs drowning the voices of the people on the platform, and far down the way behind them the noise of the draymen turning their wagons, shouting at their horses and each other, was Guillaume. He wore a heavy black overcoat of some expensive cloth that she had never seen before and a white silk scarf around his neck as grandfather sometimes did to Mass, and a smart black hat. As he came up to them his expression was grave; he didn't kiss Sophie and she stared up at him, willing him to show her the love, no matter what had transpired, that she was accustomed to from her oldest brother.

"I took the early morning train from Montréal; I'll catch the evening train back." When they didn't speak, he went on. "My firm has given me business to transact here in Sherbrooke so as I would miss you when you came through Montréal, I thought I would say good-bye here," although, Sophie thought, his expression seemed more to admonish her. He kept his distance from them, stiffly, as if they were mere acquaintances, not family, and ones not much liked at that; no kiss for Sophie, no handshake for Pierre.

"I had to have one last word," Guillaume told her severely. "You must remember that we do not abandon you, Sophie. It is the other way around," making no attempt to hide his disapproval, a steady questioning in his eyes as, finally, he shook Pierre's hand, holding on a bit too long, any hint of smiles slowly disappearing from both men's faces. Guillaume turned away then, his face closing tightly, straightening his shoulders, and in that turning Sophie remembered the day the Holy Ghost had come down and lit in her chest when she was a small child and Antoinette had said, *"It means God loves you,"* and had crossed herself, tears pouring, irritatingly, from her eyes. Antoinette would cry if a dog crossed the road, grandmother had once remarked to the air. *More of the blessed seigneuries*, Pierre had spit, when she told him, *as if good, honest feelings were a sin*. Nonetheless, she clung to this memory, telling herself, *I shouldn't be afraid*. But it was the thought of Pierre's protection that in her instant of fear, the first she had allowed herself and all the more powerful for it, that kept her from changing her mind and throwing herself on Guillaume to beg him to allow her to go with him back to Montréal. That, and his coldness that she knew she could not now do anything to mitigate. It was too late for Guillaume's rescue, if she wanted rescue, she told herself, and tossed her head as if she had spoken aloud. He hadn't even kissed her cheek.

Beside them, though, the train shuddered and muttered and people began to mount the stairs at each end of the cars. They fell in with the crowd of settlers climbing aboard, and soon were seated on the slatted wooden benches among the other terrified, thrilled passengers, the many children among them wide-eyed, silenced for the moment by the unfamiliarity of it all, while the train's iron wheels grunted and squealed, beginning to turn in rhythm, faster and faster, and the engineer pulled the whistle so that as they left the Sherbrooke station a last melancholy wail trailed, echoing, behind them.

Sophie clung to Pierre's arm, gazing exalted, out the windows while, in what seemed only seconds, they left the town behind, began the rush through the greening countryside. She would have kissed him, but he would have pulled back and looked around, uneasy by the small impropriety of it, forgetting, Sophie thought, that we are married now. She grinned instead, and squeezed his arm harder, until he grinned down at her, the light in his black eyes as good as a kiss, no, a thousand kisses. She could not believe her good fortune, that Pierre was her husband, that Pierre loved her with a love as strong as hers for him.

In only a few hours they came to the St. Lawrence River. Sophie pressed herself against Pierre as they had rattled across the long iron bridge, far below them the water glistening through a floating mist – like a fallen cloud, she thought – in the distance slowly turning to silver and melding with the white sky. There was the harbor and great buildings, bigger than anything she had ever seen before, and dome after dome after spire of churches reaching skyward toward heaven. She could barely breathe, she and Pierre exchanged wordless glances that spoke of awe, delight, mixed with apprehension. Then they were entering Montréal where the train hissed, screeched, and clanked to a stop and they were able to descend to the platform for a short while.

She had thought that possibly Hector would leave his work long enough to say good-bye. She could barely remember her brother's face it had been so long since she had last seen him, she couldn't recall even saying good-bye to him, but hadn't she gone to breakfast one morning and there was no Hector? Grandfather grim-faced, the glitter in grandmother's eyes not to be looked at. A sob, unexpected, coming out of nowhere, caught low in her throat so that she touched the place with her fingertips and turned away from Pierre so he wouldn't see. It didn't seem to have occurred to Pierre that Sophie's other brother might have come to say good-bye; it was no surprise that neither of them even spoke his name. And anyway, so brief a stop, so many people milling around on the platform, Hector would never have found them in time. Again some memory, or picture, unpleasant, wholly uncertain, tugged at her, so that she chased it away before it had time to form.

They walked the length of the platform along with other passengers from their car, children racing and screeching among them until captured by their parents, jerked into position, slapped, and momentarily subdued. Standing against the station walls, or in sheltered corners beggars stood, importuning passersby. So many, Sophie thought, surprised. Was this what Guillaume had warned her about? She shivered. I will write to Violette about this, about this whole trip, she told herself, but no, the nuns wouldn't allow Violette letters from anyone but her mother. She would have pondered on what she had seen longer, but the conductor was shouting, they were climbing back onto the train, it was vibrating with building power, it was all too exciting, then they were pulling out of the station, beginning the long trip past the increasingly decrepit outskirts of Montréal, the vision of the great city fading a little more with each turning of the noisy wheels.

A half hour or more after they had left the city behind them, a conductor came bumping down the aisle followed by two women in shabby but clean dresses, each carrying bulging cloth bags and a hat box that the conductor helped them stuff under their seats, the two empty seats across the aisle from Sophie and Pierre. One woman was about Sophie's age, the other older, the older one with light brown hair and matching light brown eyes, the other with blue eyes and the same shade of light brown hair, and both of them gaunt to the point of illness.

"We are sisters, Marianne and Adelaide Smith," the older, taller, brown-eyed one, told them, when after an hour or so of riding across the aisle from them, Sophie moved to sit facing the elder sister and took the small trove of *biscuits* that Pierre's little sister Lucie had made for them and, offering the tin to them. How quickly the women grasped the cookies, one after the other, crunching them down, crumbs slipping unnoticed into the frills of their too-loose bodices, nonplussing Sophie. She saw too, then thought she must have been mistaken, a certain trembling of their fingers as they reached in to take a cookie and to eat them.

"Where in the West are you going?" Sophie asked, first in French, then getting no response other than a widening of the eyes, switching to her few English words, as she sat swaying across from them, while outside darkness at last began to fall, small splatters of rain hitting the window beside them, Pierre snoring like an engine only a few feet away.

"My sister and I are going to the District of Saskatchewan," Miss Adelaide Smith told Sophie, enunciating precisely, presumably so that Sophie would better understand, while the younger one, Marianne – no, Mary Ann – nodded and smiled. Something wrong with her, Sophie thought: a vacancy, a flatness in the pale eyes. Ah, *les anglais* – but no, she reproved herself. Because they aren't French I will not assume they are devils. The past is past. *It is past*, she had insisted to *l'abbé*, who scolded her angrily saying she was too young to understand, that one day she would make remembering her business. *Do not forget la langue maternelle; do not forget this precious church.* She was by this the more determined to know *les deux anglaises*.

"We are getting off in Saskatchewan District, too," Sophie told them, miming getting off the train, enunciating "Saskatchewan," carefully. "We will be..." she hesitated "...*voisines*... neighbours?"

"We will get off there too, in Moose Jaw," the elder Miss Smith told her. She was not unfriendly, yet Sophie didn't like the way the woman treated her, as if behind the show of politeness, she found Sophie amusing, as if she were only a stupid child. "Our brother has land near there and we will go there to help him."

"Ahh," Sophie said, trying to think of the English words, "He has no...wife?"

"No wife," Adelaide intoned solemnly, shaking her head as if it were a great shame, and unaccountably, Mary Ann began to laugh. Adelaide fixed her now hard brown eyes on Mary Ann's blue ones and instantly Mary Ann fell into silence, her laugh cut off as if by a slamming door.

"You have come from Montréal?" she asked, but Adelaide merely shook her head, no, saying nothing, while Mary Ann reached furtively for the last cookie. Puzzled, Sophie took her leave of them, returning to her seat between the window and Pierre who slept on, not noticing his wife had been gone.

But the next morning the two women were gone from the car, their boxes and bags also, and Sophie didn't see them again. Their place was taken at once by half of a large family that had had so far to squeeze itself into two seats at the far end of the car, the older children staying behind in those seats and the smaller of the half-dozen children, moving across the aisle from Sophie and Pierre. The smallest of them now insisted on standing on the seats until their shabby, distracted father smacked each of them once, methodically. This was followed by loud crying until another blow was threatened, which dried all tears instantly, and in a moment, punishment forgotten or shrugged off as too usual, the little ones were running up and down the crowded aisles, tripping over the feet of passengers, and the sacks and boxes of belongings that no matter how the conductor scolded and threatened, the bulging corners of which continued to find their way into the aisle.

And still the train hurtled on through the wooded, greening landscape with its low, grassy hills, its cows and horses grazing in meadows, rounding corners where sunlit church spires greeted them, villages of stone houses just like the village they had left behind, forever, sat warming in the spring sun. The train was long, heavily loaded, making its loud, steady, if slow way out to the thin fringes of civilization, into Ontario, through blackwater swamps edged with a sometimes brilliant green, the dark surfaces broken here and there by streaks or pools of amber, past lakes bluer than the sky that reflected whiter clouds, around impenetrable black granite cliffs from which flakes of quartz and fool's gold glinted in the harsh light.

On it went, stopping briefly now and then to take on water and coal, and one morning when they woke, dressed, pulled back the curtains, and climbed down from the trays attached to the ceiling that acted as their beds, they had moved out of all enclosures – lakes, forests, hills, villages – into a space so vast that Sophie, standing to see better, became dizzy and would have fallen back into her seat if Pierre had not been pressed against her as he stared too. It was as if in the night the train had left its tracks and ventured into some new planet from the one they knew. *Was this the West?*

Staring out in a stunned silence, a new, unidentifiable soaring sound filled her head. It was the delicate hissing of her brain, as closed as only stone and rail fences, garden swings, rows of oak pews, years of nuns' pious sobriety and priests' thunderings, could make it, opening, now, to encompass the endless meadow – meadow? She had no other word for what she viewed before her, going on forever to the place where the earth curved down and away, and above where it had been, there was only the far-distant, pale, sky. And not a forest out there, not even – could it really be? A single tree. Again, she experienced an instant, a *frisson* of terror, suppressed at once.

But she couldn't quite catch her breath, leaned, rocking against Pierre's side so that he braced himself against the window's high frame with one arm, and slid his other arm around her waist. The waist he murmured over in the night, so slim it was, so tiny, a handsbreadth only. And now Sophie thought – even as she thought, *I must be mad* – she would wear no more stays. No more whalebone choking her, leaving deep red marks on her tender white flesh, as Pierre, unlacing her corset, had murmured to her, so that she trembled, her breath shallow and fast. Did she not know she was desired? Did she not know how beautiful was her flesh? Blood so suddenly rushing through her veins, heating her, its susurration in her ears so loud she could hardly hear his whispers which soon, in any case, became grunts, sighs, gasps, as if he had forgotten it was her, his Sophie he labored with such passion over. Then, overcoming even the tearing pain, all drowned by the cataract of sensation, so astonishing it did not bear thinking about.

But then it was the sky. All day they watched in silence as it filled the windows of the train on both sides and down the length of their enclosure. In the morning how the rising sun in the east lit the darkness with gold; ascending higher, shot beams of glowing red light into the car so strong it made the passengers look away from it, laughing helplessly, the sky gradually lightening until by afternoon it was the palest blue and measureless miles in the distance above them, as evening drew on deepening to sapphire, the highest arc of its dome too dark to see more than a white pinpoint here or there, and though otherwise lightless, all the while, everywhere, miraculously radiant. The car full of exhausted, swaying people could not stop themselves from watching the sky, the woman riding in the seat ahead of Sophie and Pierre beginning to sob, sobbed an entire day as they rocked on into the North-West Territories, tears running unchecked down her cheeks to drip off her chin, her husband turning his face resolutely away from her, to the window, and *the West*.

Dishevelled, none too clean, and aching in every limb, two days after the train had properly entered *the West*, the conductor came down through the cars calling, "Next station Swift Current," the tension in the car rising palpably, the settlers, their patience stretched beyond the imaginable, began to gather bags and small boxes, organizing, instructing each other, calling to children, straightening clothing, wiping children's faces, brushing hats and placing them carefully on heads.

"We are not going to Versailles!" Sophie muttered into Pierre's ear, her irritation or whatever it was making her want to scratch all over her own body; itchy she was, suddenly, everywhere.

No one waited patiently, for most of their number had gotten off in Winnipeg and the succeeding towns, all of the settlers left on the train, crowded the windows of the car, leaning close, stretching to see over the heads of family members, leaning against the glass so as to see down the track. Voices exclaimed, then silence fell, then an exclamation from someone else; somewhere down the car a woman had sobbed, broken off in mid-breath as if poked from behind or else grasping hard for composure. Something soared in Sophie's chest: This was it; for this they had come so far, they had left all behind, they were starting life again. *Land* was echoing in her head, but she pressed her lips together and did not say it. No one said it: It was the only thought in the car, except perhaps for young wives and mothers understanding at last that they would never again see their mothers. Remembering then their own children who clung to them, even the most disobedient chastened by the emotion in the air, dimly aware of some unknown cataclysmic thing occurring, unsure how to behave, burying faces in skirts, or gazing upward at a suddenly subdued, somehow lessened, father.

The train pulled to a long hissing stop. Sophie and Pierre disembarked in the middle of the few others also getting off. Through the drifting clouds of steam and the milling passengers and those meeting them, the several teams of horses backing around to set their wagons and drays for loading settlers' effects or other goods from the box cars, Sophie thought she saw Adelaide Smith and her sister far down the train past the engine. They were climbing into the only buggy present driven by a thick-set man whose face she couldn't see, three dark silhouettes presenting their backs to her as they wheeled rapidly away. But it couldn't have been them. Or maybe it was.

"I am still rocking in my bones," she groaned to Pierre.

He said only, "First, a team and wagon. Monsieur Taylor says we can get supplies here. Then the land." Taylor was a rancher who had, as he said "hitched a ride" on the settlers' train at Moose Jaw, having been there on business, and was now heading back to his cattle ranch. He had chatted pleasantly enough with Pierre, saying at one point that there were no "Frenchies" where they were going and Pierre had looked dismayed, while she had thought angrily, Good! and was shocked at herself.

"Is there a hotel?" Sophie asked, dubious. She tried to see the village, but only three rough buildings presented themselves down the trail, beyond which there was only the grassy yellow rise of land with only a tinge of new green. And that sky! Would it never end? Against the horizon there was nothing. Nothing at all, not even a single tree. Never such a thing as a church spire. She had never seen such a skyline, never seen such an empty ground, had not imagined such a place could even exist. She put her hand on Pierre's arm.

"It is like a sea; it is like there is no land, only sky; it is..." But she wasn't afraid so much as fascinated and awed, and dropped her hand and stepped ahead of her husband, not stopping, as if she planned to go on forever until she had seen everything there was to see.

"You should have been Jacques Cartier," Pierre said to her back, irritated. "Or Champlain." She turned to him, surprised, to find he was now staring down the train to the boxcars where men had begun to unload the settlers' supplies and equipment. As if speaking only to himself he muttered, "I like a farm, that is all. Our own land. Lots of it," and the glint she hadn't ever seen in his eyes at the mention of *the West* was there at last. At this, a tiny, festering sliver in her brain dissolved.

Then he was gone without another word to her, leaving her alone. She hardly noticed. What a lot there was to look at: the land, the endless layers of sky, great cumulus clouds setting sail above them, no hint of thunder or of lightning or rain in any of their gauzy white bottoms. The sun, too bright to look at, pouring itself over everything: horses, the hats of the men, the few women's entangling skirts, the children's round eager faces, the, although apparently newly-built, already weathered false-fronted buildings, piles of all kinds of goods on the ground from walking plows to stained sacks bulging with their anonymous contents, to the teams of horses, the train itself, and lighting again the tops of the already-brilliant clouds. Sophie was filled with light and space, no longer her heavy, earthbound Québec self; she wanted a long-handled spoon the better to eat those yellow-tinted clouds; she wanted to run miles across the pale grass as fast as she could go, to roll like a giggling schoolchild down the sloping, yellow-grassed hills.

She waited, walking the distance of the train, watching the people. Some passengers were being met: a wife with her children, by her dour husband, two grown sons by their aged father, one family by another family, while the few remaining passengers, solitary men all of them, strode or rode horseback off alone as if they knew exactly where they were going and why. A couple of wagons, that one buggy, and a dray all pulled by teams or single workhorses rattled, squeaked, and creaked toward or away from the trampled open ground that acted as the station platform.

Pierre, returning, still not looking at her, pointing, said, "We've piled our things there. They tell me it is oxen we will need."

Sophie nodded sagely, hiding her dismay. Oxen! Surely only drovers used oxen. They were going to their own land. A fine team of Percherons or Belgians, was what they needed, but she said nothing. Pierre would do whatever needed doing, in that, she had faith, even if *grandmère* and Guillaume did not. Had he not been a farmer all his life?

But land! Land first, everything else second.

"There is no one out there," the land agent told them when Pierre inquired as to neighbours. "Only cattle ranchers." Pierre considered.

"To be first is best," he said, and grinned over his shoulder at Sophie who stood beside him, a wifely foot back from where he and the land agent were studying the maps, her hands neatly clasped at her waist. But she could contain herself no longer and stepped forward to follow the agent's pointing finger.

"What is that?" she asked, her finger pointing to a small dot.

"Bone Pile," he answered brusquely. She couldn't understand what he meant, and faltering, decided against asking.

"We have nearly thirty-three thousand square miles available for settlers," he went on, but Sophie, not listening to the rest, thought, *thirty-three thousand square miles of grass and sky*. How much of creation is that? He meant only the square miles of land under his office's jurisdiction, she thought suddenly, and could not – absolutely could not – conjure eight or ten or a thousand times more than that was *the West*.

"Water," Sophie said, suddenly, her mind racing ahead as she did not recall it ever having done before, as if the pure air of the endless space that was *the West* had clarified her thought processes. But neither man looked at her, even though she was pointing to a thin line that traced a watercourse, a stream perhaps.

"That is on land leased by a rancher," the agent said, looking at Pierre, as if he were the one who had spoken. "Here is where free land begins." His finger made a line perhaps a mile or so from the line of water Sophie had found. She stepped back again, biting her lips to keep herself silent.

The agent and Pierre carried on their conversation, Sophie's mind wandering, her ear tuned to the noises outside, the men at the counter before her eventually coming to a decision. Papers were produced, Pierre lifted a pen to sign, dipping it in the ink with a flourish, whereupon Sophie stepped forward again to see what it was he was signing. A ten dollar bill extracted from his purse lay on the map beside the paper to which he was putting the pen. He gave her a sideways glance she recognized as faintly warning, and was shocked; they hadn't been married a month. Yet the communication itself, so intimate, so subtle, thrilled her in itself, made her feel an adult, and she said to herself for the hundredth time: *We are married; we are man and wife.*

"I too am bound by this," she whispered.

"Your signature is not required," the land agent said brusquely, again not looking at her, as Pierre wrote his name.

"But what did you choose? Where are we going?"

"Here," he said, the document signed, lifted by the agent so that Pierre might show her on the map that lay under the paper with its drying signature. She saw that Pierre had chosen a quarter-section almost identical to where she had pointed a moment earlier. She tucked down her chin, trying not to smile.

"Oxen," Pierre said. "Where will I find some? And a wagon?"

"Next door," the agent told him, jerking a thumb to the south.

"Best of luck to ye all," he called as they went out the door, and as the three other men waiting behind them shuffled forward to take their turn choosing land. A thrill went down her backbone that now, that simply, they possessed land that was followed at almost the same moment by that rapier-thin shaft of terror that vanished as quickly as it had come.

Outside, hardly anyone was left, and a silence broken by horses shaking their heads at flies, their halters clinking, and squalls of wind racing through the grass flattening and darkening it, prevailed. But wait, back of the expected, the usual sounds of horses, if she cocked her head just so, she could hear a faint, high-pitched ripple of sound. Birds! No trees, yet somewhere out there in the grass there were birds. She wondered how they survived without trees to light in or in which to build nests, or to keep away from predators, but Pierre was moving ahead, stepping over the rough door sill into the next building that proved to be the general store.

Already its proprietor was greeting Pierre; he seemed to be hail-fellow-well-met enough for two, eager to do business with those newcomers who had disembarked into his purview. In back, he told them, discoloured teeth appearing from under his moustache and a certain rumble back of his voice as if he couldn't get his chest clear, in fact, was a sturdy enough wagon, and the proprietor sent his son to find and bring in the team of oxen he had broken to harness and had been waiting for settlers to come so he could sell. While they waited, Sophie and Pierre joined him again in his store and began to fill the long list of needed supplies they had made sitting over the kitchen table at the Hippolyte's farm in the day or two before they left, Mme Hippolyte ticking off items on her thick fingers. A ton of supplies, Sophie standing by with pencil and list, reading it aloud, and checking off items as they went into a growing pile outside the store's front door. Flour, sugar, tea, coffee. Excitement kept her on her feet, kept her near Pierre, who didn't seem to notice her proximity.

The oxen came, Pierre pronounced them sound; money was handed over and a receipt given. It was decided that Pierre would go back to the station and load the wagon with the furniture, household goods, harnesses, traps and the single plow that had once been his Uncle Onésime's, then return to add the items they had purchased. A few cowboys had ridden up, dismounted, tied their horses to the hitching rail and, remained leaning against the building, chatting to each other from under the shade of their big hats. Inside the store the owner, his son, and a male clerk, worked at arranging supplies and answering requests for goods from men, apparently ranchers, who came and went. Since she and Pierre had clambered awkwardly off the train, their muscles slow to respond after a full week of sitting, Sophie had begun to notice that other than the few who had gone into the land, no women were to be seen anywhere. Did none of these men have wives? Were there no mothers in *the West?*

One of the men lounging against the store wall called to Pierre. "You would be needing a milk cow?"

Pierre glanced at Sophie, then turned back to him.

"Bien sûr, oui," then, embarrassed, "Yes, a cow for milk. *Non?"* he inquired of Sophie. She nodded firmly, once, clasping her hands at her waist again so as not to forget herself and touch him. The cow, a Jersey, was tied to the back of a buggy in the shade on the far side of the store. Examined, she seemed sound enough, and as the men exchanged the cow for money Sophie shivered to think how fast their supply of cash was vanishing. But they had known it would, and calculating mentally, knew there was still enough for the building materials for the house.

Uneasy, although none of the men surreptitiously studying her had been anything less than courteous, if a trifle too interested, she opted to go with Pierre to the station, even though she could tell he would prefer that she stay behind. Even he could see, though, that to leave her behind was, if not unsafe, improper as there were no women there at all, and he gave her a helping hand up onto the wagon seat where she sat as straight and tall as she could. Bouncing away the short distance down the trail to the station, she could feel the eyes of men boring into her back, imagined she could hear their low-voiced comments to each other about her. Yet she felt pleased: Was she not more than a little comely?

By the time their goods were loaded, Sophie helping with the small items, both from the station and the store, hours had passed since they had gotten off the train, and even though the afternoon was vanishing into what should have been dusk, the sun remained high. The promise of hours more of daylight was held out both by the storekeeper, and by the sky itself, whose late afternoon clarity was astonishing and beautiful.

"Now, we go," Pierre announced, finishing tying the new milk cow Fleurette – Sophie had already named her – to the back of the wagon. Sophie began to climb up onto the wagon seat, but the storekeeper protested, "It's a long way to that homestead. Why not wait? You can leave in the morning." He crossed his arms on his chest as he spoke and she became aware of how thick it was and how muscled his bare forearms with his shirt sleeves rolled as they were. She wanted to speak, but pressed her lips together. It was growing chilly, too, but she reminded herself that the woolen shawl folded in her portmanteau was thick and warm. Pierre answered, "But you have no *hôtel*. We 'ave our *tente*..." He shrugged.

"Tent," Sophie whispered, and again felt his irritation with her. He saluted the two men who stood watching him, apparently unconcerned about the disregard of their good advice, went around and climbed up into his seat.

"Indians?" Sophie murmured to him. He started.

"Les sauvages?" he began.

"Nothing to worry about," the storekeeper called up to them. "All that trouble is a long way north of here. Indians around here don't cause no trouble. Might want tea, or sugar, but that's all." Both she and Pierre knew very well there had been a good deal of trouble in the territory, now a province called Manitoba, when Sophie and Pierre were still children. The Métis, led by the great Louis Riel, who had had to run to Montana to stay out of prison, or maybe even a worse fate. Everyone in Québec knew about it, and about the settlement itself then over-run by *les anglais*, so anti-French that the French-speakers, the Catholics, had had to leave their homes and their land to go farther west. No use to think of it; they were here, they were alone, they would be fine, and stubbornly, she lowered her head, quelling a hint of nausea. In the meantime, they were rattling and swaying across what turned out, surprisingly, as it had appeared silky smooth, to be a very bumpy prairie, Pierre having located the first section peg only just laid out by the Dominion surveyors, and trying his best to keep steady in the direction of the next one. South, south by southwest. *West.*

"We must name our animals," she announced, studying the oxen, one a tiny bit bigger than the other, one with darker brown spots than the bigger one.

"You choose," he said, and for the first time since they had disembarked from the train, he looked at her with the old light in his eyes. She considered.

"I have it! Let's call them Gog and Magog!" He laughed aloud at that.

"Where did you get that? Because of where we come from?"

"Yes," she said, looking up at him, and was flushed with happiness, at her own perfect choice. "Gog and Magog, and Fleurette, *la vache*." He laughed again, but offered no objection.

By nine, the light finally beginning to seriously falter, it was May after all, they were hurrying to set up their first camp in the wilderness. Pierre had unhitched the oxen, hobbled them, and saving the few oat bundles, given them a little of the hay that he had bought from the station agent, the grazing not being good enough yet, this early in the spring, although the men lounging in front of the store had told him that the sun-cured grass even left over from last year would help fill his oxen's bellies.

Pierre had used the tent, an unexpected wedding gift from the old farmer, M. Fournier, for whom Pierre had worked now and then, as covering for their load and the tent pegs clanked in their canvas bag beneath the wagon seat. Before long he had the tent laid out carefully on the grass before them, the bag of pegs at his feet, the handle of the heavy long-handled mallet leaning against his leg, and looked around assessingly. Sophie pointed. Yes, indeed, a higher spot, but not as high as to make them conspicuous against the horizon, although there was no one to see them–except possibly Indians. For an instant, as he began working, she stood patiently, hands clasped at her waist, and then remembered that she was not standing in the convent yard now, not ever again, that she wasn't pacing demurely in *grand-mère's* garden pretending to read her missal and thinking of Pierre: She was where she wanted to be, in *la région sauvage*, *les pays d'en haut*, the North-West Territories. The sun was sinking below the horizon bathing the prairie in a rich golden light that quadrupled the lengths of their shadows. In *the West*, she too, had become a giant.

She leaped as if she had been poked, ran to the front of the bulky grey canvas Pierre was dragging, caught an edge in both hands and began to pull beside her husband. Pierre barely broke stride, glanced at her, lifted a hand as if to refuse her help, then dropped his arm and kept moving forward. Elated, for a brief instant, she surged ahead of him.

Soon they lay entwined beneath wool blankets under the canvas, Sophie's forehead tucked against Pierre's neck listening to his slow breathing. Tired beyond words, both of them, but too excited to sleep.

"As soon as we can we will get a good team of Percherons; these oxen are too slow." She yawned. "We will have a neighbour," he said. "The agent said there was nobody, but when we were loading the storekeeper said so."

"What?" She had imagined that in all of the North-West Territories, Saskatchewan District, there would be no one but them.

"Napoléon Beausoleil and his family. They moved here from the Red River district two years ago and are well-settled."

"How far?" She hoped it was a long way.

"Six miles or so, I think," Pierre said. "They came west fifteen or more years ago. I'll be glad to have somebody nearby who knows the country."

Wolves had begun to howl far in the distance, their voices faint but nonetheless causing shivers to run down her back. She hugged Pierre harder. Nearly asleep, he mumbled, "My gun…," reminding her that it leaned against their bags beside him, that he had only to put out his arm to grasp it.

Soon he was asleep, but she lay beside him, until, judging by his breathing that his sleep was deep enough that she wouldn't disturb him, she moved carefully out from under his muscle-heavy arm that lay across her chest. She needed to empty her bladder, but more than that, some authority was urging her: *Get up, go outside, see what it is you have contracted for yourself.* She gathered her shawl, pulled it around her shoulders, then sought and found her felt slippers. So still was the air and mild the night that they hadn't secured the tent flap and she crawled out, only standing when the stiff grass, an astonishing thing to her, she had never felt such grass, began to hurt her knees. She would not go far; it was too dark, and too dangerous to stray. She could hear the oxen and the cow snuffling and breathing on the far side of the tent, comforting sounds, and thought to say a prayer of thanks for having made it this far, and to ease her fears.

But when she stood and looked about her, waiting for her eyes to adjust to the night after the darkness of their tent, she forgot to be afraid, so dumbfounded was she by what she saw: Had there been so many stars in Québec? Surely not. She stared and stared, letting her head drop back until she lost her balance and would have fallen if she hadn't put out a hand against the wagon wheel to support herself. A quilt, she thought, at first, and then, a flower garden made of stars, but as she continued to gaze into the heavens, sobered: No, nothing so dainty, it was a vortex of stars, a force field drawing her upward into their ancient, eternal realm.

Something, some force, some *thing* pulling inside her chest, heretofore narrow and warm, a mere girl's; pulling, pulling, crying wordlessly to go there, back from whence it had come. What something? It was as if it was not her, Sophie Charron Hippolyte, headstrong, lovesick, but something else that resided inside that cage of bone, that perched there for the duration as if assigned and could not leave, for whatever reason until she breathed her last: her soul, her spirit, her own little speck – perhaps – of God. She fell to her knees, her head still tilted upward, as the thing inside her yearned upward with such power she felt it might burst out of her chest. No one, she thought, could gaze at this and think this vast, glittering dome could hold so puny a thing as a heaven, would tolerate a silly human paradise.

In that instant she disbelieved. Not in the moment and its truth itself, but beside this…this…how thin and small the bosom of the church she had been taught was her only and best home, the place where outside of God, all truth resided. Beside this wonder, she felt the church, its teachings, its power, slipping away from her grasp, it was like trying to catch water in your fingers, it moved on, it grew thin and pale, it vanished. It was nothing, after all. So this, *this*, she thought, is *the West*. And sank further, onto her bottom, to sit, closing her mouth that must have been agape all the while, moistening her lips with her tongue, her breath slowing at last. What she had been thinking was flooding over her, filling her with terror; she fought back against it. God would forgive; He would understand. She shook with the two ideas fighting against each other in her heart and mind, first one, the other, then she prayed: *Notre père*…until weariness began to creep through her, she remembered who she was, where she was, and rose, still shaky, went into the tent, crept into the bedroll beside Pierre, reaching for his human warmth.

THEN THERE WAS SUNSHINE, Pierre's deep voice commanding the oxen, the walls of the tent moving slowly, or with a crack and a thud, in and out with the wind. She scrambled from under the blankets, stood for a second holding her head in both hands trying to grasp again the enormity of where they were, of what they had done. She rushed outside and the chilly air shocked her back into herself and the moment.

Pierre was harnessing the oxen and didn't turn his head toward her.

"Don't look at me," she called, and vanished to the other side of the wagon where in a moment Pierre would re-hitch the oxen. There she voided her bladder as she had failed to do the night before.

"There's a small bit of water in the basin," Pierre called. He was tackling the tent pegs now, and she hurried to the spot in the earth where they had the night before dug a hole for their fire and dragged or carried rocks from wherever they could find them, not much lying loose, but mostly half-buried in the hard prairie sod, to form a ring about it. When she admired Pierre's campfire building skills, he grunted, "Did I not spend a full winter in the bush cutting trees? How do you think we kept from freezing to death?" He was unamused, barely noticed her.

Inside the ring of stones the blue granite basin sat, an inch of their precious water supply in the bottom, and she washed her hands and splashed her face, even drew up her nightdress to splash the remainder between her legs, then pulled off her nightgown and used it to dry herself. Shivering, she moved naked across the grass toward the tent. Then Pierre was behind her, his hand on her rump, the other spread against her belly. Before she could stop herself she gasped, and was about to pull away, to run playfully into the tent where he would follow her, and lie down beside her, kissing her everywhere, when suddenly he stepped back, dropping his hands, planting one long kiss on her neck where it joined her shoulder. "Dress," he said. "*Vite.* If we're lucky, by tonight we raise our tent on our own land."

Surprised at his self-denial – she'd seen no hint of that before – she hurried inside before he folded the tent down around her, gathered her clothing – refusing her stays – pulling over her shoulders her chemise and undershirt, pulling up her pantaloons and stockings, down her petticoats, then the blouse, the long skirt, the tight little boots with their numerous buttons to be done. She would have left the stays behind on the prairie, but knew Pierre would frown on that, and who knew, she told herself angrily, a Cardinal might show up for tea and I would need my stays. She pushed them into her portmanteau, and carried out the two travelling bags, returning to roll the bedroll, cast about for anything else, and emerged, nodding to Pierre who quickly collapsed the tent. Just so.

"We'll stop later for breakfast," he told her, mounting beside her, the goods stowed, the tent spread out over them and tied down. She held the edge on the far side from him and he had come around to tie the knots himself.

"Show me how you did that," she asked, noticing that his knots would hold, yet would be easy to untie. He demonstrated, but seeing he was growing impatient, said, "Never mind. I will practice and practice." How extraordinary it was that one needed to know how to tie knots!

Then they were on their way, Sophie still tucking up the last strands of her hair, pinning them in place. His eagerness for their land surpassed hers. She wasn't sure for what it was she had been so eager, and recognized that she had mostly looked only backward, at what she was escaping.

"Back to the bouncing!" she said, gaily, to evade her own thoughts.

All around them the tan and cream prairie spread, hints of green beginning to show, behind them only the ring of stones and the burnt twigs that had made their fire to show they had passed that way. Low rises mostly too small to be called hills undulated out to the horizon. But wait, wasn't that…could that be… "Pierre," she said, her voice low, her hand on his arm. Not a mile away, coming down the passageway between two hills was someone on horseback. Pierre drew Gog and Magog to a halt, his right arm going forward to where his gun stood against the front wall of the wagon box. They waited. The mounted man came forward, broke into two, a woman on a smaller horse behind him, a child riding in front of her. Indians. Sophie forgot to breathe.

Pierre murmured, "They'll be curious; tea, the storekeeper said." Sophie knew exactly where the tea was, in the seat below her, where it would be easy to find when they stopped for breakfast. The Indian family drew up, the man close to them, the woman and child on the pony staying well back, the horses motionless. Pierre did not get down from the wagon, nor did he lift his rifle.

"Bon jour," he called, tipping his hat with the side of his hand. "A beautiful morning." The Indian, medium-sized, his body the darkest brown and gleaming as if polished, no spare flesh but well-muscled, his face grooved, his hair in braids, said nothing. Pierre went on. "We have a gift for you," *un cadeau* he said, and was there not a flicker in the man's face as if this he understood? But, Sophie remembered, had not the first white men here been French? Pierre put his hand out to Sophie, who reached below to open the tin she had filled the night before so she wouldn't have to deal with the sack each time she needed it. She took a piece of cheap cotton from her supply, this one about six inches square, scooped tea from the tin into the centre of the cloth, tied it into a bundle. Pierre took it from her hand. The Indian had made a gesture without so much as turning on his mount and now the pony carrying the woman and child was moving slowly forward, past him, until it stopped beside Pierre. The woman lifted a hand, her eyes downcast, her face expressionless, Pierre set the bundle of tea into her palm, nodded briskly, formally, and the woman turned the pony and rode back to take up her position behind the man. Then Sophie saw that on her back an infant slept, strapped into a carrying case.

They sat that way for a moment longer, no one speaking, until a gust of wind came up. Pierre had to lift a hand to hold onto his hat, Sophie shivered, spring, yes, but not yet hot, and would have taken up her shawl around her shoulders, but thought it better not to move. When she had seen the woman's face near hers, the way the child, perhaps two years, had glanced into her face and quickly down again, the wonder, the light of intelligence in his eyes, she had lost her fear. Now she waited, as Pierre was doing. The Indian nodded, the same brisk, formal nod Pierre had given the woman, his horse beginning to move.

"Au revoir," Pierre said, saluting, touching the near oxen's back with his whip, that his clever brother Alexandre had made for him, and the Indian turned to ride north, the pony with its load following, calling back one deep-chested word that had the sound of farewell, and soon were gone into the landscape.

All the rest of that first long day they saw not another human. Pierre fired one shot to frighten off a wolf he saw skulking in the distance, antelope came by in large numbers, running, always running, skimming the hillsides, their white rumps shining, disappearing on the far side of whatever hill they were first seen on. No shortage of meat, Pierre told her, pleased. He would have shot one, he said, but where would they put it? They would get first to the land, then he would hunt for their meat. Birds soared overhead, shrieking, or calling in different tones, the hawks rising on updrafts, circling, driving downward, doing it again. They saw even an eagle, Pierre following it with his eyes, an omen, he said, for the good. The wind came and went, the sun shone down with too little warmth and too much brightness, clouds came, scattered, melted away. The wagon bounced, swayed and rattled, their goods clanking, thudding, pinging, the oxen's harness squeaking. Sometimes it was hard to stay awake, their wagon a raft on this sea of grass.

On they went stopping only for Pierre to gauge their position, triumphant when yet another section marker reared up through the grass, recognizable by its height and the mound of earth in which it sat. They stopped three times to eat, only once making a fire. At last, as the final light of day faded away, he pronounced that they were there, "home," he said, and they looked at each other, grinning again despite their exhaustion, "or nearly there," he added, it being too dark to go on searching for quarter section markers hidden in the grass.

Sophie was so tired that when she tried to climb down from the wagon, she fell, landing in a heap on the earth, and lay there smelling the dry soil, the stiff, dusty grass, and something else, recognizing, only feet from where she lay, the serrated small leaves and prickly stems of the wild rose bushes, already beginning to bloom. Lifting her head, she looked again, and then again, to see that they grew in the low spots all around them. It was the first moment when she was reminded of home – that surprising, unforgettable fragrance of wild roses perfuming the dry air.

CHAPTER FOUR

Sanctuary

CLOSING THE CABIN DOOR behind her, she stepped out onto the prairie and began to walk toward the buggy and its driver. She didn't recognize him, but he was continuing on a straight line toward her and her cabin and the dugout barn and the half-cut crop. She made another effort to compose herself, smoothing back her hair with both hands, capturing a blowing strand, tucking it in, straightening her apron, then turned and walked back toward the closed door of her house in as leisurely a manner as she could manage. There, composed, the *châtelaine* again, she turned to face the visitor.

At last he drew up a few feet from her, not yet climbing down from the buggy, the horse waiting patiently, flicking its ears at flies, tired from its journey from town or from wherever it had come in this heat, the younger, unsaddled horse fastened by a rope halter to the back of the buggy pulling back as if testing if he might now be free, and finding he was not, watching fearfully.

"Who are you?" the man in the buggy asked, a puzzled expression passing across his features and leaving behind a countenance that seemed to her implacable. As if as soon as he had asked the question, he knew the answer, and didn't like it.

"I am Madame Hippolyte, wife of Pierre Hippolyte. We are the owners of this homestead." His eyes had taken on a dangerous glitter: Her instinct told her to back into the cabin and bar the door, but wait, she told herself, not yet. She hoped Pierre hadn't taken his rifle; this she hadn't noticed. During the rebellion he had taught her to shoot, but since then she hadn't touched the gun. But surely Pierre, who loved his Winchester rifle and was as fine a shot – bringing in feasts of deer or antelope – as he wasn't a handler of horses, wouldn't go off without his gun.

She worked to keep her eyes steady on the stranger, who held the reins loosely in his hands, not moving, staring down at her, then lifting his head to look purposefully around at the buildings, as if she weren't there, the crop ahead and to his right, and then, further out to the wide prairie he had just crossed in the smothering, late August heat.

"Hippolyte's wife," he muttered, sounding somewhere between disgusted and resigned. He looped the reins around the rod attached to the footboard, climbed down, and stood facing her. He was of average height, but heavy-bodied and short legged, his face not as sun-darkened as Pierre's, but well-lined, although she could see no hint of grey in his thick brown moustache. She straightened even further, if such were possible, facing him squarely although it took all her courage to do so, as he took off his wide-brimmed hat, holding it in both hands with a humility that belied everything else about him. She saw he had not come to harm her, and this caused her uneasiness to grow even more.

"Pierre, *mon mari* – he is – is he hurt? Is he – dead?" she asked. At this the stranger grinned a twisted, unpleasant grin, then quickly wiped it away.

"Mrs. – uh – Hippolyte," he began. "I sure do hate to tell you this, but your husband" – here he paused – "has sold me your farm. The land, the buildings, the crop, the animals. Even the contents of your house." He had looked closely into her face all the time he spoke; now he glanced away from her.

She took a step backward, put one shaking hand against the doorframe to support herself, tried to speak, but found she couldn't control her jaw to form words. She could make no sense of what this stranger had just said to her. Or rather, she knew very well what he had said, it was only that it was such a shock, and all the many meanings and consequences of it were racing through her mind at the same time, tumbling about like swift foxes playing; she could not catch one of them and hold it; she would faint from the tumult.

"We have been here nearly four years," she managed to say, hearing, helplessly, the irrelevance. The stranger had reached past her, Sophie so overcome she didn't even flinch at the thick body inches from hers, the heavy arm brushing her forearm as he reached for the latch behind her to open the door.

"You better sit down," he said. From deep inside the cabin, Charles emitted his waking cry for her. She hurried through the main room to the bedroom behind it and as she picked him up, the shaking diminished. Holding him tightly, she returned to the other room where the stranger pulled back one of the straight-backed wooden chairs for her, indicating she should sit, which she did, although not without annoyance that he would offer her a chair in her own house.

"I'm Walter Campion," he said. "Came here from Ontario a while ago. I was looking around for land, saw your husband, he said he wanted to sell fast. Said that farming was not for him and he was leaving with his wife and he'd give me a bargain. I thought, better a place with sixty broke acres and a house and barn than one where I have to start from scratch." He smiled self-consciously, then frowned, as if reminding himself to whom it was he spoke.

Sophie said, forcing herself, "When? He was – alone?"

"Yesterday," he said. "Young woman in the wagon with him. Yellow hair," he added, not looking at her.

"He – sold our farm?" she asked, still incredulous. Campion only nodded, steel glinting in his eyes again. He had seated himself in Pierre's chair, casually, as if he had always sat there. His bulk was such that the room became smaller in a way it never did when Pierre entered it.

"Show me the bill of sale," she demanded. Charles struggled to get down and she let him, hardly noticing she had. Campion reached inside his shirt and produced a piece of paper, holding it out to her. She had trouble reading it in the dim light and with her vision unaccountably blurring, but Pierre's signature was at the bottom.

"But he didn't –" she swallowed. "He didn't ask me if I wanted to sell. And where is the money? What did you pay him?" She wanted to ask, and who was the woman?

He said, "I bought this place fair and square; we saw the lawyer in town, I gave your husband the money." Again, he didn't say how much. "Looks like he's gone with it." The last was heavy, as if for one second he had allowed himself to feel the weight of Pierre's perfidy. She was regaining some sense now.

"I do not consent," she told him in the coldest voice she could muster so that he looked at her anew, a brightness appearing in his eyes, the colour of which she couldn't determine, some kind of calculation going on, his gaze dropping to the tabletop.

"You got no choice. I can give you a day or so to gather your personal things."

She sat stiffly, not looking at him, trying to see what it was she should do. But if she resisted, he would have no trouble to force her away. She looked to the door – the gun was gone from its resting place above it.

"I will not go," she told him, her voice growing louder, barely containing rising hysteria. He only stared at her. There was a silence, she unclenched her fists, swallowed, then said in a muted tone, "I need only an hour. But taking what I can gather in an hour in no way signifies my agreement to this sale," a part of her amazed that she could find such words. But she rose, gathered Charles from where he stood, fingers in his mouth, gazing unblinkingly up at Campion's impressive moustache. With her son riding her hip, she turned to go into the bedroom to begin packing, when suddenly she thought aloud, "I have no way to travel." Turning to him, "I must ask you to take me to town."

He looked at her gravely, once again assessing her, and a knife of rage went through her so that she quickly lowered her eyes to keep him from seeing it.

He took in a long suck of air through his nose, as if exhausted with this whole annoying inconvenience. "I have business back in town too. Want to sell that horse –" he tossed his head toward the young horse tied to the back of the buggy outside the door. "I'll take you," and she felt that now he was squelching amusement, which perception further enraged her. But she had to get to town, she would find out who this woman was. She would send the Mountie after Pierre; she would retrieve the money; would go elsewhere, since she doubted she could farm without a husband. Had she already accepted that he was truly gone? That he had indeed abandoned her – his wife, his one true love?

Now, all the fear and anger, the pain and disbelief retreated. It was as if she were floating above the turmoil far below her, and she moved to gather belongings, thinking only of how best to do that, conscious – ridiculously – of her own still youthful body, of her baby's heft, of how easily her fingers worked to lift garments, to fold them neatly, to place them in her portmanteau. How cleverly her hands worked, she thought, as she lifted, discarded, chose, folded cloth creaselessly.

At first it went through her mind that she wouldn't need to take the heavier things with her, her dishes, her frying pan and pots, she could get them later, that is, if Campion would let her, or when Pierre returned… If… Yes, she admitted to herself, but distantly, idly, Pierre was capable, in a fit of rage and when she and his son were not in his line of sight, of doing what Mr. Campion claimed he had done. Maybe she would never see this place again. But even this thought failed to halt her in her careful choosing, lifting, arranging.

How well I am doing, she thought, pleased at her own cleverness. She had taken Charles' clothing and what little she had of her own, plus her two pieces of jewelry – her earrings with tiny diamonds in them that had been her mother's inexplicably she put on – and a pretty brooch, a wedding gift from Pierre's family. She was about to leave the bedroom when her eye fell on the barrel on which her few family pictures stood on a cloth she had herself, before her marriage, embroidered. The barrel contained her china dishes, Sèvres, that had come from relatives in France to celebrate her grandparents' wedding, the porcelain so thin as to be nearly translucent, painted with bright pictures, and edged with gold.

She had remembered them in those confusing days before she left, knew them to be hers because they had been given to Julie, her real grandmother, and her grandfather for a wedding gift, long before she had been born. She wondered if her grandmother had packed them away this way when she married grandfather, because Sophie knew of them, but had never seen them used and without giving it much thought, had attributed this failure to use them to a combination of grandmother's stinginess, and her love of her own dishes that had the family initial and crest on them... This man, Campion, would not have her dishes. Useless, she had to admit, as they had so far been in this wild country. The dishes themselves, though, now served to bring her back to the solidity of the rough floor beneath her feet, to the cabin's stifling heat, and she moved more slowly, the turmoil returning.

Campion had vanished. Glancing out the window, she saw his hat over the poles of the corral and she understood that he was surveying the farm that was now his. Probably watering his own horses, maybe letting them graze a little while he waited for her, corralling and putting out feed for the saddle horse, the cow, and chickens, she thought, shutting them up so the wolves and coyotes won't get them tonight, maybe even milking the cow yet again. Maybe he would bring in their five cows that grazed far out on the prairie. Who would care for the delicate Fleurette, whom she loved, and for Pierre's beautiful Tonerre?

At last, the buggy laden with the two adults and the child, and the few belongings she was taking in the portmanteau she had carried on the train West and since hardly used tucked in at her feet, the barrel of china wedged behind the seat and the back wall of the buggy, the great bay horse to whom this load was nothing, at Campion's command, pulled away from the cabin and from the farm to which she and Pierre had given, for four long years, every ounce of their strength and courage. She wanted to look back, but remembered Lot's wife, who looked back and was turned into a pillar of salt.

But she couldn't stop herself; as the horse picked up speed, beginning to jog its way onto the trail, she looked over her shoulder at the frame cabin with its yellow-grassed roof, the rough grey pole corral, and what she could see of the barn set into the hillside, and the sod chicken coop, and the half-cut crop gleaming golden in the sun. She looked back further to the place where the buff-and-cream land met the encompassing sky and her heart gave such a leap, would crack in two, the pain such that she turned back again to face, impotently, the miles before them.

The horse trotted on, the buggy swaying, the roughness of the trail causing her to jostle now and then against Campion, or he against her, no matter how she squeezed to her side of the narrow seat, until she judged it safe to move Charles from her knee onto the seat between them. Her mind had slowed enough now that she could fasten onto a thought, but all such thoughts seemed as if only distantly her own; otherwise, she was hollowed out, emptied, the emptiness vast and dark. She barely noticed Campion except as a heavy shadow on her left. Occasionally, though, he spoke to her.

"Must a' been lonely out there with no neighbours." Sophie said nothing. "But you mark it," he went on, as if she had answered, "Come spring, settlers will be flooding in. This whole big empty place – room for thousands and thousands of people." Sophie said, softly, as if testing what she had felt, "I was not lonely."

"Can you go to your family?" She didn't answer. "Are they farmers?" She saw this as his attempt to find out why she might choose not to go to them.

"They have a general store."

"Good business?" he asked, interested.

"Yes." Her ear lobes began to tingle, as if the earrings with their tiny diamonds were still imbued with the warmth of her grandmother's fingers. The dishes, riding precariously in the barrel jammed behind the seat, had never been so heavy, nor at once fraught with such delicacy. She couldn't bear the thought that her grandparents might know of her plight; she vowed she would never tell them.

Sounds seemed to come from far away: the shriek of an eagle far above, a dot circling in that space between earth and sky's edge, (she didn't search for its partner, although there would be one), the scolding chitter of small birds fluttering out of the horse's way, the lament of a coyote that followed them for a time before trotting away, pausing to look back over his shoulder, then leisurely nosing his flank for fleas. The creak of the buggy springs, harness buckles clinking, the soft thud of the horses' hooves on the ground. The sun beat down on them, and if she raised her eyes beyond the faint trail through the grass ahead of them, it seemed they were travelling on into the colourless band where the cream and tan earth and blue sky failed to meet. Charles had fallen asleep against her and would tumble off the seat. She lifted him back into her lap, shook out a shawl from her bag to cover his head against the sun. His weight, though considerable, he was big for his age, comforted her, as if, without him, she might float off the seat. Two hours passed in this uncomfortable way, the sun burning down, Sophie staring ahead, seeing nothing, until at last Campion pulled the rig to a stop.

"Horses need a rest. A few minutes." At the ceasing of motion Charles woke, and at once wanted down. Campion had dismounted from the buggy and reached for him, Sophie reluctantly allowing this, then suffered Campion to help her down, holding herself in so as to touch him only where she had to, her elbow in his palm, that was all. She held the reins for him while he went off behind a small hill and when he returned, she took Charles and went off too, although to a different rise. She laughed out loud, inadvertently, as she made her choice of a different hillock, preserving proprieties even in this wilderness, even in her situation. But the thought of coming upon Campion's leavings steaming in the grass sickened her, so she walked faster; Charles running to keep up.

She wondered briefly, herding her son back across the grass to the buggy, how it could be that someone like her, not a bad person, only twenty-four years old, should be asked to bear so much so suddenly. How Pierre could have turned away from her. This was far worse than finding him dead on the prairie, she said to herself, but even as she said it, wasn't sure, telling herself, *It is the suddenness of it; it is the unexpectedness*. But she walked on, one foot in front of the other in her worn-out boots, stumbling a little on the uneven prairie, the scent of sage, grasses, and the few wild roses sickening her, wishing the scent she had loved would end as everything else had ended. At the buggy she allowed Campion to lift Charles, and to put his thick hand under her elbow again to help her up.

"You are light as a feather," he said, grunting, as if to contradict what he had just said, but in that grunt, and in her heightened state, she heard his sexuality, gross and hard; it hit her like a blow, sickening her.

Eventually, in late afternoon on the eastern horizon, a shining white hillock rose before them, growing longer and higher by slow degrees as they inched nearer. The pile from which the village had acquired its strange name, an uneven mountain of bleached and broken buffalo bones sat waiting either for a branch rail line to be built to the village so that the bones could be hauled away to be sent East to be used in industry, or more likely, until its owner hired teamsters with wagons and oxen to haul it, load by load, to the closest rail line, north and either to the east, to Swift Current or even Moose Jaw, or to the west, to Garden City, or as far as Medicine Hat. No one knew who had laid the first bones there, that in the few years Sophie had been in the North-West Territories, had accumulated to this great mass, and her knowledge as to its uses didn't in the least diminish her uneasiness whenever she approached it, nor could she properly divine its source.

The Indians had started it, she had heard. In her strange state, altered from normalcy by shock and fear, she understood why, the knowledge seeming to swell across the prairie to reach inside her: Grief had laid them, and fear: The bones were about power. She tore away her eyes, lifted the back of one hand to her nose as if to deflect a stench, feeling Campion's dismissive glance.

In more hopeful days, Sophie and Pierre had contributed a wagon load that had brought them five dollars; *It was not worth the trouble*, Pierre had said, although Sophie had done nearly all the gathering, he had helped only with the loading of the wagon, driving the team from pile to small pile that Sophie over weeks, whenever she could find the time, had made in a circle around their land. Then he had laughed, "We're circled by bones."

"Don't say that," Sophie said sharply, and he had laughed again, in a way that seemed cruel to her, yet carried too, the sound of uneasy incomprehension. "At least now we won't always be stumbling over them. Tonerre could have broken his leg."

Before them lay a coulee, the north end deep and narrow, the south end, where they would in a moment cross, wide and shallow. Here the land folded on itself like an open mouth, lips, tongue, exposed. The town dipped out of view, then almost at once began to rise again through the stiff, dun-coloured grass: The livery stable at the north, the false-fronted general store, a few other small frame, false-fronted buildings strung out between them, and haphazardly, starting at the south and Harry Adamson's cabin, a handful of unadorned square houses built of wood, tar paper and tin, mostly little more than shacks, and scattered over two streets, the street nearest to them anchored by a large frame house. Not a single tree graced the village, there was no church spire, as yet not even a school.

But there was a water supply here in the coulee, and a few stunted trees at the deep end, which was why, people said, that rancher Quinn had built his house here, intending to make it his ranch headquarters, but just as it was ready to move into, instead, he had crashed off his horse, dead of a heart attack, people said, before he hit the ground, although others said his neck was broken in the fall, and wouldn't that kill you dead enough, never mind a heart attack? His handsome frame house with the verandah down two sides and its two fireplaces, growing shabbier and grayer every day, was now Mrs. Emery's boarding house.

Without consulting her, Campion drove the buggy straight to the livery barn at the end of the main street, Sophie barely registering that a new house had been built in the gap between the livery stable and the blacksmith's shop. Campion remarked, unnecessarily, as if to deflect her attention, "I'll get the horses feed and water while we do our business." Once again with his help, she and Charles climbed down and waited while Ambrose, the livery barn owner, came out and conferred with him. After which Campion instructed her, "Leave your things for now. Ambrose will take care of them. Right Ambrose?" Sophie understood that coins had changed hands, but as she had nothing to give anyone, she kept her back straight and gazed off at one of the front windows of the new frame house. Its lace curtain stirred as she watched.

She was holding hard onto Charles who was trying to get away to play in the hay. Impossible! Horses would not eat hay that children had played in, and anyway, it was far too dangerous to let him loose around them. To distract him, she walked out of the barn onto the boardwalk which extended a few feet across the livery barn's entrance to end abruptly on one side in what, in wetter weather, would be a muddy quagmire but which in the late summer heat was only a patch of hard, rutted, light brown earth with a few sparse heads of dry grass growing in it. A section of boardwalk had begun to be built at the entrance of the new house that would eventually meet the one at the livery barn entrance. She became aware of Campion's bulk beside her.

"It's the lawyer you'll be wanting to see."

"Yes," was all she said, not looking at him, but making her voice brusque as if she were not screwing up every ounce of her courage. They began to walk, Sophie shifting her bag to her other arm in order to carry Charles who did not want to be carried. "Hush!" she told him, her voice harsher than she'd meant, but a sound new to Charles who at once, in surprise, ceased to struggle and whimper. Never mind; he must learn too. Campion, not asking, took her bag from her and she let him. At the end of the livery barn's boardwalk, they crossed the rough patch of ground and, avoiding the entrance to the new house, crossed the street, and stepped up again onto the long section that ran continuously before the few stores. They passed the blacksmith's shop, then the entrance to the general store – odours of onion, oil, fresh cotton, spices, leather, wafting out and Sophie steeling herself against them, as if they had no right to smell as they always had – and at last reached the long set of stairs that went steeply up the side of the small wooden building that served as barber shop, to the lawyer's office above it.

Once inside the bare waiting room, Sophie hesitated, suddenly frightened, but Campion strode across the room to the closed door that, presumably, led into the lawyer's office itself, knocked briskly, and without waiting for an answer, opened it. She heard a male voice, Campion turned and beckoned to her, and mutely she obeyed his summons. Then they stood side by side in front of the desk of Frank Archibald, the town's only lawyer. Charles, having given up the struggle to go his own way, lay against Sophie's shoulder, sound asleep, making soft burbling noises; she hoped he wasn't catching a cold, although in such heat a cold seemed absurd, even as Campion set her portmanteau onto the floor beside her as she straightened to meet the lawyer's gaze. When Campion introduced her, the man's eyelids flickered quickly before his eyes descended to the paper on the desk before him and stayed there. But she was concentrating her strength on keeping her voice steady, standing ramrod straight to control the trembling running through her.

"This lady, Mrs. Hippolyte," Campion murmured, delicately enough that she was surprised, "has been abandoned by her husband who, as we know, sold his farm to me. It turns out that she didn't know about this." He looked to the sleeping Charles as if to say to Archibald, See? A child. There was a moment's silence, during which Archibald cleared his throat gently.

"There can be no question, Madame Hippolyte," he told her. "The transaction was entirely within the law. Your husband has the legal right to sell his farm." His moustache, light brown, thin, meticulously trimmed, glistened as he spoke, was motionless as soon as he stopped. She had a sense that he too had steeled himself.

"Without my consent!" Her voice, to her satisfaction, came out strong and clear; she hadn't been sure it would. "It is my farm too, did I not give four years labour to it? Did I not leave my home and family to come with him here?" Aware, even as she said it, of her hypocrisy, for hadn't she been the one who had persuaded him to come?

"He does not, by law, need your consent, Mrs. Hippolyte."

"But certainly he needs my consent! I am his wife!"

"You must understand," the lawyer replied, his voice gentle again,"that the dower law has been struck down here in the Territories." When she said nothing, staring at him, her disbelief and consternation diminishing with the dawning of the full nature of her predicament, he went on more naturally, as if she too would be interested in his lawyer's considerations. "Yours is one of the first cases I've dealt with, although it's unlikely to be the last."

She faltered. "What do you mean?"

"Please, sit down, Mrs. Hippolyte," he urged her, his gaze faintly alarmed, as if he might need to rise to help her, and Campion stood ostentatiously behind the chair beside her, his hands resting on its back. Her knees were threatening to buckle; she sat more heavily, partly because of Charles' weight, than she would have wished. For the first time, real anger rose in her, spreading heat through her face and throat, and it propelled her, child and all, back to her feet. Oh, yes, she had thought sometimes when Pierre was in the midst of one of his rages – she could rage too. But Archibald, seeing again what was in her face, spoke quickly. "Let me explain. It was the law that gave a wife's right to a share in her husband's property." He cleared his throat carefully, glanced at Campion standing behind her – Why is he still here? she wondered – stroked his pale moustache briefly, and went on, "It was only last year the government…struck it down."

Sophie was stunned. "All over Canada? In Québec too?" The lawyer looked down at his desktop before he answered.

"No, Mrs. Hippolyte. Only here in the North-West Territories." He moved his fingers slightly this way and that, then held them still. She had observed that he was, or could be, a handsome man, tall and straight-backed, his pale thinning hair carefully brushed to one side, and held in place with a discreet amount of pomade. There was not the tiniest piece of lint on his dark blue jacket, and a distant part of her marveled at that tidiness, unobtainable on a dusty homestead. Which brought back the smell of the cabin in the early morning, Pierre's heat against her's, that he had gone…

She struggled for composure, breathing deeply through her nose, lifting her head again and straightening her back, holding her child more tightly. She could see in his eyes how he watched her, his face composed into politeness of the sort the better men reserved for their dealings with women: excessive courtesy, which as a girl she had thought beautiful, veiled watchfulness, a hint – she could never rid herself of this perception – of amusement.

"I see there is no help to be had here." Her voice had softened to a whisper. The lawyer stiffened, his face smoothing to a mask of politeness, and came round his desk to escort her and Mr. Campion from the room.

"There is no recourse in law for what your husband has done, indeed," he told her, "And I deeply regret this. Had I known, perhaps I would have refused his business. Nor did Mr. Campion have any idea that the…uh…person with him was not his lawful wife." At the door to his empty reception room, his stiffness relaxing slightly, he added, "I have heard of the most deplorable cases – a Galician mother of six little ones abandoned and utterly penniless. At least you are –" he hesitated again, "not without resources."

She wanted to ask how much money Pierre had received for their farm, animals and crop, knowing it had to be worth, she had estimated this quietly on the long ride into town, perhaps two thousand dollars, but she knew if she asked the lawyer he would refuse to tell her, and she wouldn't give Campion the satisfaction of telling her what her very life had cost him. As little as he could get away with, of that she was sure – a thousand dollars, maybe, or twelve hundred. She knew Pierre; when it came to money, if it were up against a stronger desire, he had no sense at all, he would throw money away, whereas being raised in a household supported by direct commerce, she supposed she had imbibed a certain attitude without even realizing she had.

When they were in the waiting room, the door behind them closed, Sophie stood, her son still dozing on her shoulder, her back beginning to ache from carrying him, but with no place to put him down, and the weight of the portmanteau suddenly too much for her so that she took an uncertain step to one side, as if she had lost her balance, then regained it. She realized with a start that Mr. Campion remained to her left, quietly, waiting on her.

"Monsieur Campion?" she queried, hearing the note of desperation in her own voice and cursing it.

"I'll take you to the Mountie. You're lucky – he's in town today." She was about to refuse, then thought that with a man of his substance beside her, she might fare better with the Mountie. Without speaking she began to descend the stairs slowly, hugging Charles closely with one arm, peering over his rounded back to see where she was stepping, lifting her skirt with the other the bag hanging uncomfortably from her forearm. Campion gave a slight tug at the portmanteau and again, she let him take it. At the bottom of the stairs, she recovered it from him, refusing his offer to carry it.

As she and Campion walked back down the street the way they had come, past the general store toward the blacksmith shop, in between which stood the small building they were looking for, he inquired of her, had she any friends in town? She didn't want to answer him, yet all her girl's training in courtesy to her elders forced an answer out of her.

"No," she replied. "I seldom came to town, and my husband preferred we spend our free time with other settlers like ourselves. I mean – French–speakers," she added.

"One of them, maybe?" he asked. She shook her head, no, then managing, "The Le Fèbvre family left for the north I was told."

"There are some new people in town, came a month or so ago, I'm thinking – the Tremblay's," he suggested. "That is French without a doubt." Tremblay! That was the name, and their oldest daughter was Marguerite. Hadn't Pierre spoken of meeting the family not long ago at the Beausoleil's? And once, after that hadn't he said he'd dropped in on them when he had come to town for the mail? And Charles feverish so she had stayed home? Aloud, she said, keeping her voice light. "I do not know them." First, she told herself, she would talk to the Mountie. Then she would go to Mrs. Emery's boarding house. She clung to this thought as a kind of salvation from the company of this man, helpless as she was against the necessity of acting before she had even properly assimilated her own plight. She would go to Mrs. Emery's, and Mrs. Emery would take them in. Surely she would.

How she would pay for the night there, if indeed Mrs. Emery would have a room free for her, she didn't know. Work, maybe? She had only a few pennies, a fact which her intuition told her no one must know. Pride yes, but also she recognized how vulnerable she would be should anyone know; she vowed then to claim that she was only waiting for money to come from her family in Québec. No one would ever know that there would not be money coming from Québec, because she would never ask, would never reveal to her grandmother or her brothers that they had been right about Pierre, and she, wrong. She clung more tightly to Charles. No, appealing to her family would be her last resort before starvation. In a flash that came and went so quickly it barely registered, she longed for the comfort of Antoinette's bosom.

The Mountie, luckily, was in his spare, unlined shack that, on the days the family with the mail route brought it, also functioned as a post office. His papers were spread out over the table and irritation appeared on his face, as she pushed open the door, that evaporated when he saw Mr. Campion enter behind her. He stood, a short man, with an officious manner and military carriage, his lips pursed as he pushed his papers this way and that with his fingertips, without making any perceptible progress in arranging them. She could feel his contained fuming from across the table between them and her familiar woman's patience in dealing with difficult men settled into her chest and forehead, even brought a measure of calm, as something she understood.

"Constable McMann," Campion said heartily, extending his hand. "Glad to find you in. Wasn't sure this was your day to be here."

"Just finishing up my patrol, Mr. Campion. In the morning I'm for Garden City and a few days leave." He didn't look at Sophie.

"New house in town," Campion said. Something passed between them that Sophie couldn't divine, but the Mountie nodded, smiling faintly, and not replying, yet the new house with its lace curtains was only yards from where they stood. "This is Mrs. Hippolyte." Sophie waited, but he said nothing more. Now, she thought, she was to speak for herself, and a flash of hatred for both these men startled her even as she suppressed it.

"Constable McMann," the officer said. "May I be of service?"

"Mr. Campion has been kind enough to accompany me here to see you," she said, forcing her voice into a clear light tone, aware of her accent, and cursing it. In this world, she would be better without it. "My husband –" She paused, swallowing. "My husband, Pierre Hippolyte, has deserted me." In this new, light voice, it was possible to say things she couldn't say in her own, and having said it, continuing was easier. "Worse, he has sold our farm to Monsieur Campion and I am without a home for myself and my son. We have just come from the lawyer who tells me my husband acted within the law."

"Oh," the Mountie said, noncommittal, then shifting his tone. "You're not the first lady to come to me with such a story." Then, another shift into firmness. "There's nothing I can do."

"He has abandoned us," Sophie repeated, not changing her tone.

"Can't you pursue him?"

"When did this happen?" the Mountie demanded, as if she were the criminal.

"I saw him yesterday," Campion intervened. "Here in town, when I bought the farm from him. Yesterday morning, to be exact." It suddenly occurred to Sophie to wonder how Archibald could not have known that the woman with Pierre was the pretty daughter of the new family in town. Perhaps he didn't see her in the wagon? And Campion might truly not have known as she was fairly sure he didn't live in Bone Pile, and as they had never seen each other before this morning, a blonde woman with Pierre would mean nothing to him. Or was she, appallingly, inventing excuses for him? And why was he staying with her when all he had to do if he really wanted to help was to hand her back the deed to the farm? Yet she knew, as well as she knew herself to be Charles' mother, that Campion would never return the farm to her, hadn't a qualm about what had been done to her, probably viewed all this business as tedious beyond words.

"So he has had the better part of two days and a night," the Mountie noted. He shook his head. "He'll be over the border by now. He has broken no laws. There is no reason for me to chase him. I might have tried to reason with him if I'd known, but..." he shrugged his shoulders. "It's too late now." Sophie didn't know whether there was something the Mountie could do or not, only that there was nothing he would. She was about to turn away, Charles beginning to wake, twisting in her arms so that she hummed softly to him in reassurance, jiggling him a little and patting his back, all the while with her eyes fixed on the Mountie's face. "Now, if you'd run out on him that would be different. I could go after you. No wife can just up and run off and take a man's children." Sophie drew in her breath quickly. She could tell by the Mountie's abrupt change of expression that she must look as stricken as she felt. Now he looked concerned, although she had noted too, the look of exasperation that had passed fleetingly over it before his face softened.

"Wait – do you need a place to stay for the night? Are you destitute?" It was the first time he had really looked at her, and she saw his eyes pass swiftly from her bosom, mostly hidden by Charles, to her waist and then up again to her earrings where they lingered for less than an instant, but enough that she saw interest, even perhaps a hint of respect. She ignored his question about her financial situation.

"I am going to Mrs. Emery's for the night," again working to keep her voice steady. "I will make other decisions tomorrow."

"You have family here?"

"I have not," she replied. "But my family in Québec will m'aid." Annoyed, she corrected herself, "Help me. They will help me."

He nodded, relieved. Clearly, he didn't want another penniless woman and her brood on his hands, had already begun calculating what he would do if she hadn't a roof over her head and no help she could turn to, and the fact that he would have to do this was annoying him no end.

"Now, you never know," the Mountie said to her, smiling in a false way, she could see him washing his hands of her, "your husband might be back in a few days or a week, and even if he doesn't return, he may send you some of the money." She wanted to strike him, speaking to her as if she were a child, and she shifted Charles a little, moving her eyes away from the Mountie's so he wouldn't see her anger.

"I will not wait for that," she said, grimly. No, Pierre wouldn't be back in a week or ten days, although – now that she thought of it – maybe he would send her some money, if not for her, at least for his son's sake. She turned from the Mountie without speaking again, deliberately not thanking him.

Outside again in the stifling early fall heat, the air laden with dust and the sun lowering in the western sky, turning it bronze and yellow, she said to Mr. Campion, "You have been very helpful. I must thank you." She didn't smile, but couldn't stop herself from adding, "Despite your being the agent of my –" she struggled for the English word, "misfortune." Charles was begging to be allowed to walk, so she set him down. Her arms and the small of her back ached from his weight, as well as from the bag she carried. *"Ne bouger pas,"* she said, and then from habit, "Stay here."

Campion had again removed the hat he had taken off in the lawyer's office and then in the Mountie's. She could see he had something he wanted to say to her, and anxiety arose again. Indeed, she half knew already what he was working to say.

"Mrs. Hippolyte –"

"*Oui*, Monsieur?" she replied, gravely, as if she were not fighting a sudden rise of gorge into her throat, as if her heart hadn't begun to trip quickly there, making her swallow.

"You know I have to either go back to the farm right away to milk the cow, and in the morning to let the horse and chickens out to graze, that I have to find them five cows and bring them in, or there'll be a disaster. Never mind get that crop off while it's still standing. I'll find somebody to do all that, but right now I have business to attend to. I – I have a proposal –

"Yes, Monsieur?" coldly, now.

"I need a cook; I need someone to keep the cabin clean, to wash the clothes, to look after them animals when I'm elsewhere." His words hung in the orange-tinted, dusty air between them.

"I know exactly what you need, Monsieur," she said, with every ounce of repugnance she could muster, and turned on her heel, Charles trundling after her. Her face burned, her entire body glowed with heat. He came after her, caught her by the sleeve. Her instinct was to pull away, but who might see this? Better to make it look as though they were having a friendly discussion. It stunned her, how quickly she had become prey.

"I didn't mean to offend," he said, humble now, but she could see what was in his eyes.

"Leave me now," she said, "before I return to the Mountie." Although she doubted the Mountie would lift a finger to help her, and indeed, hadn't a touch of amused contempt entered Campion's face at this threat? She was a mere woman, and a penniless one at that. She was trembling again, but this time it was with a billowing anger that threatened to engulf her, that should she unleash it, would burn this very town to the ground. "Go," she told him, in a low voice. "*Vite!* Before I scream." He flushed a deep red.

"Now wait a minute," he told her, and would have said more, but her countenance appeared to stop him. He gave her a slight bow, as if their conversation had ended, and walked away.

Her mind churning with disgust and fear, she moved her bag to the other hand and began to hurry toward Mrs. Emery's house. She marched for a moment, Charles catching her skirt and beginning to cry so that she had to stop to pick him up again.

Lâche! Coward, she told herself. *Idiote!* If you make a mistake, you correct it. You do not let it lie and ruin your life. *Le bon Dieu* – she was even beginning to think in English. How could she correct this life-ending mistake? But wait! What *was* her mistake? she asked herself, putting down her son again, taking his hand and slowing to his speed. That I didn't see how weak and selfish Pierre really was before I married him? That I did not know the law? That I didn't keep some cash for myself when I had the opportunity? Yes, to that, and she cursed herself again for believing in Pierre's love and in their mutual desire, never seeing how things between them had changed. Their precious moments together as they came to know each other, the kisses they shared in her grandmother's garden – all came back to her. Would she never have that again?

But she had arrived at the Emery house, seeing how shabby it had become, although it had been only two or three years since the rancher had died and Mrs. Emery had bought it. She was thinking how best to approach the woman as she climbed the few steps onto the open verandah, set Charles down, and knocked nervously on the big front door with its oval bevelled glass that spoke of a house built for better things. In a moment she heard heavy footsteps coming down the hall, and the door swung open to reveal a short, stout woman well into her sixties whose inquisitive gaze from behind round spectacles caused Sophie to unexpectedly flinch, even as she remembered hearing somewhere this woman's own name was Charlotte, and surely a Charlotte couldn't be anything but kind?

"Mrs. Hippolyte, ain't it?" "Yes, I am Madame – Mrs.– Sophie Hippolyte," Sophie replied. The other opened the door wider, silently inviting Sophie to enter. The hall was redolent of cooking food, and something that she found unpleasant underlying that, the lingering odour of a hundred meals before this one, and it was untidy with boots and coats, although seeming clean enough. Many a settler who had no friends or family in town spent the night here, although she and Pierre never had. This was the first time she had seen the house's interior.

"Don't mind the mess," Mrs. Emery said, noting Sophie's quick glance down the hall. "I have my hands full just keeping the meals on time." She gave a wry snort. "You looking for a room for the night?" Without waiting for a reply she said, "Come into the parlour," and stood to one side indicating the room on Sophie's left, which Sophie entered, Charles following closely, clinging shyly to her skirt and making it hard for her to walk. The parlour was also clean despite the shabbiness of the furnishings, the rug underfoot threadbare.

"Yes," Sophie answered. "I am looking for a room for myself and my son."

"Sit, sit," Mrs. Emery said, and Sophie sat, grateful to be in an environment that did not feel so masculine and bare as the lawyer's and the Mountie's offices had been, and with a woman older than her mother, were she still alive, would be. Charles plunked himself down on the rug, gazing around at all the new wonders, and Sophie handed him the small mirror she had taken from her bag so he would be occupied. He began at once to study it with care, turning it this way and that to make it flash, talking to himself all the while. Soon he would be crying for food, and terror struck Sophie again so that she forced herself to look down at Charles so that Mrs. Emery wouldn't read her face.

"A pretty boy," Mrs. Emery said, smiling at him in a cursory way. Sophie saw at once that this was a woman who was done with children, and wondered how many she had given birth to and raised. How many had died. And where the living ones were now. "I keep an empty room for just this kind of thing. I could rent it out to a bachelor, but you know them bachelors, not so steady a lot of them, and a nuisance." Sophie smiled. "I rent it out most nights," Mrs. Emery added, nodding. "So it does me no damage – in a business way, I mean. Except for that Mrs. – what did she call herself – Mrs. Smith. I know a doxy when I see one. She wouldn't be staying here." She smiled angrily at Sophie, and went on, "Between them blessed drunken bachelors and the doxies looking for a place of business –" Sophie decided to ignore this.

"I am temporarily without funds," she began.

Now Mrs. Emery started, and would have spoken, but Sophie went on quickly. "I wish to work for our room and board for perhaps one week or two, maybe longer, until my family sends me my remittance from Québec." Mrs. Emery observed her carefully, her eyes bright. "This is a big house. You must have at least a half-dozen boarders. I see you keep the place very clean and I know from my own life that that is very difficult, especially if you have no help."

"You're right about that," Mrs. Emery agreed warily. "Dawn to dusk and no stopping. And try to find a woman to work. There's so few of 'em to start with, I no sooner find one and train her and some bachelor carries her off, be her stupid or ugly – it don't seem to matter. As long as they can work." She nodded to Sophie's unspoken question. "If they pay me extra, I do their laundry too." She gazed down at her hands, knuckles enlarged, fingers swollen, the skin roughened and red. For an instant, the spirit seemed to go out of her, as if the sight of her own hands said such things to her as she could not bear to know. "Mr. Emery and I come from Ontario," she remarked, her mood shifting. "The land rush was just getting started out here on the prairies. Free land! We thought we'd found heaven." She sighed heavily. "Maybe we would have, too, but Mr. Emery, he had a bad heart and we didn't know it. Or else it was just plain hard work did it. He didn't make it through our first winter. He was the first one in the new cemetery. You might say we started it." She thrust her hands up under her glasses, to wipe her eyes with their backs, not even bothering to search for a handkerchief, nor did her expression change even though for an instant her tears had run freely. She straightened her spectacles as Sophie watched her with a combination of pity and puzzlement. "So I took everything we had left in our savings and I bought this house for a song," she continued, as if there had been no interruption.

Sophie said, "You didn't wish to –" she hesitated, "– go back home?"

"Mr. Emery and I had four children," she said. "The oldest, Jerome, he decided to stay back east. Didn't even come with us. But my youngest died when we first got here. Elizabeth. She's buried out in the grass on the farm. My only girl. Never did get her moved to the cemetery."

"I am so sorry," Sophie said.

"The next-oldest boy, Henry, he took on the farm. Milton, he went south, to California. Looking to get rich, I reckon he was. Hasn't been back." As she added the last she turned her head and gazed at the closed door that led into the long, cluttered hall, blinked once or twice, and turned back to Sophie.

"Such a large house," Sophie remarked, to divert Mrs. Emery from her litany of loss.

"A rancher named Quinn built it – before there was a town here. I expect you know that. He passed away sudden, his widow she wanted to go back east. She sold the deeded land easy, wasn't much, his cows just grazed out free, lots of land and nobody put their name to it, but the house went for a bargain. Furniture and all. She was in a hurry. Hated it out here. When I saw that Henry and his new wife didn't want me on the farm, I bought this place – Henry, he wanted me to go back to Ontario, but I dug my heels in. Couldn't leave my sweet girl all alone out there." She spread out her hands as if to say, what could I do? "Land belongs to men, I reckon," she said, not looking at Sophie.

Just then, from above their heads, came the creaking of floorboards. Sophie had been dimly aware for some moments of heavy, slow footsteps overhead. Mrs. Emery gazed upward. "That one don't work no more," she said. "Sam Wetherell, you heard of him?" Without waiting for an answer, Mrs. Emery said that he was an American, had ridden with American cavalry and fought in the Indian wars there, that he had gone to the California gold rush in 1859, and when they'd opened the land there for homesteading, he had filed. Then something had happened, she didn't know what, and he had come north and started a ranch somewhere far to the west of Bone Pile. She didn't know what had brought him to her boarding house to live out his last days. She appeared to have a sort of grudging respect for him mixed with a certain indignation that she made no attempt to hide.

In her pain, Sophie waited, as patient as Job, then realized that this chatter had been to give Mrs. Emery time to think about her answer to Sophie's proposal. If the answer would be no – she caught her breath, tried to cover this with a throat-clearing – and waited.

"All right," Mrs. Emery said. "I need help, you're right, and you're right, too, it ain't easy work, and it don't end. Days are long. You'll get tired. But then, you been on a homestead for a while now. I reckon you know how to work." Sophie nodded, not able to speak in her relief. Just then loud footsteps, this time on the wooden floor of the porch on the other side of the parlour wall, could be heard, then the thump of something heavy being set down, followed by the boots marching off the porch. The parlour windows were thickly curtained, but suddenly Sophie knew who it was.

"I believe it is the gentleman who brought me to town bringing me my things," she said carefully. The barrel of dishes.

Mrs. Emery said, slowly, "Your neighbour?"

"No," Sophie said, "The new owner of our farm. Mr. Campion?"

Holding herself steady, her voice calm. She saw Mrs. Emery look away when she had indicated what had happened to her, and she just as suddenly was sure that Mrs. Emery already knew about it.

"Oh, Campion," Mrs. Emery responded, as if it were only to be expected. "I hear he's buying up anything he can get his hands on. You didn't know? When he's not buying and selling horses and cows, he's buying land. Thinks there's going to be a rush once they build us a branch line down here, figures he'll get rich, I guess." Sophie said nothing, thinking, so he will sell everything on our place as fast as he can. So he *was* making me an – she hesitated, trying to find the word – immoral proposal. Pretending he was helping me. She kept her eyes down and waited until her anger slowly ebbed away, leaving behind disgust that prickled at her cheeks and forehead.

She forced herself to say, "My husband –" She hesitated. "My husband – went away. Without me. I don't know when he will return –" Mrs. Emery interrupted, giving a slight wave with one hand as if to say, don't bother telling me, it isn't news to me.

"Heard that old Mr. Jean Tremblay went after them." Again, she looked away while imparting this information. So he had gone with that Marguerite as she had thought at once, although hoping against hope that she was wrong. Marguerite who was perhaps seventeen. And not only Mrs. Emery had known this, everyone in the village would know it. And now they would also know that he had sold the farm out from under her. That he had spurned her wholly, had so scorned her as to leave her destitute.

For a moment she thought that this was more than she would be able to bear, that every step she took from now on would be monitored and whispered about, everyone waiting to see if she would go back home or if she would – fall – would move in with any man who would have her and her child so as not to starve. This was worse than the judging eyes, the censure, of the village she'd come from. Mrs. Emery continued, either oblivious to Sophie's state, or thinking it better to ignore it.

"I saw him ride back into town this morning. Guess they made it across the border." She looked hard at Sophie who sat rigid, clinging to fistfuls of skirt that she didn't know she had gathered in her hands. Mrs. Emery shifted her gaze to the wall behind Sophie's head. "Could be old Jean realized that was one less mouth to feed. Or –" she paused, while Sophie, suddenly feeling the cloth in her hands, opened them, began smoothing the fabric with her palms, again and again. Still looking at the wall, her tone hard and low now, Mrs. Emery said, "I know you feel shamed. How do you think I felt when Henry chased me off my own place? Oh, he was all for helping me, but what he done was he chased me to wherever he could get me to go." Sophie wanted only that she stop saying these terrible things out loud, her own shame was so complete. The woman sighed. "To tell the truth, I been halfway expecting you."

Charles, as if suddenly growing tired of all this palaver, pulled himself upright, and reached for his mother, with a loud wail, then began to sob in earnest. Sophie could feel Mrs. Emery's irritation at the racket. She began to rummage in her bag, extracted the last bit of bread and gave it to Charles who pressed it against his lips at once, as if to make sure it really was food, and then pushing it into his mouth.

"He's hungry, that little one," Mrs. Emery said. "We got to be friends," she said. "Or this ain't going to work. I help you, you help me. Now we got to get supper on the table." She pulled herself to her feet. "First I'll show you your room and then you give me a hand in the kitchen. Supper'll come that much faster."

Charles quieted and in her arms again, Mrs. Emery moving into the hall, even exhausted as she was, Sophie saw herself in a new town, somewhere she had never been before, where no one knew her or what had happened to her. In her desperation, imagining herself walking smartly down the main street in the sunshine, smiling at the ladies she met, wearing a handsome new dress, her wide-brimmed summer hat with its bright ribbons setting off her dark hair. Even as she patted Charles' back and murmured soothingly to the exhausted child whose weight seemed to have doubled, tripled even, over this long day, even as she saw the childishness of her vision, she couldn't suppress a small surge of excitement. To re-create herself, she, Sophie Charron Hippolyte – what a thought! But Pierre hovered there, a shadowed presence still around her, and alone, she would have cried out, *Pierre, come back to me*, even as she wondered if she would ever find another lover, another husband, to take his place.

But then, they were mounting the stairs, both of the women as if they carried the weight of the world on their backs, she thought only of the hours of work ahead and then food, and bed, and Charles asleep so she could think.

CHAPTER FIVE

Introibo ad Altare Dei

I WILL GO UNTO THE ALTAR OF GOD

It seemed to Sophie that Sunday would never end; it seemed this way every single Sunday since she was old enough to remember. First, Mass, then lunch, then grandfather to his study, grandmother to her room to rest, and Sophie to her own room where she was supposed to read religious books or tracts, whatever grandmother might have found for her, or the nuns sent home to her grandmother so that Sophie might learn from them. She was sometimes so bored by her reading material that she fell asleep at the desk that had been her father's and was now growing too small for her, her head resting on the open pages. When she was younger, she had spent her Sunday afternoons playing with her doll that *oncle Henri* had brought from Sherbrooke for her that grandmother, unaccountably, had not taken away.

"Naughty girl!" she would scold the doll. "You have dirtied your dress. No supper for you!" But then she would relent, and hug the doll to her chest, and kiss it all over its face, and feed her an imaginary supper, carefully, bite by bite. "How good it is, yes? I have cooked it just for you, *ma petite Lilie*," and so on. But now she was too old to talk to her doll, at eleven she was not sure she should even have a doll, and had with great reluctance put her precious Lilie away into a box Antoinette had given her that sat under her bed. Sunday afternoons became even longer after that. She supposed she should tat; *grand-mère* was teaching her to tat. How she hated tatting, yet at some point this afternoon she would have to do some work on the doily she was making or grandmother would scold her and make her do twice as much before she would even let her go to bed.

Unless she was very lucky, and once in a long, long while she was, grandfather would announce at lunch that he was going visiting in the country this afternoon, and she was to come with him. Off they would go down country roads, the birds singing in the trees beside them as they trotted along, the buggy wheels spinning in delight, or so it seemed to Sophie, and at the end of the rutted lanes, a farmyard with its low whitewashed or stone cottage sitting under trees, its rickety log outbuildings, its yard full of animals and children. On such excursions he would send Sophie out to play with the children of the house. He didn't chide her to look after her dress, or not to step in manure and dirty her boots, nor force her to sit in another room while he and the grown-ups talked. She longed for such days, if he had said nothing at lunch about such a trip, she found herself listening for his footsteps on the stairs. How long had it been since the last time?

The afternoon dragged on. She read her tract so as to be able to tell grandmother she had, then read it again in case grandmother asked her questions about it. If she couldn't answer them, grandmother would send her from the table, or she would not let her have dessert, or scold her fiercely in front of grandfather, Antoinette, and whoever else might be around. Sometimes she punished her as the nuns did, sending her to kneel in the corner and say her rosary. But then she thought, soon it will be dinnertime and I can go downstairs and perhaps I will be allowed to help Mme Gauthier in the kitchen. It was not that she liked kitchen tasks, but only that then she was doing things, moving around instead of stuck sitting at her desk. In the kitchen she could sometimes even sing a little, if she wasn't too loud about it and grandmother heard and made her stop. One did not sing on Sundays, except in church, although singing didn't seem to bother Mme Gauthier.

Finally, judging by the noises down below, it was time for her to make her slow, careful way down the stairs and into the dining room where the table would be covered by the thick damask cloth with its frayed hem and two large, faded spots that nothing Antoinette tried ever succeeded in fully removing. The table would be set with heavy silver cutlery elaborately engraved with *fleurs-de-lis* and an initial Sophie had always found unreadable and wondered about until Antoinette told her it was a "T" from her grandmother's family name, and the thinnest of porcelain dishes trimmed with gold, while lamps radiated a steady yellow light, the flames not daring to flicker. Even then the room with its heavy velvet curtains was gloomy as always, whether morning or evening, winter or summer. Grandfather would begin with a mumbled grace, then there would be silence broken only by grandmother's sharp orders to the cook, or the cook's little granddaughter Manon, who sometimes came to help, or even Antoinette after she had returned from her Sunday afternoon visits to relatives. Sophie's gratitude at having escaped her room never lasted very long, for in moments after arriving there she would be longing to escape the dining room.

Grandfather's fork clinked against his plate and grandmother's head snapped up: Eating should be silent. But she said nothing – if it had been Sophie who had clinked her fork, she would have been reprimanded or sent from the table. Grandmother even scolded fierce Mme Gauthier if she made too much noise in the kitchen, but Mme Gauthier only banged her pots and pans more loudly, knowing grandmother needed her to cook the meals. Tonight the vegetable was mashed turnips. Sophie did not like mashed turnips, but went on slowly putting forkful after forkful into her mouth, trying to swallow without gagging. There could be no question but that she must eat every bite, unless grandfather said she didn't have to.

As Sophie contemplated the diminishing mound of the pale, now watery vegetable on her plate so absorbed in the task before her that she had heard nothing, both grandmother's and grandfather's heads went up, then turned toward the kitchen as the door opened and Antoinette stepped into the room. Before grandmother could speak Antoinette said, "Madame, a gentleman is here to see Monsieur." She was twisting her hands in front of her in a way Sophie had never seen before.

"Now?" grandmother hissed, as if such an outrage were entirely Antoinette's fault.

"Monsieur," Antoinette said, turning to grandfather, pleading.

Letting air out heavily through his nose, he asked, "Who is it, Antoinette?"

"It is Plamondon, Monsieur Plamondon," correcting herself. "It is..." she hesitated, "It is..." and, astonishingly, began to cry. Grandfather rose abruptly, even grandmother's face showed alarm, her fork going down to her plate, Antoinette, apron at her face, pushing the door open to go back into the kitchen, grandfather rising to follow her, then stopping, calling into the kitchen, "Send him in, send him in!" then returning to his place at the head of the table, composing his expression as if there had been no alarm, no astonishment.

Plamondon, Sophie knew, was an *habitant* who farmed the land that belonged to Sophie's *oncle Henri* who was grandfather's younger brother. Now he stood before them, ignoring Sophie, ignoring even grandmother, not even greeting them. He held his hat at his waist, his large, greying moustache quivering as his lips worked, no sound emerging; unaccountably, his face seemed to be wet, yet surely it was not raining. A calamity, obviously, to bring him here now, in such a state, the two elders waiting for his message. Grandfather's face was changing again, the colour rising in it, as if he were coming to some understanding as he stared at the farmer in his rough Sunday clothing. As silently as possible Sophie set her fork down on her plate and waited.

But this tiny gesture did not escape grandmother.

"Leave the table, now!" she commanded. Tears sprang to Sophie's eyes at the suddenness of this, but forcing them down, she rose, not looking at her grandmother, and went out of the room, grandmother saying to her retreating back, "To your room and stay there." But once in the hall, having shut the door behind her, she moved more slowly. M. Plamondon was speaking, she could hear the halting rumble of his voice, a sound from grandfather of wordless consternation, a sharp cry from grandmother. Her astonishment at hearing the latter rose goose bumps on her arms and sent her rapidly down the hall to the stairs which she rushed up despite knowing she was never to do so, closing her bedroom door behind her, standing, frozen, in the centre of the room, her heart thudding so hard it stopped her from catching her breath.

What had happened? She went to her window, saw people passing by on the way to evening Benediction, saw them noticing Plamondon's stout workhorse tied to one of the trees that lined the road in front of her house, and was not too upset to fail to notice the people noticing the horse and cart, knowing to whom the rig belonged and wondering, no doubt, what it was doing here early on a Sunday evening. She went back to her door, without making a sound, opened it and listened. Nothing, then voices, her grandmother's, her grandfather's, then grandfather rushing through the hall below – she knew this by the sound of his footsteps although she couldn't see him, and behind there was a lighter tap of grandmother's steps – opening the front door, going rapidly out, shutting it loudly behind him and grandmother standing still for a moment, then going back down the hall into the dining room, calling, "Antoinette! Antoinette!" Grandmother did not call; it was rude to call aloud. It was a peasant habit.

She hurried back to her window. Grandfather was getting into the cart to sit beside Plamondon as the *habitant* swung himself up, his whip in his hand, turning the *équipement*, and off they went out of the town toward the west, out of her view. After that she waited and waited for someone to come and tell her what she must do, Antoinette especially, who would explain to her why grandfather had rushed off like that. Later, she heard her grandmother and Antoinette going into the *salon*, where they seemed to be moving furniture. Impossible! What were they doing? But still no one came, no one told her what she must do. When at last it grew dark and neither Antoinette nor grandmother had come to prepare her for bed, she undressed, put on her nightgown, knelt to pray, and climbed into bed herself. And still no one came.

Somewhere in the night she was wakened by muffled thumps in the *foyer* below and male voices she didn't recognize. At first she was confused waking from so deep a sleep, thinking that there had been loud voices in the night before, first her own door closing, her pillow damp – why was her pillow damp? Grandfather and grandmother speaking loudly – but no, that was some other time, all shadows, out of which nothing clear emerged, Antoinette had said it was a dream, and this was now: Plamondon had come to the house, grandmother was angry, grandfather had run to the cart… She got out of bed, moved on tiptoe out of her room, and crept as close to the stairs as she dared, stopping well back so as not to be seen from below, saw the heads of three men, one was Plamondon – the fourth she realized was grandfather himself – manoeuvering a long wooden box in through the outer door, on the other side of which was only the blackest of nights, not a star shining – how it took her breath away to see the vastness of night intruding into their dwelling that way – turning the box with difficulty, grunting, muttering, taking very short steps crushed as they were into so small a space, and disappearing inch by inch into the *salon* with it. At the sight of the box they were moving, and both grandmother and Antoinette's heads appearing below her as if they had been in the *salon* and had come out so that the box might go in, she rushed backward into her room forgetting even to be quiet, climbing into her bed, pulling the covers up high over her head.

Then Antoinette was in her room, forgetting even to open or close the window, her eyes reddened, her face pale. She didn't speak, but pushed back Sophie's covers so that Sophie sat up reluctantly and swung her legs over the edge of her bed as she always did.

"Is it morning?" She knew it was morning, and was puzzled by such a question coming out of her own mouth.

"Yes, it is morning. We must get you ready for school." They began Sophie's *toilette* in silence. Then she remembered, pulling away from the hair brush.

"Who came last night? What…?" But grandmother was entering her room. She never came into the room on ordinary mornings. She carried with her a black garment that she set on the bed beside Sophie, who slid down to the floor as neatly as she could manage.

"Bonjour, Grand-mère," Sophie said quickly, gazing into her face in

hopes she had come to explain things to her.

"She will not go to school today," grandmother said to Antoinette. "You are to tell her what has happened." She made an abrupt gesture with one hand held at her side, as if to say, *finished. Say nothing more.*

"Oui, madame," Antoinette murmured. Grandmother went out of the room without having so much as looked at Sophie. Sophie turned her face up to Antoinette's, who had let the hand that held the hair-brush fall to her side while tears emerged to trickle down each cheek and using her free hand, raised her apron to wipe them away.

"I can do my own hair," Sophie said, too loudly, and reached for the hair brush that, surprisingly, Antoinette relinquished without resistance. "What? What is it?" she demanded. "I am not a child anymore. Tell me what?" It came to her then what she had known all along, that the box was, of course, a coffin. Her breath poofed up into her mouth, she took a step backward so that her *derrière* bumped against the bed, the garment grandmother had brought slipping off the bed where it lay, a black puddle on the yellow pine floor. "Someone...has...died?"

Antoinette said, breaking into a sob so that it took Sophie a second to understand, "Your Uncle Henri."

She noticed then that outside the window in the branches of the maple that had stood there all her life, and that in autumn was as if on fire day and night too, a troop of birds had set up a choir: *Chirp-chirp-chirp-chirpety-chirp-chirpety-chirpety-chirp-chirp-chirp*, a din of birds, an uproar, a bedlam.

She had meant to cry out, "Antoinette!" but only a whisper emerged, and hearing it, or not hearing it, seeing only her lips move, Antoinette took two strides to the window and slammed it down in its sash. Then there was only silence in her bedroom, Antoinette's uneven breathing, the heat in her own face, her own mouth open, trying to speak, no sound exiting.

SHE HAD NOT HAD BREAKFAST, she wanted to protest, where was her breakfast, but Antoinette, behind her, had both hands on her shoulders urging her forward into the *salon*. The heavy velvet side curtains, always open, were shut now, candles glowed at the head and down the sides of the wooden box she had seen them in the night, grunting and muttering, carry into the room. Someone was kneeling at the box's head, someone very large and black: It was grandfather, she realized with a start. And on the other side, seated on the faded and worn yellow satin *divan* was grandmother.

"Kneel," Antoinette whispered. She had taken her hands from Sophie's shoulders in order to cross herself. Sophie dropped to her knees, crossed herself, bowed her head, a reflex so long impressed in her that she hardly noticed she was doing it. The coffin lid was closed, how was she to know who was in it? No, no, it was *oncle Henri*, it was grandfather's brother. She was aware then that grandfather was making strange noises, had been making them since she had come into the room. She crossed herself again, knew she was to pray, but no prayer came to mind, no words at all, only the sharp, hot scent of the burning candles and the sound grandfather was making. Grandmother said, whispering, *"Assez!"* Then Antoinette was lifting her by her elbow, turning her as if she did not know how to turn herself, ushering her out of the room, closing the door behind them both.

"Breakfast," Antoinette said, wiping her eyes with a damp handkerchief. Meekly, Sophie followed her down the hall and into the dining room, sat down at the table, waited for food to be put in front of her, began to eat her eggs, bite by bite. Before she had finished grandmother came and sat down without speaking at her usual place on Sophie's right. Mme Gauthier brought her a pot of tea and grandmother filled her cup, but Sophie didn't see her even sip it. Both of them heard grandfather leave the *salon*, go down the hall past the dining room door, and into his study where he shut the door quietly.

Just as she finished her breakfast, *l'abbé* Deschambeault came rushing, heavy-footed, down the hall into the dining room, not even waiting for Antoinette to lead him, speaking rapidly to grandmother as she rose from the table, *"Désolé, Madame,"* taking both her hands in his, "I came as quickly as I could. Madame Girodat will go to the Lord today, I think," then, seeming flustered, said, "He is…?" and not waiting for answer, left the room to disappear into the hall and grandfather's study.

Grandmother said, "Antoinette is cutting the white lilies. They are for the altar. You are to take them to the church."

"Yes, Grandmother."

"Go," grandmother said. "The kitchen, they will be in the kitchen." Forever after the scent of lilies would make Sophie ill.

When she returned, *l'abbé* and grandfather were still in *grandpère's* study, while *grand-mère* paced in the hall outside, muttering as she fingered her rosary, repeatedly crossing herself as if she had forgotten that she just had, pausing to straighten the long wine-coloured carpet with the polished toe of her black boot, then straightening it again, fiercely, as if no matter what she did the length of carpet would not straighten. Seeing Sophie, she said, "Go and read your catechism." Sophie went as quietly as she could up the stairs and closed her door soundlessly, sitting on her bed, although that was forbidden as it wrinkled the coverlet, and tried to think about what was happening. Antoinette came in again, her eyes, if it was possible, even redder.

"Study," she said. "Study, little one. It is better if you study." She took Sophie's arm and moved her to the low chair in front of her desk, then pushed Sophie's books forward, opening pages randomly with her rough fingers.

"No, no, Antoinette!" Sophie cried, irritated, shoving back the heaviest of the books and leaving only the catechism before her. So many years later, in another world, she would realize that Antoinette had not known how to read, and she would be ashamed, and filled with a frustrated pity for the woman who had been the closest thing to a mother she had ever had. Antoinette sniffed, blew her nose loudly into a fresh handkerchief she drew from her apron pocket, and left the room as if she hadn't even noticed Sophie's rudeness. Sophie thought, still angry, that she was no longer a *little one*. She was eleven years old, nearly a grown-up. But, still, she sat on, not reading. Where were the birds? She listened, but no sound came from the maple tree outside her window, not even of leaves turning, brushing against each other in the breeze.

Oncle Henri is dead, she told herself. He was dead, whatever dead was, and yet he was in the room below her, in that box, her *oncle Henri*, who laughed and gave her *bon bons* to put in her pocket. A new thought occurred to her: Guillaume, she had no doubt, and also Hector would be on their way home for the funeral from faraway Montréal where they were both in college. Things would be better then. She thought that perhaps she should cry like Antoinette and get red eyes too. Would *grand-mère* scold her for her red eyes, or not care? It was impossible to tell. In any case, even though she tried, she couldn't seem to squeeze out a single tear.

From the moment she had wakened the day had been extraordinary, nothing happening as expected or as usual, being made to stay home from school, then being sent to read her catechism. What would happen next? She had no sooner thought this than her door opened and Antoinette, not stepping inside, said to her, "Come now, Your *grand-mère* needs you to go to the church."

"But why?" Sophie asked, not rising, but half-turning her body toward Antoinette.

"Vite!" Antoinette hissed, glancing over her shoulder as if grandmother would come at once and be angry. Reluctantly, Sophie rose, secretly relieved not to have to read anymore catechism, not that she had so far read a single line, and accepting the coat Antoinette held out, did as she was told, going back to the church to help the nuns polish the altar's oak railing, and sweep under the pews to make sure that no speck of dust remained anywhere in the entire church, she supposed in preparation for Uncle Henri's funeral. The nun who looked after the church during the week was old, enfeebled, and very slow. She was also deaf, Sister Marie-dumpling, Sophie called her privately, her real name being too long to say or even remember, and not necessary anyway, as long as Sophie did as she was told and said nothing more than "Yes, Sister," or "No, Sister." Finished, she went back to the house

and to her room where Mme. Gauthier had left a tray with a glass of milk, an apple, a slice of fresh bread, a chunk of white cheese for her. No lunch in the dining room then. She was beginning to wish she'd been allowed to go to school, although she hated school, and the nuns, and even some of the stupid girls.

As the day wore on a few people came to the house – the man who owned the apple orchard on the edge of the village, the lawyer Chouinard, *l'apothécaire* – arrived one by one, went silently, stiffly into grandfather's study, stayed only a moment before going away again. She monitored all this from her bedroom door, opened a crack, or by tiptoeing to the stair railing and listening attentively as the visitors spoke in brief whispers to grandmother. A tradesman came to the back door; when he came into the hall Sophie knew him to be the man who worked at *le cimetière* with his burly son digging graves. She had seen them there more than once on the way to Mass. He and his son went into her grandfather's study and emerged only moments later, the father sliding something into his pocket, touching his cap, bowing just a little. She wondered why no women came, no ladies, or families, why no one stayed. *Oncle Henri* had no wife, he had no children.

Then, at last, it was dinner time. *Grand-père* ate nothing, nor did he speak. Sophie sat silently down the side of the table from him where she always sat, but he did not look at her, even once, not even to wink at her, and *grand-mère* and *l'abbé* Deschambeault who ate with them, after he said a long grace and added to it some words about the difficulty of this day and God's trials to test the faith that Sophie recognized as being about her great-uncle's death, spoke only a little, and when *grand-mère* had seen Sophie glance at her, had sent her from the table yet again, even though Sophie hadn't finished her meal and she was supposed to – usually – eat every bite on her plate. And neither of the men rescuing her or even seeming to notice the small drama she and her grandmother enacted most mealtimes.

Again, she went meekly enough, but something hard was beginning to live in her chest, a knot, a nugget; she suspected it might have been there for awhile but only now was she noticing it, and sometimes, when her grandmother was particularly unfair to her, she would feel its hard edges that nothing would soften, not tears, not a sweet from her uncle, or even a wink from her grandfather, not even being allowed to run in the garden. If she never again looked at *grand-mère* could she make that black-gowned shadow disappear?

It was early evening, outside the window the songbirds twittered noisily to one another, then as dusk came, turning slowly to darkness, grew silent. When again no one came to help her with the nightly ritual, she undressed by herself, put on her nightgown, said her prayers, at once pleased with herself, but pushing down her confusion and something that might have been fear at the unaccountable and sudden difference in her life, again put herself to bed. *When you are eleven years old you can put yourself to bed*, she told herself, but she wished she had Lilie to hold, or even that Antoinette would come and kiss her forehead as she often did. She supposed that Uncle Henri's funeral would be the next day, or perhaps the day after as that would give more time for her brothers and other relatives to come. And there would be prayers at the church for him, perhaps tomorrow night. But why not tonight, she wondered? The church was ready, she had helped ready it herself.

THEN IT WAS MORNING AGAIN, Antoinette at her window, raising it, then closing it, as if her mind were on other things so that she didn't notice what she was doing, telling her to hurry or she would be late for school, and the nuns would berate her and slap her hands even if she was eleven and hardly a child anymore. "Is the funeral today, Antoinette?" she had asked, rubbing her eyes. Although how could it be if she was to go to school?

"Don't ask me that," Antoinette answered as if she were angry, and rushed out of the room, saying over her shoulder only, "Breakfast will be ready." Puzzled, Sophie suddenly thought that she could ask Mme Gauthier if the funeral would be today, and so she hurried even faster than Antoinette expected her to, went softly down the stairs seeing no sign of either grandmother or grandfather, hurried through the empty dining room, and into the kitchen.

"Mme Gauthier, please, is the funeral today?" The woman, who was mixing something in a thick crockery bowl, looked at her, exasperated, as she so often was, but Sophie did not quail.

"I am only the cook! Who would tell me such a thing? Ask your *grand-mère*," she said, knowing well that Sophie wouldn't. She turned away from Sophie, not looking at her, banging pots and pans and saying she was too busy for foolishness, that the meals would not cook themselves, and *le bon Dieu* knew there was only herself to do all the work. She went on muttering to herself and Sophie went back into the dining room to eat her breakfast, again by herself. Guillaume will come home, she told herself, forgetting about Hector, and Guillaume who was so nice to her, nicer even than *oncle Henri* had been, would give her the answer that she craved.

Why was *oncle Henri* dead? What did it mean to be dead? Not long ago they had taken her to Madame Girard's funeral: It meant you wouldn't be seen again, except at your funeral, then the grown-ups would carry you away in your wooden box, *l'abbé* Deschambeault at the head of the procession in his white and gold finery, and they would bury you in the cemetery and then everything would be the same. She could taste a strange unpleasant flavour in her mouth, especially at the back of her tongue. She did not know what it was. Was it only that no one would talk to her about *oncle Henri?* Was it that noise–that only now she remembered–she had heard last night coming from behind grandfather's closed study door? But she wouldn't think about that, even though her palms were abruptly damp and her stomach queasy as if she were sick, at its very memory, and nothing, not deep breaths, not swallowing her spit made these symptoms disappear.

HÉLÈNE TOLD HER, whispering as they walked two-by-two down the convent's dark-panelled, windowless hall that smelled of oil and dust, past plaster saints gazing, woebegone into the distance or contemplating the dark wood floor, toward Sister Marie-Catherine's classroom, that Sophie's *oncle Henri* had died. Sophie resisted telling her that she knew this, and pulled away, a minuscule gesture no one else would see, but Hélène felt, not moving her head nor answering, even though she knew that Hélène had something more to say. Sister Marie-Thérèse was watching them, her eyes glinting a hard light to see them even in the dark, but Hélène had already bowed her head just the right amount, her hands clasped meekly at her stomach, managing to give off the aura of good-girl muteness and pliability. Sophie felt some strange new emotion rising up in her at the glimpse of her friend's pious demeanour. It was so strong, this abrupt, inexplicable desire to strike her, that her chest rebelled, rising suddenly to force air out through her nose, and in an act of such boldness, it happening before she had thought of doing it, she let her eyes meet for an instant those of Sister Marie-Thérèse.

To her amazement, the nun blinked, looking away from Sophie and grasping the child nearest her by the upper arm, uttering some shrill admonishment, then standing back so the rows could turn beside her into Sister Marie-Catherine's classroom. Sophie waited, breathless, as she and Hélène passed the nun, for the hard palm on the cheek or the back of the head, the rough grasping of her arm, the shove or pull of her hair, but – they were past and – nothing. She thought, does she know my uncle has died? And for one stunning instant wondered if the nun had let her get away with the audacious act of meeting her eyes because her uncle had died and she was in mourning. Or was it something else? What else had Hélène been going to say? It would not be something kind, she knew by the strange twist of her classmate's mouth.

Catechism class had begun, the nuns were preparing them now for their Confirmation and suddenly, that moment at her First Communion when her chest had filled with a cloud of light seeping into her consciousness, catching her by surprise. So precious a thing, her own private moment it was, as if somewhere someone knew who she was. Was it her mother? The nuns would say it was the Holy Spirit. Sister Marie-Catherine was speaking, telling them to recite after her: *The seven gifts of the Holy Spirit: wisdom, understanding, counsel, fortitude, knowledge, piety, fear of the Lord.* Obediently they recited together, eyes fixed on the nun's lips.

She wondered if, landing in her chest such a long time ago the Holy Spirit had deposited there its seven gifts to help her now as the nun had said they would, but she guessed not, because she had no sense of help being given her. It occurred to her then that kindness hadn't been on the list, and even though she was nearly grown, and understood the list's seriousness, she could only guess that kindness was somehow not important.

She came back to herself at the muted swish and click of the other girls arranging their books, moving into line, ready to go to their next classroom, Sister Marie-St. Antoine's where they would study arithmetic. She moved quickly enough that even this ever-vigilant nun did not notice she was seconds behind the others as she took her place. When all of them were seated in their customary places in the next class, books open on their desks in front of them, Sister Marie-St. Antoine, hands clasped inside the long sleeves of her gown, said sharply, "Sophie Charron!" Startled, Sophie stood by her desk as you were supposed to do when a nun called your name. Sister Marie-St. Antoine lifted a hand, index finger pointing, "Gather your books." What could have happened now? Had someone else died? She had begun to tremble, but not so much that she couldn't reach for her books, close them quietly, pick up pencil, pen and ink bottle, and hold them to her chest while she waited for the next order.

Instead of speaking Sister Marie-St. Antoine walked very fast, her black gown pouffing heavily out around her with each footstep, down the aisle, past Sophie to an empty desk in the corner at the back of the classroom. She turned to look at the backs of her students, none daring to turn their heads to follow the nun, not even Sophie, but the nun then said, *"Vite,"* and Sophie knew she must be speaking to her as she was the only one standing. She turned, her heart quivering, to find the nun standing by the empty desk, pointing downward to it while her eyes were fixed on Sophie's face. Sophie, not quite understanding, walked down the aisle and then along the back of the room until she had reached the desk beside which the nun stood. Still the nun pointed downward. Sophie set her books down on the desk's lid and slid into its seat, making herself as small as she could. Without a word Sister Marie-St. Antoine then strode back to the front of the room and the class began.

At the end of the school day as her friend Hélène walked beside her down the hallway she whispered to her, "Why?" But her friend said only, "It is your uncle." Sophie was baffled. Her uncle had died, her grandfather was in mourning. Maybe children in families where people had died were sent to the back of the room until they felt better. But when Agnès had lost her mother she hadn't been sent to the back of the room, and even though she cried all the time no nun scolded her.

At the end of the day she and Hélène walked together out of the school, crossed the convent yard at a steady pace, not speaking again, and the minute they had gone through the wide gate knowing themselves to be hidden by the two oaks that flanked it and stood at the head of the long bank of lilacs down each side of the narrow dirt road that led into town, they grasped hands and began to run. They ran as fast as the book bags carried over their shoulders, and as the grasping of hands that made running awkward, would allow. They didn't speak, both knowing exactly where they were going and why. They outran even the flies, their neat chignons loosening with the jarring, their skirts requiring lifting now and then, dirt scuffing up in puffs behind them. When they heard a horse and wagon approaching around the bend ahead, again without speaking, they rushed to the side of the road, wading, laughing, through the tall grass and hid in the many-scented, flowering bushes growing wild there until the wagon had passed, then came, laughing, back out onto the road and carried on as before. When next they heard the voices of children far behind them calling to each other in English, they ran into the ditch again to hide, but the handful of children turned before they reached the two girls crouching among the plants and in the wild grasses by the roadside.

In a moment they had come to the place where a narrow road crossed the trail from the convent and they made a wide left turn, book bags thumping against their shoulders. The town lay spread out before them, much of it obscured by tall, thickly-leafed oaks, beeches, alders and maples, interspersed with fir trees of various kinds. Up the first hill they went and as they descended the other side the village vanished and they were alone, cows grazing in the field beside them. They stood panting for a moment, dropping their book bags, slapping futilely at the long ends of hair that had come loose – Sophie's black, Hélène's a light brown – and gazing, bright-eyed into the other's eager face. In an excess of ebullience Sophie did a little dance that made more dust rise to cover her boots and in response, she scuffled even harder so as to dirty them more, emotion rising in her up from her stomach into her chest and she stamped and flailed her arms like a windmill and even threw back her head and screamed wordlessly at the billowing white and yellow-tinted clouds sailing playfully overhead. Beside her, Hélène eagerly followed her example.

As soon as they stopped voices could be heard from the other side of a second hill; they called, "Simone! Suzette!" and heard their own names in response. Already they were racing up the second hill, had crested it – it was higher than the first so they could see the great lake in the distance, a long glint in the bright sun, and beside it the blue mountain that sometimes seemed to smoke or was veiled in white mist, and the two stately rivers flowing through the countryside. Below them stood Simone and Suzette, as grubby as they were themselves. Shrieking, the two girls raced down the second hill, going so fast they could hardly stop themselves and both nearly went tumbling head over heels. Indeed, held themselves back from doing so only by dint of the trouble they would be in if they couldn't get the dirt off themselves or their dresses, or actually tore stockings or skirts.

Gasping for air they came to a stop. Already Simone and Suzette were tossing rocks at each other as if they were balls to be caught, deliberately making them fall short of their goals. Then Suzette turned and threw a stone as hard as she could toward a fir tree that stood next to the trail beside them. Hitting her goal, she shrieked in wordless delight.

"Hey, Suzette, how strong you are!" Hélène called, her voice deepened, coming from her chest, a different voice than the one she spoke from at school, and Sophie, only because she could, found a similar-size stone that fit the palm of her hand just so, and threw it as hard as she could, screaming as she threw, toward the same tree, missing it. Then all four of them were scrabbling to pick up stones, heaving them, screaming as they threw. They howled until their throats were sore, flinging stones until their arms and shoulders hurt too much to toss one more. Then they threw themselves in the grass along the roadside and lay gazing up at the sky, waiting to catch their breaths, for the beating of their wild hearts to slacken.

"I must go home," Sophie said, finally. "Antoinette won't tell anyone, but if grandmother sees how late I am… "

"No, no!" Suzette shrieked. "The third hill!" At once all of them were on their feet, their book bags still lying on the road where they had dropped them when they began their fusillade of stones, and began to run up the last and longest hill. When they crested it, they stopped and began to turn themselves in circles, slowly, to look around at the horizon in three directions, yet as if in ritual that they knew to be such, but for what purpose or to what end, they didn't know, or care. Trees, trees, and more trees, every shade of green and blue and black. Beyond the trees, they had heard, lay the wider world, the great city of Montréal too, where Sophie's brothers lived, but from even this high a point – the top of the world – they could see no trace of it. Perhaps it didn't exist; perhaps it was a folktale, like the ones Sophie sometimes heard when her grandfather took her to visit at the farms of his customers. From this vantage point the lake lay a shining dash of silver far away at the edge of the sky.

Simone moved first, then all of them raced down the steep hillside together and no sooner reached the bottom, than they turned, made the long run back up the second hill to the top where they raced down the other side, still trying their best not to fall. Once Simone had fallen and torn a hole in the knee of her stocking. They had stopped, all of them panting loudly, staring in horror at the ragged hole, the bleeding knee beneath. Suzette had said, "My mother isn't angry if I tear my stocking," and she had given her good one to Simone to put on, and put on her own leg the torn stocking. Shrugging, she said, "I will tell Mama that I tripped on a stone and fell. I will limp," and she gave a demonstration, saying, "ooh," and "ouch," so that they all laughed derisively at invisible mothers as if they were not afraid of them or anything else. At that moment Sophie had been able to believe that either she too had a mother, or that she did not need one, she could not have said which it was.

Scuffed, dusty, wrinkled, sweaty, and out of breath, they finally stopped and without speaking, bent to pick up their book bags and dust them, then went about tucking their hair into place, straightening the skirts and long sleeves, brushing off dust and smudges, presenting themselves to each other for inspection. Calling *à bientôt* and au *revoir*, Suzette pausing to say over her shoulder, "Sorry about your uncle," to which Sophie did not reply, they walked soberly back to the village, at its edge separating, each making her solitary way home.

But as Suzette had called to her this sympathetic remark said almost in bravado, in that unguarded moment, the sound had come to Sophie again, a cry, high-pitched, short, of such a texture and intensity that Sophie's stomach had plummeted as it did when she was dreaming she was falling off a cliff. Who was it? Not someone she knew; not grandfather. It was night; she was asleep; she had dreamt it. But no, now, she heard it again, it echoed in her head and her heart and her gut, a sound that came out of a universe of which she knew nothing, did not know even existed, and that terrified her so that then she had pulled her pillow up over her head, pressing it on each side against her ears. Now, at the memory, sweat having broken out on her forehead and palms, she walked faster as if to outrun it.

Oncle Henri was dead. That meant she would never see him again, that meant he would never again come in the front door, kiss *grand-mère* on the wrinkled cheek even as *grand-mère* pulled back her head from the second kiss as if he would spit on her, and he laughed, then went on past her without waiting for her to lead him to his older brother's study, from where would come loud male voices and laughter. If he saw Sophie, he would sometimes lift her, swing her around once, kiss the top of her head, call her *ma chère petite-nièce* Sophie before he put her down again. Often he brought her a sweet that he tucked into her apron pocket, one finger to his lips to indicate she should say nothing, a quick wink like his older brother, her grandfather, then he would be gone again. *Grand-mère* knew about the sweets, but she never took one from her, a puzzle, because she was allowed sweets otherwise only in the spring when the new batch of maple syrup and sugar would arrive in the kitchen.

He would be in heaven by now, she surmised. Heaven was a good place, he would be happy there, not pale and anxious as he had been the last few times he had visited. No kiss for grandmother, no sweet for Sophie, only a touch to the top of her head as he passed, as if an accident, as if he hadn't seen her at all. And for some time, now that she thought about it as she walked alone from school through the bright afternoon, when he visited there had been no laughter and loud voices from *grand-père's* study.

Dead. He is dead, she whispered to herself, and waited for the sky to crack open because she had dared to say this out loud. She wasn't allowed to say that her mother was dead, or that her father was dead. Or her little brother Achille who had killed her mother somehow, or her older sisters she had never known either, Françoise or Édith, were dead. She had to say that they were in heaven. And anyway, she couldn't remember a time when they were all alive. She twisted her head to one side, and then turned it upward to the burning blue sky as if should she strain hard enough, she might see her uncle, her mother, her father, her brother and sisters smiling benignly down on her.

Before she was aware of crying she felt tears on her cheeks and for an instant, an instant only, she wished she were dead too, and up there in heaven with them where there was no Sister Marie-Catherine, no grandmother, no hours to spend motionless, kneeling in church or sitting between her grandparents not daring to so much as move a finger. She couldn't breathe; terror at what she had just thought seized her, she was panting, trying to catch a full breath. She would go to hell; *le curé* Deschambeault would see to that, burning in the fiery pit for all eternity, such torments she would suffer, never to see heaven. Never meet her mother there. She would confess; if she confessed and said many, very many *Avé Marias* she would be spared. But oh, how she wanted her uncle back; how she missed him.

But when she finally reached the house, bracing herself for the scolding and punishment, a lie on her lips about being kept behind at school, trying to think of a reason for this that would not attract more or harsher punishment, no one was about. The door into the *salon* where the coffin sat was closed tightly and not a sound emerged from behind it. Antoinette, she discovered, was in the back garden, her grandmother nowhere to be seen. Perhaps she was in the *salon*. And where was grandfather? By their absences reprieved, she rushed up the stairs as silently as possible, threw off her school dress, put it away in the closet, changed quickly to her after-school dress, and sat down at her desk to pretend to be studying. Although there was only silence from below she had a sense, perhaps from half-heard whisperings and swishings of garments, faint clicks that meant doors shut as quietly as possible, that there was much activity going on in the house, although when she deliberately listened she heard only silence, and later, the faint pings of pots and pans being moved in the kitchen. She wondered if this strange time would ever pass, if the coffin would remain forever below in the *salon*, if her uncle would ever be buried.

Yet Antoinette called her for dinner and both her grandmother and grandfather were at their customary places at the opposite ends of the table, neither eating, sipping at water from their heavy glasses, grandmother toying with her cutlery, rearranging her napkin, grandfather as heavy and dark as a block of obsidian, not moving at all or speaking.

Sophie ate carefully, the thick bean soup sticking in her throat, requiring much swallowing, and tiny sips, until grandmother finally gave her permission to leave the table, although both her grandparents remained there as she, with infinite care to make no noise at all, shut the heavy dining room door behind her.

That night she again put herself to bed, no one came to help her, she knew only that she must have gone to sleep because she had wakened to the faintest hint of light creeping along the windowsill, stretching a finger to touch her pillow. She had not known if it was morning or still night. A horse whinnied somewhere close by, she would have snuggled further into her warm bed and drifted back into sleep, but there was something strange about the horse whinnying, she did not know what, but let her mind examine the problem in a half-interested, drowsy way. It had come to her that their horse, when she wasn't in the pasture outside of the village, was on the far side of the house from where Sophie lay, she should have barely been able to hear her.

A sound from below woke her further and she pushed her quilt away from her face, sat up on her elbows. In the full silence then, no heavy cotton rasping against her head, no whisper of feathers, holding her breath, she knew there were people again below in the hall. She was too sleepy to get up out of bed, the room too cold so that even her curiosity wasn't strong enough as it would once have been to propel her up. Instead, she listened, her child's hearing so acute that she could see pictures with each tiny, muffled sound: the front door opening, the squeak of wood against wood, a faint grunt, hinges rasping as if something were pressing too hard against the door, more shuffling noises, then the door shutting so quietly she hardly heard anything at all.

She got out of her bed and at the window, leaned against it so as to see as much as possible of the road below. It was the box, the lamps in the *salon* and the sitting room along with the pale yellow glow behind the darkness that was the forest on the edge of town revealed a wagon, two horses, four men carrying the coffin, with visible effort lifting it into the wagon, then climbing in themselves, two on the driver's seat, two of them at the box's head, the horses moving slowly away to drive quietly out of town into the blackness that was the west.

SOPHIE PUT DOWN HER NAPKIN, glanced inquiringly at her grandmother, receiving a brusque if barely discernible nod in return, when without looking at his wife, grandfather announced to his dinner plate, "The child will come along with me." She didn't know where they were going, but could guess: It was Sunday, grandmother, who hadn't spoken, wasn't going with them: They would spend the afternoon in the country visiting at the farm home of one of his better customers, or even – because this had happened before although rarely – perhaps they would drive to two or three different customers' homes and at each place the men would smoke pipes together and discuss the weather and the roads while the women bustled about passing mugs of beer to them, or fussed over the many small children, and she, happily would be allowed to run about with those her own age. She could barely contain her excitement and smiled in the direction of her grandfather who didn't so much as look at her. Nonetheless, she left the table as silently as she could to run upstairs to change her dress to a light muslin one and to gather a shawl just in case they came back late when the day had cooled. She did this mostly so grandmother would have nothing to complain about, no excuse to keep her from going.

When they were safely seated in the buggy and the horse was pulling them along down the winding road that led out of town, through the forest, and into the countryside past small farm after small farm, she asked, "Where are we going, grandfather?"

"To mes cousins," he answered. "To the Hippolytes." She didn't know the Hippolytes were cousins and would have asked about it, but supposed that he might just as well have said, *mes copains* – my pals, so she didn't bother to inquire as to how the family came to be cousins and whether or not they were her cousins too. And anyway, if they were really cousins, wouldn't grandmother have sent some small gift with them if she would not come herself? But who understood grandmother?

Certainly not Sophie. The buggy rolled on through sunshine and shadow, the birds making an uproar as they passed, and deer twice leaping across the wet trail before them. Even the very air smelled free to Sophie and she breathed it in deeply, smiling without realizing she was.

"I am so glad to see you!" Violette cried as the mud-splashed buggy rolled into the Hippolyte farmyard. As she put up her arms to help Sophie down – Violette was inches taller than petite Sophie – her parents already on the other side crying greetings to grandfather as if he were the returned prodigal son, and the oldest son, Alexandre with his tousled mop of dark blonde hair, ready to hop up into grandfather's vacated seat to drive the horse to the barn, unhitch it, and give it feed and water although it needed neither after so short a run and having been fed before Mass that morning. Violette went on, hugging Sophie as if they were indeed cousins or maybe even sisters, "I was so bored! Sister Marie-Catherine says it is a sin to be bored, but I was bored anyway!" She laughed a delighted, full-throated, child's laugh to which Sophie couldn't help but laugh herself, and as for the hug, it was something she so seldom received it made her shy.

Violette Hippolyte was only a year older than Sophie and attended the convent too, although Sophie didn't know her beyond passing her in the hall where they were not allowed to speak. Even though she was only fourteen, there were rumours that she had a vocation, that as soon as she finished her last year at school she would go to the Grey nuns in Montréal to whom she was already bound. In her own farmyard and among her brothers and sisters she seemed less formidable, warmer, and more open. Her long dark hair wasn't in the convent's chignon either, although Sophie's was at grandmother's insistence, and hung down Violette's back, its unruly abundance tied loosely with a pale green ribbon that went well with her blue cotton dress. Sophie felt a pang of regret on Violette's behalf, who would be required to cut it all off when she arrived to join her order.

After she had made proper greetings to the elder Hippolytes, Sophie and Violette linked arms and went off together to perambulate the farmyard and then the small, well-kept orchard behind it, and behind it, the Hippolyte family's thick woodlot. Violette's younger sisters followed them, but not too closely, sometimes being distracted from their close study of the two older girls, by interests of their own. There were three of them: the youngest Cécile who kept a finger in her mouth and her big brown eyes fixed on Sophie, plump Lucie, so much like her mother already, and tiny Marie Ange who, although smaller, was older than Lucie. Soon the little girls were running about playing a game they seemed to have devised themselves during the long days when no visitors came, and no other children. It involved a lot of calling and chasing each other in and out of the trees so that often they ran ahead of Violette and Sophie, sometimes circling them, sometimes disappearing entirely to reappear, giggling with each other so that the older girls, watching, laughed too.

The older Hippolyte boys, Marcel, the tallest of them, and Alexandre, paid the girls no attention, going about their business from barn to house or out to a nearby field where they almost disappeared in the tall hay, then could be seen on the other side of the field smoking pipes as they lounged under the branches of a massive oak. Herménègilde, the youngest boy, had gone to the nearby stream to fish, Violette informed Sophie, and wasn't seen all afternoon, but Pierre, a little older than Sophie, was hanging about the farmyard, not talking to the girls, but watching them as they made their slow way back into the farmyard proper. Sophie couldn't stop herself from staring at him, wondering why he was lingering, going neither with the men in the house, nor his older brothers under the tree, nor fishing with Hérmènegilde. Was he being punished?

Violette said, "Ignore him, Sophie. He is always looking for attention." But Sophie found she couldn't. His eyes, blacker than *grand-mère's* even, but at the same time light-filled, seemed to her to sparkle, and his teeth were so white in his brown face when he smiled, which it seemed to her he was always doing, that she kept glancing toward him in hope of seeing the beauty of that smile again, and to experience again that strange feeling in her gut when she saw it.

"Why does he want attention?" she asked Violette in a whisper. Violette shrugged, then said, staring ahead as if she were talking to herself, "He is the third boy. Papa hasn't much time for him. Alexandre and Marcel tease him." She sighed. "He likes mischief." Sophie was unsure why anyone would like mischief, but then, he was a boy and she knew nothing of boys, at least, not of ones near her own age.

The girls made a slow circle around the old house, chattering about the convent and the sisters and the other girls, and then made a second circle, ignoring Pierre. Growing bored or, as she had said wanting some attention that Violette refused to give him, he rooted about in the tall grass near some lilac bushes and came out with a half-dozen large duck eggs, that judging by the smell when they broke, were old and had failed to hatch. He began to throw them toward Violette and Sophie, deliberately sending them just short so that they splattered on the ground near where the girls walked sending up the most appalling stink. As if that were not bad enough, miscalculating, or so she thought, he threw one that broke against Sophie's skirt, sending stinking orange rivulets down it.

It was all she could do not to cry. Violette, seeing her dismay, said, "Never mind, Sophie. I will clean it for you."

Sophie whispered, "It is only that grandmother likes me to keep my dress clean," lamely, unable or not wanting to say just how angry grandmother could be, and perspiring a little at the apparently hopeless situation in which she found herself. Now she felt herself a child and Violette the kindly mother, which only added to her confusion.

"It's nothing," Violette insisted. "He is such a rascal!" She threw up an arm and made a pushing gesture in Pierre's direction as if to tell him to leave at once, at which he only grinned.

How Sophie blushed as at the water trough in the yard Violette raised the stained part of her skirt to eye level and scrubbed at it with a brush that hung on a hook from the pump until there was only the faintest yellow mark left in the muslin, although now it was wrinkled where when she had arrived there had not been a wrinkle.

"It will dry in a minute," Violette assured her. "No one will ever know there was an accident." She turned to Pierre, calling to him where he lounged against the open barn door. "If you did the washing you wouldn't be so careless!" but he only laughed, looking into Sophie's face with those eyes still sparkling with mischief, then turned away to pick up dried balls of horse dung, pitching them as hard as he could against the barn wall where they exploded into golden dust. Violette shook her head in exasperation, but left him to his own amusement, saying, "Useless to scold him," with an expression somewhere between annoyance and puzzlement as if she were his mother instead of a sister actually younger than he was.

Soon Madame Hippolyte stood at the low kitchen door calling, *"Voyons! Vite!"* and all of them came from around the yard, the little girls running ahead of everyone, while Pierre and his brothers strolled behind. In the crowded kitchen there was buttermilk to drink and *gaufrettes* Madame Hippolyte had made. How delicious they were, melting on her tongue like the Host. Oh, no, she mustn't think that thought, and tried to erase it.

She wished then that she might never go home, but could sit forever in that crowded, low-ceilinged room with huge blackened hearth all along one wall and children everywhere giggling and teasing one another, while the two men sat at the scarred wooden table, smoking their pipes and sipping a hot brew from thick mugs. And their mother, short, stout, red-faced, rushed about simultaneously scolding and praising, throwing out orders to the boys who paid no attention, but that Violette did her best to carry out. Sophie sat in silence in her corner on a low stool, her mug of buttermilk on her lap, basking in the warmth that filled the room. Across the way now Pierre avoided looking at her, giving all his attention to the men, but Sophie was unable to stop herself from glancing at him every few minutes, fascinated by the gleam of his white teeth when he smiled, and the curl of black hair that hung over his forehead. Eventually the small girls began to grow restless and were sent outside to play, but the men and boys hung on, deep in conversation while Mme Hippolyte, sitting at the end of the table, lost herself in her knitting. Finally Violette asked, "Should we go outside too?"

Outside, she said, "I am tired of walking around. Let's go up into the loft and sit in the old hay. Papa won't mind, and we can hear everything there. You'll know when M. Charron is ready to leave." Sophie had never been in a hayloft before and climbed the rough ladder with some excitement. When both of them had stepped from it onto the floor of the loft the first thing that struck her was the delicious smell of last year's hay, and then the wonder of the way beams of dust-filled light poked thick fingers here and there through openings in the walls. Following Violette's lead, she went with her to a place where the hay was still thick on the floor and stretched out on it beside her friend who was already lying on it. They lay beside one another staring up to the rafters and for a long time neither said a word. Sophie was growing sleepy. She lifted her hand, put it into one of the light-rays and wiggled her fingers to watch the shadow fall on the thick post at their feet.

"Do you remember when my uncle died?" For a long moment Violette said nothing, then she stirred, turning on her side to face Sophie, the loose hay crackling under her.

"Yes," she said, in a tentative tone.

"Do you know what happened to him? No one will tell me." Sophie was careful not to look at her friend, not to touch her, not to stop wiggling her fingers in the ray of light that cut across above her own bosom. Violette rolled onto her back.

"You don't know?" She asked the spiderwebs in the beams above them.

"Know what?" She wanted to stop making shadows, she wanted to roll against Violette and be held by her, she wanted to ask Violette to help her, although with what she was unsure. "There was no funeral for him, my brothers didn't come home. Nobody ever spoke of him again." She put her hands down, linked them on her chest, took in a deep quavering breath, still not looking at Violette, but gazing instead at the far barn wall where below which she could hear mice stirring in the loose hay. Violette didn't reply.

Abruptly, she turned onto her side facing the older girl, lifted herself on one elbow from the sweet-smelling hay, and commanded, "Tell me!" Then, hesitating, "It is time I knew, don't you think? I am thirteen. I am not a child."

Violette let out her breath, ran fingers through the hay beside her, lifting a strand or two, then dropping them. "Your uncle, he...he hung himself, Sophie." Sophie's arm that had been holding up the upper half of her body gave way so that she fell back against the hay. A few seconds passed; she began to shake. Seeing this, Violette moved against her, lifted Sophie's head to rest it against her shoulder.

"Hung himself?" The words didn't make sense; she couldn't imagine this.

"That is why there was no funeral." Sophie would have asked why not, but she knew the answer: *Only le bon Dieu gives life: only He can take it away.* It was the greatest of sins, greater even than to kill someone else – to kill yourself. She heard herself make a cry, not loud, a sound she did not know she owned. It made her think of grandfather's cry so long ago when he had been with *l'abbé*. An infinite number of dust particles still danced in the streams of light, outside in the yard the little girls called to each other, laughing, a horse whinnied from the nearby pasture, and crows cawed loudly, nastily, as if to mock her.

"I have never seen his grave," Sophie said, turning her face away.

"It is behind a stone fence, under a big beech tree."

"How do you know this?" Sophie cried out at the injustice of Violette's knowing while she did not.

Violette said softly, "Everyone knows."

She had no resistance left, and puzzled over the other question: How could it be that everyone knew such things and she did not?

On the way home in the early twilight, she longed to ask grandfather why his brother had hung himself, what it meant to hang yourself, and where exactly he was buried, and how it was that everyone knew things that she didn't know. But looking up at his strong jaw, his wide cheek under the black hat, the thick grey moustache moving up and down as he hummed a tune or clucked to the horse, even at his carefully groomed hands holding the reins, she knew she could not. She allowed herself only to put her head against his upper arm and hold it there, as if she had fallen asleep.

And yet, it was at dinner that same evening that grandmother, who had seemed to Sophie for reasons she didn't know, more agitated than usual, also angrier than usual with grandfather, had suddenly said, "When you are fifteen you will go to your brothers' houses in Montréal. We will have looked after you long enough."

It was as if she had gathered all her ire, all her bitterness at the world and placed it on Sophie's head. She gasped aloud as she grasped what grandmother's remark implied, that she had never been wanted here in the only home she had ever known. Hot blood flooded her face, neck and chest, and she gazed at her own napkin spread on her lap, swallowing hard so as to be able to breathe. Grandfather's head snapped up, there was such tightness in his throat when he spoke that Sophie hardly recognized his voice, squeezed as it was by something.

"She will stay with us until she is married."

Grandmother looked at her plate, saying nothing at all, although red spots appeared high in each cheek. Sophie left the table then without asking; no one stopped her. She moved lightly, as if she no longer weighed anything at all, going down the hall, up the stairs, into her room where she sat down at her desk, opened her school books and studied without lifting her head until Antoinette came to tell her it was time to go to bed. She didn't think about what she had heard, not even when she was tucked into her bed, her lamp out, and Antoinette gone. But she lay for a long time, dry-eyed, staring at the shadows on the ceiling, thinking hard of nothing at all. Or perhaps she thought a little of her mother, whose face she could only sometimes remember, but whose warmth she sometimes – rarely – felt around her. She even cried out, once, softly, *"Maman!"*

CHAPTER SIX

Angels

WITH THE FIRM INSISTENCE of her grandfather who had said that he would take her himself as it was his duty to attend all of *la fête de St.-Jean-Baptiste*, she had been for the first time given permission to attend the late afternoon and evening parts of the day-long celebration.

"She must never leave your side!" Grandmother turned her face to Sophie's then, Sophie watching as her mouth elongated, lips pressed together, chin lifting upwards, eyes hardening. "Stay with your grandfather at all times. Do not shame us."

Sophie nodded, whispering, *"Oui, Grand-mère,"* shifting from one foot, carefully, onto the other, hands clasped meekly at her waist, and managed not to glance upward to grandfather for reassurance. Very unwise, she knew, when grandmother wore this face and held Sophie's in its grip. Her eyes lowered, she waited until she heard the sibilation of heavy fabric that meant it was safe to look up, or better, to turn to grandfather where he stood gazing after grandmother as she went out of the dining room, a slight smile playing on his face, then tilting his head so his eyes met Sophie's.

"We will go soon," he told her, lifting a finger. "Are you ready?" Shivers raced up her spine.

"Yes, grandfather." She already knew that grandmother would not so much as put in an appearance herself at the *fête* – *uncouth habitant wildness* as she had put it, even though *l'abbé* Deschambeault would preside over the festivities and, through the Bishop, the church had sanctioned them. As they went out into the hall Sophie treading lightly for fear her grandmother might change her mind, Antoinette came bustling from the kitchen holding out a woolen shawl for her.

"It will be chilly when evening comes," she declared. "You must carry it with you." Sophie was indignant: The house was sweltering, it was June, how could she carry around a silly shawl all through the late afternoon without being laughed at by the other girls? But grandfather, seeing her petulance, looked gravely at her, saying, "This is very thoughtful of Antoinette, *n'est-ce pas?* Of course she will take it."

"Merci, Antoinette," she said, wondering already where she might hide it to keep it safe through the hours ahead.

Her experience was that mostly on any of the rare occasions where only grandfather had taken her, having arrived at their destination, he simply forgot about her. That is, until it was time to go home. Then it was wise to be within his sight if she surmised he wanted to leave in order that he never had to look for her, such an annoyance perhaps having the effect, next time, on whether he would take her along.

Already this morning there had been a parade, although with only one float, a tableau of St. John the Baptist, the figures made of straw except for the saint himself who was represented by *le notaire's* tall, fair-haired son, André, that is, while the saint still had his head, at the front of which a half dozen altar boys walked carrying the large wooden cross, and behind them *l'abbé*, then, singing, the nuns from the convent, and after them the children who lived as orphans in the convent, walking in pairs and singing bravely along with the nuns. Next to last the float itself, and behind it, the parishioners, suppressing any signs of anticipation of the gaiety to come, but excited enough not to mind even when their feet found themselves in puddles or mud caused by the warm early morning rain.

When they reached the church, all paused, the singing stopped or in one or two cases trailed away, the priest went slowly up the church's wide front steps, waiting until not a sound could be heard save the birds chirping so gaily in the trees that surrounded the churchyard; he blessed everyone, and the float itself, which had stopped to one side, the owner of the horse pulling it taking the animal by the bridle to hold it still. As soon as the priest finished the blessing and everyone followed him and the cross into the church for the special Mass, the farmer and his son would unhitch their horse from the dray that it pulled, hurry the animal off to a nearby small pasture where it would be left for the day, and would come rushing back so as not to miss a moment of the Mass or the celebration that would follow. By then André would have jumped down from his perch and taken off his costume, a long piece of dark blue cloth patterned with silver that was wrapped around his lanky body that resembled, suspiciously, a curtain from a fine house, and that had been worn for many years by successive St. John-the-Baptists, folded it away, smoothed down his blonde thatch, and joined everyone in the church too.

Grandmother had not walked through the town with the procession as Sophie and grandfather had done, but gauging the moment, had arrived precisely as the procession did, so that she walked into the church with them, and sat down in their customary pew just below the altar where all the towns' dignitaries had places. A low-grade buzz of excitement filled the church even among the very pious and the priest, normally given to long sermons and many admonishments about the behavior of his parishioners, seemed to be infected too, if not exactly rushing through Mass, wasting no time about it and cutting short his sermon on the saint and what he had to teach the people of *la patrie*, Quèbec, remind them that God was watching and He did not like drunkenness nor fornication, the latter a sin apparently so grave that Sophie could only hope it was one of which she hadn't been guilty.

After Mass most of the townspeople went home for a light *repas* and a nap in preparation for the night of festivities ahead, but the country people who had poured into town in wagons and buggies, on single horses and by whatever other conveyance they could press into service would stay lolling in the grass wherever there was a high spot where the ground was dry, or finding shade under a tree from the hot afternoon sun for a nap, while others were picnicking, playing games and making music with fiddles, spoons, and flutes until it was time for the feast. And after the feast, the bonfire! It was for this highest point of the day that Sophie had braved her grandmother's ire to ask if she might attend, and grandfather had intervened saying she was now old enough to attend and he would look after her.

But first, the feast. Most of the villagers and those from the countryside were there, she had even caught a glimpse of Pierre Hippolyte standing with a group of boys his own age. As many as possible of the crowd were seated at the roughly-made long wooden tables on which sat trenchers piled high with bread, platters of meats of one kind and another, others creaking under mountains of biscuits, cakes, pies and sweating pitchers of lemonade for the children, women and old people, and beer for everyone else. Already people were eating and when they were satiated, they rose and wandered away to visit with relatives, neighbours and friends, or if children, to play noisy games in the grass, to run in and out among the trees shouting, hiding and being found, and boys tripping each other, running away, being chased. Grandfather, remembering at last that she sat quietly beside him, released her with a pat to her shoulder so that she might join in the fun. Far down the tables she spotted Violette Hippolyte and her mother and sisters, thought she would go to them and sit with them.

It was slow going on the uneven ground in the twilight that was beginning to rise up from the grass and with the stars not yet out nor the bonfire lit. People were beginning to come and go, the long tables emptying and women to gather dishes and leftover platters of food to cover them until another supper would be required after the bonfire had died away – a last sleepy lunch before the slow trip home, drowsing in the wagonbox or the buggy. Some boys too, had lit firecrackers and they were pop-popping on the far side of the square beyond the great pile of wood. Sophie slid between a group of men who stood together smoking, tankards in their hands that were thick and gnarled from work, and when she emerged, twisting past the full skirt of a dignitary's wife, she saw that the Hippolytes had left the table and in the growing darkness, she couldn't pick them out from the female figures milling about in front of the trees. She came to a stop, considering, looking about, then back the way she had come where she saw the figures of girls her own age, although she couldn't make out who they were. Never mind: They would be friends, or at least, acquaintances from school. She began the trip back, once again dodging among adults and avoiding little boys whose eyes burned with their own fire, clearly intent on mayhem. Her grandfather was no longer at the table, nor was the mayor, nor the town clerk.

Shortly she located some of her convent friends and ran to be among them, at first only listening to their excited chatter, not taking part. Out of the corner of her eye she noticed her grandfather standing well back from the tables that the women were so quickly denuding of dishes, saw that he stood next to a woman, although she couldn't make out who it was. Not grandmother who never attended and in any case this woman was full-breasted, her skirts flaring out over her plump *derièrre* as she stood sideways next to grandfather, her bonnet more elaborate than most of those about tonight. Sophie peered over her classmate Aimée's shoulder, just as Aimée moved away, so that Sophie caught a full glimpse of the two adults standing so near each other that their clothing touched.

Now she recognized who the woman was: the widow Bénédicte Bilodeau. Just as Aimée moved back to block Sophie's view again, she saw grandfather catching and holding Mme Bilodeau's fingers and that Mme Bilodeau was turning to him and he was looking down into her face with an expression Sophie had not seen before, as if this woman took up every iota of his attention, as if there were a magnet between their two sets of eyes. He had never looked at Sophie that way; he never looked at grandmother that way. A tiny shock ran through her of surprise and some not quite coalesced understanding. She could feel, unaccountably, her cheeks burning and would have said to Aimée, "Look!" but her friend was shouting to the girls around them to be heard over the racket of the crowd, including Sophie in her call, "Let's go! Let's go! *Allons y!* They are starting the fire!"

Swept up in the excitement, linking arms with Aimée and Catherine; they began to run through the crowd, everyone moving in the same direction toward the massive pile of wood and the men who stood at intervals around its base holding torches, whose flames were thick and bright and reached over their heads.

L'abbe stood on a high point by the fire. As the girls approached running, they came to a dead stop as he lifted both arms in a gesture that said that everyone should kneel because it was a part of the celebration, it was imperative that he pray with them and remind all of them that this wasn't just summer fun, but a serious occasion, that the church must be honoured too. Those at the front of the crowd fell to their knees, those behind stumbling a bit, a few accidents occurred and the crowd piled up tightly against each other, then spread, and all knelt. When he had obtained silence finally, except for the light breeze high in the treetops, the birds setting up a racket, then abruptly stopping, and the usual distant animal sounds coming from the thick woods that surrounded the village, he began to pray. For once, it was a short prayer and when he had finished blessing the wood, "the light that is Christ," he intoned, he again raised his head and made a gesture toward the woodpile and the men who stood around it. At once, in unison the torch-holders stepped forward, crossing themselves with their free hands, and lowered the flares to the perimeter of the pile. As soon as the wood at each place caught fire, each man threw his torch into the pile and a cheer went up through the crowd. Sophie and her friends began to jump up and down screaming and clapping their hands, their bonnets bobbing askew.

It is here Sophie began to be confused. Somehow she lost track of her friends Aimée and the other girls, although how that had happened wasn't clear to her. Of course she would never forget watching *le feu de joie*, the powerful roar and upward thrust of flames stretching so high they reduced the town to a toy village, the wood crackling and snapping, fountains of multi-coloured sparks, sometimes more than one at the same time, shooting upward and falling, falling, not to wink out, but simply to be absorbed by the night. She remembered too that at the same time, or maybe it was later, there had been shouting and singing to loud music from fiddles, harmonicas, flutes and musettes, as well as much dancing on the grass among the grownups, although she had seen children dancing with each other too, holding hands, jumping up and down and laughing. She couldn't remember if she had danced or not, but she had seen, maybe even more than once, a dancer or two falling down. This had frightened her so that she sought out her grandfather, he no longer standing with the widow but close to the fire among his friends. She clung to him and he looked down at her, laughing.

"Il a trop but, c'est un pochard," he told her but she didn't think she knew exactly what that was; it did not explain anything; it did not explain what frightened her. "Don't be afraid," he said. "They won't hurt anybody but themselves," but, still, he seemed to find her fear amusing. She remembered, too, seeing crockery jugs being passed among the men, but then, hadn't there been something like a fight between two of them? Both of them rolling around in the grass with women shrieking admonishments at them, men, bafflingly, calling instructions, until the priest had come and demanded that they stop at once – although he himself might have been laughing – which, nonetheless, they did.

She was clear that then her friend Hélène came up to her, there with her younger sister Thérèse; they had come by where she stood on their way to find a better place from which to watch the fire without it being too hot or too close to the sparks or occasional shards of glowing wood that would explode out of the flames.

"Sophie! Sophie, come with us," Hélène screamed, shaking with excitement and with a stare that moved from place to place and person to person without stopping to recognize anyone or anything. Sophie grasped the sisters' hands and hurried with them as they thrust their way through the people gathered several deep at the perimeter of the fire. The three of them stood, arms linked, rigid with mixed fear and awe, watching the fire as it consumed slowly at first, and then faster and faster the mountain of wood that the townspeople and country people alike had been gathering and bringing to the centre of the village for a week or more now until the pile was manor house high and as wide. Moment by moment it grew until it turned into a conflagration of such size and power she could not quite assimilate it mentally. Sophie turned her head to her friends, looking for comfort or explanation, but seeing them open-mouthed, bright-faced and shiny-eyed from the reflection of the flames, fixed in fascination, transported even, she dropped the sisters' arms, they not noticing she had, she could only think – something about hell – hellfire – that even now, somewhere, souls were roasting slowly in such flames. Her great-uncle Henri! Perhaps her mother? Or her father? Perhaps someday even the widow Bilodeau? And – no, it could not be – grandfather? Horrified, already beginning to pant with fear, she backed away from her friends, and from the bonfire, while such thoughts sped, terrifyingly, through her mind, even as she tried to stop them. Not great-uncle Henri who hugged her and gave her candies. No, it couldn't be.

Behind her was the night, pitch black and full of the rush of undefined and unnamed figures; ahead was the fire, by the second growing louder and burning more ferociously. It was too brilliant to look at, its noise too loud to tolerate. It was unstoppable, an engorged, fire-breathing dragon, twisting and yawing about; it would consume them all whether sinners or not. *But we are all sinners!* She spun about and ran, into the cool darkness of the night, through the blackness under the trees, up the stone steps of the church, pushed open the heavy wooden door, slipped inside to stand trying to catch her breath, overcome by the tumult in her brain and heart, in the vestibule's shadows.

Oddly, the church was not in total darkness: a dim silver light came from the sides of the altar straight ahead of her, and a reddish glow from the high windows on the side nearest the bonfire even though tall trees stood between the two. In the centre of the church a softness that was neither darkness nor light bloomed so that the wooden floor gleamed darkly, seeming to float. So inviting was it that Sophie, her heart still tripping too fast in her throat, was drawn forward to it and began to walk without meaning to or noticing that she was, up the central aisle, past the crudely-built wooden pews, one by one, toward the altar, below which she stopped, genuflecting, and crossing herself as if her knee had been bent and her hand lifted by someone else.

Behind her trembling shoulder blades there was only darkness, not black and forbidding, but alive with miniscule quivering particles that seemed filled with – something – intelligence, wisdom, a presence that waited in hushed suspension. How small she felt, infinitesimally so, the shadowed rafters soaring high above her and before her, the white-clad altar glinting with gold, vases of lilies and roses sending out their scent to saturate the air. All around her the whispering grew into a rustling. In its Presence even hellfire retreated, withering. But still, she was afraid, and in her terror she might have called out, *Angels!* Exalted, she fell to her knees on the wooden floor, beat her temples with her fists, not able to assimilate the two visions of the world that she had been taught. How could it be both? And where was her place in this – but her ears were once again filled with a roaring, choirs singing perhaps? She could not – she could not…

Had she fainted? She wasn't sure.

She sat wrapped in a quilt, although fully dressed, in a big armchair in the *salon* so that the sun could shine on her. She wasn't sure what summer it was, had expected it to be winter when Antoinette had carried her downstairs the first day she was well enough to leave her bed, grunting falsely, saying, "How big you have grown," to her even though she knew, because everyone had told her, that she was very thin and must eat to regain all the weight she had lost. She remembered with certainty a vast winter storm that for days had left the countryside frozen and still, snow coming up over the windows and she was afloat on a scintillating sea of white, snowflakes drifting around her, and her mother floating above her bed, disappearing as soon as grandmother or the doctor opened her door.

"Do not forget the water," her mother, whose face was the one in the only photo she had ever seen of her at the same time as she could not quite see it, instructed her, and another time, "Be the sure the lake…" and even, "Where is the…" but Antoinette came into the room then carrying something white on a tray and Sophie's mother had vanished, her voice trailing away, and Sophie had cried out, "Antoinette! Antoinette!" angry because Antoinette's entrance had blotted out her mother's last word and now she would never know what it had been. Then there was a cool dampness on her forehead, her chest was on fire, she couldn't breathe, and twisted her body, beating the bedclothes with her fists to make the air come back into her lungs.

There was winter, she instructed herself, she had been sick.

"You nearly died," Antoinette told her. "It was very close." She remembered that the doctor had said, "Well, you are back with us again!" as if he were surprised, crossing himself, then stroking his stiff grey beard with one hand, his other in a fist at his waist, holding back his long coat so that his trouser leg in corded grey wool was revealed. But Antoinette said that it was not winter when she had grown ill, that it had been summer, "Not long after *la fête*," she explained. "You were overtired, you lost your shawl and got yourself chilled." She paused from where she was holding a length of white Turkish toweling having brought the clean laundry into the *salon* to fold so that she might keep Sophie company, shaking her head solemnly, her lips pursed as if about to chastise her.

"Yes," Sophie answered, uncertainly. "Grandfather said I must take the shawl. Where is it?" fearful that it was lost permanently, that if grandmother found out she would be angry. Antoinette went to the *armoire* that sat in the hall, returning with the pale brown shawl draped across her forearms for Sophie to see.

"*La sœur* Marie-Mathilde brought it for you. It was in the church," and she cast Sophie such a look that Sophie knew that Antoinette knew that Sophie herself had hidden it there. That was now though, when all of this had happened in the previous six months, or so she thought because now it was summer and time to stop being so confused. Then she remembered, or thought she did, that Hector had sometimes come to see her in her room when she was ill, and her mother had talked to him, because she was Hector's mother too. It seemed to Sophie that she could remember Hector weeping by her bedside, or was that grandfather?

"Was Hector here?" she asked.

"Hector came home for one day," Antoinette answered briskly, not looking at Sophie. She had finished folding the toweling and now was rearranging the parlour lamp and the glass figurines on the table beside her, all glittering from the beam of sunlight that bathed them. Her voice changing, she asked, "Do you remember Guillaume coming home? He brought medicine from the famous Montreal doctor, *le docteur* Roche that Dr. Belanger asked him to bring. But then the doctor," – Sophie did not know which one – "said it was useless, you would live or die on your own according to the will of *le bon Dieu*, and He decided you should live and here you are." She tapped Sophie on top of her head, then unexpectedly bent and brushed her hair with her lips. When she stepped back, crossing herself, there were tears in her eyes, but then, Antoinette always cried over nothing at all. Crying from Antoinette didn't mean a thing Sophie reminded herself.

Snow over the rooftops shining silver in the high sun, fields of snow spreading out in blue waves for miles in every direction. Trying to remember, she grew uncertain: Had those been clouds? Had there been fields of clouds? Impossible, clouds didn't come down and make fields, she told herself dreamily. She thought that she could remember floating over frozen clouds, that she had been suspended in the frigid air by the white puffs of her own breath. Through her wonder, she laughed out loud at the impossibility of it, so that Antoinette paused in her folding and gazed assessingly at her.

"Has it been winter?" Sophie asked. Antoinette stood motionless, letting the length of toweling fall back onto the chair, her brown eyes widened and grew darker. Then she came to Sophie, placing a warm palm against Sophie's forehead. Irritably, Sophie jerked her head away. Antoinette said, "It is summer still, Sophie. You have been sick for a month or so." Her voice, unusually, was gentle. Sophie dropped her eyes, embarrassed to be so mixed up.

"Was there a storm?" she asked, but if it was still summer there could not have been a snowstorm, and tears sprang to her eyes.

"Don't worry," Antoinette told her, going back to her folding. "You will get stronger and then you will remember everything. Your grandfather found you in the church, you had passed out, he brought you home. Already you were wheezing in your chest," and she did an imitation of how Sophie had sounded. The sound terrified her, if only Antoinette would stop, she pulled the blanket up under her chin and would have hugged herself under it, but she was too tired.

Once she had opened her eyes and saw grandmother standing at her bedside, staring down at her with a look that said she was thinking of her, Sophie, but of other things as well and could not separate them so that sometimes Sophie seemed to be her focus and other times that she did not see Sophie at all, but was looking through her or past her into another time, one that made her sad. Had grandmother lost her mother too, when she was only a child? But when she had tried to ask the question the only sound that came out was thick and not what she meant to say, as in a dream, when in the midst of one she thought she had screamed but all that emerged from her throat was a sickly croak.

She remembered then that she could hear her own breath rattling in her chest, rumbling like grandfather's sometimes did when he fell asleep and snored in church until grandmother kicked his ankle, her expression not changing an iota. Then she remembered how she couldn't breathe, struggling for air, thrashing in the bedclothes, trying to call for help, but able only to make the rattling half-wheezes. It was the shadows in the corners doing this to her, she tried to push them back so she could get air. Her door opened, that she remembered clearly, and Antoinette in nightdress and slippers entered carrying a candle, cried out at Sophie's struggles, there had been noises, doors, the window being opened, her own absolute terror engulfing her; she was lifted up, someone was striking her hard on her back until she coughed and coughed and choked and coughed some more, and then, breathing again, the world went black.

In the early evening when she had been carried back to her own room for the night, Grandfather came upstairs to sit with her for a while before she fell asleep.

Sophie told him, whispering, "I thought the angel would carry me to heaven." Grandfather let his gaze rest on her face, gently, but then, seeming to dismiss what she had seen in her fever, he teased her, "How do you know it would be heaven?" At first she didn't understand him, and then she had cried out in terror at the thought of hell, so near, hovering in the hall, and its implacable flames roaring on the other side of the maple tree outside her window. He stood quickly, pulled back the covers, put his arm behind her shoulders and helped her sit. She was quivering all over, her chest dampening with sweat, and he held her close to his chest and engulfed her with the smell of his tobacco and his warmth.

"Sophie, Sophie," he told her, "Children do not go to hell. The church wouldn't allow such a thing. You must not be afraid." He put another pillow behind her head, helped her to a higher place against them, stroked her forehead, then sat again holding her hand.

She said, "But the church – May I go visit Uncle Henri's grave? May I, Grandfather?" He wouldn't look at her.

"Your grandmother would not like it," he said, shaking his head slowly and not looking at her. "When you are older you can go yourself. But now? No." She thought, I will go after school one day, when no one knows, but such exhaustion was sweeping through her that her hand fell from grandfather's and she was asleep.

Later, she didn't know how long it was, she woke again. He stood with his back to the window so that the light was blotted out, she saw only a grandfather-shaped shadow and then she remembered the widow Bénédicte Bilodeau, and was about to ask him why he had been holding her hand; why had he kissed her? When she turned to him out of the blackness of the shadows under the great trees of the churchyard and saw them standing so close together, then kissing, and how they had looked at each other.

Now, suddenly, she remembered running into the church, the bonfire roaring maniacally behind her, the silence in the church that was filled with – she did not know what: Angels, she supposed. Was that when I got sick? But her thoughts were all mixed up. Why was I in the church in the middle of the night? *La fête de St. Jean-Baptiste*. With this straightening out of some of her confusion, her memory of the widow and grandfather grew stronger, both hellfire and salvation diminishing in the face of what she had seen, she knew at once, clearly now, that she must never ask grandfather about the widow, must never let him know what she had seen, must never speak of it to anyone else, not even Violette Hippolyte.

CHAPTER SEVEN

Beginning

SHE HAD COME TO KNOW the stars: To the south Orion, by his three-studded belt, above the sword that since her marriage she had come to understand was not a sword at all; to the north the pole star and the dippers, and in the west, well, nothing much in the west, she told herself, and the east was for the rising sun. She wished she had a book so she might identify more constellations. But there was no book to be found here on the prairie, nor any library from which to borrow one, and no neighbour who might be more knowledgeable than she was about the stars. Here, even the skies are wild, they are like an undiscovered continent, she thought, pleased, as she rose from her squat, lowered her nightdress and made her way back into the tent, and the makeshift bed beside Pierre who didn't stir, as he hadn't when she had crawled out moments before.

Mostly, the nights were silent, even the wind taking an hour or two to rest, and the only sound that came to them as they lay side by side or curled around each other was the faint, distant wail and barking of coyotes, and the howl of wolves that never failed to make shivers run up and down her back, or once in a long time, a snarling hiss that caused them both to stiffen, because a mountain lion stalked the night-dark prairie nearby where they lay inside their flimsy canvas house. They listened, not breathing, but no further screech disturbed them, and they relaxed and fell back into sleep. One morning, unnervingly, they found what had to be bear scat not far from their camp and staring at it, black, crumbling, and laden with berry pits, turned to look at each other with wide eyes, not speaking, until Pierre said, "I have my gun, Sophie," and she had nodded, reassured. After that, even while they worked on the cabin, he kept the gun within reach, although mostly, during the day they didn't even think of it, or of wild animals, or maulings, or death.

They rarely thought of what they had left behind only six weeks earlier: a village, families, church, priests and nuns, streets and sidewalks, stores and hospitals and mayors and police. If they were reminded, they would turn and gaze into each other's eyes at the reminder, start to smile, then laugh aloud, a delighted, even ecstatic laugh that came out of their understanding, now, of what freedom consisted. Even if it also consisted of seeing no one but themselves for days and weeks, of thinking that this blessedly good weather would surely be broken one of these days by a storm or a stretch of damp and cold that would tire them more and further exhaust their resources. For now, it was fine, and they were fine, and the world was fine as fine could be.

THEY HAD BROUGHT a walking plow all the way from Québec. The first thing Pierre did when at last they had found their own quarter section, one day later than when they first thought they had, and Sophie had decreed that the house they would build would be *there*, pointing firmly, and *the door will face the east.* As Pierre had finished the hitching and grasped the plow handles experimentally, she had felt something was missing, almost called, wait! But then realized she was so used to the priest blessing any new venture, that it felt very strange to be beginning so momentous a thing without any ceremony. Shaking herself, she felt that need too diminish if not vanish, and making a hasty sign of the cross as Pierre was also doing, but he without even thinking about it as it seemed to her that she always did about everything, she let her hand drop to her side. Pierre set the plow blade down, spoke to the oxen and farming began. With Sophie walking with him as the sods fell aside from the blade, the grass turning over so that the light brown soil revealed itself, glistening and giving off a faint, unnamable odour, the iron ringing and sparking against the occasional stone, the muscles of his back and shoulders moving as he fought to maintain the plow upright, to keep it deeply in the soil, the line he walked straight, he plowed their first long furrow.

She looked back at the tent – even from the far end of the long furrow it looked tiny in the immense space of grass, hills, sky – wondering what she ought to be doing: organizing supplies, setting up the stove, if she could discover how, they couldn't cook on a campfire the entire summer, arranging their trunk of clothing, making a place for morning *toilettes* inside the tent; setting up a makeshift cupboard where she could keep handy her plates, cutlery, pots and pans, but covered with a cloth to keep out the flies and mosquitoes, not to mention mice and even gophers and the small foxes that ran about; gathering – she paused. Gathering what? No chickens, so no eggs – they would have to remedy that very soon – no animals as settled farms had and they would someday soon too, the oxen already fed, watered and working, Fleurette, hobbled and nibbling tentatively at the grass. Needing to be milked for sure.

She started, remembering this, and left Pierre at once, he appearing not to even notice she was going. Finding one of their two wooden pails, also hand-me-downs from one of the Hippolyte neighbours, she went to the cow, speaking quietly to her as Mme Hippolyte had shown her she must do, but firmly, even though her palms were damp with anxiety. She set the donated milking stool at the cow's flank, mercifully Fleurette seemed to know what came next and stood quietly, switching her tail against the insects while Sophie took teats in each hand, and doing her best to hold them just so and to draw as she squeezed, began to milk their cow. What ridiculous triumph she felt as milk began to cover the bottom of the pail.

The farmer said Fleurette had had a calf not long before, although he had kept it, so there would be milk for a while, but then, they would have to find a bull somewhere, so the milk supply could continue. In the meantime, no way to keep the milk cold, no cool dark well into which to lower it in a bucket where it would be out of the sun, no ice box, no delivery of ice, no ice. Her butter churn, Mme Hippolyte's old one that M. Hippolyte had hurriedly repaired for them, was somewhere in the pile of goods tumbled onto the grass, but without a way to keep butter cold...They would have to dig a hole for it, that was all. She wondered if the oxen could drink the leftover milk. Fleurette made a hard, wide swipe with her tail, catching the side of Sophie's head. She blinked, leaned away, tears starting at the sting. But no, Mme Hippolyte had told her that she must take charge.

"Fleurette, stop that!" loudly, angrily, as if she were indeed in charge. Fleurette subsided, it was as if she had been trying this out to see if her new owner would allow it, and finding Sophie would not, desisted. A lesser victory, but one nonetheless, and feeling suddenly competent, she relaxed into the job. We will get along, Fleurette, *non?* she inquired of the cow.

The milking done, she puttered about trying to put things to right again, laughing because overnight the prairie had become her house, the four walls made of air, the cupboards wooden boxes where things could be shut away at night, the stove sitting majestically against the sky in a patch from which they had scraped away all the grass so as to avoid starting a prairie fire when she cooked. I have the biggest kitchen in all of Christendom, she remarked out loud, and stood listening to her words riding on the steady breeze. She wished Pierre would take the time to hunt – in a few days he would have to – she didn't choose to eat cured meat forever and they were running out in any case. A garden! How could she have forgotten? She must start a garden at once, for without one, they would starve come winter.

For the first time, trying to get the tip of the shovel into the root-matted, dry sod, the reality of the hard work she would need to do began to sink in. If it seemed too much today, how would she manage for the many summers that she saw lay ahead of them? She would, that was all; she would not fail, but in her fear that she would fail, all the past came welling up over her, all her many losses, parents, brother and sisters she hadn't even known, Sophie no longer first in dearest Guillaume's heart, her grandfather who had done his best for her, great-uncle Henri. Had the sun not clasped her so fast in its bronze grip, so strong it was almost visible, the smell of grass and sage not filled her nostrils, had her beloved Pierre not been plowing so nearby, she might have collapsed onto the hard prairie and beat her head against it. She might have wailed and screamed; she might have died from her own terror and sorrow. She sought frantically for something, anything to grasp that would make it possible to go on. No words came to her, no memory of anyone else's, but instead, in her violence of emotion, she raised the spade and with the aid of her foot pressing with all her strength on its shoulder, she succeeded in getting it into the hard, gritty soil, again, and again, and again, sweat pouring down her temples, along her spine and under her arms. She slammed the shovel into the ground, wrenched it, pushed it forward, until she had no breath left and had to stop, panting, leaning on it. *I will have a garden*, she told herself, through gritted teeth, or maybe she was speaking to those unseen forces that would let her have nothing unless she forced it out of them. *I will not fail Pierre. I will not fail.*

She thought then, *winter will come*. Had not the *voyageur* Jacques Le Blanc told Pierre of the ferocity of the winters in *le pays d'en haut*, claiming them worse than even in the north of Québec, the week-long blizzards, the temperatures so cold you could freeze to death in minutes, made the more terrible for lack of towns or houses on any of the trails in which to take shelter?

Winter. From now on, in a flash more like a knife cutting through her bridal dream, her dream of freedom, she understood that winter would be their darkness, their ultimatum from which there would be no escape, their final test. Every year from now on they must be ready for winter, or die. She lifted a quivering hand to her face, closing her eyes, breathing in through her nostrils, trying to shake this unwelcome wisdom, trying to encompass it with her own will, one that demanded that she be stronger even than winter.

Out there against the sky Pierre was plowing, wrestling with the plow, his voice reaching her faintly as now and then he cursed at his oxen, stubborn as they were, but powerful, another furrow unfolding behind him straight as the first. Behind her, the sides of the tent snapped or cracked dully, heaving with the wind that rose and died and rose again. Pierre would plow from dawn to dark, *while I putter away prettily.* She had not succeeded in breaking down more than a couple of square feet of sod. Prettiness will not help me now, she told herself, disgusted by her own, heretofore unrecognized vanity, nor will it help my husband. As she watched him work a half-mile from where she stood in her frustration, she was awed by something she could only call his manhood. How different we are, she thought, and a thrill ran through her in celebration of the difference that she had not mentally examined before, allowing it only to settle in her body. She thought of her grandfather bending down to her when she was a child, smelling of his pipe, grunting as he bent, his hand so big and heavy on her head that she nearly buckled under its weight. How then she had loved what grandfather was, although she did not *know* what it was: his size, his deep voice, the way he smelled, his whiskers, all were part of it, but were not *it* itself. Watching Pierre she felt she could not now fully grasp what a man was, and was grateful that this *man*, so different from what she was, belonged to her, that he adored her, that he would never hurt her, but would protect her forever, as her grandfather had done from her birth twenty years before. Is this what it is to be a woman? She supposed that it must be.

When Pierre came back across the prairie to her just before the sun reached its zenith and the heat came up in waves off the earth, and fell onto his side on the ground, groaning, she said, "We aren't enough people. We need a hunter, a builder, a plowman, a chef, a house-keeper…" She sat down beside him.

"And a parlour maid," Pierre said, touching her ribs with his elbow, teasing her because she had lived in a house with Antoinette who was both something of a parlour maid and a housekeeper, and with a cook.

"I will be the parlour maid," she said, starting out in a high-pitched, pretty voice, then dropping the joke as she would indeed be the parlour maid, whenever she acquired a parlour. But her hands were blistering from her garden work. When Pierre, lying exhausted and wet with sweat on the grass in the shade of the tent while she prepared his meal of the last of the canned beef and the biscuits she had made on the top of the stove for lack of wood to fuel the oven, saw what she had done, he had looked at her with something new in his eyes, frowning a little, watching her, as if to ask himself, who is she? But all he said was that after he had eaten and had a nap he would plow some ground for her garden, then she could break the sods down with her shovel.

"That will be easier than trying to cut through that matt of roots with only a shovel," he told her. "A little rain would make breaking the sods easier." Inadvertently, both glanced at the sky, then looked down again. Not so much as the shadow of a cloud broke the even blue.

"Then we have to get water," Sophie declared.

"I need to build a stone boat, but I can't do that without wood and some iron for the runners, or I buy the runners in the town."

"And wood," she said, "for fuel, when we get the water." He said that surely there would be a wood supply along the stream where they filled their barrel with water.

"I need chickens."

"Maybe we can get some hatchlings or chicks in the town too, or..."

"She didn't tell him that after his break, when he would go back to his field, she would take one of the wooden pails and go out across the prairie to get more water, being careful to stamp in her mind the bump on the top of a hill that she knew was above the stream nearly a mile away to the north, the one she had pointed out on the map with her own finger, and then to survey carefully the terrain around their tent so as to know what to look for on the way back, she would take one of the wooden pails and go out across the prairie to get more water. She would take two pails but knew she would never be strong enough to carry them both back at once. If only we had a saddle horse. Soon, she told herself. Next year at the latest.

She knew that the stream ran through a shallow ravine where some shelter from the sun might be found, and perhaps some berries too. What had the grocer in Swift Current called it? *Couler*, she thought. A French name, butchered in English; he had said 'coulee' with the accent on the first syllable. The word meant running, so...ah, she thought. A place where water runs. That must be it. Or did he only mean the French Canadian word "coulee"?

It occurred to her to wonder what would happen if she hadn't chosen a destination and had merely wandered out from their camp to walk, but thought that if she had no destination, how would she ever find her way back again? She pondered this fact as she walked, that already what had seemed beyond endless, an infinity of gently rolling plain covered with grasses soughing delicately in the steady breeze, she had found, or made, markers. A human thing, she told herself, just as at night we find stars to tell us where we are. She tried to imagine a featureless world, but frightened herself, and stopped. She walked slowly glancing at the horizon to re-orient herself.

The thought that she might find berries at the stream heartened her, and she imagined presenting Pierre with a freshly-baked blueberry pie. But she hadn't nearly enough wood to keep an oven hot for the time it would take to cook the pie. Worse, she had never made a pie all by herself, and knowing what skill was required, quailed at the thought. Pie, too, would have to wait. She would make biscuits.

Behind her there was a narrow gap in the line of mauve hills far beyond their tent and the new long scar in the grass; she would use it to mark the way back. Every once in a while she would stop walking and turn in a slow, full circle studying the vista of grass in each direction, marvelling at the subtlety of colouring, the way the slopes of the hills, a soft ecru at the top, changed as her eyes moved down them to a faded blue-green and, at the bottom where water sometimes gathered, there would be a streak of brilliant emerald, incongruous in the otherwise subtly-coloured landscape. The beauty of the scene in all its softly-radiating distance suffused her; she could not *think* of it: it *was* and she *was*, but as she moved slowly forward, her skirt trailing in the stiff, dusty grass, she was stopped by a flower gleaming at her feet. She bent to look at it, faintly surprised, this didn't seem to be a landscape for flowers, but there it was, a daisy-like plant, bright yellow, but tiny compared to the daisies she knew from far-away Quebec.

After that, every fifty or so feet she bent, or even knelt to study tiny flowers reaching up through the short grasses, for she recognized by name only the sparse scattering of pink or white roses that grew a few inches high here and there in the grass. The other flowers were yellow, blue, white, purple, and even once a true red: She was amazed at the plethora of flowers she saw if she looked closely, and although most of them with blossoms not bigger than her smallest fingernail, how lovely they all were, when she had thought there were no flowers at all, and would have missed their presence if she had had time to think of it.

Two kinds of beauty, she thought, and wished for an instant she had someone to say this to: the long view, and the very short view. And look! Wasn't that lichen? Growing right on the ground. How colourful the few scattered rocks were, and examining them closely, saw that the colour wasn't the stone itself that made them so bright, but lichen of many shades from rust and orange, to gold to white and black. And surely that was moss with those tiny white flowers blooming on its palest grey-green surface, moss growing right on the dry ground. How could that be? She touched it, rubbed it gently with her fingers, wondering at it stiffness, from which sprang this tiniest perfection of blooms.

She had not at first paid attention to what seemed to be bits of old, stringy, dark brown wood half-buried in the grass and dirt that she sometimes saw by the flowers she examined so closely. On impulse she reached for one, scratched it up with broken fingernails from the dust and the previous year's semi-cover of beige-coloured blades of matted grass. But no, as it came free she saw that she held in her hand, not a piece of wood, but instead, a short curved animal horn, or rather, the bark-like covering of a horn. At one end it was at least two inches wide, its edges ragged and it curved to a sharp but broken point at the other end. The horn itself, she supposed still attached to the skull, was nowhere to be seen. She rose from her knees holding it up before her eyes, turning it slowly, shifting hands, then putting it back to rest on the palm of her right hand.

But what animal, and looked about nervously, half-laughing at herself. Antelope horns were black as ebony, and the horns of deer darkened ivory. Then she knew: It came to her in a rush that started in her abdomen and flushed upward into her chest where it held for a breathless second: She was holding the horn casing of one of the legendary, vanished buffalo.

She walked on, glancing up for the three hills and the middle one with the bump on the top, so as not to lose her way. A breeze came up and she pulled on the strings of her bonnet, tying them more tightly, brushing away a buzzing fly. She heard, far above her head, but faintly, a piercing falling sound, half-whistle, half-screech and raised her head, back, and then further back than that. A hawk circled, and as she gazed, far higher even than the hawk and a long way ahead of them she made out a black speck and then another: A pair of eagles, she knew at once, circling too, looking for prey and wondered how big she looked to them. Too big to be prey she hoped, and would have stopped, perhaps even turned back, but the blue-green space ahead of her called. On she walked, carrying her pail in first one hand and then the other, the wind singing in her ears, her whole being held fast by the yellow-white sun, until she saw in the near distance a dark green line that she knew to be shrubs and knew too, that she had found her way to the only surface water she and Pierre knew of on the prairie near them.

She thought then that she'd been foolish not to bring any food with her, or a jar from the last of their drinking water, and wondered at her carelessness. She had been so intent on this new life and this strange new place, that she had somehow, without realizing it, in the perfection and wonder of this precious time with him, her beloved, in this wide, barrierless Eden, she had moved into a dream. Although she would have argued that it was the old world that was the dream and that she was now, for the first time in her life, fully alive, and wide awake.

At last, she arrived. What she saw was a narrow ribbon of clear, brownish water bubbling over rocks embedded in or lying on a smooth clay-like bottom surface of a perhaps ten-foot wide and six-foot deep raw cleft in the prairie. The stream ran swiftly because the cleft in the earth angled slightly downward at the point where she stood. She dropped the pail down the cleft's deep side and clambered down herself, pausing only to free her skirt from the grasp of a rose bush and to brush off the bits of grass and dust. How cool it was down here, and how still, except for the hiss and burble of the water as it swept by her. No river this, she thought, but she bent and filled her pail at a spot where the water pooled on the downward side of a deeply-embedded, larger, flat-topped rock. Finished, she wanted to follow the stream, to see if perhaps she could find berry bushes, or to rest on the bank below the sharp edge where the short prairie grass nodded in the breeze, lying against the crumbling beige wall of the bank with the occasional stunted bush that she didn't recognize growing more horizontal than vertical out of it, its trunk the size of two fingers, but as gnarled and grey as if it were a thousand years old, its greenery not even proper leaves, but a sort of fuzz like a pussy willow, and not a proper green either, but closer to the faded, dusty green of the prairie moss. But she didn't; she had to walk a mile back in the sun and carrying a full pail of water at that. This wasn't going to be easy, and she needed to start at once.

It took her a full hour, or so she estimated, to return, and when she arrived, she had perhaps slightly more than a half a pail left, what with the missteps she made that caused water to rise over the pail's edge, its small tendency to leak, and with its evaporation in the heat. But she was proud of herself. Pierre was still in the field, still wrestling the plow, sometimes she could hear him shouting at the oxen. She took a glass jar, filled it with water, took two of her breakfast biscuits from the tin, and carried them to where he sweated and panted in the heat. He stopped plowing then, giving the oxen a rest, and sat on the grass beside her to devour the biscuits and sluice down most of the water, then lay on the grass, tipping his hat over his face to keep the sun from his eyes and after a pause, reached out one hand to her.

Surprised, she took it, he pulled her against him, then rolled them both over so that they lay full-length against each other. He kissed her softly, his hand on her breast. Before she knew it he was pulling her skirt up, whispering to her to remove her underwear – she had taken to wearing only one plain petticoat so as to save the others and because of how silly she felt in this place empty of people in all her standard layers of proper clothing – and in barely a moment they were rocking together, crying out, as if they hadn't seen each other in months, or it had been a thousand nights since they had last made love.

"Sophie," he began, and fell asleep in mid-sentence. She pushed herself upright, rearranged her clothing, and sat beside him gazing at his beloved face: his black eyelashes, long and thick for a man, and eyebrows threatening to thicken when he grew old as her grandfather's had, his straight, strong nose, the hint of curl in his glossy black hair even where he had unbuttoned his shirt at his throat, and she could see the sun-bronzing that had darkened his face, hands, and throat stopped abruptly and where his skin with its olive tone was fine and pale. Just gazing at him while he slept stirred her. How I love him, she said to herself, and then, out loud, "How I love you, my Pierre." Not long after that he got up, pulled his clothing together, and went back to the field where the furrows he had plowed lay shining in the sun.

Evening came, she was preparing to take his supper out to him since he showed no sign of stopping, but then she realized that he was plowing toward her, was nearing the end of another furrow, and that probably he would stop then, when he was nearest their camp. She waited. As she had expected, at the end of the plowed land he stopped, unhitched the oxen from the plow and began to lead them to the barrel of water. She knew, just looking at him, that he was thinking how he needed to build a water trough as soon as he could find the time.

She was alarmed at how slowly he moved as he came toward her, how under the sun's darkening she could see a hint of ashen pallor. He ate groggily, together they went to do their few chores, then he went into the tent to undress and lie down while she made sure the fire was out, and that things were tidied and covered, and whatever needed to be kept safe from marauding animals or weather she had carried or drag inside the tent.

Tomorrow, she knew, she would have to go back to the crevasse in the prairie to pick up more wood, having stripped the prairie near their camp of any burnable twigs, and knowing she would have to resort to buffalo chips, which lay all around them, although there was not a buffalo to be seen, nor would there be, she had heard on the train. All gone, no one knew where.

FROM THEIR FIRST BRIGHT DAY Sophie had wanted to know what they might see from the top of hills that lay a couple of miles to the northwest. She had at last prevailed and made Pierre take an afternoon away from work so that they might explore the landscape around them a little. "If winter comes and the cabin isn't ready we won't be able to stay here," he warned her, "we would freeze to death," but she said, pleading, "One half day, that's all," and eventually, curious himself, he had given in.

Now, Pierre reached the hilltop first while she, surprised by their height, at least a hundred feet above the prairie, was still struggling up the hill's steep side. "Hurry, *vite*," he called down to her, and she called back, panting, "It is not a race, sir," and they laughed together out of delight in each other and excitement at what they were about to discover. But when she reached the top of the hill, the one with the bump on it that broke the softly undulating line of the horizon to the north of their homestead, that at last, after days of staring at it, they were finally investigating, he was yards away standing before a big pile of stones. She paused to catch her breath.

"Mon Dieu!" she said, awed, with a touch of sudden fear, for were they not alone out here? "So that is what the bump is." Pierre was silent as she hurried to stand beside him. The pile of stones was perhaps twenty feet in diameter, the bottom layers nearly buried in the earth, and at its highest point it rose as high as Sophie was, at least five feet

and possibly more. Thin bunches of awkward yellow grass grew up around the pile, and more stalks thrust upward from the layers of dirt packed between the stones by centuries of wind and snow and rain; many of the stones' exposed surfaces had white stains on them and partially-eroded trails down their sides, bird droppings, the size of the chalky worms of excrement speaking of great birds, hawks or even eagles; the surface of more than one stone had resting on it the feathers and bones of small birds or tiny animals torn apart by predators. Oddly, Sophie thought, for the most part the stones were smooth, often oval in shape, and she wondered fleetingly what had polished them so. Some were too big to be lifted by any but the strongest man. Many were smaller, and embedded in the earth were a couple of boulders, one of them as high as Pierre's waist, as if the pile or cairn or whatever it was had been started around them. The stones were dull greys, biscuit-coloured, charcoals, and some with fine, sandy surfaces as if they were soft, a faded ochre or a powdery near-white, all the stones' very paleness melding into the landscape of soft blues, greens, and cream and dun-coloured grasses.

"But who...?" She moved closer to him, touched his arm to reassure herself of his protection.

Pierre said, "Who else but the Indians. There is no one else, and what white man would waste his time carrying so many rocks up so steep a hill when he has ground to plow and crops to seed?"

"And houses and barns to build," she said, not stifling a small sigh. But she was whispering. "Do you think it is...a grave?"

A wind came and pushed around them, rippling her thin skirt, blowing loose strands of hair into their faces, then passing on. Into the silence he said. "Unless we throw aside the rocks and dig, we will never know."

They didn't speak then, studying what lay before them, alive to the mystery of it, Sophie shivering briefly even though the sun beat down on them and the world melted at its edges with heat. They walked the full perimeter of the mound of stones, looking for what they didn't know, and finding nothing, turned then, to gaze out around them from where they stood in the centre of the universe.

Nothing, nothing to be seen for miles in any direction: only grass and more grass, hills and more low, softly sloping hills repeating themselves until they reached the far, light-filled, wavering horizon. Beyond all that, lifting a thousand times higher than the highest hill, the wide sky, a light blue that deepened at its fathomless apex to take on a purple tinge, a few wisps of cloud hanging motionless far above where they stood, two specks in the immensity of plain and sky, light and wind. And the sun, too brilliant to ever look directly at, its rays burning through their clothes, commanding all that lay before them.

ONE MORNING IN MID-JULY, they both saw at once a wagon and team approaching from the southeast, the direction of town. They waited as it slowly drew nearer, saw that many heads bobbed around in the wagon, that there were three people on the wagon seat. Staring hard at the people on the seat, Sophie thought joyfully, merciful Virgin! A woman! Before the horses were even stopped, (Percherons, both Sophie and Pierre noted), three of the children, all girls, dropped one by one to the ground, running to where they had come to stand side by side by their tent, then stopped abruptly a safe distance away and stood there shyly, hanging their heads, peeping up to look at the newcomers before dropping their heads again, the oldest girl scuffing in the dirt with her boot, as if she were at home standing in front of the pen of chickens with not a soul between her and the faraway town.

The man holding the reins called, *"Bonjour, bonjour! Comment allez vous!"* – they were French! – and was climbing down from the wagon, reins still in his hands and shaking Pierre's hand as if to pump his arm off. Pierre, at first tense when they saw the wagon coming, now grinned from ear to ear. Before they had even stopped, Sophie, and certainly also Pierre, knew them to be the Beausoleil's whom they had never met, nor gone to visit themselves because of lack of time–they had to get the crop in as soon as Pierre had broken a small patch of ground – although they kept hoping to go "any day now," as Pierre would tell her if she asked.

Sophie had gone to the other side of the wagon and was helping the woman down. She was stout, at least fifty, an old woman, Sophie noted, too bad, she'd hoped for a friend, but despite her age, the horde of children of all ages leaping from the back of the wagon, and her corpulence, she was strong, so strong Sophie wondered if what she had taken as fat was instead muscle, like a man. Smiling, the woman shook off Sophie's helping hand on her elbow.

"Oh, that prairie!" she exclaimed, "My back is broken in ten places!" But then, changing her tone, she went on, stiffly, properly, "I am Madame Beausoleil, Séraphine Beausoleil, and you..." here her serious expression dissolved into a grin, and she threw her arms wide, "You are our new neighbours! *Bienvenue, bienvenue!* How I have longed for neighbours! We meant to come sooner but what with all the work and winter never too far away..." She apparently planned to go on, but had taken Sophie in her arms and hugged her as if she had known her all her life. Sophie, out of surprise (or so she would tell herself), could not stop herself from hugging her back. "And these," she went on as she stepped back, sweeping her arm around to indicate the children, are, "Théophile, Rémy, Martine and Marie-Anne, Aurore and Jacqueline."

Huge tears abruptly began to run freely down her cheeks, and Sophie, to her dismay, found tears had started in her own eyes. At the same time she couldn't stop herself from recognizing the Beausoleils as one of the *habitants* families she thought she had left behind in Québec, nor could she quite quell a touch of unease that she recognized as coming from her grandmother's attitude toward such people, people from whom she had tried to keep Sophie separate. And now, in all places, the middle of nowhere, Sophie seemed to find herself one of them.

On the other side of the wagon the men were still talking loudly, their voices overlapping, questions being asked about where in Québec the Beausoleils had come from and then the Hippolytes, and mention being made of this relative or that who might once have lived where the other family lived. Soon the horses, still pulling the wagon, were being led to the corral, barely begun and with its too-small wooden trough, where they would be unhitched, given water, and using hobbles, be allowed to graze.

"No fences!" Sophie heard the man whose name she now knew was Napoléon, shouting, "I will come and help you. Fences, you can't do without them. We can be of help to each other, *non?*"

"A garden! You have begun a garden, so good, good for you!" Sophie was already leading Séraphine over to have a look at it.

"If only it would rain," she said. "Then I could put all the seeds in, but right now, the ground is still too lumpy and it is too hard to chop it down into good soil. I've done some," she pointed out, and looked questioningly at Séraphine, wanting advice from the older woman, who stood, elbows extended, fists on her wide hips considering the situation.

"Time for all that," she said, turning away. "Now, the children must eat," and began to walk toward the wagon, calling to the oldest girl, "Martine, Martine, bring the basket."

The basket contained two loaves of fresh bread and a jar of Saskatoon berries that Mme Beausoleil had brought as a gift for their new neighbours.

"The last one," she declared, and when Sophie remonstrated, she said that soon there would be a fresh crop and she would can them and they would have their winter's supply.

"It's going to be a good berry season," Napoléon announced, puffing at his pipe as they sat, the men and children on the grass, the two women on empty packing cases.

"We can meet at the berry patch north of here," Mme said. "We can all pick berries together. Like at home." There was also home-canned beef to eat, from a steer butchered from the Beausoleil's small herd.

"We need *venaison*," Pierre murmured, gazing out across the prairie to where, faintly, they could see a few antelope who seemed unaware that nearby were humans who would see them, not as a party of the beauty, but as a meal. "Our supply of meat is almost gone, but I've been so busy..."

"We need to make a hunting party," Napoléon said to him, "Like our cousins, the *Métis*. We pack up camp; we all go; we hunt for weeks and months. Sophie and Séraphine there, they can skin the animals, gut them, slice up the meat and hang it to dry in the sun on racks." He was laughing. Sophie stared at him in surprise. *Our cousins? What could he be thinking of?* Still, fresh meat, even if the day would never come when she would skin and gut an animal. What nonsense he talked, she decided. The basket had also contained a bottle of home-made wine and he had been drinking freely from it. So had Pierre, now that she noticed. Even Séraphine had taken a small glass and Sophie had accepted one out of politeness, but so far hadn't even sipped at it.

Next from the capacious basket came oatmeal *biscuits*, large and a bit hard, but when she bit into them, the flavor of Québec came rolling out to fill her mouth and throat.

"You used maple syrup!" she cried, her mouth full. Séraphine merely nodded, frowning, as she tasted her own *biscuit*.

"It used to come into the settlement," she said, meaning, Sophie understood, the Red River settlement. "So we get a tiny bit shipped to us sometimes." It was in the flavor of the cookie that Sophie came at last to understand how important this visit was to the Beausoleils, never mind to herself and Pierre.

"You are so kind to bring some to us," she cried, turning to Séraphine, blinking in her sudden emotion.

"New neighours, well…" Séraphine said, the corners of her mouth turned down, thrusting out both hands, palms up. "And a woman to see sometimes. I will feel better just to know you are here, hoeing and digging and cooking, like I myself am doing, just over the grass from my house. How good it is to have you here!"

"I have a million questions," Sophie told her. "I don't know where to start."

Pierre said, "Sophie comes from a house with a maid and a cook." He laughed, teasing her, but she thought in surprise, with a faintly derisory note. Was he mocking her?

"Oh, Pierre," she said, chiding. Séraphine was staring at her as if seeing her for the first time.

"I thought...I wondered," she said, staring back, her eyes wide, searching Sophie's face. "Oh, *ma pauvre petite*, how hard this is for you!" If Pierre had expected laughter or angry sneers at the product of the *seigneurys* from the Beausoleils, he was not getting it. Even Napoléon gazed at her with wide open eyes, then turned his head away, saying nothing.

"I can work just like...anyone," she said, angry, but with a hint of her surprise at Pierre's suddenly turning on her. All three voices agreed with low murmurs, and Séraphine looked hard at Pierre as if to remonstrate with him for being cruel to his young wife. Pierre was stretched out on the grass, lying on his side, supporting himself with his elbow so that the upper half of his body curved upward.

"Did you see her garden?" he asked, falling on his back so that he could look up at the sky instead of at the rest of them.

"Oh, yes, *certainement*," the Beausoleils said.

"She has done hard work," Pierre muttered.

But Sophie was wondering in what way she had failed him, but could not, no matter how she searched her memory, think of anything she might have done that she hadn't, or that she might have done differently.

"Séraphine," she cried, "you must tell me what I need to do!" She gazed about the camp, all the sacks and boxes neatly arranged, the kindling for the stove kept in the tent, the now empty bucket for water waiting at the open flap into the tent. She could think of nothing. Was there some mystery here that needed solving? But Séraphine had her lips pressed in a tight line.

"You are doing very well," she said. "I see nothing forgotten here, or undone. The Blessed Virgin knows you have been here only a few months and there is plowing and building to be done first." She threw out a hand as if to indicate the impossibility of this vast place and its distance from civilization. "But I will help you."

The Beausoleils were gone by mid-afternoon, having cows to milk, animals to pen, and the long, bumpy ride back across the prairie to get through. Before they drove away Napoléon insisted that he and Pierre and the oldest boy, Théophile, would take Pierre's oxen and the wagon and help him fill the barrel. "We have used up all your water!" he cried, and would listen to no objections. How relieved Sophie was, although she had objected briefly too. When the family was no more than a tiny black dot across the yellowed grass, a new mood descended on Sophie, who was at once elated, exhausted, and for a few long, bad moments, feeling thoroughly abandoned. How can this be, she wondered, when before I saw them coming across the prairie I was happy as a lark all alone out here?

The following morning, though, she rose into the clear, early morning, the air cool and lighter than silk on her skin, and could not believe that no children would come shrieking past her, chasing each other. How still it was, only the faint calls of the tiny birds that lived in the grass disturbing the silence. The sun was barely breaking the horizon to the east, sending long fingers of gold across the grass to where it reached her standing alone beside the tent, her elongated shadow stretching like a dark finger behind her. A few feet out from the tent a gopher popped its head up from its hole, looked about – Sophie held still so that it wouldn't see her – then pulled itself out to stand upright, surveying its kingdom. She wanted to laugh; how self-important it was, like Napoléon Beausoleil. She lifted a hand to cover her laugh at this absurd thought and the gopher was gone in a flash.

Pierre got up, moving slowly, stretching and yawning, but with a look of his old near-contentment on his face that she was relieved to see, washed himself in the puddle of water Sophie had heated for him over the small fire she had built to allow him a few more minutes sleep, and after eating the last of Mme Beausoleil's bread and meat, went back to plowing. He looked fully into her face before he went to hitch the oxen, holding her with his arms around her shoulders, lifting a hand to play with her still-touseled hair. She remembered then how he had been cruel to her yesterday and wanted to ask him how she had failed him, but could not bring herself to say anything. His eyes this morning, she thought, were again full of love for her, and seeming to know what she was thinking, he said, "Sophie, you are the best wife a man could have. I would not be here with anyone else," and kissed her full on the lips before dropping his arms and going away. Contented by this, it was a long time before she began to wonder, just a little, what he had meant by that last remark. If it hadn't been for her, he wouldn't be here? He would be home with his family, married to a solid *habitante* who...who...could do the plowing herself, she thought, for an instant angry again. Who would have dug up that entire garden all by herself on the first afternoon, but after she had delivered a baby first. The ridiculousness of this made her laugh, and her anger, or unease, or whatever it was, dissipated.

She wished that the men had gathered a real pile of wood while they were at the stream, instead of the armful they had brought back. But she had been so pleased about the water, and they had been doing so much talking – and, it must be admitted, drinking – that they seemed not to have thought very seriously about what else was needed. Never mind. She would go herself, and went into the tent to transfer contents from a sack into an empty packing box so that she would have something in which to carry back the wood. When I return, she told herself, I will dig in that cursed prairie if it kills me. I will break those infernal sods to infernal powder. No one will be able to say I'm not a fit wife for a homesteader.

When evening came, Pierre stopped early, before his supper was even ready. Tomorrow we go to town, he told her. I am too tired even to hitch the plow for another day's work. Even the oxen are tired. He didn't look about to see how much work she had done in the garden patch, or even to notice how much wood she had gathered, having made two trips instead of the one she had originally planned. She thought to herself that Séraphine Beausoleil would not expect her husband to notice every bit of work she did; one worked, that was all.

One worked as hard as one could, every day, forever. The thought chilled her momentarily, but then, Pierre rose, mumbled something to her, and went into the tent where she could hear him undressing. By the time she had extinguished the fire, put the food and dishes away, and undressed herself, he had been, for some time, snoring loudly.

So their first summer on the prairie went, work and more work, although neither of them flagged for longer than a second, in love with this strange new landscape and each other, and the promise of a prosperous future if they could just accomplish all that lay before them. First, the cabin and at the same time, a dugout barn for the oxen and Fleurette, and then the animals they saw themselves soon acquiring: a pair of workhorses, the beginning of a small herd of cattle so they would have something that could be sold quickly to raise a little cash if they needed it. There would be fences, and a farmyard alive with chickens, ducks and geese; there would be a flower garden, not just the vegetable garden that would keep them from starving during the coming winter. On and on it went, all of these needs beyond the plowing of the land that never stopped except for the building, and if either of them paused at all to think of what lay ahead of them, they soon chased away their fears, believing in themselves and their youth and strength.

FOR SEVERAL WEEKS, as fall drew on toward winter, Pierre had been making time to take the team and wagon out onto the prairie to find firewood before snow came and covered up whatever there was left. In the end, he had gone to town and bought a load of wood from a settler who had driven down from further north where there are trees, trying to make a little money by selling roughly chopped loads of dead trees he'd picked up on the forest floor. These Pierre had brought home and spent an hour every night chopping into lengths to fit their stove, and so that he could pile them more efficiently against the side of their rough cabin, with the help of the Beausoleils, finished before winter set in. Whatever Pierre did, Sophie thought admiringly, he did well, partly because M. Beausoleil knew so much about the best way to do things, and partly from his life on his family's farm. Her admiration for him grew, her love increased, and even as she immediately quashed even the slightest doubt or uncertainty about his uneven temper, and his sudden fancies: the way he would suddenly throw down whatever tool was in his hands and with a quiet curse, walk away to begin another job. As long as he loved her, she thought, his idiosyncrasies meant nothing, as surely as he forgave her hers, whatever they might be, this latter thought making her frown a little, for a second.

With what was almost the last of their cash he had also brought home a small supply of coal, "For the really bad storms," he said, "the ones that go on for days." She had pretended she hadn't heard this last, but a chill of fear went down her spine and she had to remind herself that storms in Quebec also often went on for days and she had barely noticed them. In response to this thought, she had gone all around the interior of the cabin again to make sure she hadn't missed a spot where there was a crack or a hole that needed chinking with a mixture of clay from the streambed and ashes from their fires.

And now, it was on them, had been on them for six weeks, Sophie carefully marking the days on the calendar, and now it was Christmas and what might they call Christmas when they were alone and far from home and couldn't even go to Midnight Mass? They were to have spent it with the Beausoleils, but on the afternoon before Christmas Day when they were to leave, both of them anxiously watching the sky the whole morning, the first bad storm of the winter had blown in from the east, growing worse by the minute until even Pierre had to say that it would be too dangerous to go. It was a terrible disappointment to them both, Sophie had even cried when she realized this, but carefully hid her tears from him when he came in from settling the oxen and milk cow in the dug-out barn, leaving them with a good supply of feed in case for a day or more he couldn't get across the yard to them.

"Maybe we can go tomorrow," she said to him, uncertainly. He slammed his hand against the window frame where he had been standing peering out into the whistling white that obscured the world outside the cabin.

"Not this time," he muttered. "This is here for days," and she had said nothing, afraid to make him explode as he sometimes did when things went especially wrong. While he had been attending to their animals, she had put on her heavy mantel and boots, hat, scarf and leather mitts and had brought in several armloads of firewood, knocking off the encrusted snow first, and piling it neatly near the stove. She filled the coal scuttle too, to overflowing. He had seen all this, she saw his eyes go to the woodpile and the dull gleam of the coal, but he hadn't spoken and she wondered if she had made a mistake, taking on one of his jobs, and leaving him with nothing to do when he was so full of barely suppressed anger.

As if to resolve her concern, the wind gave a great howling bellow, and blasted snow and ice particles against the walls of the cabin so that they shook and rattled and groaned, she was afraid the roof would be torn off, and she dropped the broom she had been holding to stand, frightened, listening. He came to her then and held her. "Sophie, Sophie, we will be all right. We have prepared for this, we have shelter...we even have firewood right here so I won't have to go out again before daylight tomorrow." Safe in his arms, her contribution acknowledged, she clung to him. It came to her suddenly that her very need was steadying to him, so she held him tighter, and didn't move back until, gazing gently into her face, he unclasped her arms from around him and said in a mock roaring voice, teasing her, "Quick, woman! Stir yourself! I am a hungry man!"

All night they lay clasped together, still in their clothing to keep warm despite the steady fire in the other room, the noise outside so great sleep was hardly possible. If they had had another bed or a divan to sleep on they would have spent the night in the main room where the fire was, but everywhere the floor was colder than a block of ice and small gusts of freezing wind came up through cracks as well so that they had no choice but to go to their bed and pile on every blanket they had, even their two small rag rugs Pierre's mother had given them.

Pierre drifted off, exhausted as he always was, and she lay thinking of their animals – how terrible for them – out there in their fragile shelter, and of the wild animals further out on the prairie who could be freezing to death even as she lay thinking of them. Then she thought for the first time that maybe she had made a bad mistake, a life-threatening mistake to cause them to leave their long-settled village with people around to help them. If they survived this cataclysm, there were still another three months of winter to get through, and she wondered if they could do it.

As if he could read her thoughts, Pierre spoke into the darkness and the steady roar of the storm, in a strange, hollow voice, as if she had somehow entered his very dream, "Not every day will be like this." But she couldn't, at this moment, believe what he had said. Now she knew that she and Pierre were nothing, they were nothing out here in the West, they were barely human beings here, just helpless animals in thrall to the unimaginable, implacable force that nature was showing itself to be.

In the morning, the wind still battering their home, they woke to a film of dry snow on their bed coverings, the air so cold despite the fire, that they could see their breath. All that day, Christmas Day, and that night they rose, taking turns at Sophie's insistence, only to replenish the fire, or to go into the other room and use the pail that was their chamber pot, or for Sophie to bring them something to nibble on, bread or dried fruit or lukewarm porridge, waiting for the storm to end. Each time she entered the other room she couldn't even bring herself to look at the basket of her baking and the venison roast, all frozen despite being on the table and covered with a length of toweling, that they had planned to take to the Beausoleils.

SHE SLUMPED AGAINST the cabin's outer wall where there was perhaps six inches of shade to be had. The hoe fell from her blistered hand, and she didn't stoop to retrieve it. She placed her palms flat against the small of her back and pushed, trying to find relief from the steady ache. Should she go in and rest? But Pierre didn't rest, she could see him out there, plowing, always plowing, and then he would haul water from the stream, a hard job, for it was the end of the summer and the stream nearly dry, except where, with infinite slowness, a spring seeped water. They would begin the well as soon as help was to be found. Pierre would pay back the help, not with money, but with work of his own. In the meantime if, rarely, they went to town for any supplies, they always brought back a barrel of water pumped from the town well. Yet, it was beginning to seem to her that the harder they worked, the farther behind they found themselves, their money supply all gone and waiting to be replenished by the sale of their small harvest still ahead, and another winter on them before they had time to turn around.

But the garden – which thought brought her back to herself, and she bent and picked up the hoe, breathed deeply a few times, walked back into the rows of vegetables and began to cut the ground, her hoe striking stones and devilish weeds with roots that must descend down to hell itself, puffs of light-coloured, fine soil rising with each strike. When Pierre brought the water in the wooden barrels, she would carry pail after pail, watering carefully each single plant so as not to waste a drop. Soon there would be potatoes, and God willing, also corn, the peas having been a failure this year, but the carrots, turnips and beets a success. We must have a root cellar, she had said to Pierre at the end of their first summer on the prairie, and he had nodded in agreement, but looked away toward the horizon with an expression that said digging the root cellar would be the last straw that would finish him off. She had dug it herself, in the evenings, when the air cooled a little, and she could think of herself as having finished her long day's work. Then Pierre had come and shored it up for her with planks and the trunks of bushes he had found lying at the stream. Without it, they would have starved come winter.

Once again Napoléon Beausoleil's bull would service Fleurette, but she must, this time, be brought to the Beausoleil's instead of the bull and the Beausoleil family to them. The men having settled this on their last visit together when they had met by chance in town, it was decided they would make a good visit of it, and even stay overnight, and maybe they would have music and perhaps dance a little and then eat Madame Beausoleil's good Québec food. It would take a half day or more to get there, as they could hardly expect Fleurette to run all the way, or even part of it. And Sophie had been feeling a little unwell this last little while; the jolting of the wagon would be hard on her, although she vowed to be strong and not complain no matter how nauseated she might become.

Séraphine was ready for them when they arrived and had a feast spread out on their homemade table in their shack which was one room bigger than Pierre and Sophie's. Meat pies! Sophie hadn't seen them since she'd left home, but no, one of them was a Saskatoon pie, and Séraphine had just pulled four roasted grouse from the oven. Napoléon also had a shotgun, besides his rifle, and often shot prairie chicken and grouse and would sometimes send a brace of them home with Pierre whenever Pierre dropped in to give him a helping hand.

"Such heavenly scents!" Sophie cried. Suddenly she felt her cheeks flushing and perspiration popping out on her forehead. Pierre had driven the team to the barn where Napoléon and his two oldest boys waited to unhitch the wagon and unharness the oxens that would be put in the corral for the night. She put out a hand to support herself against the door frame.

"My dear girl!" Séraphine exclaimed. "You have been working too hard, non? I know how it is. Never-ending and then some more after that. Aurore! Go – pull out the chair for Madame Hippolyte!" Little Aurore hastened to do as she was told, her sister Jacqueline trying to help, although she was too little to do much good. The door opened and Martine, the oldest of the girls at fourteen, entered, carrying a bunch of carrots from the garden. Her twelve-year-old sister Marie-Anne followed with a sack that Sophie supposed would be full of potatoes from the root cellar. Séraphine bustled over, batting away flies and children as she came, and helped Sophie sit down.

"It is nothing, I am fine," Sophie protested, and swallowed hard to keep down the bile that wanted to rise and spill all over the hard-scrubbed wooden floor. Suddenly Séraphine drew back, pausing, arms akimbo, mouth fastened in an 'oh' as if she had just understood.

"Tu es enceinte!" Then put her hand over her mouth as if to hold back the news. Sophie burst into tears, why, she couldn't have said. They wanted a baby, yes, Pierre, a boy, while she didn't care which it was. But now, when there was still so much work to be done, even a year after their arrival? And no doctor, no midwife – she cried because she was afraid. And she was surprised, not recognizing that this was the reason she hadn't bled this last couple of months, thinking that the flow had stopped as it had during the trip West and the first six months of such hard labour and so many shocks to her system, the ferocity of the winter being, she felt, the worst. But no, it was true: She was carrying a child. A Western baby! And was caught between more tears and sobbing, and laughter. As if it had never before happened that a woman became pregnant with a child for a fleeting instant some closed thing in her solar plexus opened wide and her whole being cried out for her mother. Now, to be with her now, her mother. This fathomless sorrow threatened to engulf her utterly at the same time as something else, a huge joy, grasped her body and shook it as if a slow lightning moved up and down it.

"Oh, my," she said, gasping, "Oh, my God," while Séraphine crossed herself so rapidly it was comic, and sought her rosary that she kept in her apron pocket at all times, like a nun. Pure joy was flooding Sophie now, at the same time as she sobered, thinking of the added labour ahead, and all the many things she lacked for a baby. No nursery or nursemaid, never mind so much as a cradle or a cot. "I am perhaps two or three months along?" she asked Séraphine when she regained control, who nodded, tears running down her face, as if she were the one pregnant yet again.

"I have a few baby things that aren't worn to absolute shreds," Séraphine told her. "And I will help you deliver him – or her. I have had enough of them myself to know something about how it's done," this last sounding both very determined, and a bit angry, although at who or what, Sophie wasn't sure. Séraphine was old enough to be her mother, Sophie thought now, she will have to do.

But Séraphine said nothing about it for the rest of the day or during the long evening, nor did Sophie say a word, as Napoléon screeched out tune after tune on his banged-up fiddle, and the children swung each other around heedless of dishes, or furniture, or adults' toes, and the men quaffed a certain amount of homemade alcohol. After Sophie was in the children's bed with Pierre, the two little girls in their parents' bed, the older girls sleeping on blankets on the kitchen floor, and the two big boys on straw in the barn, she whispered to Pierre, thinking perhaps she should wait until they were alone on the way back to their farm, or when he hadn't had so much to drink, but unable to keep back the news a moment longer, that they were expecting a child.

He groaned, then hiccupped. "I was afraid of that." She drew back from him. "I mean, so soon. I'd hoped to have one more year to ready things for a family." Placated, she told him, "Never mind, you know we will manage as we have managed everything so far." Then both of them lay on their backs, side by side, not touching, thinking of the year they had just passed that had been so hard, and changed even their physical bodies, all lumpy and hard now, with sore spots and bruises and scars, even Sophie's pretty hands thickened, the skin darkened and rough. And of what they had left behind: Pierre sadly of his parents and all his many siblings, their farm, and the village, and Sophie, bleakly. For her to come West had been an escape, and all the hardship – still – worth it.

"Do you want to go back to Québec to have the baby, and so you can have him properly baptized?" He said this as if it had just occurred to him that having a baby in this wilderness would be a dangerous enterprise.

"Of course not," she answered, a little too sharply. "I will never go back." She breathed in tightly through her nostrils her mouth set. "Séraphine will be my *sage-femme*, and we will find a priest to baptize him when he is old enough to travel." He sighed loudly, starting to turn on his side away from her.

"Do you doubt me? Do you think I am not strong enough for this?" It was not usual for her to talk to him in this tone. A long silence followed, while she waited for his touch, his kiss.

"No, Sophie," he said, finally. "I do not doubt your strength." His voice had in it a hint of something she couldn't quite place, but that did not gladden her heart. Resignation? And back of it something that might have been...distaste? No, she told herself instantly, it is only that he is tired and has had too much to drink. That was all he said, and though she lay awake a good part of the night thinking of the little one coming soon, trying not to give in to the sudden arrows of fear that pierced her, trying to believe that this at last would not be too much, because she knew nothing about babies, or children, or... Pierre fell immediately to sleep, and snored. At first she was hurt at what seemed to her his indifference, but after a time, as she listened to his breath, heavy with what she knew to be more than just drink but from sheer exhaustion, and then to its loud expulsion, though never so loud as Napoléon's in the next room, her annoyance slowly dissolved. Was he not still her beloved? Was he not the man for whom she had given up everything?

But no, she had to admit it, that wasn't true. They had not run away from things so much as they – or she at least – had run *to* this life that was their own, where no one made rules for them, where they made their own decisions, their own choices, and built their own life together, stick by stick, furrow by furrow. And now, what was always inevitable: a child. Thinking of it, she suddenly realized that even the youngest of the Beausoleil's children had been born in Manitoba; in their district their child would be the first Western-born baby. She lay awake for a long time, her mind reaching out beyond the bed in which she lay, beyond the cabin walls, and the few plowed acres, out across the miles of grass, and over the distant hills, crossing streams and gullies and wild, animal-filled coulees, lifted out of herself by the momentousness of this thing of which she was the fundamental part.

CHAPTER EIGHT

Bone Pile

NIGHT CAME; the residents retired, the house gradually falling into silence as everyone from Charles through Mrs. Emery to the boarders drifted into sleep. But Old Man Wetherell could still be heard walking about, his footfalls, steady, but not loud enough to keep anyone awake. Sophie lay, despite her exhaustion, staring into the darkness as the long hours of the night began to pass and Wetherell walked ceaselessly back and forth. Who was he? Had he killed someone? Was there some other crime in his past? Where was his wife? His children? He had come West before Sophie was born, according to Mrs. Emery, but he had ridden south, crossing the border to the United States before the border was even demarcated, when the Indians were still wild and dangerous, and to run into them alone was certain death. She saw him racing through the night, the moon lighting his solitary course across the hard pan and burnouts of the territory south of Bone Pile, his horse foaming from under his saddle. She imagined that terrifying, exalted passage south and ever more west, crossing the Missouri, through the Bitterroot that she had only heard of but thrilled to the name. Were there even towns in Montana then? Fort Benton, maybe. However he would not be quivering with fear as she had been all day, but flooded with some strange wild toxin. No, not toxin – joy, *une joyeuse sauvage*. Her mind went out to the long fields of dark grass spreading for miles out beyond the bed where she lay, peaceful, quiet, only animals crouched in burrows or bushes, or running soundlessly, their eyes glowing – how he would have galloped past them, seeing or not seeing them, he wouldn't care either way. His rifle tucked against his thigh, his bowie knife against his gut. Of course he would have a bowie knife, she told herself and laughed out loud, one quick ungovernable snort, and stunned at herself, pressed her lips together, holding her breath. Oh, such stories as she had heard of that wild West. Thinking of Pierre again, and sturdy Beausoleil who could barely stay on a horse, a farmer in his very soul. Maybe it was all lies. And all the men she had heard speak of it as if it were some male Eden, were duped by men like Wetherell. But even she didn't quite believe this. And still he walked, as if to see that none of them forgot what the West had been. It is as if he is keeping guard, although against what, she couldn't think. Then, as if the words had come from elsewhere: *He is guarding against you.* What? Me? What am I? But she knew very well: Softness, femininity, home, hearth, family. She had been sucked out of herself; not frightened, but she nonetheless felt pinpricks of perspiration popping out on her brow. A day like this, she thought, the things that have happened, twisting her head on her pillow, her eyes grainy for lack of sleep. She had to think.

She had gotten them a roof over their heads and food, but she couldn't stay there forever being a housemaid in exchange only for that. She needed clothes for Charles or the cloth to make them, shoes, medicines, perhaps even to pay someone to care for him while she worked. She couldn't manage for more than a few days without money.

She thought of the money they carried when they arrived in the West – more than a thousand dollars that had come from hoarding Sophie's small dowry left for her by her parents, a few wedding gifts of cash, and from Pierre's savings, earnings from working for a local farmer during seeding and harvesting, and lumberjacking for a couple of the winter months before they had even promised themselves to each other. *I knew I would marry*, he told her. *It takes money to marry*, and he had laughed, and she knew he wasn't thinking of her. It had all gone in paying the fee to acquire the land, buying the animals, the wagon, the plow and binder, the materials for their buildings and corral and the tools to build them with, the seed wheat and the store of household supplies – one hundred pounds of flour, fifty pounds of sugar, twenty pounds each of tea and coffee, table salt and rough salt, yeast cakes, baking soda, even laundry blueing and coal oil for the lamps. In what seemed no time, not a cent was left. Here in the West Pierre had earned a little now and then working for a few days on this ranch or that, or for a new homesteader building his house, or helping somebody harvest, leaving her alone on the homestead sometimes, or if his work was closer, riding back each night. They had been careful, had made no mistakes, and yet, the money was gone.

It was Pierre himself who turned out to be the mistake. Now she thought, still waiting for the great gap to close that had become her interior, trying to smother her aching for him, that soon, when she was able, she would rue the day she had met him.

She would have to sell some of her belongings. What did she have that had any value? Her earrings, her dishes. *I will never sell my earrings*, she vowed, even as a part of her registered this as foolishness. There was the brooch Pierre's mother had given her, a pretty thing, gold, studded with seed pearls and with a sprinkle of the tiniest diamonds to catch the light. She had always wondered, if the truth were known, if those sparkling stones were perhaps only glass. The Hippolytes were poor farmers, where would they find the money for jewelry? Pierre had been his mother's favourite son though, and she knew that his marriage to the granddaughter of one of the village's prosperous families had been considered a *coup* for him, no matter what the circumstances. She wondered briefly if she and Pierre were still a topic of scandalous conversation in the village they had come from. She doubted it; by now surely there would be other scandals to occupy the countryside.

Still, even here in tiny, unprosperous Bone Pile, there might be some woman who would want the brooch, whose husband had money to spend to please her. Tomorrow she would inquire – no, she corrected herself. No one must know her true situation. It wasn't in her nature to be secretive, she had learned to hate secrets and secretiveness; was it only her pride that insisted on silence? But everyone in the village already knew that Pierre had run off with Marguerite, had known long before Sophie did.

But they did not know that I have no one to turn to, and not one cent of money. *But they will assume that*, she realized. No ordinary married woman in the North-West Territories has money of her own, or at least, money left over after her and her family's needs have been met. She remembered Campion's overture, indecent, she had thought, and then that perhaps she had mistaken him, that he was offering her salvation in allowing her to stay on in her home, while also freeing him to go about his business, which she knew now was land speculation.

If she had accepted his offer, at the first opportunity he would sell the place out from under her a second time. Then where would she go? Ruined as she would be. Besides, to be hired help on the farm she and Pierre together had laboured to turn from wilderness into civilization... She'd rather start again on different land, and imagining plowing virgin prairie by herself, twisted in the bed with the bitter knowledge that she could never do it alone. Nor could she stay out there all alone even if she could do the farming herself. This knowledge was cruel, hopeless.

Above all, she was prey: If she let them – she did not define *them* – they would turn her into a slave, a drudge, into a...but the last thought, she could not quite bring herself even to articulate, although she knew very well such women existed, even here on the very frontier of civilization. Hadn't Pierre told her that such a woman had arrived in Bone Pile? She saw the women at the station when she and Pierre had passed through Montréal on their way West. Dirty, bruised, ragged, some of them with small children, some of them clearly mad. Now, hearing Charles's even breath beside her, she understood that mothers would feed their children, whatever they had to do to get that food.

The West was full of young men without women; if she couldn't support herself by honourable means, she would be a bought-and-paid-for bride, slave labour on some homestead, or else she would fall and become a *putain*. There it was, she thought, although her bitterness was mixed with a kind of amazement that she had never seen this before, that if the man a woman had cast her lot with was not honourable, this was what her life would become. In three days, a day, an hour.

Even as she lay there though, wide awake in the darkness and deep silence broken only by the faint, long-drawn-out howls of wolves in the far distance, and the constant background of Old Man Wetherell's footfalls, so relentless and she thought, malign, that she covered her head with her pillow so as not to hear them, she struggled back from the bleakness of this understanding. Surely the world was not so cruel. Pierre had loved her once, she had loved him. It was Pierre she wanted. Only him, and was ill with longing tainted with the shame of her desire for someone who had so wronged her.

There was no choice. She would have to present a face that said that she wasn't helpless, but could go back to Québec any time she chose. And she would act carefully and wisely to save herself and her child. She would find someone who will tell no one – maybe even the lawyer – who could advise her or even buy her brooch himself for his wife. She thought of Adamson, that kind giant of a bachelor who had forced a reckless and inexperienced Pierre into caution so long ago, when they had first come and he was trying to go home in the middle of a blizzard. Perhaps Adamson could advise her, and keep silent about it. Still, the hope that Pierre would send money, she could not quite eradicate.

Her wedding ring: A flimsy gold band with another tiny diamond in a delicate setting. Oh, she would part with the ring with no difficulty, she said to herself, even as every part of her from her fingernails to her womb cried out against it.

Perhaps the lawyer would buy her china for his wife? She had once met Candace Archibald, a woman in her forties, slender to the point of thinness, and if you looked closely, who must once have been very pretty. There were two children, both in boarding school in the East, home only for short periods at Christmas and in the summer. Sophie had met her at the summer's pony races a year or two before.

"Madame Hippolyte, *bon jour, enchantée*," she had said, her accent precisely correct, but in its precision declaring her to be an

English-speaker who must have learned her French in some young ladies' school. How fine and delicately wrinkled her skin, as if she were ill; how very thin she was.

"So beautiful a day," Sophie had replied in English, "And so pleasant to be out with so many people. Do you enjoy the pony races?"

"Hmmm?" Mrs. Archibald had answered Sophie's efforts, and Sophie saw that this woman thought her of no consequence, was barely listening to her. She blushed to think of how poor her English had been then, and how thick her accent. Now, wondering if she should go to her, she was too ashamed of her clothing, her shoes, and worst of all, to have her situation exposed first-hand to such a woman.

Dawn came and she had fallen asleep only once. She lay quietly, Charles stirring beside her now and then, meaning that he would soon wake. Out in the darkened village a rooster crowed, then crowed again. Now she closed her eyes; she had been too distraught and exhausted to pray before she lay down; now in her near-despair, the thin warmth of a dream lingering, she who had for some years now merely gone through the motions, thought to pray:

Notre Père, qui es aux cieux
qui ton nom soit sanctifiié....

The words dried in her mouth. But surely, she told herself in her misery, if the church cannot be trusted, God can be. Still, the rest of the prayer would not come. She foresaw the years ahead as she worked night and day to keep herself and Charles alive. She thought of her girl's dream of wifehood, of marriage, of family, how she had deferred to Pierre, and still he had gone – and she cried out against her own new wisdom. But she couldn't go back; she could only go forward. What began now would be her first trials at managing her own life, in her own way. Today, now that she thought of it, perhaps her emancipation would begin. But she trembled all over as terror swept through her, then passed, leaving her shaken to her core, a grey residue left made of sorrow and her new knowledge of the darkness underlying the hopeful world she had mostly occupied until this terrible day.

"Maman?" Charles cried, getting ready to wail, and she reached for him, holding him tightly. Then she rose, changed his soaking diaper, bathed him, put fresh clothing on him, performed her own perfunctory toilette. Her child in her arms, she descended the stairs as silently as possible, and after the necessary morning trip to the outhouse, made her way back to the kitchen. From here on, she thought, she would have to work and at the same time watch Charles like a hawk or he would wander off or burn himself or fall downstairs...or Mrs. Emery would tire of his endless needs and would send Sophie and her boy away.

Dawn was breaking and Mrs. Emery had not yet risen. Sophie spooned a bowl of porridge out of the pot that she and Mrs. Emery had started the night before and gave it to Charles to keep him busy while she descended to the cellar to bring up the milk, butter and eggs. While she fed Charles, she ate a slice of buttered bread that sat in a lump in her stomach while she made a large pot of coffee, put the kettle to boil, and began setting the table in the dining room for breakfast for the five people Mrs. Emery had told her would be down. When that was done, she sliced the slab of salt pork and lay the slices in one of the two large frying pans, and to heat the second pan for the eggs she would cook whenever she heard the boarders descending for breakfast. Everything ready for the morning's meal, she began to prepare the yeast and to mix bread dough, it being one of the two days a week when Mrs. Emery had told her she made a dozen loaves of bread. By the time she was giving the dough its first kneading, Mrs. Emery had arrived in the kitchen, rubbing her eyes behind her glasses and bustling overly-much out of embarrassment at having slept in.

"I ain't had such a good sleep in ages," she remarked to Sophie. "Guess I thought, for once, somebody else was making breakfast." She poured herself some of Sophie's coffee and not even sitting, sipped at it. At the sound of footsteps on the stairs, she drew in her breath, put the cup down, and joined Sophie at the stove, frying salt pork, breaking eggs into the pan, while Sophie toasted bread, Mrs. Emery giving instructions and Sophie following them, as one by one the boarders descended and found their places at the table in the dining room.

"Who might you be?" Sam Wetherell of the creaking floorboards demanded of Sophie, glaring at her from under his overgrown white eyebrows as she carried in the steaming pot of coffee. She didn't care for the way he looked at her, but it was a gaze that made her straighten her back and ignore him rather than reply. It surprised her how much in that instant, she found she disliked him, as if he stood for all that was wrong with men. Thinking of her own people, the *voyageurs* and their great, open hearts, their love of food, drink, song, and good times, even while they did their backbreaking, life-threatening work. Old widows in her village whose men had drowned in rapids or been torn apart by bears as they carried their loads through the wilderness. Beside them, Wetherell, the lone hero, she could not admire at all.

"She's my new helper, Mrs. Hippolyte," Mrs. Emery said.

"French, then," he remarked, and looked down at his plate, as if she was by her Frenchness of no interest to him after all.

"I speak English, sir," Sophie said softly, but she had waited until she was walking briskly from the room to say this so that he couldn't reply. She had seen glances exchanged between at least two of the boarders, all of them men, when Mrs. Emery had given her name. She hadn't thought to expect this, although the instant it happened, she realized that she should have. Her cheeks burnt and she thought that she couldn't go back into the dining room, that surely Mrs. Emery would understand... She drew her breath in sharply enough through her nose that Mrs. Emery, taking the fried salt pork from the pan, glanced at her, but then Sophie clenched her jaw, thinking that if she could not withstand a glance between two so far nameless young men, then she might have just as well accepted Campion's offer. I am blameless in this, she told herself, not without a measure of ferocity. I must remember that *I am blameless*.

Mrs. Emery had introduced Sophie to the other, younger men, although Sophie had difficulty straightening them all out, mixing up in particular Mr. Henry Ogden with Mr. Harold Olds, not only because of their names, but also because they were so alike physically – short stature, fair-skinned, with slicked-back blond hair – that they might have been brothers. When she entered the dining room carrying food, or tea or coffee, or clearing away, she never once saw or heard them engaging in the general conversation which could be lively, and which was often punctuated by loud pronouncements by a red-faced Wetherell – *balderdash, horse manure* – always, momentarily, silencing everyone at the table. Ogden and Olds, she knew, worked in the village, one as a clerk at the general store, and the other as a private tutor since there weren't yet enough children to warrant a village school. And although they didn't seem to speak to one another during their meals, Sophie had the impression that they were particular friends.

The remaining two men weren't difficult to distinguish. Percy Haslam was taller even than Mr. Wetherell, with black hair, eyes and moustache, and there was something about him Sophie didn't like, finding him – *louche* – shifty, for want of a better word. He worked for Ambrose – Sophie didn't know if this was a first name or a last – at the livery barn, and in the ensuing days she would find that always, no matter how clean he appeared to be, he smelled faintly of hay, manure, and horses. Instinctively, she kept her distance from him.

She would save her warmth for the last boarder, Monsieur Guy Roche, a francophone like herself although neither of them ever spoke French to the other, not even when Sophie found herself longing to, and she thought, he too longed to, countrymen after all, in this Protestant, English land. He would treat Sophie with absolute courtesy, and she him. A man of average height, a good figure with broad shoulders lacking in the other boarders, and a taste for quality clothing, he was married and a father, but had left his family behind as he came West to search out business opportunities. Soon, he told them, he would return home to Québec and would probably stay there as he had so far found nothing out West to attract him. It was he who had come upon Sophie, late on her first evening there, trying to get the barrel of dishes from the verandah into the house and who had insisted on carrying it to her room for her.

"I like my comforts," he would tell them, laughing. "I do not like sleeping out on the ground or eating food so bad that only the spectre of starvation puts it in the mouth. That is why I make this house my headquarters – because of Mrs. Emery's excellent cooking." And Mrs. Emery's cheeks would turn pink, although she would frown fiercely as if to say they needn't think she would be taken in by compliments. While Wetherell's unspoken contempt blighted the conversation, except for M. Roche, who seemed to be somewhere between amused, puzzled by, and dismissive of the old man. After one of Wetherell's sneers, Sophie and M. Roche would glance quickly at each other. Aside from mealtimes, she would hardly see the boarders, except to pass them once in a while in the hall or going up or down the stairs. But as a housekeeper, which struck her as odd, she would become intimately acquainted with their belongings, their clothing, their habits, even while they remained strangers she saw only at meals, too tired in the evenings after Charles was asleep to think of joining them in the sitting room.

When early afternoon arrived that first day, after Sophie had cleared and cleaned the dining room, finished washing the dishes, and tidied the kitchen, she told Mrs. Emery, "I have errands that I must run and as soon as possible, Mrs. Emery. I'll be gone only an hour and a half, and then I'll make the pies." Mrs. Emery studied her, and for a second Sophie thought she might refuse to let her go, but a certain understanding seemed to dawn on her face and she said, "I always have a rest right now, anyways. You go, and good luck to you." They were standing in the hall at the foot of the stairs, but rather than going upstairs, Mrs. Emery turned into the parlour where, Sophie knew from cleaning, behind it there was a small bedroom Mrs. Emery used, thus saving the mostly larger upstairs bedrooms for her boarders.

Sophie went upstairs, patiently moving behind Charles who was determined to mount them on his own, giving him a boost whenever he flagged or was distracted by even a loose thread in the carpet, or a shiny nail holding it in place. In her room she removed her large apron, folded it carefully and left it on the bed, tidied herself and Charles, and with hands that shook faintly, took her wedding ring, her brooch, her precious earrings, from their hiding place tucked against the back of the mirror's wooden frame. Each was wrapped in small squares of cloth she had torn from Mrs. Emery's worn cleaning cloths, and she put two of the packages in her pocket, but unwrapped the earrings and put them in her ears. She would have preferred to leave Charles behind, but he was so agitated by the abrupt changes in his life that she knew he wouldn't sleep, and that keeping him from irritating Mrs. Emery was vital to their welfare.

The afternoon was again very hot, the light almost unbearably piercing to the eye, and although there was not a breath of wind, the air was filled with fine dust. For a moment, Sophie stood breathing it in, dust and all, welcoming it after the general stuffiness in the house, comprised of too many bodies in close quarters, when she was used to only herself and Pierre and small Charles, with the outdoors in their flimsy cabin nearly as present on the inside as out. In her moment of inattention, Charles had made his way up the path beyond where she stood getting her bearings. She let him go, looking at the town with the eyes of someone who would not be leaving it again in an hour or two, but who, willingly or not, suddenly finds it her home.

In the entire village not a tree grew for shelter from the sun, or to soften the village's rawness, to remind the homesick of the green places from which they had come; nowhere was there a single patch of well-watered, soft, green grass. Hitching rails or single posts stood at intervals down each of the two, sun-bleached streets, and in the afternoon heat no one stirred; it was as if the village was deserted, the few whitened wood houses flattened by the unrelenting sun. All with a rickety air about it, as if a good wind might come one night and sweep it away, leaving behind only a churned up patch of earth, the stars in their black shroud glittering down, brilliant points of silver glowing in a few mud-brown puddles. Behind all of this, far back on Sophie's left, the great pile of white bones stood brooding over it all.

The village's few places of business began with the livery barn at the north end, which, rather than facing the buildings across from it, looked south onto the length of the street before it, as if the most important place in town. On the east side and proceeding south in a less haphazard manner than the houses on the first street, were the blacksmith, the butcher, the general store, the barber. The village had grown rapidly since the first time she had seen it four years before. But still, between the livery stable and the blacksmith shop, broken only by the new house, there was an open area where the grass-covered plain flowed into the town like a tide at the beach, but where, instead of engulfing it, the townspeople, their horses, dogs, cows, cats and oxen, wagons and buggies had trampled it into mud, now dried and crumbling, as rough as if some farmer had plowed it with his heavy breaking plow. While all around the village lay the prairie, serene, sun-bright, aloof. Their sixty plowed acres that had seemed to her and to Pierre to be a vast mark in the until then ungovernable wilderness, she now saw for what they were: Barely a pin's head in size in all the acres of wild prairie.

Midway between the livery stable and the blacksmith shop, but back from it, stood the new dwelling Sophie had noticed the day before, with its lace-curtained windows on either side of the front door, and two upstairs not quite evenly spaced, as if the builder was an incompetent or had played a practical joke, giving the house a slightly comical air, or an aura of things in a general way being askew. Facing the row of businesses, on the west side of the street, were a few more small frame houses, standing with their backs to the backs of the few houses on the other street. One of these was also a two-story, and therefore larger than the others. Sophie thought at once that it must be the Archibald's, because of its freshly-painted white and blue – none of the other buildings had ever been painted – and its verandah on two sides with turned, white-painted poles supporting its low roof, and gingerbread trim in the eaves of both the verandah and the house proper. Shrubs were planted out front, too, and a row of parched-looking little yellow flowers marched up either side of the narrow boardwalk that ran straight from the gate to the steps leading onto the verandah.

Not a soul was about, the men all out on their land seeing to the harvest, or else at work at various jobs, the women either with them or preparing food in their kitchens, minding children, taking a few minutes for a rest on this stifling hot afternoon. Where were the children? She supposed they were with their fathers running errands, or working with their mothers in the kitchen. When evening came and the day cooled, she told herself, people will be out, calling to each other over fences, working in the gardens, dropping into each other's houses for visits. For now, she was glad she could see no one on the streets or in the yards.

At breakfast she'd heard one of the men say that the evening before some wagon loads of Indians had come through town, stopping for the night in the coulee, looking for water there and maybe getting some game. Heading on into the hills they supposed, maybe a big pow-wow going on there, although they doubted the Mounties would allow that, and where was Constable McMann when you needed him, at which Wetherell had snorted loudly without speaking. Now she saw no trace of them, or of the fact that they had come through town, and she began to catch a glimmer of what Wetherell was, why he seemed to hate all of them. He thought *he* was the real West, she told herself, and we are all interlopers.

That there was no church eased her mind; as long as there wasn't a church to go to, she didn't have to battle with herself over it. She thought of her grandfather's pain when his beloved younger brother had died, and the entire household was in deep mourning, and the priest had come and locked himself and her grandfather in his study with the pearl and gold cross hanging over the desk and the shelves of religious books, her grandmother walking about tight faced, pale, her lips constantly moving in prayer as she fingered her rosary, unaccountably not seeing Sophie as she slipped by. She would not soon forget her grandfather's pain, visible even to her, a child, and a few years later when she at last understood why the priest had come, and that finally her grandfather had acquiesced to the church's decree that his brother couldn't be buried in consecrated ground, the ground under her feet had shifted, just a little, and on that matter, had not yet righted itself. It was better there was no church in Bone Pile; she didn't think she could walk through the door of a church again now that she had some idea of the freedom without one or without a priest keeping a watchful eye on her every move.

She caught up with Charles, took his hand, and travelling at his speed, moved the short distance east across the rough trail to the main street, and then up it toward the livery barn, although her actual destination was Mr. Archibald's office across the street. She was deliberately taking a round-about route in order to think of precisely how she would broach the subject of selling her jewellery.

Just as Sophie was about to cross the street to the eastern side, ahead of her, the door of the new house opened and a woman stepped out onto the short strip of boardwalk that fronted it. She hesitated, then turned in Sophie's direction, crossed the street to the side where Sophie moved at a snail's pace with her child, mounted the boardwalk there, and began to walk toward her. She was tall, her buxomness accented by her tightly-laced stays, clad in a mutton-sleeve blouse and a skirt, similar to the ones Sophie wore. But Sophie's were once bright blue, now faded by washing to a blue-tinged grey, while the stranger's blouse was made of a light fabric, dimity perhaps, and narrowly striped in yellow and brown, her skirt of a heavier fabric in light brown, both skirt and blouse crisp and fresh-looking, their hues still bold. Around her waist she had tied a bright blue satin sash whose ends hung down nearly to her knees. On her head was a large hat, on the brim of which bright yellow and blue silk flowers rode, quivering with each confident stride. Perambulating as she was through the dust and heat of this wilderness village, she was a startling figure.

Now Sophie saw that she was a redhead, her hair carefully pulled back from her face and piled in intricate curls the hat only partly covered. The hair colour, Sophie noticed, was far too bright. As they met and passed the woman glanced at her, offering her a slight smile, and Sophie, at the same time as she smiled in reply, seeing the woman wasn't as young as her figure, her costume, or her hair suggested, and realized with a start that this was the village's *putain*, its fallen woman, surely the one Pierre had mentioned as they lay in their bed after lovemaking, whispering softly to each so as not to wake the baby. "Adelaide," he said. "They tell me her name is Adelaide."

"She has no last name?"

"She calls herself 'Smith,'" he said. "Nobody knows where she comes from and she refuses to say." For some reason, Sophie thought of the two women, sisters, who had sat across from them so briefly on the train west.

"But, is she pretty?" she had asked, puzzled why any woman would do such a thing if it weren't out of immediate need.

"If she weren't," Pierre said, yawning, "who would go with her?" Sophie had been too shocked to say anything more, and Pierre had soon drifted into sleep.

They passed, not speaking, the showily-dressed prostitute, and the younger, prettier, but drably-dressed homesteader. Around the village the prairie danced, soft aquamarine and the palest yellow, and glistened in the great heat of the early afternoon, the sky retreating far above them, pale as the last crocus. Sophie did not change her pace, crossed the rough street carefully, while the other woman kept going toward the south, apparently just out for a stroll. Sophie wondered if this was why the woman chose such an uncomfortable time for strolling – she herself preferred the much cooler evening – because now no one would accost her. Then she thought, a little shocked, and her work is at night. And yet, from the moment she and Charles had left the boarding house Sophie had had a sense of being watched, and she thought that behind the drawn curtains of the town's few houses people were curious, taking note, for all she knew where Adelaide was concerned, cursing her.

She lifted Charles into her arms despite his protests, and walked faster, careful not to look back, although she wanted to. But even as she began to walk toward the barber shop and the lawyer's office above it, the two women she had met on the train west came into her mind: sisters, they had said, going west to join their brother who had a homestead, the location of which they said they knew only vaguely. Sophie was vague herself about precisely where she and Pierre were going – but now she knew that the two women, whether sisters or not, were prostitutes, heading West to ply their trade. She would have thought more about this, but the nearer she drew to the lawyer's office, the harder it was to think of anything but the task before her.

She mounted the stairs doggedly not glancing around, because anyone could see her and would know she was seeing the lawyer, and would take it for granted they knew why, that one way or another she was trying to salvage something from her humiliation. She continued to carry Charles, shifting him to her other hip as she climbed, and at the top, opened the screen door, entered the lawyer's waiting room, letting the door close behind her with a light clap that would announce her presence. Setting Charles down, she waited. A moment passed before Mr. Archibald opened his office door and peered out.

"Mrs. Hippolyte, good afternoon," he said, coming forward. "I thought I heard someone. Such a warm day, I hope you are not fatigued from your walk, and with the little one." Charles stared gravely up at the lawyer.

"I have come for advice, Monsieur – Mr. Archibald," Sophie told him. "I have no money with which to pay you –" she had not meant to say that, "but – it is only an inquiry, in any case."

"Come in," he said, his face composing itself into professional courtesy, standing aside so she might pass into his office. "Please, do sit," he said, indicating the same chair in which she had briefly sat the afternoon before. She had forgotten Charles, but he had followed them in and now was at her knee, asking to be lifted. She picked him up and then sat gratefully in the rich brown leather chair with its decorative brass studding that she hadn't so much as seen the day before even when she sat in it. He went around his desk and sat down too, and waited, while Sophie, casting about for the right words, stared at his gleaming oak desktop that hadn't so much as a fingerprint on its surface.

"May I ask for your silence on this matter?" she said at last.

"I am a lawyer," Mr. Archibald said. "Not even Mrs. Archibald is privy to what goes on behind this door."

"I am – destitute, Monsieur," she said. Then added hastily, "I have not come for a loan of money –"

He interrupted, "Surely, your family –"

"I choose not to ask," Sophie said. "My parents are dead. There is no one else." She chose not to mention who had raised her, nor her brothers; she would never tell them, especially not Guillaume, what had happened; it would just be adding fuel to the fire of his rage at her. Mr. Archibald murmured something politely that she couldn't make out, then cleared his throat in an embarrassed way. "I must wait for my husband to remember his duty and send me money for his son, if not for me." She was about to go on, when he interrupted her.

"I might be able to help you." He leaned forward, his elbows resting on his shiny desk, making a tent with his clean white fingers. "My wife is...not strong. Perhaps you would be interested in...ah...a position as her, shall we say, housekeeper? Her," he paused, "maid?"

"Oh, sir!" Sophie said, without even thinking. "I could never..." Never what? Never be someone's 'maid?' Even desperate as she was? Or was it that she would be too humiliated to live with the family as a maid, in a house not as nice as the one in which she'd been raised? In a tiny attic room? And what about Charles?

He said, as if she had said Charles's name out loud, "I'd forgotten you have a child. Mrs. Archibald would no doubt find the noise too difficult. Maybe it wasn't such a good idea. I should try to find her a young, unmarried girl, perhaps. Forgive me," he said to Sophie, seeing perhaps, the strong emotion on her face, and misreading it.

"I...thank you for offering me work," Sophie managed to say. "You are right – small children can be very noisy." She could barely speak, trying to grasp that she had fallen so far as to be maid material. She said nothing about working for Mrs. Emery; everyone in town would know that, or would expect it. There was nowhere else for a decent woman to go.

"And the room we have wouldn't be big enough for both of you in any case."

This didn't require a reply. Speaking haltingly out of her embarrassment, forcing herself to go on, she said, "I have come to ask you for advice as to who might wish to buy – might have sufficient funds – to buy a few of my – trinkets," here she dropped her eyes, "So that I might begin to make a fund of money, for Charles and myself."

She wasn't too upset to perceive the slight relaxation of the stiffness in his shoulder. She said no more, keeping her eyes on the pronounced grain of the oak desk between them. "These, ah, trinkets? They are?" he asked.

Inadvertently Sophie touched an earring. Mr. Archibald's eyes followed her hand and light came up in them when he saw the small jewels in her ears.

"No, no, not my earrings, or at least, not yet," she told him, and heard herself laugh, a sound which she shut off at once. She reached into her pocket, taking out the two cloth-wrapped pieces, set them on the desk between them, putting Charles down again so that she might unwrap them.

"Trinkets," she said, apologetically, "but not easy to buy out here." He gazed at her treasures. "This brooch is perhaps not valuable. This ring." She did not say, my wedding ring, but saw the lawyer glance at her hand.

"I must say, Mrs. Hippolyte, if you'll forgive me, that perhaps it's not the best way to bargain by saying that the things you have are not valuable." Smiling, he reached for the brooch and lifted it, raising his eyebrows as he did so. "Gold, of course," he said. Sophie didn't answer, but thought that perhaps the setting really was gold, although at this moment she suddenly doubted it. As for the stones, she didn't know, but following his good advice, kept silent.

"I believe my wife would like this brooch. It's very pretty. Just the other day she remarked –" He broke off. "I'm not well-versed in the value of jewellery." She held her breath; even Charles was silent and motionless, as if he, too, felt the weight of this moment.

She said, apologetically, "It was a wedding gift –"

The lawyer reached inside his coat and brought out a leather purse, glanced at its contents, then swung his chair around so that his back was to her, and bent from the waist, his dark coat straining between his shoulders. She had thought him thin and was surprised by the breadth of his back the strained fabric revealed. By the slight click and whir of the lock turning, she realized that there was a safe installed behind his desk, and she waited again, holding her breath, her body rigid with anxiety.

The safe door swung open, Archibald rummaged about for a moment, then pushed the door shut and swung his chair back so that he faced her. "Will you accept twenty dollars?" Tears started in Sophie's eyes: nearly a month's wages for a labourer or a washerwoman, or – "I had no idea," she said, meaning that the brooch was so valuable. "You are too kind, Monsieur Archibald –" She hesitated. "Perhaps you should take the ring too?"

"No, no, my wife wouldn't want the ring." He added, hastily, "She has several. Anyway, I don't want to rob you of your ring," and he laughed in something that might have been, again, embarrassment.

"That is a most satisfactory price," she said, carefully. "I am very grateful to you for –" she struggled for words, wanting to say, for not trying to take my brooch for as little money as possible. "You are very generous," she said finally. As she spoke, he was extracting an envelope from a desk drawer and placing the money into it. He closed it and pushed it toward her, not looking at her.

It occurred to her that it might be that he was ashamed of helping in the selling of the farm out from under her, and was trying to soothe his conscience, but she reached out, picked the envelope up with care and put it into her pocket, while he refolded the cloth around the ring, and pushed the small package toward her with his long-fingered, clean hands with their white-tipped fingernails. She hadn't seen such perfect hands on a man since she had left *l'abbé* Deschambeault behind in Québec, and found herself distantly indignant again at the priest.

"Merci, Monsieur," she said, flustered, taking the package, and thrusting it back into her skirt pocket. "I must ask you also," she said carefully, "Do you know anybody who might wish to buy some fine china – a Sèvres porcelain dinner set that came from France during..."

"Fine china," he said, his voice falling on the last note. "Fine... china..." She waited. He pushed a paper on his desk forward an inch, and then back an inch to its original position.

"There is a woman," he hesitated. "This woman, she's called Smith, I believe. She might perhaps – But no, this isn't a good idea." He appeared rattled at this. "Hmmm, let me see." Knowing at once who the lawyer meant, Sophie herself was confused. The woman, come to think of it, didn't dress like a poor woman. Maybe that was all he meant, that she could afford to buy Sophie's dishes, and then realized how improper it would be for Sophie to have any commerce with her. To have her precious dishes end in the hands of a prostitute!

"A certain rancher and his wife from far west of here will be coming to see me later this week. I'll ask them if they would be interested in some excellent china dishes. From France," he added. "Sèvres."

"I would be most grateful," she said. "And, of course, if I hear of any suitable young girl for your wife, I will tell you at once." Having recovered her dignity just a little by this offer, she stood, smoothing down her skirt, clasping her hands together at her waist like the convent girl she had once been, although now so he wouldn't see how they trembled.

He had already risen too, and she set Charles back on her hip, nodded gravely to the lawyer, who had gone around his desk to the door into the waiting room, and held it back for her to exit.

"Be careful, Mrs. Hippolyte," he said to her softly as she passed, "Where you put that money. There are – thieves." She had broken her step as he began to speak, and when he had finished, she merely nodded, not looking at him and went on through the chairless waiting room, out the screen door, and carrying Charles, crept down the none-too-solid wooden steps to the ground below, satisfaction and a nebulous, free-floating anxiety at war in her chest and head. And she was fighting back tears, not a few sentimental drops accompanied by lady-like sniffing, but chest-heaving sobs, a deluge of water from her eyes. *I must not; I must not*, she told herself, and did not, and was surprised by her own small strength. No, she would learn to act as *les anglais*, did: As if pain did not hurt; as if blows could not make one stagger.

She let her eyes wander from house to house across the way from where she stood. One of them, she knew, was the Tremblays'. She looked sharply at this one, then the one next to it, as if by dint of sheer examination she might discover it. But a woman was bending over in the midst of a large patch of potato plants to the side of one of the nondescript wooden houses, nearer to the livery barn. Sophie could see her back rising and falling as she worked, probably digging a few potatoes for supper. A small woman, thin, as far as Sophie could see, and with greying hair pulled back in a sparse bun. She felt certain, although she couldn't have said why, that this was Madame Tremblay. But she looked away quickly from the green dress and faded hair.

Well down the street ahead of her was the house that belonged to the bachelor, Harry Adamson. Had he not saved Pierre's life? She began walking in that direction, slowly, as if she were merely out for a stroll. Charles, who had missed his nap, had fallen asleep on her shoulder and she walked carefully, trying not to jolt him, while also trying not to turn an ankle on the rutted ground or catch a heel in a crack on the few strips of boardwalk. Her boots, that she had come West in, were so worn that they no longer provided support for her ankles, the soles so thin she felt every lump of earth, every pebble. It shamed her to think of her and Pierre's poverty, a perspective from which she had never before viewed their lives, seeing it as temporary if she thought about it at all, or else as interesting, another challenge, how to make something out of nothing, as if the whole venture were merely a game that she could end with a snap of her fingers. No, no, she told herself; it was that she saw only the land and the future it promised then, soberly, allowed in just a tiny ray of truth: She had seen it all as a romantic game; she never saw how *real* it was. But Pierre did; *he saw the truth of it from the start*. Nausea struck; she thought she might vomit, before it passed.

Adamson's cabin door was shut, the curtains on the one window firmly closed so that she could not peek in had she been so inclined. She knew that he had filed on a homestead, so of course he'd be on his land on this perfect harvest day, cutting his crop or stooking, or forking the stooks into a wagon to haul them somewhere for threshing. She glanced back down the street but there was no one about, and although it seemed hopeless, she knocked on his door anyway. To her surprise, she heard someone stir, the inside door opened, and a gaunt Harry Adamson leaned against the door frame, his head only inches below it, squinting through the screen door into the light. She saw at once that he was ill.

He stepped outside into heat, closing both doors behind him, a gesture for which she was grateful, knowing that the easy ways of the West, no longer applied to her. How pale he was, still blinking in the light, his cheeks hollow.

"Will you mind if I sit?" he asked, lowering himself carefully onto a broken-back wooden chair by the door. Here he must lounge evenings and watch the people of the village going about their business, she thought, and a warmth grew in her face again, that she had lost such comforts. "I'm sorry not to offer the chair to you. I am –" He began to rise again.

"No, no, Monsieur. I shouldn't be seen –" She glanced around again. He said quickly, "Of course, Mrs. Hippolyte." So he remembered her from a chance meeting, had perhaps seen her in town with Pierre. "What brings you to my door?"

"I'll come to the point," she said, "As I must get back to Mrs. Emery's." She noticed the fine line of sweat that had broken out along his hairline, that his breath was shallow and quick. "You know…" she hesitated, swallowed, then finished her sentence briskly, "what has happened to me." He nodded, yes, gazing over the prairie to the east, lifting and falling gently in the waves of heat, not raising his eyes to her. "I choose not to bother my family in Québec to send me money. I will solve this problem myself." The last came out more firmly than she had meant it to. He again said nothing, his eyes flickering upward to her face and down again quickly. "I've decided to sell what few – what valuables I possess." She reached into her pocket, setting Charles down again, who, still groggy from his little sleep, stood blinking into Adamson's face, as if trying to discover if this man was his father or not, as she produced the carefully wrapped package.

"Have you any use for this?" She held it out to him. He took it and slowly flicked back the wrapping to expose her ring. His fingers were pale and wrinkled as if he'd been soaking them in water. In such bright light, though, the ring looked better than she knew it to be, the gold gleaming, the diamond sending out a minuscule rainbow that rested on his index finger.

"Your wedding ring," he said quietly, and lifted his head to gaze into her face, his expression changing so that she had to look away. She said, "I have no need for it." Then cursed herself for sounding self-pitying.

"Pretty," the bachelor said, then, apparently not hearing that note, laughing, "I can't say I need it." Her heart sank. "But, I'm still young, still hope to find a bride." He smiled at her.

"You are ill, Monsieur," Sophie said. "I am sorry to trouble you –"

"It's nothing. A summer cold. Tomorrow I'll be back at work." He had, after all, always been thin; he had no one to cook proper meals for him. "Yes," he said. "If we can agree on a price, I'll buy it from you and put it away for the day when I need it. I hope soon." He held the ring in his large fingers and turned it slowly. "Or, maybe, once you're on your feet again you'll come and take it back from me." Such a thought hadn't occurred to Sophie and it caused her no pleasure. Why would she want back something that spoke to her only of betrayal? While she was considering this, he had risen shakily and gone back inside his cabin, emerging a moment later.

"Will this do?" he asked her, holding out coins. He was offering five dollars, which neither surprised nor disappointed her. The diamond was small, and although the ring was gold, it wasn't heavy gold, nor was it engraved. Still, she had no doubt he was a poor man, and five dollars was a considerable amount. This thought made her hesitate – hadn't he saved Pierre's life? But then, he would have other money, he had no child to care for, he could earn money if he needed it. Not without a qualm, she said slowly, "Wouldn't four dollars be fairer?" He had seated himself again, and laughed out loud, which made him cough. When he had caught his breath, he said, "A bargainer should bargain up, not down. Look, it has a diamond."

"It's very tiny," she demurred.

"If anything," he told her, "five dollars isn't enough. Now, I want the ring for my bride-to-be, whoever she is, and I'm offering you five dollars, not four." He spoke as if their transaction was a game they were playing, and she found herself smiling back at him, then blushed. Charles was gathering small stones from the road, making a pile of them, and seeing how dirty he was getting, distracted by this, she said, "Thank you with all my heart." She put the coins in her pocket and was about to walk the few feet to Charles to dust him off, when Adamson said, "I think I'd better lie down again." His face gleamed with sweat, blanched even more than when he'd opened his door to her. She put a hand under his elbow to steady him as he pulled himself to his feet, feeling a slight trembling, and his unnatural body heat radiating through the thin fabric of his shirt. Alarmed, she reached to open the screen door and then the inner one so he might go through. His weakness surprised her; Pierre was never ill, and Charles seemed to have inherited his father's strong constitution, a fact for which she could never be grateful enough. Besides fire, her greatest fear had always been that she might lose Charles, a fate for most mothers even in the great cities; how much greater out here without doctors or hospitals nearby.

"How long have you been ill?"

"A week, no longer," he replied. He grimaced slightly as if in annoyance at having to admit it, or else that it had been longer. "I'll be all right as soon as I lie down." Half inside his house he paused to rest against the door frame. Sophie didn't know whether to go inside with him to make sure he got to his bed, or whether she would be better to leave him to make his own way.

He began moving again, so she said, "I will come with Mrs. Emery tonight to see how you are." Not waiting for an answer, nor taking any time to glance around his room – in any case, it was so dark inside, and the light outside so bright, she could see nothing but blackness – she pulled the door shut behind him, let the screen door close, and turned away to pick up Charles. Part of her was concerned for Adamson, but the other part was filled with elation. I am no longer destitute! She crossed herself with her free hand, murmured aloud a prayer of thanks, then stopped in surprise, her hand still raised at her breast. Blinking back tears – no, not even tears of happiness, she scolded herself – she hurried back to the boarding house.

AS SHE AND MRS. EMERY worked together in the kitchen making the evening meal for the boarders, Sophie said, "I passed Mr. Adamson's house while I was out; he had stepped outside for a minute and I saw that he was ill –" She couldn't say she had knocked on his door, and remained convinced no one must know that she now had a small cache of money – not that Mrs. Emery would be a threat – and was beginning to think that the villagers would forget her presence faster if she melted into the background as that shadowy woman who worked for Mrs. Emery. She, who had scorned secrecy as the resort of scoundrels, and as unworthy of her, was learning its value. "I was alarmed. I thought that maybe we should go back tonight to make sure he is not getting worse? Or should we try to reach a doctor for him?"

"He's that sick? We could send somebody to get the doctor over to Garden City, I suppose," Mrs. Emery said. "But I better see him first. Is there any of that soup left?"

They hurried through the cleaning after the last meal of the day, even leaving a little to be done the next morning in order to get to Adamson's house before he fell asleep for the night. Sophie put Charles to bed, and exhausted as he always was by evening from the strenuousness of his days surrounded by, as he had never been in his short life, so many people, he fell asleep at once. She judged it safe to leave him alone for the short time they would be at the bachelor's house, but she warned one of the young boarders, Harold Olds, (she had called him Mr. Olds and he hadn't corrected her), whose room was across the hall, that she was doing this, and making him promise to come running for her should he hear Charles cry out. She gave a brief thought to what she would give him to play with tomorrow while she worked beside him, but put this aside for later.

They set out, Mrs. Emery carrying a loaf of bread wrapped in a cloth, while Sophie stepped carefully, holding a bowl of hot soup with a plate set over it to keep it from collecting insects or spilling over its sides as they traversed the short, but rough distance between the two houses. It was early evening, the mosquitoes descending in clouds and flies buzzing about attracted by the smells of the food they were carrying. A few people puttered about in their yards up the street, and a team and wagon creaked and jolted its way toward the livery barn, its driver waving perfunctorily to them. Somewhere, nearby, a night hawk could be heard whooping as it dipped through the dusky air catching insects, and back in the coulee an owl called softly, over and over again, until a dog barked and was silenced in French: Monsieur Tremblay, then.

Adamson answered their knock, blinking as if he'd been wakened or hadn't been out since Sophie had stopped by a couple of hours earlier, and despite the fact that the harsh light of the day was softening.

"Imagine not telling anybody you're sick," Mrs. Emery scolded, pushing past him so that he had no choice but to go back inside, with Sophie following him. "Now you sit right down here. We brought you some hot soup." He had begun coughing, and she paused to listen to the noise. "The heat will loosen up that chest of yours –" She fussed about him in a way that had about it the quality of a well-known role that she fell into at once with a certain eagerness, coming to life in a way that surprised Sophie.

As Mrs. Emery fussed Sophie occupied herself tidying the room, not speaking as Adamson ate his soup and bread. Observing him more closely now, in his own environment, she had begun to see that he was less ill than she'd thought, although, worrisomely, his cough was in his chest, the sound tight and hard. So nervous was she, she barely saw the room she was trying to tidy, listening so as not to miss a word of the conversation he was having with Mrs. Emery.

"We never brought water," Mrs. Emery exclaimed.

Sophie said, "I'll go and get a pitcher of it. It will give me a chance to check on Charles, too," thinking but not saying so, that she was worried about fire. The stove in the kitchen was out, she had put it out herself, in this heat nobody would have a fireplace or a parlour stove blazing away, and there was no thunderstorm to send down lightning to set the grass alight. But people would light lamps, there was no stopping that.

Back at the house, she hurried upstairs to find that Charles hadn't so much as turned his head on the pillow since he'd fallen asleep. In the kitchen she pumped a pitcher of cold water and set out with it for Adamson's house. Halfway there, she met Mrs. Emery returning. Surprised, she asked, "Is he all right?"

"He don't need a doctor, I reckon," Mrs. Emery said, "There's no fever tonight. But I thought we should maybe get him in some food – he's got to eat to get back his strength. I'll get one of my boys (referring to her young boarders) to bring over a pail of water for morning. And he can empty Adamson's slops too, won't hurt him none." She hurried on. Sophie hesitated, but then, she had the pitcher of water that Adamson needed – the village would assume, she supposed, that he was too ill for there to be any misbehaviour between them.

He was in his bedroom when she knocked briskly and opened the door, not waiting for his reply.

"Here is your water," she called to him cheerily. She went to his cupboard where she took down a glass and filled it, then carried it into the other room, where she set it and the pitcher down on the chair by the bed. He lay fully clothed on his narrow bed – what had she expected?

"Thanks very much," he said, pulling himself to a sitting position and reaching for the glass. "I was plenty thirsty."

"I hope you'll be well soon," she said, retreating a careful distance.

"Couple more days and I'll be right as rain." He repeated, "I can't thank you and Mrs. Emery enough."

"It's nothing, you'd do as much for us if we were sick. I'll come back tomorrow and get your sheets. Tomorrow is wash day."

He slumped back against his pillows, sounding, that quickly, exhausted. She came forward to fill his glass again, and as she did so, allowed herself a quick glance into his face. In the dim light she was unsure of his expression, although she knew he was looking at her, neither of them smiling, but something passed between them, she could feel it, strong enough to disturb her so that she turned quickly and left, murmuring an *"au revoir,"* the only other sound her rapid footsteps and the rustling of her skirt. Then she was outside, shutting the doors carefully behind her. She had to restrain herself from running through the fading light back to Mrs. Emery's.

That night, in the stuffy darkness of her bedroom, Charles lying motionless beside her, she woke with a start. *That brooch that Madame Hippolyte gave me that I sold to Monsieur Archibald was not gold. I'm sure it isn't.* Which could only mean that the money he had given her for it was a gift given out of kindness. For a long time she lay awake thinking of this, first hot with humiliation, followed by a resolve to return the money to him for a fairer price, and then, slowly accepting that she couldn't afford to reject whatever kindness might come her way. How rich he must be – yet he helped Pierre sell our farm to Campion. Perhaps the twenty dollars was what Pierre and Campion had paid him for the exchange of the deed, and now his conscience wouldn't let him keep it. She no longer knew what she should think, and it surprised her that assessing blame and defining what was right and what was not in this situation should be so difficult. Then she remembered the spark that had passed between herself and Harry Adamson, but pushed it away as a fluke or her own mistaken apprehension.

Each evening for the next week after the day's work was done, Sophie and Mrs. Emerson strolled the short distance to Adamson's shack, bringing him a hot meal, fresh sheets and towels, and any other item they thought that might make his sickroom more pleasant. On the third day when they entered his kitchen, a small bouquet of pansies glowed in a glass jar in the centre of the table, and a plate carefully wrapped in a clean cloth sat beside it.

"Mrs. Archibald and the preacher's wife, Mrs. Oswald, came by this afternoon," he explained. "Said they'd heard I was sick, didn't know I already had nurses." He grinned briefly at them.

Mrs. Emery said, "Pooh, they knew, everybody knows we come every day. Saw a chance to get inside your house." She was clearly annoyed that her bounty was considered insufficient by the town's first lady. Adamson raised a hand to hide a grin, ending by rubbing his forehead. Sophie peeked under the cloth.

"Cookies," she said. "They look good."

"Have one," he said, "I'll never be able to eat them all. The mice will get them." Sophie took one, then passed the plate to Mrs. Emery who refused as if insulted at the very suggestion, then held it out to Adamson, who took one, but set it down without eating it.

On the sixth evening when they arrived, they found him sitting outside his door on his broken-backed chair, his long legs stretched out in front of him. He took the plate of food from them and would have risen to carry it inside to eat later, so as not to eat in front of them, but both of them insisted that he stay where he was, Sophie going inside and returning with cutlery and a glass of water. She went back and brought a chair for Mrs. Emery to sit on, and leaned against the unpainted wood of the outer wall while they chatted, and he ate, apologetically at first, and then heartily, a fact which both women noted with satisfaction.

"What year was it you come?" Mrs. Emery asked him, frowning, as if she'd been doing mental calculations that weren't working out.

"Two years ago," he told her. "I haven't accomplished much," he said, mildly rueful.

"You need yourself a wife," she answered. "Them with wives gets settled faster."

"When did you get here, Mrs. Hippolyte?" he asked.

"Eighteen eighty-four. I will never forget that trip south from the train in Swift Current. It was so rough, and we were never quite sure we were going in the right direction. Our wagon loaded down – I mean *loaded* with provisions and equipment…" She waved her hand and both Mrs. Emery and Adamson laughed in agreement. "It took forever. And then the plowing! Nothing would do but Pierre would start at once. The very next morning after we arrived. We didn't even have a house to live in." She said this as if Pierre were back on the homestead waiting for her. She lowered her head in embarrassment, and yet, pleased, that she had managed to sound normal.

"Most of 'em do," Mrs. Emery said, dreamily, doubtless remembering the day she and her husband had first reached their land.

"It marks your place as your own – your own land at last," Harry told them, and both women glanced curiously at him, as if they hadn't thought of it that way before.

After a while Mrs. Emery said, "I reckon you'll be fine in a day or two," rising clumsily, as if the weight of her own body had become too much for her. She said to Sophie. "My bed is calling me, but you stay on if you want, bring back the dishes to wash. I'll make sure Charlie is all right." Sophie said nothing, and Harry gave his plate his full attention. Mrs. Emery strolled off, as if she were too tired to walk faster. Harry and Sophie watched her until the corner of Adamson's house blocked their view.

"Don't know how I'm going to manage with nobody bringing me my supper each day," Adamson said.

"How did you manage before?" she asked, halfway between tartness and teasing.

"Bachelor grub is not the same thing," he told her. "It'd be nice to have a dining room in town so a fella could buy a good meal once in a while, but, I reckon we're too small for that."

"I should go back," Sophie said. "When you're finished – I'll take your plate with me."

"Got to get back to my crop," he remarked, looking off into the distance. "Haven't had a drop of rain, it should be fine. Not much anyway." He didn't speak, finishing up the last of his potatoes and gravy. "Who is taking your crop?" He asked this tentatively.

"It's not my crop," she said. "It's Mr. Campion's problem."

"He bought the crop too?"

Sophie, not trusting herself to speak, merely nodded.

"He's probably sold the whole thing by now," he remarked.

Sophie straightened, reaching abruptly for his empty plate to take it from him.

"Sorry," he said. "I didn't mean –"

"It's all right," she said. "What's done is done. I am...all right." As she touched the plate her hand grazed his, and she drew back as if she'd been burned. He laughed uncertainly, coughed a little, raised the plate shoulder high not looking at her so that she could take it from him.

She walked back to the boarding house too quickly, stumbled in a rut, nearly fell, but managed to hold onto the dishes. She looked back over her shoulder, embarrassed, but Adamson's house had blocked her from his view. She noticed for the first time how the setting sun had retreated further from the west toward the south, that dusk was drawing on earlier and earlier. The last rays of the day were spreading like water out across the prairie far beyond the boarding house, a rose colour, beginning to deepen to purple back along the faces of the hills, and the evening stillness had descended, as if they were caught, all of them, in this little moment of paradise, the ramshackle town, the shoddy buildings, the poorest of the poor in their shabby clothing and their fences, wagons, buggies all rattling themselves to pieces on the prairie. So tiny, all of it, in the midst of this wild splendour. Had she time to think she might have wondered if they might be better in settled places, rather than despoiling yet another Eden. But her fingers still tingled where they had touched Harry's, and she scolded herself for that smaller, more natural foolishness, even while an irrepressible part of her remained pleased, so that she had to stop herself from smiling. She knew full well that in the eyes of her church she was married to Pierre forever, could not take another husband until Pierre died. Another husband! Had she really thought that? Pictures poured through her mind at this: The profound pleasures of the marital bed, then Pierre's raging at her, as if coming West had been her idea alone and she had dragged him all the way; the always endless, often cruel work of the homestead, and now, its futility – to have it all given to Campion, and she left without a cent or a bed of her own on which to lay her head. But if she let herself think about this, she would be ill.

She grew sober, the fact of her desertion by Pierre seemed even crueler than it had at first, no longer to be assuaged by angry outbursts, by sobbing, fainting, screaming – by any histrionics at all. Her response now was heavier, darker; her misadventure had entered the realm where it was merely truth, one that she was still unable to grasp fully, as she was unable to take the measure of her own failings that might have helped bring on her catastrophe.

CHAPTER NINE

Introibo ad Altare Dei II

HER GRANDPARENTS AHEAD of her, she came slowly out among the other parishioners, her missal held carelessly in one kid-glove-covered hand, the cloying scent of incense slowly being replaced by that of the honeysuckle near the church door, and the roses beginning to bloom along the church wall, now mingling with clover wafting from the hay fields behind the church. A fat bee bumbled among the straw bonnets and pomaded male heads, and threatened her new spring hat with its lilac silk flowers sprinkled along its curve that only yesterday, out of the blue, grandfather had brought home for her. She lifted a hand to brush at the bee, shielding her eyes with her other hand against the onslaught of light, and as she dropped her hand, such buoyancy spread through her that she felt she might lift off from among the voluble farmers and their pious wives, the stiffer townspeople, the impatient children, and simply float away across the houses, barns and sheds, and fields of hay, and the two rivers and the tree-clad banks until she had shed the last of the chains that all her young life had held her earthbound. All this in less time than it took to raise her right foot and begin a step forward, before she had even set it down again.

She was at last finished with the convent. What a joy it was in these first few days away to know she would never again have to set foot in that gloomy building that smelled of oil and floor wax and burning holy candles, all mingling with the faint odour of cooking food drifting into the classrooms from the nuns' kitchen. It was no wonder the village bloomed with such beauty on this early summer morning, nor that the usually dull parishioners today wore such glowing faces. She walked slowly down the stone steps of the church as, behind her *le curé* Deschambeault could be heard clearing his throat loudly, people moving back from him to give him room to address his flock as they stood in the churchyard, as he always did after Mass, with requests for things the church needed, or the nuns, or reminders of meetings, services and ceremonies: weddings, funerals, baptisms, First Communions and Confirmations. Sophie would pay him no attention, as she had always done, or failed to do. As he began to speak, she kept moving slowly through the crowd.

Violette Hippolyte had left just after the New Year to join the Grey Nuns in Montréal where she would learn to nurse the ill, but the nuns had not even bothered to talk to her about her vocation; they did not think a girl as bold as they claimed she had become as she grew older would make a nun. *No order would have you*, Sister Marie-Catherine had spit contemptuously at her, and Sophie, no longer the terrified child, had allowed herself a faintly insolent smile in reply, and did not lower her eyes. The nun laughed in a disconcerted, faintly helpless way, then, recovering herself, hissed, *You will come to no good, my girl*, her eyes hard and small, glinting darkly, and had thumped away, her heavy black skirts flapping dully around her legs as she turned, as if Sophie were not worth the trouble of punishing.

But finally, over the last years, Sophie had seen why where she was concerned, the nuns had always drawn back from the raised hand, the harsh scolding. Despite the only slightly mitigated scandal of his brother's suicide years earlier, Grandfather, with his ponderous, grave air, and his commercial interests that concerned everyone in the community, had maintained his place among the village's *bourgeoisie*. Sophie saw this was why she was saved from the worst, and was grateful at the same time as she was angry at the hypocrisy of it. But even though grandfather was indeed a man of substance, an *homme d'affaires*, his brother's suicide had, in a small way, set him apart. It was not that anyone blamed him, but some of the townspeople and farmers stepped carefully around him, even – one or two of them – crossing the street to avoid him, as if his brother's crime would infect them if they went too near. But business at the family general store seemed to be as good as it had ever been. No one snubbed grandmother, though; she would not have noticed if they had.

How thin she had grown. Always a slender woman, she now ate little beyond bread with milk, a few strawberries, raspberries, and blueberries when they were in season, a thin piece of chicken or beef now and then, a few spring vegetables from the garden. Her health seemed good despite her stringent diet, and grandfather had long ago given up trying to persuade her to eat. Always, grandmother glanced at Sophie's plate with that look weighted with a sort of contempt as if Sophie's appetite were somehow disgraceful, even though Sophie was as slim as a willow, and young and, as Madame Gauthier said disrespectfully to grandmother, needed a healthy diet. On a day like this even the fierce Mme Gauthier made Sophie laugh. And yet, that tiny nugget of – what? – still stuck in her chest, scraping her heart whenever she looked at her grandmother.

She paused in her quiet movement through the crowd to look around to where members of the congregation stood under the elms and ashes that bordered the churchyard, the men smoking their pipes, all waiting for the *curé* to finish so that they could begin exchanging gossip, chatting about weather, cows, crops and business. The Hippolyte family stood in their customary place to one side at the outer edge of the crowd, and Sophie edged past her grandparents who were in conversation with the owner of the new inn, *l'auberge Saint Louis*, and his elegant if worn wife – rumour had it she had come directly from France – and made her way through the crowd until she reached the Hippolytes.

She saw them all turning and smiling at the sight of her. Little Cécile of the big brown eyes was a tall, thin twelve-year-old now, a sober, unusually studious pupil at the convent; Lucie, at fourteen, was also still in school although no one would accuse her of being studious. Marie-Ange, now sixteen, was married – *So young!* her grandmother had gasped – that familiar contempt settling into the knife-like lines of her face. Earlier, in church Denise had whispered to Sophie that already Violette had made her first vows, and that Marie-Ange...but grandmother had cast one glance in their direction and both were silenced, turning their heads as one dutifully toward the altar, l'curé Deschambeault, and his servers.

"Madame, Monsieur Hippolyte," Sophie said, nodding politely to them. Pierre and his brothers had been standing among the farmers who were laughing together a few feet from the rest of the Hippolytes, but when he noticed her approaching, out of the corner of her eye she saw him slip away to stand with his own family. For the first time she wondered why grandfather liked so much to visit the Hippolytes when there were so many families who were good customers at *Charron frères* he might as well have stood with on Sundays, but for whom he had only a few words. "I have come to congratulate you on Violette's first success in the Order."

"We are so proud," Madame Hippolyte declared, her old-fashioned once-white bonnet unadorned and slightly askew, her greying hair mostly stuffed into, but leaking an unruly strand here and there. "But oh how I miss her. She was the best daughter. Such a help she was to me." She sniffed, tears gathering in her eyes, escaping to trace down her plump cheeks.

Monsieur Hippolyte said, heartily, "Come now, my dear, she is still our daughter..."

"Non, non," Madame Hippolyte sobbed. "She is Christ's daughter now..." Monsieur. Hippolyte, undeterred, went on, "And we have still our three girls."

"Two!" Madame Hippolyte declared, as instantly as angry as she had just been sad, but nevertheless, the tears began to positively pour from her eyes, she withdrew a large cotton handkerchief from her reticule, about to blow her nose, when a bee landed on her fingers and she brushed it off brusquely as if it were no more than a speck of dirt. Flies buzzed, all the parishioners were brushing at them without even noticing they were, and mosquitoes, already a plague, required slapping and brushing also, while in the trees around them birds were in conversation with each other so that the humid air was embroidered by their sound. The scent of wild flowers blooming at the edge of the field behind the line of great old trees filled Sophie's head, and from somewhere, perhaps across the road muddy from the night's refreshing rain, a bank of profusely-blooming lilacs tried to outdo the roses in casting their heady, female scent among the parishioners.

Sophie kept resolutely smiling, Marie-Ange or no Marie-Ange. She was not supposed to know about such things, but she did, a little, learning them from her convent classmates who came from the small farms that surrounded the village. Marie-Ange, she supposed, had been at Mass with her too-young farmer husband, but had already crept away. Probably she wouldn't stand with her family until she carried her baby in her arms, when Madame Hippolyte, in the face of her first perfect grandchild, would forget all about the transgression.

Again, bees circled them, everyone waving them away, Monsieur Hippolyte tipping his head back to look up into the ash tree that spread its branches above them, as if to check for a bee hive. Finding nothing, apparently, he said, his expression deadpan, his tone jocular, "And you, Mademoiselle Charron, when do you leave for the convent?"

Even Madame Hippolyte, forgetting for the moment Marie-Ange, smiled at this sally, and Sophie, pretending sorrow, said, *"Hélas,* I cannot be spared," then smiling, so they would all know that she understood that they knew she was making a joke, that everyone knew she was emphatically not nun material, not to mention that she could be spared readily as she did nothing in her grandparents' house, or next to it. She didn't mind the joke, yet the familiar tug of shame she would never vanquish punctured her ebullience, that among these people she was considered privileged – *was* privileged – despite carrying about every day the heavy burden and most terrible secret of all, that she was not wanted. She turned her head to the left and then to the right, frowning without realizing she was. But Monsieur Hippolyte was speaking to her.

"Lucky for all the young men," he declared, grinning, wagging a thick finger at her and, embarrassed, Sophie looked down to the ground. Eighteen was marriageable, it was a wonder grandmother and grandfather hadn't already found someone they would insist she marry: Was it not, after all, a good way to get rid of her? In an effort to forestall this she had suggested *higher education*, but grandmother had only glared at her, and grandfather had laughed, as if she were still six years old. She had no idea what to study anyway: She had no talent for painting or drawing so going away to a young ladies' art school was out of the question; she had no musical talent either, although she had been forced to take piano lessons and to practice every day, no matter how badly – and while Violette craved a life of piety and service, this was the last thing, God help her, Sophie wanted. Grandfather would let her help with the bookkeeping in the family store, and she supposed she would do that, at least for a while, but forever? A unease, like an itch deep inside her abdomen, its location unreachable, not even quite identifiable, gnawed at her, so that she looked across the group and found Pierre Hippolyte's eyes, and in the sudden encounter forgot the conversation, forgot everything she had been thinking.

"Perhaps I will go to Montréal instead," she said, daring a glance at Pierre. He was watching her with a light in his eyes that made a warmth creep back into her cheeks. "Perhaps I will live with my brother Guillaume for a while, see the city, go to Mass in *basilique Notre-Dame de Montréal.*" The idea had just occurred to her; she didn't know if she meant it or not.

"How lucky you are," Lucie said, wistfully. Lucie had both parents, had lived with them all her life, she had three – no, four – brothers who lived in the same house too, as well as her sisters Violette, Cécile and Marie-Ange. No, not Marie-Ange. But Sophie's indignation at the very idea that she who was parentless and sibling-less was lucky was fleeting; it angered her that because she had not ended in a work-house when her parents' died, or as a drudge in a nunnery, or – heaven forbid – begging on the streets in a city, something about which she was supposed to know nothing, that she was a lucky girl.

"I'll help with the babies," she declared, thinking of Guillaume's and Hector's households in the city, but a swell of uncertainty rose at the thought. What did she know of babies? Thinking of them, screaming and smelling, involuntarily, she shuddered. Pierre, she noted, was still watching her and as if he could read her thoughts, a flicker of amusement, or so she thought it was, crossing his face.

Her grandfather was coming across the lawn toward her, so grandmother must be in the buggy now, waiting to go home for the lunch that Madame Gauthier would have waiting for them.

"Madame, Monsieur Hippolyte," grandfather said, bowing, then smiling at Cécile and Lucie, nodding in a less friendly way at Pierre. *"Mes chers cousins."* She hadn't heard him come up, but here he was, at her elbow. "How is everything on the farm? Did the new bull work out?" Monsieur Hippolyte had been standing slightly behind his wife, but now he stepped past her, his chest swelling as he moved to one side of his family so that he might begin a gentleman's conversation with Grandfather Charron. Pierre appeared to be following his father, but Mme Beauchamp and her three daughters clad in matching white dresses with blue sashes and bonnets had arrived to say hello, and all female attention went to them, so charming were the little girls.

Sophie, lost in the newly formed group, was unsure what to do. She turned then, still smiling, and began the walk she had been avoiding back to *grand-mère* and the buggy and another cold Sunday lunch in the dining room, the walls' dark paneling giving off a surly gleam in the poor light from the velvet-draped windows. For some reason grandmother loved the room, Sophie could only guess because it reminded her of her first home in her grandparents' seigneurial mansion, long gone to damp and rot, or fire, or to *l'anglais* Robert Harrison who had bought the *seigneury* when grandmother was still a child. Sophie hadn't gone three steps, the chatter of the Hippolyte and Beauchamp females trailing brightly behind her, when she felt a light tap on her shoulder.

It was Pierre Hippolyte, not bowing, looking frankly – too frankly – into her face, so that for an instant, her breath caught so that she touched her throat with her fingertips as if to free it.

"You dropped this, I think," he said. It was a woman's pale kid glove, although not Sophie's, and she indicated this by lifting the two of her own that she held between her clasped hands, mutely showing him. He held up the one he had found, grinned – her heart jumping at those white teeth and light-flashing eyes – as if he had just had a marvellous idea, and keeping his gaze on her face, tossed the found glove over his shoulder. It landed a short distance away on the grass. She laughed aloud, then covered her mouth with one hand before dropping it

"May I walk with you to your house?" Confused, she looked around at her grandfather, who was still lost in his conversation with Monsieur Hippolyte, now joined by *monsieur le docteur* and M. Beauchamp.

"You will miss your ride home," she said, wanting to, but uncertain as to whether she could agree to this or not.

"I can walk," he said, slapping his hand against his thigh as if to indicate the muscles, which she inadvertently found herself gazing at until she realized the impropriety – an instant, that was all – and looked quickly back up to his face. He was more than a head taller than her, not as tall as her grandfather, but taller than his own short, thickset father. His hair, blacker than her own, had a slight curl in it, a lock fell onto his forehead, partly covering his eye, and he tossed his head to throw it back. She clutched her embroidered reticule, her gloves, and the missal in both hands, trying not to look into his face, so he wouldn't know how his unconscious gesture had affected her.

She saw then over Pierre's shoulder that grandfather had finished his conversation with the farmers and was coming to where she and Pierre stood facing each other. Seeing her expression, Pierre glanced backwards and whispered, hurriedly, to Sophie, "Meet me here at the church as soon as you can after *le déjeuner,"* then straightening, smiling at her, just as grandfather arrived who, touching Sophie's forearm with his carefully groomed, pale hand, said cheerfully to Pierre, "Well, young man. Time to go home for *le repas,*" both dismissing him and making clear that he gave no credence to the young people's conversation, though neither was he angry. Pierre nodded, took Sophie's hand, made something approaching a bow over it, that caused her blush and smile secretly.

"Next Sunday," he dared to say as he bowed, and in grandfather's presence, but so softly he probably hadn't heard; she couldn't quite believe he had said it.

At the buggy grandmother sat staring straight ahead, annoyed. Grandfather ignored her, helping Sophie up and climbing in himself, taking the reins, starting the horse. As their buggy fell into the line of buggies leaving the churchyard, Sophie wanted to look back, to see Pierre again, but she didn't dare: *Grand-mère* would be watching. If it were not for grandmother, she and her grandfather would probably walk to and from church as so many of the parishioners were inclined to do, if only because they lived nearby and it was a nuisance to hitch the buggy. As they passed, Sophie watched them wistfully, seeing school friends linking arms, groups of interesting young men laughing together, their jocularity loud, adults calling cheerfully back and forth across the road where each family group walked. Children, as always, played noisy tag, ignoring the half-hearted admonishments of their elders, dodging in and out among them, and little girls scowled and complained to their mothers when their boots were muddied or their skirts splattered by the boys.

Home they would go, Sophie thought, where the mothers would set down their babies and put on their aprons, the fathers would light their pipes and relax into their rocking chairs on the porch or next to the hearth, and any farm chores not yet done would be attended to by the older children while the younger ones played, and the older girls helped cook the big meal. She sat patiently, not moving, thinking of this, that she knew about only because some of her friends from the convent lived in this way, and from her few visits to the Hippolytes with her grandfather. She suddenly remembered that he had greeted them today as "*mes cousins.*" Was he only being extra-friendly? She supposed that was it.

How she wished to be allowed to get down from the buggy and walk among the families, but grandmother was not like most *Canadiens* and set a standard for Sophie, quite different from that of everyone else in the village, that grew more unbearable – it was stifling – to Sophie every year. But already, they were drawing toward the back of their lot at the edge of the village where the small barn that housed their horse sat, the wide door open. She thought, as grandfather helped his wife down from the buggy, and she waited patiently for him to help her, stifling her urge to jump down herself, *I am not a child anymore*, and then, in a surfeit of impatience and irritation: *I will meet Pierre Hippolyte.*

The idea swelled, took form, grew into firmness and solidity. After lunch grandmother would nap or read her prayer book, grandfather might go out to visit the notary, M. Chouinard, or he might spend the afternoon with his books in the study, or perhaps *le docteur* would drop in to see him, and she would be sentenced to her room and the study of religious books, lately it was Thomas à Kempis's *Imitation of Christ*, until dinner was called, to be followed by the trip back to the church for Benediction. She would not stand for it; she would go out, and hang the consequences, although her chest trembled a little at the thought of her own daring.

At last lunch ended, no one having said anything of import about anything, except for grandfather making some mention to grandmother about the Ménard boy who had disappeared, and found again finally only by the note he sent back to his terrified parents that he was on a train for the West and did not plan to come back. Their mutual disapproval wafted down the table, no comment being necessary. Grandfather rose at last glancing directly at Sophie as she and grandmother rose simultaneously, grandmother's black silk gown rustling, Sophie's softer dimity dress barely whispering.

"Sophie, come with me." Startled, she opened her mouth to speak, would have turned to grandmother for an explanation, but already the woman was going out the door that led into the kitchen as if she knew very well what grandfather's summons was about, and grandfather was standing back at the door into the hall, one arm stretched gallantly, palm open toward her to indicate she was to go through first.

In his study seated across his heavy mahogany desk from him, her knees trembled; she bunched her skirt over them to hide the shaking. All sorts of awful possibilities flitted through her brain, the worst that he was about to marry her off to some old man she had never even met. *I will run away*, she told herself, but to go where? Only Montréal and the homes of her brothers came to mind. She had no one else and nowhere else to go.

"You are eighteen now," he said, "Soon to be nineteen years, I believe." She held herself motionless. "You have no vocation..." he lifted his eyes to hers at this as if to make sure. Mutely, she gave a quick shake, no. "And there seems to be nothing you want particularly to do, is there?" She had dropped her eyes to her neatly-clasped hands resting on her lap and didn't respond. It was hard to breathe. She wanted...she wanted... She did not know precisely what it was she wanted, but with such a profound yearning that mostly she dared not think of it. He waited, but nothing came into her mind to say. "You must marry then," he said, and sighed. She wondered, was his sigh because of the difficulties he would have to deal with? Or was it – could it be – some sort of regret? Through her shame that she was now discovered to be so useless, and fear of what he would propose, a finger of anger began to stir.

"I want..." she said, trying desperately to think of something to ward off whatever he was about to say.

"Yes?"

"I want...to visit my brothers in Montréal." He had raised his thick white eyebrows and gazed over her head at the ecclesiastical books in Latin on the shelves behind her. She had never seen anyone take one of those books off the shelf, except for Antoinette, who dusted them carefully, holding each as if it were the Monstrance itself. In the silence she became even more aware of how the thick wood of the door, the wall paneling fronted by bookshelves and glass-fronted cases containing mysterious objects she had never been given the chance to study, served to mute all other sound in or out of the house. It is like a tomb, she thought, and the shaft of anger pierced again, that fate had brought her this. She vowed again: She *would* meet Pierre Hippolyte.

"We can consider that, I suppose," he said at last. "But I have other business to discuss."

She waited. "I have had several expressions of interest in you as a potential…wife." Not one young man had spoken to her or even looked in her direction, and yet "several" wanted to marry her? Or did this mean only that the young men's parents thought she would be a good choice for their sons, having a prosperous family behind her, and grandmother's seigneurial background providing a rise in social status for members of the *bourgeoisie* and *habitants* alike? *But I am too young!* she wanted to shout. *I don't want to marry yet!* She swallowed, keeping her eyes down.

"Who?" Her tone was surly, her eyes fixed on the polished edge of his giant desk. He cleared his throat, as if suddenly embarrassed by his mission. A long hesitation, then he said, "André Chouinard, (she knew him a bit; his father often visited grandfather), Mathieu Grandmaison (she had never heard of him), Jacques Allard." Oh yes, his father had a lot of land scattered about the parish. Him, she might have seen once or twice, where exactly she could not recall. Without softening her tone, she asked, "Whom have you chosen?"

Surprised by her ungraciousness, he said, "Sophie, you must look at me." Reluctantly, she raised her eyes to meet his. "I thought you would be pleased to establish your own home," his tone mild. She hadn't thought of such a thing, only of the man he would choose to be her husband, only of the tyranny of marriage to someone she didn't love, didn't even know, when she was herself bursting with pure desire despite having no idea for what. "We might choose together," he offered. "They would all make excellent husbands for you, I believe. No ...difficulties...taint any of them, and all are...gentlemen." What did she care for gentlemen? In fact, they were all members of the *bourgeoisie*; none of them would be gentlemen in grandmother's eyes. *Poof*, she thought, in her consternation daring to dismiss grandmother.

"But, I don't want to marry – yet." It disconcerted her to hear how childish she sounded now. He tapped his fingers on his desk, considering, gazing into the shadows behind her.

"You *are* young," he said. "I know that, yet your grandmother..." He fell silent, then took in a long breath through his nostrils, still not looking at her. "I want to make sure you are safe," he said, "Should anything...happen to me." Sophie couldn't imagine what he meant; she wanted to ask, but was suddenly afraid.

"Grandfather," she began, but he interrupted, smiling pleasantly at her as if there had been no earlier dip into some other subject which neither of them wanted to approach. He said, heartily, "We must make plans. The most suitable young men will marry elsewhere if we don't make our arrangements. I want the best for you, of course, among those who are marriageable." She didn't answer. "We make our choice, do the...ah...business, and then we wait."

"How long do I have?"

"Your grandmother tells me that first we invite the suitors and their families so we might meet them. We make our choice, then your suitor and you would meet now and then... A year, I think, would be about right." They sat in silence, not looking at each other. "You must prepare your *trousseau, n'est-ce pas?*" His attempt at jocularity passed Sophie by. In a year, unless she took some steps of her own – and what would they be – she would be a married woman. It was too shocking; she thought for a moment that she might faint, black pinpricks swarmed before her eyes, her breath was coming too quickly. She whispered, "May I go, grandfather? I need...to think about this."

"Yes, yes, go, of course, go." She started to rise, the dizziness assailing her, slowing her. "I hope you haven't any foolish ideas about choosing your own husband," he said, his voice wavering between firmness and humour. "Your choice must be from these three."

Her dizziness had retreated, but she could feel colour rising in her face, wanted to protest, to refuse firmly, but some wiser self prevented her, knowing any protest now would only harden him in his resolve. And he had to deal with grandmother.

"Yes, grandfather."

When he didn't speak, she went to the door and, her hand on the knob, suddenly, angrily, trying to find a way to hurt or even just startle him so that he would have to acknowledge that she was a person too, "Why did you call the Hippolytes *mes cousins?*" She could feel some strange emotion coming from him, his hand arrested for an instant on the piece of paper he held.

"You had better sit back down." She moved back to his desk, stood instead of sitting, her vision suddenly hyper-clear, dizziness gone. "They are not exactly cousins," he began. "But your grandmother Julie –"

"What?" Surely grandmother's name was Henriette.

"My first wife," he said slowly. "She was named Julie. Julie Roland. She was the mother of my sons Emanuel and Honoré." Emanuel was Sophie's long dead father, the other was his brother, Sophie's uncle, dead at fifteen of a fever. "You didn't know?" She shook her head, no, then sat down before him, staring. "Someone should have told you." He was speaking to himself, it seemed, but then he gave the faintest shrug to his heavy shoulders, and not looking at her, went on. "Julie was a distant cousin of M. Hippolyte's father. She lost her parents and having nowhere else to go, came as a young girl to stay with the Hippolyte family, when M. Hippolyte was only a little boy." He paused, seemed disinclined to go on, sighed heavily, and spoke. "We met long before any of you were even thought of. We married. Some years later…" here he paused again, then drawing in a long breath, went on. "She died giving birth to a child."

Sophie wanted to ask, who was the child? But her grandfather said, "The child died too." He didn't seem to want to look at her. "She was… your grandmother."

Sophie said, finally, "The Hippolytes…"

"Not really relatives," he said. "I choose to remember." She couldn't quite make sense of this. For a long moment both were motionless and silent. Then, without even murmuring thanks, Sophie went out into the hall, closing the study door softly behind her. She half expected to find grandmother waiting, but there was no one there and as she listened, no sound on the stairs or in the *salon* assailed her. She kept on moving down the hall to the wide front door, opened it, and went outside onto the *véranda* and out onto the street. No one seemed to be about, all still at their after-Mass meal or perhaps having *une petite somme*.

She could not think what this news meant; something beyond having had a different grandmother once; something beyond grandfather's relationship to the Hippolytes. She began to run, her confusion spurring her until she remembered how unseemly this was, and slowed to a fast walk. At one point she stopped dead, half-turned, looked back over her shoulder as if to see if she were being followed, but in reality, because she thought she would go back, ask someone, anyone, to tell her what this news meant. Then, re-thinking this impulse, forcing herself not to run, she walked rapidly the rest of the short way to the churchyard. From a few feet away, she saw Pierre emerge from the shadows under the trees as if he had deliberately been keeping out of sight, and was surprised, having for the last few seconds forgotten he was the reason she was here.

She didn't even slow, not remembering they hadn't walked together before, or that she was engaging in an activity that would be utterly forbidden if her guardians knew of it. Pierre seemed now someone she had always known, someone she might trust. The absurdity of this didn't strike her until hours later.

"Come," he said, smiling in a delighted way as she reached him.

He took her hand in his, how warm and thick it was, and led her quickly down the side of the church where a high hedge prevented anyone in the nearby houses from seeing them. Down the tight passage they went, Sophie having to run to keep up with Pierre's strides, then through the back lot behind the church that ran along the edge of the cemetery, through the gate, across another empty lot overgrown with waist-high grass but in which there were narrow walking paths, and then they were on a country trail. He pulled her a few steps further so that they were both leaning, panting, against an oak whose trunk was so wide that both could lean side by side on it and not be seen by the eyes of the village behind them. He started to laugh, but seeing her face, stopped at once.

"Sophie, what is it?" He grasped both her hands in his.

"Grandfather is arranging a marriage for me," she told him. Then grew embarrassed, thinking, it is nothing to him. She wanted to say something clear and strong, but she couldn't yet even separate all the parts of this development, knew only that it was as if a hurricane or a flood threatened her and she could do nothing to save herself. And yet, how was it that it seemed as if she and Pierre had known each other forever?

"Who?" was all Pierre said. He moved to stand in front of her, fixing her eyes with his two flashing dark ones so that she couldn't look away.

"He...has...choices," she said, and began to draw a line in the dirt with her boot. This made Pierre laugh out loud.

"Then I'd better stake my claim, eh?" he said, teasing her. She dropped her head, didn't answer and he put his fingers under her chin to lift it again. "Let's walk," he said. They stepped back onto the road, so little used now that a newer, wider road ran into town from this direction, and now thick grass grew between the wagon ruts, and rivulets of rain had cut finger-wide channels here and there at right angles across it. The ditches were choked by flowering honeysuckle, tall grasses and weeds, a riot of colour. She felt only the heat of his hand covering hers, heard only the sound of his boots on the soft loam of the trail. Bees and flies buzzed in the ditches and mosquitoes stung now and then. She kept finding herself back in grandfather's study, the air thick with old cigar and pipe smoke, the dull, padded silence of it, and grandfather, a dark shadow looming across the desk, deciding her fate.

In the afternoon sun the leaves of elms and ashes shimmered, and the dark blue-green boughs of the many firs seemed for once airy and buoyant with light. Fat white cloud ships perched in the blue above the yellow fields, seeming docked, although she knew that in a couple of hours their bottoms would darken and fill, then open to drench the countryside with a warm rain before the sun came out again to heat the ground so that in places steam would rise from the wet earth and cloud the surface of the pools of warm water. As they strolled she felt herself beginning to regain a sense of normalcy and, looking to the left and to the right as they topped a low rise and could see around them, beginning at once to descend, she stopped walking.

"I know where we are!" she declared, studying the stone wall, parts of which showed either above and occasionally between the exuberant growth that otherwise hid it.

"Where?" he asked, as if to test her.

"That must be Uncle Henri's land – grandfather's, I mean." She pointed to their right.

"C'est exact," he said, and waited while she gazed up the stone fence ahead of them and then backward along its face, what little of it she could make out. A few small trees had fought their way up through the heavy growth of the ditch, but on the opposite side of the wall someone had either thinned the natural growth into a neat row, or had planted trees as a boundary – someone a long time ago as they were mature trees. *'Beech'* came into her mind: *a beech tree*. Who had told her that? Ah, Violette, some years ago. Uncle Henri was buried on the other side of this fence.

"I want to see his grave!" She looked at Pierre, thinking he wouldn't know what she meant, opening her mouth to explain. What is the matter with me, she asked herself, feeling she had lost something today, some line of sense that had been her life until now, the end of which she couldn't catch so that she felt herself bouncing from subject to subject, and emotion to emotion like a runaway ball in the schoolyard.

"It is further down," he said, reaching again for her hand. At its touch, this time she felt a shock – *Pierre is holding my hand* – and instead of pulling away, moved closer to his side, panting a little at her own daring, and at some other, new excitement. He gave her fingers a squeeze, didn't look down at her, yet she could feel the small touch of joy that had leaped inside him at her movement, and feeling it, was calmed. They walked on, their bodies touching now and then in answer to the uneven ground, slowly up and down the hills and troughs of the rough trail. She remembered running here with her school friends, caught between smiling and frowning in perplexity at how they had once behaved, and how good it had felt. She didn't know why they had done that. She and Pierre didn't speak, but once in a while he would shift his light grip on her hand, just slightly, and a thrill would go up her body. They walked on.

She had rarely been allowed to go for walks through the village or out in the countryside without an adult, and she could remember fairly clearly the few times she had gone with only school friends. Once, on such a walk with Rose-Claire and Yvonne, perambulating the village one Sunday afternoon, arm in arm, they had met three English boys walking together down the road and, as no adults were present, had smiled at them, and the boys had smiled back, and Rose-Claire, Yvonne and Sophie had all given small bobbing curtsies, while giggling behind their gloved hands.

The boys had said, perhaps mockingly, "A lovely afternoon, *mademoiselles,"* and *"Comment allez-vous,"* and Sophie had laughed aloud. She wanted to learn English then, had wanted to for a long time.

"'ow are you?" she had dared to ask aloud, her voice perhaps a bit strained in her amazement at what she had ventured, and the boys, one tall one in particular with a smooth cap of pale yellow hair, had laughed, and replied in an imitation of her stilted greeting, although in a not-unfriendly way, "I-am-well." Then they had passed on, and the girls had sobered and grown silent. So much of the village still English, descendants of the British who had run from the American States a long time ago, before even grandmother was born, and who led their own lives entirely in English, girls their own age also out on afternoon strolls, and in that moment of sobriety, their voices still lingering in the damp, sunny village air, Sophie had glimpsed another world, bright and gleaming, beckoning her.

Suddenly Pierre stopped, pointing. She saw nothing, only an enormous old beech tree, its lowest branches stretching out far on every side. Since the time before her birth, farmers had swelled the area clearing acre after acre of the finest trees, from yellow birches to aged oak to mottled sycamores, so there were not that many great old trees left in the immediate vicinity of the village. How was it she didn't know of this one?

Already he was wading through the thick growth in the ditch, looking for an opening in the fence.

"There." He pointed to their left, some distance down the stone line. They kept walking, and when they reached the point he took her hand again and helped her. Waving her handkerchief about with the other hand to ward off insects, she crossed through the tall grass that bounded the trail into the space between fence and road clotted by wild rose bushes and the full branches of late-blooming red and yellow columbine interspersed with mauve-flowering bergamot over which butterflies, bronze and gold, fluttered and wheeled.

She said, "I wanted to come, but grandfather wouldn't allow it. He said that grandmother would disapprove." She suspected that grandfather came here, perhaps even often. He would have come by road, through the farmer's yard, she supposed, then down the fence line to his brother's grave. They waded through the prickly, entangled shrubs as if through deep water, pushing them aside, until they came through the gap into the field to stand, panting – at least Sophie was – under the spreading, thickly-leafed canopy of the ancient beech.

The now-speckled grey granite gravestone, slightly aslant after years in the rich soil of the field, sat under the tree, a rough stone cross polished only on the side facing the field, on which was carved, *Henri Émile Charron, 1820–1871*. No carved angels, no Bible verse, or line of poetry. But wait, a closer look revealed one simple word, nearly smoothed from view despite the relatively few years it had been there: *Loved*. The letters more crudely made than the others, and cut less deeply. Pierre said nothing while Sophie traced the word with her finger, hoping to confirm that the word said what she guessed it to say. Only grandfather, surely, would have done this. Who else might have loved Henri Charron so much? She knew of no one.

And yet, how very beautiful the setting, the roughly-textured wall behind it nearly chest-high on Sophie, the branches of the beech spread over it, its shade keeping down the growth on the grave itself. She crossed herself, without noticing she had, as the memory of the grim horror that permeated the household at the time of his death came back to her. How long had it been since Violette had told her that her uncle was a suicide? A long time, she thought, and she had failed to think of it again because it was too terrible; she could not comprehend it. Now, she would have knelt to pray, but the ground was damp, in places downright muddy, there was nothing about she could use to keep her knees dry, so she stood, tears dripping off her nose and cheeks, using a handkerchief from her reticule to sponge them away. Pierre scuffed his boots in the earth, waiting, reached to touch her arm, then came closer to put his arm around her shoulders so that she turned her face into the coarse cloth of his sleeve.

She wondered why he had killed himself, but no reason came to mind, no reason had, in her memory, even been hinted at. For the first time it occurred to her that her Uncle Henri was actually her great-uncle and that without noticing she had done so, she had long imagined him as a copy or near-copy of the father she had never known. Surprised, for an instant her tears ceased, then started again as she tried to imagine her own father as a much younger man than her great-uncle had been. Tried, but drew only an Uncle Henri-sized blank.

"He was my great uncle," she told Pierre. "He was very kind." Pierre said nothing, pulling her against him, filling her with both gratitude and fear, so that she resisted, ever so slightly, and he didn't insist. "I don't know why he...killed himself. Do you?"

"How would I know?" he asked her, but gently. "I was a child too." A silence. "I suppose I could ask the old man." She drew away from him then, wiping her eyes, blowing her nose, struggling to compose herself. Indeed, the cool shade under the tree's great branches, and something else, something gentle in the air soothed her. And Pierre at her side.

She knew that *M. l'abbé* Deschambeault had come and come again and had stayed for long hours with grandfather. And that cry she had heard that she knew came from grandfather. Uncle Henri was here and not in the cemetery with the rest of the family because – it came to her in a nun's voice – *We cannot judge the greatness of the One True Church*. It was no wonder that grandfather could not prevail in the matter of where his beloved younger brother would be buried. She wished she knew if the Holy Spirit had come down from on high and lit in the Pope's chest to tell him suicides could not be buried in consecrated ground, as the Holy Spirit had long ago done to her. But no message had been left her, only that ineffable lightness, that wonderful as it was, did not explain itself.

She stared up at Pierre, his face light dappled between the shadow of the leaves. She turned from him then, went to the trunk of the beech and ran both hands across its grooved bark, propping her feet against one of its thick, exposed roots. She became aware of birds singing merrily in the trees up and down the fence and the incongruity of their chorus in this place struck her even as she listened willingly to it. She tried to remember her uncle, his kindness to her, the *bonbons* he had placed in her pocket or tucked into her palm as he passed. His air, she saw now, of distance broken only for that second that he saw her. She was filled now with a deep unease: Her great-uncle's exclusion, for all eternity from heaven, her fear, perhaps, of her own fate in some unimaginable future. Or the shadow of it, a prophecy.

"Maybe some woman he loved wouldn't marry him," she suggested. Pierre shrugged, put his hands in his pockets and looked away, then offered a hand to her so that she would come away from the tree trunk. She couldn't resist, even though she knew she should, and stretched her hand to meet his. He took it and kept pulling her gently toward him until their bodies met, then bent his head and kissed her on her mouth. For an instant she allowed it, then pulled away, laughing in an embarrassed way. Chills ran up and down her body interspersed with little spurts of excessive heat.

"Has no one ever kissed you before?" She shook her head, no.

"I am glad to be the first." She remembered then that grandfather wanted to marry her off to some man she didn't even know, and both hands went up to her face.

"How will I escape...?" She didn't need to explain. He turned away, reached up, grasped a low branch with one hand and hung from it. He had no answer either, apparently. She thought, what if I didn't know Pierre, had never met him, what would I think then? She was jolted a little by this, seeing for just an instant, but also for the first time, the pleasure she might take in the process that grandfather had initiated. But, she thought further, *I have known Pierre since we were children; I have always...* but she could not allow herself to say what it was she had always felt for him: Love? Her first inkling of a destiny for herself? He was taking her hand again, and in his touch, all her thoughts vanished from her head to focus into the heat and heaviness of his flesh engulfing hers. Shivering slightly, her entire body quarrelling with itself as to whether she was hot or too cold, light or heavy, she began to walk beside him.

Having moved out from under the bows of the great tree, they paused to take a long look across the rising field of bronze-coloured barley soughing in the breeze that had come up while they had been meditating over the grave, then up to the sky where the clouds had thickened and were moving faster now. They made their way through the gap in the stone fence again, waded through the ditch of tall grass and flowering plants back onto the track that they had come along. He said, “Sophie…” She waited. “How can we meet again?”

“Next Sunday?” she suggested. “We could walk here again. Grandmother thinks I am reading my missal in my room.”

“Too long,” he said. “Far too long to wait.” He gazed up and down the over-grown trail, then, not looking at her. “We could see each other after dark.” She waited, not sure what he meant. “In your garden,” he said, “at the back of your house. We could meet there.” She couldn’t imagine what he meant; grandmother would never allow it, nor would grandfather. “At midnight,” he said.

“Oh, I could never…”

“On Wednesday. I’ll be taking oats into the village with Alexandre. I’ll just stay on and walk home afterward.” She thought, grandfather will marry me off without my having a word to say about it. Pierre was hope – wasn’t he? For the first time she noticed that now and during the time she was with him, that inconsolable, indeterminate yearning that plagued her, that she could not name nor understand and that was sometime larger than she was herself, had dwindled and almost disappeared.

“Yes,” she breathed. They walked on then, not speaking, until at the edge of the village where the new road met the remnants of the old on which they walked, they paused again briefly.

“I will leave you here.” She nodded, not taking her eyes from his face. “Your eyes are beautiful,” he said. Had she heard him right? She wanted to speak, but was afraid to, found herself nodding, once, twice, nearly imperceptibly. “I will come,” he said. “Wednesday?” Again she nodded. “Midnight,” he said, and turned, began to walk away toward the road that led into the forest, not waiting for further assent, nor looking back.

BUT AT TWO OR THREE in the morning she woke suddenly, not with thoughts of Pierre Hippolyte, but instead of the woman Julie who was her grandmother also. *This means*, she told herself before she was fully awake, *that grandmother is not my blood relative*. And further, her thoughts coming so clear it was as if a voice were speaking them aloud in her ear, she had to raise Julie's children, and then her grandchild. *It means that she hates me not because I have been such a bad child, but because grandfather loved Julie first, and I – I belong to her eternal, never-to-be-equalled rival, Julie.* Then she realized with something approaching awe that grandmother must have loved grandfather.

CHAPTER TEN

Night Music

SHE ROSE RELUCTANTLY through layers of sleep until, awake, she lay gazing into the darkness, puzzled, listening intently for what had wakened her. She put a finger gently against Charles' nostrils to feel his steady, shallow exhalations. Not him, then. She held still and listened for sounds from Sam Wetherell's room. Nothing. So sometimes he did lie in his bed. But he would be awake and listening too. Gradually, through the stillness came the faint sound of music: a piano, voices singing – no, a woman's voice, joined now and then by a man's, phrases broken, fading eerily to silence, the sound returning, only to dissolve again into the faint near-humming that was the noise of the night's silence. She wondered if she were still dreaming, but the sound returned, louder this time, only to fade again, then returned once more. Sophie got out of bed, threw her mantel on over her nightclothes, and went silently into the hall, past snores wafting from behind the closed doors of the boarders, to the end of the hall where a small ornamental window looked out over the verandah roof, giving a narrow view onto the street. She pulled back the curtain and gazed down and to each side as far as the glass would allow, but not a figure appeared in any direction, no dog or horse, wagon or buggy, or even wild animal disturbed the blue-shadowed emptiness.

Still, there it was, that faint music: tinny, dissonant, and now, broken by a man's shouts, followed by laughter both male and female – drunken laughter, she thought, suddenly. Her curiosity growing, she descended the stairs to the main hall, and placing her ear against the outside door, listened again. Here, the noise was a fraction louder, and after a second's indecision, she opened the door, leaving it ajar, and stepped out onto the verandah.

This air was cool enough that no mosquitos seemed to be about, so she pushed the door open behind her further to let a little fresh air into the stuffy house. Listening again, she turned her face toward the north end of the town. There, at the far end she could see an irregular rectangle of yellow light blazing into the darkness from the open front door into Mrs. Smith's house where the party raged, uneven because of the same light bleeding from the windows on each side of it. Appalled yet curious, she watched and listened, wondering – until she caught herself – what it would feel like to be a part of that gaiety, then, unsettled by her own thoughts, went inside, shutting the doors, mounting the stairs soundlessly, passing the snores, having a sudden intuition that nothing escaped Wetherell, not even her wakefulness, but believing him to be as impotent as she was to alter anything, had no fear of him, went back to her bed. It was not that he did not like women, she had concluded, but that there was no place for them in his conception of the world; he saw them, ate the food they cooked, took his clothes cleaned from them, even desired and bedded them, but they were never real to him. An intuition that did nothing to cheer her as she listened still to the faint sounds of revelry disturbing the silence of the prairie night.

She couldn't understand why Adelaide would run such a risk, wondered if perhaps the woman didn't understand how vulnerable she was to being arrested and going to jail. But she had seen Adelaide close up. Fear was the last emotion she had projected. Or was she herself the one who was wrong, living in something close to terror that at any moment the tiniest indiscretion would bring about her total disgrace? Was it possible that she could risk more and stay on the safe side of the world? Or did Adelaide think there was nothing left to destroy her? Not disgrace, not jail, not – What? Sophie's thoughts ranged through stonings and even hanging, before she shook them off as exaggerated and foolish.

Then she began to wonder who the people were at the party. Maybe prostitutes from Garden City or further away. As for the men, it wouldn't surprise her if the boarder Percy Haslam was there, or – Would Harry Adamson go to such a party? She wanted to believe that he wouldn't, but what did she know about him, really? More likely he was lying in bed only yards from where she lay, awake and listening to the music and wishing – what? That he had a woman with him? Probably he was still on his homestead and had no idea that Bone Pile was, however reluctantly, hosting such a party.

In the couple of weeks since she had last taken supper to him, she hadn't returned to visit him, nor had he stopped at the boarding house, probably because he had gone back to his farm as soon as he was well enough, and wouldn't be seen in town again, unless he had a machinery breakdown, until the crop was harvested, hauled to the nearest elevator or rail line, and sold. Not trusting herself to say his name without giving a hint as to her feelings, vague and unnamable as they were, she didn't mention him to Mrs. Emery, wanting to appear to have forgotten about him over there being any suspicion of being too interested in him. She kept silent, and worked, while she waited and hoped for a letter, or even some news from Pierre. But the sound of the party continuing to ebb and flow through the softness of the fall night, she remembered their mutual shock when their hands had grazed each other, and the moment in the half-darkness of his bedroom when they had looked into each other's eyes and a warmth had passed between them. She wanted very much to see him again, and forgetting Charles beside her, threw herself roughly onto her side to blot out his face. She was married to Pierre forever, and she was overcome again by longing for him.

She expected to hear the boarders talking about the party, or Mrs. Emery perhaps mentioning it, but to her surprise, the next morning at breakfast, as if by mutual agreement, no one made a single remark about it. It was wash day, so she had to hurry through the serving and the washing up and couldn't linger to listen to conversation; she needed to get a fire going inside the circle of rocks in the backyard over which the tub would sit and, once the fire was steadily burning, to fill the tub with pails of water from the pump.

An hour or so later she was descending the stairs carrying a load of bedsheets to set into the water-filled washtub, when Mrs. Emery emerged from the kitchen, and said, not looking at her, "Come. Put down the sheets," and passed her to stand in the door into the parlour. Unnerved, Sophie did as she was told, the thought of the twenty-five dollars, (now twenty-three), she had hidden away muting the worst of her fear. She followed Mrs. Emery into the parlour and sat down across from her on the prickly horsehide sofa with its crocheted doilies resting on the arms and spread across its back.

"Don't look so scared," Mrs. Emery said. "I ain't about to ask you to go." Sophie became aware of the tight grip of one of her hands on the other and loosened it. "No, I just want to say," Mrs. Emery paused, began again. "I'm tired out."

Sophie said, "You work very hard. You should let me take more of the load."

"You already do, Mrs. Hippolyte," she said, turning her head to gaze at the unused fireplace with its dark wood trim, so elaborately carved, that teamsters, it was said, had brought up from Fort Benton. "Having you here doing so much of the work makes me feel how tired out I am." In this clear light, softened by the lace curtains, Sophie could see that what Mrs. Emery said was true. "I want to take it easier," she went on. "I been trying to think how…"

"You are thinking about selling this house?" She had seen at once where this was going, and thought it best to simply say it, even though her heart had speeded up in fear. What now?

Mrs. Emery nodded, then sighing, said, "But who is there to buy it?"

"It is a good business, I think?" Somehow, she doubted this, but still, she wondered.

"Keeps a roof over your head. Not much profit for all the work, but I managed to get some set by." Her expression was dubious, and a sudden pity struck Sophie. To work so hard and leave with next to nothing.

She considered. "Your sons would want it?" Mrs. Emery snorted, causing Sophie to look away from her in embarrassment at seeing such pain.

"They'd sell it – they might keep the money." She laughed without amusement. "Got to look out for myself." She lowered her gaze to her gnarled hands resting loosely on her lap.

Sophie said, helplessly, "You are wise to think of your future."

Mrs. Emery smiled unexpectedly, looked up somewhere near Sophie's face and said, in a voice that shimmered with emotion, "Never thought I'd end like this." The air between them had grown fragile.

"I did not think so either." For a long second neither of them spoke.

"You still want to leave here?" Mrs. Emery was still gazing at her hands.

"I do," Sophie replied, "If – my husband doesn't – return –" it was her turn to avoid looking at the other. "If he does not send Charles and me money…"

Ever since the day she had seen Madame Tremblay digging potatoes in her yard she had been wondering what the woman knew about Pierre – where he was, or what his intentions were, even if he was still with Marguerite or if, having abandoned his real wife, it would be easier to abandon his paramour. A part of her wanted nothing so much as to speak to Mrs. Tremblay, and armed with whatever information the other woman could give her, use it to track down Pierre in order to confront him. But she felt guilty too, thinking that Madame Tremblay might be very angry with her because she hadn't been able to keep her husband, and the consequence had been that she lost her daughter. At this thought, Sophie felt an agony of shame mixed with rage at Pierre who did not care what he had done to her, who did not even write her a letter, much less send her money, if not for her, at least for his son. But when it came to actually walking down the furrowed, dried-gumbo track that passed for a street, to knocking on Mrs.

Tremblay's already-weathered door, she had not yet been able to bring herself to do it.

"Now you know what I'm thinking," Mrs. Emery said firmly, looking Sophie in the eye, something she rarely did, her habit being to fix her eyes on the view out the window or at the work her hands were doing rather than on the person she was talking to. Sophie realized with a start that Mrs. Emery was suggesting that she might buy this house and take over her landlady's business.

She said, haltingly, "I have nowhere near enough money." Mrs. Emery nodded carefully, as if she were having thoughts she wanted to express, but wouldn't.

"Leave it alone for a while." Dismissed, Sophie rose, was about to go out of the parlour when Mrs. Emery said to her back. "But if somebody comes along wants this place – and you know they say that when the railway branch line comes here in the next couple of years or so property will be worth something – if somebody comes along with the money, I ain't in no place to turn it down."

"I know it," Sophie murmured, bending to retrieve the soiled bedsheets. She imagined writing to Guillaume asking for – what – a thousand dollars? Five hundred dollars? The very notion made her rush out of the hall, catching the trailing ends of sheets and angrily stuffing them into a ball in her arms. Guillaume would never help her.

She recalled then that although Mr. Archibald had said he might find a buyer for her china dishes, no one had come for them or so much as inquired. She knew without asking that Mrs. Emery wanted a cash payment so that she could wash her hands of the house. Sophie didn't blame her, and the woman was right, if a branch line arrived, every single person with property in the town would do very well indeed. Especially a boarding house, which could more profitably – it occurred to Sophie – operate as a hotel. A hotel for all the speculators and settlers and other business people who would flock to the town once it had a railway. Endless work, of course, but with the possibility of a much better income, for didn't hotel-stoppers pay every single night, while boarders paid monthly fees that she knew barely covered the costs? But all that cooking, and daily washing of bedsheets and towels…

She had hit on something, could feel it in the pit of her stomach, but really – what good was such an insight if in the first place she had no money to buy the house? She had no clever ideas as to how she might add to her tiny store of cash. She was thinking all this while, hardly noticing where her feet were taking her, as she moved through the house intending to return to the back yard where the water in the large washtub steamed, and the fire below it would need more wood.

But at the door into the kitchen she came to an abrupt halt. Wetherell, tall, gaunt, a bit shaky on his feet, was standing over Charles who was sitting on the kitchen floor with the wooden horses the boarder Monsieur Roche had given him only that morning scattered around him, M. Roche saying that he had too much luggage, and that anyway, by the time he got back to Québec, his smallest son would be too old for them. Sophie had looked askance at him, but could detect no other motive in his manner and, in the end, had accepted the gift. She was even more grateful for a full morning without Charles pulling at her skirts for attention or begging for bread or milk when he had already had a full breakfast. The child's appetite was endless; she didn't know whether to be glad or to be worried, settling finally on gladness, that he would be a big man, that he needed all that food in order to grow.

Neither Wetherell nor Charles was aware of her as she stood with a touch of dismay, gazing at them. Wetherell held one of the horses in his gnarled hands.

"This here is a Thoroughbred," he was saying to her little boy. "Fast, my boy. But big. You need long legs to ride one of them bastards." Sophie gasped at the word. But Charles was pointing up at the horse Wetherell was balancing on his palm.

"Toor-bred," he said. "Ride horses. Fast." Wetherell laughed.

"That's it. Ride 'em fast. Get a jumper so you don't have to open them goddamn gates them goddamn farmers are putting in everywhere, ruining the goddamn country." Horrified, Sophie hurried into the room, glaring at Wetherell who paid her no attention at all, but dropping the horse to the floor in front of Charles, brushed past her without looking at her, on his way out of the room. She rushed outside, dropped her armful of sheets on the ground beside the tub and hurried back into the house where she gathered a protesting Charles up in one arm, while collecting the horses with her free hand, and brought him outside where she plunked him and his toys onto the ground a safe distance from the fire and the steaming water.

"He is a bad man!" she said fiercely to Charles. "He uses bad language!" But Charles wasn't interested, engaged in throwing his horses one by one as far as he could, then hurrying to pick them up, saying, "Fast, fast, fast!" each time. Sophie muttered to herself, "That West is over! It is over! Charles will never, never know it!" And finally, "I have got to get us out of here!" Meaning, out of this house where bad influences seemed to be everywhere.

Plunging the sheets into the steaming water and reaching for the paddle to push them down, for the thousandth time she asked herself how she might acquire more cash. Teaching school would have been a good possibility, but unless she found someone to care for Charles, no one would hire her. And when she considered who might be found to care for him for the pittance she could afford, she rejected school teaching. She would not have her son coarsened – or worse – neglected, even abused. These were not people who let children be children. Here they were put to work, their labour taken for granted. Even though she supposed she and Pierre would have had Charles working on the farm too, when he was still barely out of the cradle, even though she understood the necessity, she deplored it. She had been raised with a cook and a housekeeper, her only duties to attend school and church – and even that had been too much for her, she thought wryly. Altogether too much church. No, Charles would stay by her side. Fear struck and she gripped the paddle too hard, then told herself that Mrs. Emery would never abruptly toss her out on the street. Not as long as she could work.

As she stirred the kettle of soaking sheets, forgetting even to scrub them, she pondered the problem, while the small prairie birds chittered in the grass beyond the sagging picket fence and the sun, rising towards its zenith, caused a breeze to rise, blowing loose strands of hair into her face, at which she pushed absently. A meadowlark called and a second one answered from beyond the town behind her where the pile of bones sat brooding in the sun. She swatted a mosquito on her cheek, then waved away flies. In her exertion sweat had begun to trickle down her neck, and she used a sheet still sitting in the grass to wipe it away, hardly noticing that she had.

There was no other work to be had in the town – just cleaning houses, doing laundry, baking, cooking, and dishwashing. Mostly only for room and board, as she was doing for Mrs. Emery. How did one do the only thing one was trained to do – keep a household – and make money by doing it? She thought of the women at the party, how much they earned, was shocked that she would even wonder such a thing.

Perhaps she could borrow the necessary amount? But from whom? The banker was in Garden City, but he would never lend her money. A mere woman, and worse, young. She allowed Marguerite's appearance to surface at last: pretty, with the delicate white skin and the slenderness of youth. But Pierre can't marry again without renouncing his faith – unthinkable – he would first have to divorce her, Sophie. Marguerite didn't know it yet, but by taking her away when he couldn't marry her, Pierre had stolen her life from her. Perhaps he would tire of her too, before too long, and then what would the girl do? Especially if she were with child, a thought so unexpected that it caused Sophie to halt in her labour.

She dropped her paddle, collected the washboard that had been lying in the grass, set it into the tub, and began pulling at a sheet until she had it in position to begin scrubbing. It was then that she remembered the spinster sisters who ran a tearoom in her village back in Québec. They not only ran the business themselves, but baked many of their own pastries. For them, her grandmother had once told Sophie, it was not entirely a financial necessity as their parents had left them a house and some land which a neighbour farmed for them. They took pleasure in their business, and did it to fill their days, and for the company of others it brought to them, their lives otherwise being circumscribed by the church and, Sophie surmised with a shudder, the stifling propriety of their own front parlour.

She imagined the tearoom from her village transplanted here where she stood in the backyard washing the bedsheets of strangers, shooing away insects, trying not to inhale smoke from the fire that she kept forgetting to renew, and saw that in this community such a business would be ridiculous, even an object of fun. People here didn't want fancy pastries or cups of tea served on elegant china. They wanted hearty meals of roast beef, or steaks, and potatoes, ending with thick slices of fresh pie, or hearty bread puddings. They wanted home-baked bread and buns, and home-made preserves, and baked beans studded with chunks of good salt pork.

A café? Could she do it herself? What would she need to do it, and would it be any easier than the boarding house ? And would there be enough customers? Instantly, she thought, if she kept the prices low enough, everyone would come, just to experience something new. Then – oh, appalling, but interesting thought – she could slowly raise them.

"You'll wear out that sheet," Mrs. Emery said, startling Sophie so that she dropped it and had to reach into the water to retrieve it. "We'll never get 'em all done today." She went on muttering as she took the paddle from the ground and used it to search out a sheet, lift it, and catch an end.

"I am so sorry, Mrs. Emery. I was thinking and thinking –" Mrs. Emery had succeeded in pulling loose one sheet from the soggy tangle in the tub and said only, "I reckon you got things to think about." Quickly Sophie caught the sheet's other end as it emerged, and together the women, each holding an end, backing away from each other, began to twist the dripping sheet, wringing the soapy water from it, then dropping it into the unheated water of the rinse tub, before going back to do the same with the next sheet. The rinse tub had a mangle attached and when the two women judged most of the soapy water had been removed from a sheet, while one turned the mangle, the other straightened and fed the sheet between the rollers.

Mrs. Emery said, as she grunted away at the mangle's handle, "Heard the noise last night, did you?" For a second Sophie couldn't think what she meant. "That one is heading for trouble," she went on, pausing to push her hair back from her face and to straighten her glasses, pushed crooked by her efforts. "I heard there's talk of running her out of town."

"What?" Sophie said. "Is that legal?" And then laughed, a quick, sharp sound.

"The Mounties will send her away quick enough if she upsets things too much."

"Where would she go?" Sophie wondered aloud, thinking back east? Into the United States?

Mrs. Emery said, "To the next town, I reckon. Maybe to a city. Calgary, maybe."

"Such a hard life," Sophie grunted. "Always on the move. My turn." They switched places, Sophie beginning to turn the mangle's crank.

"She'll be lucky if something worse don't happen," Mrs. Emery said darkly, grunting.

"What?"

"Burn her out," Mrs. Emery said. "I've heard of it done. Them kind, you don't want them in your town. They attract the wrong kinda people. So bad for the children." At which Sophie had to restrain herself from laughing. As if anyone even noticed what the village children, few as they were, saw or knew. She thought ruefully of her days on the homestead, cooking meals for Pierre, making biscuits for him and carrying them out to the field where he laboured, resting with him in the shade of the binder or the plow while he ate and Charles played nearby. What an innocent I was, she thought. To live in such happy peace and only a few miles away the world was busy with its mischief. And I knew nothing of it.

Over the last few days Mrs. Emery's rheumatism had been acting up and, after they had finished cooking and serving the noon meal, Sophie saw how reluctantly she took money from the coffee can in which she kept it to go buy yeast for the bread making that would begin the next morning early. She insisted instead that she would go.

"You rest," Sophie told her, although she hated going into the general store, feeling that everyone stared at her and whispered about her as soon as she was out of hearing, and sometimes before. Maybe today they would have the party to think about and her own shame would seem too mild to remember.

Before she left the house, she put Charles down for his nap, and for once he had fallen quickly into sleep. She glanced in the mirror, rearranged some of her hair pins to catch the long ends that had come down during her morning's exertions, untied her apron and placed it neatly over a chair back, and went quickly down the stairs and out onto the street.

In a hurry, but afraid of turning an ankle, she kept her eyes on the rough patch of dried mud she had to cross to reach the main street then, without raising them, stepped up onto the boardwalk, almost colliding with a woman, who, she saw as she drew back, apologizing, "I'm so sorry," was Mrs. Archibald. A few steps behind her a thin young girl of perhaps fifteen in a pretty but badly-fitting dress stood, her hand over her mouth as if to suppress a giggle.

"No harm was done," the older woman said, pleasantly enough. "Fortunately, I saw you coming. It's Mrs. Hippolyte, isn't it?" She gave the name its proper French pronunciation.

"Yes, I am Mrs. Hippolyte," Sophie replied, then, recovering, "How nice to see you, Mrs. Archibald."

"I hope you are well," Mrs. Archibald said, "And not working too hard – there," glancing in the direction of the boarding house. Sophie knowing by the glance that Mr. Archibald had told her of Sophie's near-refusal to be her maid, deflected by Mr. Archibald's decision that Sophie's child made such a role impossible. How far she had fallen, to be so patronized.

"Mrs. Emery and I share the work," Sophie said. "I hope that you are well."

"Oh, I am," Mrs. Archibald replied. "This is my new…helper… Lily. Say hello Lily." Lily, admonished, dropped her hand from her mouth, nodded shortly at Sophie, muttering a greeting. Far too nervous, Sophie noted, and wasn't that a bruise on her forearm, just below the ruffled pink sleeve of the dress that might have been charming on Mrs. Archibald, but on Lily was clumsy, calling attention to some quality in her that utterly refused the pinkness and the ruffles? And a certain – for want of a better term – deviousness in the way she couldn't seem to meet Sophie's eyes?

"We must go on," Mrs. Archibald said to the air over Sophie's shoulder. "When I'm well enough, I enjoy a short walk, but I must say that even though it is fall, I find the sun too hot." Without looking directly at Sophie again, murmuring, "Good afternoon," she walked on past her, Lily following, with that same half-amused, half-anxious expression on her face, as if she couldn't quite believe where she had found herself, and couldn't decide whether she liked it or not. But Sophie was in too big a hurry to consider this, and several days would pass before she even thought to mention the encounter to Mrs. Emery. Mrs. Emery though, already knew about the girl Mr. Archibald had found to help his wife.

"Some old farmer passing through looking for land left her behind," she would say. "Said she was no good for work, and he'd had enough of her. Even though she was his daughter," this last indignantly. "I would have taken her, but –" meaning that with Sophie there was no room left for the girl. Or possibly, that, sizing her up, she had concluded as Sophie had, that the girl might be more trouble than she was worth, despite her obvious need for rescue. "Oh, you know, Sophie," Mrs. Emery would tell her, "It was more than him beating her, I hear. People talk." This last a phrase she often used to explain where she picked up information.

Sophie hurried on to the general store, seeing no one else, and was greatly relieved to find herself the only customer, bought the yeast cakes quickly, and scurried back to the boarding house as if she were a fugitive. She was out of breath as she opened the door, and had been clasping her hands so tightly as she rushed through the town, that when she took the yeast cakes out of her bag, discovered that she had cut small crescents into her own palms with her nails. Gazing at them, she felt nauseous. She could not live like this, although what precisely she meant, wasn't clear even to her. No, she told herself. She must find a way out of this boarding house, and then, out of this town. She must. She would.

She had at last found an island of privacy. The first time, not long after she had come to the boarding house in August, had been an impulse, that quickly grew to a habit and then to a need. Every evening, sometimes as late as nine, but the second Charles was safely asleep, regardless of how exhausted she was, she left the house to go walking on the prairie. Sometimes she was gone only half an hour, once nearly two hours, but usually an hour was sufficient before her fatigue, so deep that she couldn't sleep, at last passed into something more natural, allowed her muscles to loosen and begin to ache, then her eyes become heavy with the need for sleep that took her back to the boarding house and her bed. She was sure she'd never been so tired on the homestead. Or was it only that she shared it with Pierre? That they helped each other and understood that their labours that so tired them would one day transform their world into prosperity?

She had walked out of a stuffy prison replete with the odours of stale cooked food, of coal fires, and carbolic cleaning fluids, into a fresh, free one. And calm rose from the land itself that as she walked, seeped into her too. If it was still early, the little prairie birds would rise away from her to skim the grass, whistling their delicate songs, so that, listening to them, for a little while she could forget her plight. Even the howling of wolves and coyotes far out on the darkening plain failed to deter her. She walked on a line parallel to the town, able all the time to see its few lights shining through windows and screened doors, but far enough back to be lost in the shadows herself, taking pleasure in knowing the villagers couldn't see her. She walked slowly, breathing in the fragrance of the grasses, feeling them prickling her stocking-clad ankles, and welcoming the slight give of the earth underfoot. She stayed away from the pile of bones, feeling still that something emanated from it that was not benevolent, and never failed to wish someone would haul them away.

She paused often, to stand motionless, feeling the warmth or the coolness of the night air on her skin, listening to the wind soughing through the grass, or coyotes or wolves calling in the distance, sometimes a nighthawk softly whooping. More than once she had known an animal was nearby, heard it scurrying away in the grass, or the soft pat of its rapid footfalls as it retreated from her. Then, slowly, as she walked, stood, breathed in deeply, her muscles unclenching themselves, she would begin to remember what it was to be herself, grateful that she could still find that place where she recognized who she had always been. After that, she would feel able to return to the village and the boarding house, and her servitude there.

Yet the problem remained: How would she provide for herself and Charles? All the ideas would present themselves to her once again, beginning with a job elsewhere, running through trying to buy the boarding house, and ending with the one she found the most difficult of all – starting a café. During the day, whenever it crossed her mind, she would move to another job to distract herself from it. She would think about it later, but when she fell into bed after her walk, she dropped instantly into a deep sleep, too exhausted even to dream. Sometimes on her evening walks, though, she would imagine her café as already accomplished, a large, brightly-lit room with white-painted walls, rich, dark wood trim, pale rugs on the floors, flowers on the tables, and the steady murmur of voices of her well-dressed patrons, this latter always breaking into her imagining, making her laugh at herself.

Another two weeks passed and September had come and was gone, and although the October days remained clear and warm, the evenings had begun to be chilly enough that she had to wear a shawl on her evenings walks. One evening just as she was about to turn back for Mrs. Emery's house, she heard hoofbeats coming from the west through the falling dusk. She looked nervously over her shoulder and quickened her steps toward town. Almost at once a horse and rider emerged, throwing aside the shadows like a cloak being left behind. The rider pulled up his horse alongside her, laughing, and saying, "You gave me a turn, Mrs. Hippolyte. I almost ran you down." Although she couldn't make out his features, she knew by his voice it was Harry Adamson. As he spoke he dismounted, and holding the horse by the bridle, he pulled it around so that its hind quarters were facing the village and she could stand where she was in safety from any errant impulse the horse, intent on the barn and feed and water, might have.

He leaned toward her in the dusk, the horse's head silhouetted against the glowing sky just behind and above his right shoulder, and she caught the horse's smell of grass and clean sweat, and then something that she recognized as Adamson's perspiration. Rather than stepping back as she would surely have done in full daylight, she made no move, but pulling the shawl more tightly around her shoulders against the growing chill, looked into his face, which she could barely make out in the shadow, as he looked into hers.

"You did startle me," she said, her voice softer than she had meant it to be.

"I'm sorry," he said. Neither spoke for a second until Sophie said,

"I was going back."

"I'm glad to see you," as if she hadn't spoken.

"We should – walk – someone might see us."

"No one can see us in this poor light," he told her. He moved a step closer to her, until she could feel the faint warmth radiating from his body, and smell the dust in his clothes, and grease from working with machinery. He had taken off his hat; now he lifted it to shoulder height, which was where her head reached, and turned it to use as a screen as he bent to brush her lips softly with his. She had wished to resist, had thought that she should have known such a thing would happen, but when it did, his lips gentle against her mouth, instead she found herself responding, and raised her right hand to touch the rough cotton of his shirt where it lay against his chest.

He stepped back, she lowered her hand, and he his hat. He said, "I am – I…"

"No," she said. "I…"

"I think maybe –" he said, "That – both of us…"

"We have…" They laughed into each other's faces, and she thought with a pang, followed just as quickly by one of anger, of Pierre.

"Let's walk," he said. "I'll take you home."

"Thank you, sir," she said, realizing how coquettish she sounded, and wishing perhaps she hadn't, although her choice of tone had been deliberate, just as her lack of resistance to that unseemly kiss must have been – mustn't it?

But he walked her back only part-way, leaving her at the point where any villager gazing out a window to the west would have been able to make out who the two figures walking with the horse were. He said, glancing over his shoulder to the village and back at her, "I'll leave you here. Good night." She replied only, "Good night, Mr. Adamson." And he, "You might call me Harry when we're alone out here." And she, "Please call me Sophie." But he didn't answer her, and had soon become only a moving shadow, circling to reach his house from the south, until even it melded with the night, and she was alone.

After she had undressed, bathed sketchily in the basin of water she had heated in the kitchen and brought up to her room, and climbed into bed beside her child, she found that sleep wouldn't come. She had responded to a man, more, she hoped, than he knew – her entire body had responded to him, her reaction taking her by surprise and upsetting the equilibrium she sought that took her out onto the land in the first place. She and Pierre had had an intense physical relationship and in her anger and her pain at his rejection she had thrust away any memories of it, all desire – or so she thought – murdered by the violence of his actions. *I am still a woman*, she whispered to herself, *my body remembers it all.* It occurred to her then that if she couldn't marry again, and Pierre never returned to her, she would have to do without this thing between men and women. For the rest of her life. But she was still young, she thought, it isn't fair. There was no answer for that, no one to beg mercy of, no way around this that she could see. While one half cursed herself for responding to Adamson, the other half was filled with desire that would not be stifled.

She continued to go for her evening walks. She did so defiantly, knowing she was putting herself in the way of trouble, that, although she was fairly sure no one had seen her return that evening with Mr. Adamson, if he should meet her again and insist on escorting her back into town, soon everyone would know about it, and in no time at all, everyone would assume that she too had fallen just as far as Adelaide Smith, or whatever her true name was, and then what? And yet, she risked it.

Again, as she must have hoped, only a week or so later, Adamson came riding quietly up to her one evening, and dismounted to walk along with her.

"I was hoping I'd see you again," he said, and his eyes shone in the last rays of light as he turned his face to look at her. "I think all the time about when I was sick and you came every day with bread or biscuits and soup."

"Mrs. Emery's kindness," she demurred.

"But you came," he said. "I got so I waited for you every day." The fear she had kept at bay touched her, and she answered,"I am a married woman. I have no choice. I can't divorce, I can't marry again." She was aware of the primness in her voice, and embarrassed by it, even as she wondered at her own objection. But still, to re-marry when your husband was still alive was beyond unthinkable.

"Pardon me," he said. "But that's nonsense." He paused, calming himself. "People come West so they can get a new start. Out here people don't keep on living by the same old rules." She heard such anger in his voice, and wondered where it had come from. But she would never ask. Out here, it seemed, everyone had a story. Even me, it occurred to her.

He raised a hand to stroke her cheek. From that touch, she began for the first time since the day Pierre had left her, to doubt again all she had been taught as a child and a girl. She thought of grandfather's suffering over his brother's death – worse because the church cast him out – cast out his very soul from the paradise she'd been told waited for them all one day. But what had this to do with that? Confused and faintly afraid, she thought, *but when I left that life behind, didn't I also leave behind the rules in which I was raised?* People live here in ways she had never seen before, had never thought possible, or even considered that anyone might want. She hadn't seen a priest in months, there was no church for her to attend, no village of people who have known her family since they arrived there after the *dispersal* more than a hundred years earlier. There is no one to take notice and accuse her; she felt herself falling into a sea of doubt and above all, was the intensity of her desire that would not abate or leave her.

He grasped her elbow, stepping in front of her so that she couldn't walk away.

"Mr. Adamson – Harry –" she began in an admonishing tone, but even to her own ears her resistance was feeble. He bent and kissed her, harder this time. She pulled away, "If I fall," she cried. "If I lose my good name, Mrs. Emery will turn me out…"

"Nobody is going to know," he said. "Especially not Mrs. Emery." His frankness gave her pause.

"I can't marry..."

"I'm not proposing." She did not think this a very gentlemanly thing to say – but – she looked about her: Darkness had fallen; no one was out; a few lights glowed in windows nearly a mile away across the prairie, the only light to guide them back to their homes. Behind them was the deep "coulee" as the people called it, speaking French without knowing they were, where animals lay alert, their eyes glowing yellow or green in the darkness, or they stalked silently, searching for prey. The day's heat still radiating off the earth warmed her feet and legs even as her arms beneath her shawl were goose-bumped with cold. And her face, her throat, even the skin of her chest burned.

"You want only... "She stopped, not able to go on, torn between her desire and her fear of discovery, her fear that he would use her and then abandon her too. Perhaps would tell others – but no, she didn't believe that of him.

"That we do what men and women do," he said. "What they've always done, will always do. That would be enough for now. We don't have to talk about anything else." He kissed her again.

She half-resisted when his hands touched her bosom, and then moved downward, pushing at her dress, but her own desire finally overruled what she knew was the only thing to do, the right thing – to wrench herself away, to run as fast as she could away from him. Even when he had helped her down onto the stiff grass, lifted her skirts, and with her help, removed her long cotton drawers, even when he was inside her and groaning softly into her ear, she utterly abandoned her wiser self and clung to him, her mouth on his neck, his shoulder, his lips, and gave herself to pleasure, for after all, by this time it was too late to go back to what she had been only moments before. Then she thought of pregnancy, and would have shoved him away from her, so terrified was she, but as she thought this, he was already moving to let his fluid spill onto her thigh. In gratitude she clung to him harder until, breathing heavily, he rolled aside. The thought of pregnancy, which ought to have come to her much sooner – she was puzzled by her own recklessness, it wasn't as if she didn't know – had for that instant cut into her longed-for pleasure, nearly, but not fully, spoiling it.

As she began to speak while they sat side by side on the grass both adjusting their clothing, he interrupted. "No one will ever know. I promise you, no one will know. I swear that no one will ever know." She hated him speaking of this; it was demeaning. She got shakily to her feet. He rose too, and kissed her again.

"I have to get back," she said, urgent now.

"Yes," he said, his breath still uneven. "Don't take your eyes off the lights in the village. I'll be behind you, don't be afraid."

"We mustn't be seen together."

"I'll stay with you to the village," he said. "Then I'll circle back and come up from the south into my own house in a half hour or more's time. Nobody will guess we've seen each other." He kissed her one last time, and she turned unsteadily, and left him.

But as she hurried back across the prairie, stumbling now and then on rough spots or small dips that she couldn't see, her eyes on the fewer and fewer lights of the village, she could hear his horse snorting a few yards behind her, or the muted chink of its bridle, or even Harry's muttered expletive at a misstep. Then she passed the bones, a looming shadow on her left that she could have sworn emitted a faint murmuring – but no, it was only the wind. She was at the edge of the village when she looked back, and Harry was gone.

She lay beside her sleeping baby, her body suffused with remembered pleasure. At one minute she was both frightened and repelled by what she had done, horrified she would be found out, that Pierre would – *Pierre?* – and at the next, raged at God for having made such unbearable rules, followed at once, by joy at the memory of Harry's body on hers, his mouth against hers, and a certain – she couldn't deny it – satisfaction that a man had so desired her when Pierre had – then the cycle would start all over again, until at last she fell asleep.

Morning came, and as she hastened to rise, bathe in her basin, dress, clean Charles, feed him breakfast, and begin her morning work in the kitchen, the evening's exchange faded, and as it faded, she saw it as less the occasion of her fall from grace, or as her salvation, as merely what had happened. No one knew it had happened; she would not be pregnant. She was safe.

"Did you get lost last night, Mrs. Hippolyte," Mrs. Emery inquired as she tied on her apron. It seemed to Sophie that Mrs. Emery's voice was unusually subdued, as if she weren't really asking a question. But then she went on in a more natural-sounding tone, "I heard you come in quite late; I'd been a bit worried."

"Why yes," Sophie said, helping Charles down to the floor, handing him a crust to suck on. "I walked out too far, it fell darkness before I could get back and then I stepped into a dip and lost the lights of the town – I was quite frightened for a moment." She laughed. "I think I will be more careful about how far out I walk."

"There are wolves about," Mrs. Emery warned her. "Some of 'em are human. After dark – it ain't safe. It truly ain't."

"I am so sorry for worrying you." Sophie risked a quick, side-long glance at her.

"They say there's hardly no grizzlies left," the woman went on, slicing salt pork at the wide table as she spoke. Sophie turned to the stove, lifting the kettle and setting it back down, ostensibly to measure whether it was full of water or not, although she had just finished filling it when Mrs. Emery had entered the kitchen. "But –"

"I will be more careful," she murmured. "Grizzlies, what a thought," and she shivered.

THE FALL SEASON WAS ENDING, winter with all its difficulties and hardships would soon be on them, and still she had heard nothing from Pierre, was no longer sure that she ever would. It was not just that his absence saddened her because she had loved him, but that Pierre's son would not know his father, would quite possibly never have a father. When Charles asked for him, as he sometimes did, she not answer him directly, but would deflect his attention. It baffled her, too, that a man could simply walk away from his child and his responsibilities to him. That, she found more unforgivable than that he would walk away from his wife, would abandon her utterly – steal from her – shame her with another woman – not a woman, a mere child. He had loved his little son; even in the face of what he had done she didn't doubt it. He would play with Charles when he had a few moments, would pick him up, hug him, sing a snatch of song to him. She felt that perhaps, in some way she didn't have a name for, she was coming to terms with her own tragedy. But she gazed at Charles as he slept or played quietly in the boarding house's back yard with its already decaying picket fence. How he had grown, so quickly, what a big child he was, how clever, speaking in complete sentences and picking up a dozen new words a day. Only yesterday he had said in English, "Mother, I need my horses, please," to her enormously pleased surprise, before he lapsed back into broken phrases. But every once in a while he would announce something to her in a full sentence as if, if he could be bothered, he could do it all the time. He would need school very soon, that was plain, and Bone Pile had no school. Why could Pierre, at the very least, not have thought of that?

Now that the tremendous shock from his betrayal had gone, she often found herself remembering moments of their lives together, small things, such as the way he had turned his head away from her when he had remarked on the need for more and better fencing, or the way he had worked with his horse, quietly, in the corral, doggedly, but with minimal success, and she had seen by his face that he knew the failure was his own – because he was impatient, didn't know how to wait, how to repeat gently – although he would never say so out loud, and how she had pitied him then, and wanted to comfort him, but knew better than to even let him know what she had seen. She saw then, not for the first time, how puny they were in the face of what they had come West to do, in the face of the West itself – the vastness of the land, the ungovernable power of nature itself. And more, that they were not, had never been, not Pierre, not Sophie, in any way invincible, no matter how they beat their chests and crowed that they were. And yet, they stayed, or she had, while he had walked away. Was he defeated? Or was he merely bored?

It had snowed once, only to melt before noon. Sophie, as with everyone else, dreaded to think of winter, the previous one having been so harsh, but that scant snowfall, quickly melted, gave her a new thought: It was that maybe the very ferocity of the winter past had had something to do with Pierre's departure. Already exhausted, he had harvest to finish and a thousand other tasks before winter came upon them, and maybe, in his deep fatigue, he had looked into the long winter ahead and decided he had had enough. But why hadn't he told her? Why had he gone without her?

She remembered how sometimes over those years of hardships she had thought he would simply walk away, take her and Charles and go back to Québec, but each time she had feared such a happening, she had been able to dissuade him. *We have worked so hard, Pierre. We have almost reached our goal; soon this land will be ours.* And when even then he had paced and shouted and even sometimes swore, she would remind him, carefully, while never actually saying it, of the shame of returning home, having failed. *"Your family will take us in again until we find our way. You can go back working for old Fournier. He loved you to work with him. How good it will be to return to our birthplace, all the people we know..."* That, usually, would calm him, because she knew that he was as happy to be away from that constricting world as she was, and then she would touch him – his cheek, tracing his mouth with a fingertip, she would slip her palm inside his shirt, laying it flat against the heat of his chest, knowing he couldn't resist her womanhood – and soon he would be soothed enough in her hands that he would sigh and mutter, and eventually go back outside, to the plowing or the building, or post-pounding, or the cutting. And in doing all of this, believing she was holding him there with her, she had convinced him only that she herself would never leave, and never let him leave.

Was he not incurably excitable, enjoying his own excitement, wanting more, always more, and had not their life become settled, more or less stable in the steady round of work? Hadn't he talked about adventures with Indians, and were the Indians not mostly settled on their Reserves after the rebellion? And he, wanting to take part in the fighting, couldn't go because he couldn't leave her and his baby alone and had no one to leave them with? She had asked, "And on which side will you fight? With the Métis? They are our own people. Or with the soldiers from Ontario?" Come to think of it, hadn't he spoken to her about the gold fields of California, and even of Barkerville in the Caribou, and hadn't she laughed? His complaints had been saying this – that he felt he had made a mistake, that he didn't want the life of the settler-pioneer after all.

During this period of intense questioning she happened to enter the general store on an errand for Mrs. Emery just as the mother of her rival, Madame Tremblay was leaving, their shoulders nearly touching as each slipped through the wide doorway. Their unexpected proximity made Sophie dizzy, the air seemed to bubble, for an instant, she thought she might faint. Sophie and Madame Tremblay didn't so much as glance at each other even as the fabric of their garments brushed. It took a second for Sophie's eyes to adjust to the store's dimness, but she could feel the suddenness of the hush within. She continued as if nothing had happened, said good morning to the shopkeeper's angular wife, Mrs. Kaufmann, who stood behind the long counter piled with bottles of medicine, jars of jam, stacks of torn ends of cloth, cans of fruit, needles, pins and thread, and various and sundry other items. Thankfully, Harold Olds or Henry Ogden, she still couldn't keep them apart, was out on an errand, and didn't see the encounter which he would surely have reported back to the boarding house. Yet how she wanted to speak to Madame Tremblay, wondered even if perhaps Mrs. Tremblay wanted to talk to her.

Madame Napoléon Beausoleil – Séraphine – was sitting on a chair at the far end of the counter next to a window that let in enough light that she could see to knit, but that opened only onto the worn wooden wall of the building next door. Sophie knew she was waiting for Napoléon to finish his conversation with Mr. Kaufmann, who never failed to engage his male customers in dialogue while his wife or his clerk went about filling the customers' orders, and the wife or wives waited patiently. Often as many as a half-dozen men stood or sat together on unopened barrels of pickles, or sacks of flour, or chairs, or leaning against the counter, while they chatted and smoked, arguing about the weather, the price of wheat, the government, the possibility of new settlers coming, and of the railway branch line that would soon be theirs. On this day though, there was only Napoléon Beausoleil and Gerald Kaufmann. First nodding hello to Mrs. Kaufmann, Sophie, still trembling from the brush with the mother of her rival, went at once to Séraphine.

Madame Beausoleil, whose needles clicked briskly over what appeared to be a man's sweater, lifted her head from her work, gasped and dropped it, and clasped Sophie's proffered hand in both of hers. *"Ah, ma pauvre Sophie –"* she began, her eyes filling with tears that spilled over and began to run down her cheeks, but Sophie interrupted, speaking in English. In English she was in less danger of throwing herself, sobbing on Séraphine's bosom.

"No, no," she told her, sniffing back the hint of tears. "I am well, Charles is well, we are..." But she couldn't go on.

"Bien sûr, of course," Madame Beausoleil answered, wiping her eyes with a tiny handkerchief she extracted from her pocket. "I am so happy to see you. Why did you not come to me? My dear, I would have helped." Tears spilled again and she wiped them away again, then lowered her voice to speak as only an old friend could do without trespassing, "Have you heard any word from Pierre?" Sophie, regaining her calm, shook her head, no.

"Madame, I know you would have helped me, but – I was not myself. I couldn't think. I knew only that I had to get to town..." She tried to remember why that was – because maybe Pierre was there? Séraphine interrupted.

"By the time I found out that he – what had happened, we were told by a pedlar who had stopped by your place that you were gone, and for a long time I did not know where until one day Napoléon brought me the news that you were still here. I thought that you would return to Québec. "How I would wish to return someday..." She was about to begin sobbing, but Sophie said, hastily, "You know where I am, *chére* Séraphine. I beg you come to visit me at Mrs. Emery's the next time you come to town. I would stay here now, but Charles is napping and I must get back before he wakes." If they had been in Québec, there would have been a room serving cakes and tea or coffee where they might sit together for an hour renewing their friendship, but in this godforsaken place, there was no such thing, and – once again it was brought forcefully to her attention – that even though she had invited her friend to come to the boarding house, such a visit would be brief, that Sophie no longer had a home of her own to which she might invite her friend.

When, having made her purchase, Sophie said good-bye, Madame Beausoleil was still seated, still waiting for her husband whose conversation with the shopkeeper showed no signs of flagging. Sophie reflected that when a woman finally had an opportunity to leave the homestead for town with her husband, unless she had family or friends there, she had no place to go, nothing to do once she had made her purchases, no place to sit in privacy or with an acquaintance except in the wagon, no place even to find privacy for her bodily functions. More than once Sophie had glanced out the kitchen window to see a woman she knew only by name exiting the boarding house's outhouse or entering it. Mrs. Emery said nothing at this unauthorized use of her facilities, but Sophie had often thought how a public washroom was needed in the town, or even a small café with its own outhouse, so that women in town for the day might have a toilet designated for them to use instead of having to shamefacedly borrow a homeowner's private outdoor toilet. And there was no other kind because there was no sewer system and wouldn't be until kingdom come, Sophie thought. In Bone Pile there weren't even bushes to hide behind where a woman might relieve herself. Seeing the unguarded glance of exasperation Madame Beausoleil had made in the direction of her husband, and Sophie's own rush of sympathy for the woman who had helped her deliver Charles, the idea of starting a tea room or a café seemed even more urgently to demand consideration.

Back at the house, as she stood peeling potatoes and listening to a long story Charles was telling her apparently about a farm with "free cows and two-six fast fast fast horses and lotsa babies," only half of which she understood although she was momentarily arrested when he included a father (*papa*) in his story, her mind was once again on the café. She had wasted all these weeks since the idea had first come to her, partly out of caution, partly to give herself time to get used to the idea, but mostly, because she was afraid; her skin goose-bumped with fear at making such a leap. This time, though, she told herself, she must face this squarely and either act, or give up the idea entirely. If she were to do it, what would she need?

A house with a good cook stove and enough room to seat as many as a dozen people; then dishes, tables and chairs, pots and pans for her cooking and baking; she would need supplies: tea and coffee, flour and sugar, all the items she and Pierre had bought for the homestead. Without a cow or a garden of her own she would be forced to buy milk, cream, butter, vegetables, fruit, and meat. For all of that, she would need money – cash – and she was sure that so far, she hadn't enough. She remembered that there were still the porcelain dishes.

"Maman," Charles complained. *"Tu ne m'écoutes pas."*

"I am listening, my sweet," she told him, handing him a long unbroken piece of potato peeling and he grew interested in straightening it. Perhaps she could trade that china for the less elegant dishes she would need to run her café. The thought caused her some grief, but not as much as it once would have, and she was pleased, then fought off a wave of sadness.

But it was now into the last days of October. For weeks on end during the previous winter no one could get into town because of the deep snow and the blizzards that seemed to follow one after another through all the long winter and into spring. Visitors would come to town only when the trails were clear enough to pass over, or when the weather relented, as it did now and then, most winters. Should she perhaps wait until spring?

Should she speak to Mr. Archibald again, and then – she hesitated – should she approach Harry Adamson? After their last encounter, rather than going out onto the land, in the evenings she had satisfied herself to stroll up and down the newly laid wooden sidewalk that went past the few houses that comprised the second street, anchored at the south end by Mrs. Emery's house. She wasn't sure if this was to prove to herself that she wasn't merely a wanton woman, or if it was out of fear of causing people to talk, or even that Harry might see her out there on the prairie night after night and think that she was waiting for him. But once winter set in, snow would prevent her from walking out there, as it would often prevent Adamson from riding his horse across it.

Seeing Mme. Beausoleil and Mme. Tremblay the same afternoon had shaken her. So great was her need to think unencumbered by the imperative of her work, or even her child, that she risked going out before Charles was quite asleep, murmuring softly to himself in their shared bed as she left the room, telling him she would be back in a moment so that he wouldn't know she had left the house. She was so deep in thought as she wandered down the boardwalk near Adamson's cabin, that not until it was nearly on her did she hear a wagon coming up from the south. Startled, turning quickly, she saw that it was Harry Adamson himself, driving his team and wagon with a load, judging by the chair legs in the wagon box pointing to the sky, of household items. She would have walked on, but he pulled his team to a stop beside her.

"Evening, Mrs. Hippolyte," he said, a hint of amusement in his tone, or perhaps, she thought, it was pleasure at seeing her that he didn't want to show.

"Good evening, Mr. Adamson."

"It's been awhile since I last saw you," he said, grinning now. She turned away, nervous about the familiarity in his tone, if not his choice of words, but he climbed down from the wagon and stood by his horses, one hand reaching up to hold the bridle of the horse nearest them. "I've missed your company," he said. Then, seeing her anxiety, "There's no one about. We can talk together for a few moments without…"

"I've been busy," she said, "And as the days grow shorter it is harder to get away early enough to walk out there as I used to do." She glanced toward the contents of the wagon box. "Are you closing down your homestead?"

"Just for the winter. I decided to bring some furniture and supplies into town, keep them safe here." He dropped his hand from the bridle. "I'm going East for a few months," he said. "I might find work in Regina or Winnipeg. Might not get any farther than that. No use hanging around here starving."

"I have wanted to talk to you. I –" she hesitated, afraid to say out loud what she had in mind lest it seem silly. "I want to start a small business…" She looked up into his face, trying to gauge his reaction. He was listening with interest. She hurried on. "I have no experience at all of such a thing, I thought – I wonder – I need advice."

"Don't have experience with such a thing myself," he said, giving one shoulder in its faded brown canvas jacket a slight shrug. "But, sure – tell me about it."

Hesitating at first, then as her excitement caught hold, she told him of her desire to start a café, "Or perhaps only a tea room to begin."

He listened, at first gazing into her face, and then turning his head to stare down the street, as if he were weighing the potential of her idea against what he knew of the village. No one was about on the boardwalk, but she could see a couple standing talking at the Archibald's gate far up the street, although in the dusk she couldn't make out who they were. Closer to them a couple of children played tag, running and shrieking. There was no light in the windows of Adelaide Smith's house.

"I think," he said, slowly, "This could work," he said, "Maybe only as a stop-gap, until you earn enough to…" He paused, scratched the back of his neck, then said nothing more.

"Enough money to leave," she finished for him. "To go to a bigger place where there might be better opportunities for Charles and myself." She gazed down at the boardwalk between them, and he at the sky above her head. The horse on the far side of them sighed, moved one plate-size foot, then blew out air, making his lips vibrate. Harry turned his head, laughed a little, and when she caught that he had thought the horse as offering an opinion on human affairs, she laughed too.

"I need a house," she told him, "I need a kitchen with a stove and – other items. And then I need perhaps three tables and perhaps a dozen chairs. Eventually – not so many at the start."

"And dishes," he said.

"And cooking pots."

"Nothing left from your farm?"

"My husband sold the place with everything in it. The animals as well. I own only my clothing and Charles' and the few items Mr. Campion didn't prevent me from taking."

"Hmmm," he said, the lines in his face deepening, or was it only that night was beginning to fall? Was he thinking that he would perhaps find Campion and try to get back those things?

"You need a house first," he said. "One problem at a time."

"There are no empty houses in town that I know of," she said. "But," she hesitated, afraid to say what she had just realized, "did you say you…you are leaving for the winter?" He nodded slowly, studying her face in a way she found both gentle and a little too penetrating, as if he were curious, but admired what he saw there, and was trying to find its source. She would have thought of love, but was too intent on her café. "Would you consider renting your house to me for the time you are away?"

"It isn't much of a house. Would you live in it too?"

"I hadn't thought about that," she said. "But if I don't work for Mrs. Emery anymore, then I have to pay her to stay in her house."

"You wouldn't be any further ahead then," he said. "I think that, maybe, this might work. But I'd need to get back my house when spring comes." He was smiling; she smiled back.

"Of course, Monsieur," she said. "I would keep my eyes open for other houses, or a better idea, or …" She spread her hands out widely. "It is all so uncertain."

"Yes," he agreed. "You rent my house for the winter. I won't ask for any payment in advance, but when I come back in the spring to seed my crop, I'll ask for payment then."

"What if I have made no money?" she said, and the thought caused her to lift one hand to her face.

"Then you won't owe me anything." He wasn't looking at her. She was overcome with gratitude and then, suddenly, she was flooded with heat and desire, shame and…"

"I don't know – I can't…"

"Careful," he whispered. "People could be watching." She looked up, blinking, could feel that he was restraining himself from stepping closer to her, or touching her, or both. She forced herself to slow her breathing.

"Thank you with all my heart," she told him. And then, more softly, "I wish – I yearn…" She put out her hands as if in supplication, then quickly drew them back.

"Me too," he said as softly, looking off down the street as if he were speaking to someone else. Silence, then, "There may be a way."

"You leave soon."

"I leave when I want to," he answered her brusquely, as if annoyed that she would think he had to answer to anyone. "Bring Mrs. Emery with you. Tell her you want her advice about the house. When she says she has to go, you stay on, maybe, to clean a little. We can leave the door open."

"You'll be here tomorrow?" she asked.

"If you can come tomorrow, I'll stay."

Their eyes met, an instant or less, then Sophie left him standing by his horses in the near dark, stepped off the boardwalk, and walked away across the patch of grass struggling upward through the dried mud, now dead from cold, toward Mrs. Emery's. She forced herself not to look back, could feel the jerkiness of her steps, but couldn't make her body relax, as if it belonged to someone else. All the short distance she felt his eyes were on her, his hands resting on her body.

Afterward, as she undressed and got into bed beside Charles, she thought not about Harry, but about Pierre. It occurred to her for the first time that maybe it was her failure to listen, to think about the meaning of his outbursts that had brought her to her present situation. She had, she realized a streak of – she couldn't think what to call it – stubbornness? Pierre had said that: *When you want something, Sophie...* In her desire to fulfill her homesteader's dream, in her great love of her new, free life on the Western prairie, she had blinded herself to Pierre's needs and wishes. What he had done to her and Charles in the end was unforgivable, but she had, to some degree, brought it on herself. It was true, she saw now, that she had loved herself and her own desires more than she had loved him.

Still, shocked as she was by this understanding, filled with dismay at what she had done that she now couldn't alter, she found that under her shame and sorrow she also felt something that might be strength: If she was in part to blame for Pierre's turning away from her, then it would be easier to accept this outcome, and not keep on wasting all her energy on this nebulous cloud of misery because he had spurned her, and in futile anger at Pierre and God for what had happened.

CHAPTER ELEVEN

Saecula Saeculorum

FOR EVER AND EVER

WHAT TIME WAS IT? Eleven only? How would she endure to wait another hour, when she had already waited days for this moment? And how would she get out of the house without being caught? There could be no way but to go very slowly with long pauses between steps on the outer edges of the stairs where no one walked and thus, they didn't creak. The door into the garden was through the kitchen, and Antoinette's room was off the kitchen. If Antoinette caught her, she wouldn't tell her grandmother, Sophie didn't think, but she would bar the door and not let her out. Therefore, Antoinette must not hear her.

She had avoided thinking about what would happen when she and Pierre met, but now a fine perspiration broke out over her body, her cheeks felt hot, she seemed to be breathing from a spot higher in her chest than she normally did. He would kiss her. She would be kissed. He would clasp her to him. Would she allow it? What if they were caught? The very thought halted her in her pacing and her hand went up to cover her mouth. There was a footfall outside her door: grandfather on his way to the bedroom. Thank heaven she hadn't lit a candle; he might have seen its light and wondered why at nearly midnight she was not asleep. She held perfectly still until she heard the handle turn on her grandparents' bedroom door, and the click of the latch as it closed.

After a moment, while she waited for silence to descend again, she went to her bed and disarranged the bedcovers so that anyone thinking to look in on her would guess that she had perhaps gone downstairs for milk or some other reason she wasn't able to think of, this because once she had gone into her bedroom for the night she had never left it that she could recall in all her years in this house. A bad dream? Yes, that would do. She had often had bad dreams as a child and would scream and wake Antoinette or grandmother who would come to her. With grandfather gone to his bedroom it would be safe to light the candle, if only briefly, just to look at the clock.

At last it was only a few minutes to midnight, Sophie left her room, taking infinite care to make not a sound, taking forever to go down the stairs avoiding every creaky floorboard, moving like a ghost through the hall and the kitchen, and going as silently as possible through the door from the kitchen into the garden where she paused, breathing in the warm, heavy night air, waiting for her eyes to adjust. The moon was at half, giving off a good light, but the garden was shaded by tall old trees along its borders and impenetrable darkness bloomed below them like the wide skirts of women. No matter, she could find her way out here blindfolded. She paused again, listening intently. In the night's clear silence, any sounds seemed to her sharpened and precise. Holding herself motionless, alert and tuned to every tiny click, or ping, or whisper, it came to her that perhaps it was not the sounds that were different, but that somehow she herself was different.

Her senses turned inward for an instant, probing, assessing. Yes: That tense unease, that steady irritation that had begun to plague her some months ago, growing worse every day so that it took all her resources just to spend an evening sitting across from grandmother doing needlework, not to run away screaming, was now not to be found, had vanished in the intensity of this enterprise. Grandfather's plan to marry her off to anyone but Pierre hung always in the back of her mind; she knew only that she would not acquiesce, they would have to force her–but she knew too how easily that would be done. For her there would be no escape short of running away–to go where? She would have thought immediately to go to Guillaume and Claire's but felt sure that as much as her brother loved her, he would send her back. Or if she became very ill so that no one would want her – or – the thought caused her to catch her breath: If I were already married. She steadied herself, taking a deep breath, tuning herself again to the night, to the resting flowers and trees, to the air. Was Pierre already waiting in the shadows and she so silent he didn't know she had come?

Then came the softest of whistles from somewhere near the centre of the garden, but off to her right. A wide thrill swept through her, a current, a tidal wave, and she almost called, "Pierre! I am here!" restraining herself just in time. She started down the flagstone path that ran from the kitchen door to its wooden gate at the end, no longer trying to quiet her footfalls or to silence the whisper of her gown. When she was abreast from where she thought the whistle had come, she called in a whisper, "Pierre!" Before the sound was fully out of her mouth his arms encircled her, he was pressing his face against hers, his mouth on hers, then on her cheek, her forehead, in her hair, then on her mouth again.

So this was what she had come for. She was stunned at how overcome he was by his own desire, and how powerful he was, not just physically from his hard labour on the farm, but also in this maleness she had never before in her life seen or known even existed. It left him no room for thoughts of ruination, or of hellfire, no room even for thoughts of what would become of her. She pressed her hands against his chest as hard as she could but without struggling, only to remind him that he had to regain control of himself, that he was frightening her, that whatever she might want, this was too soon. His breathing began to come less quickly, his stance relaxed, and she felt safe to put her arms down. He knows, she thought, goose bumps breaking out all over her body, my arms are not strong enough to stop him if he couldn't govern himself. She couldn't stop him. He came closer to her again, but this time when he kissed her it was more as she had imagined such a kiss would be: tender, an expression of his love without the demand that had been his first response to finally being alone with her. He was saying her name over and over again, softly, "Sophie, Sophie, Sophie."

They made their way to the bench under the fruit trees and sat side by side, pressed against each other, his arm around her, her near hand spread flat on his knee, Sophie thrilled by and welcoming the warmth of his very body seeping into her palm through the rough weave of his trousers. They talked freely for the first time in all the years they had known each other. She said, "Pierre, I cannot…I am filled with…" trying to tell him how it was as if something inside her swelled and grew larger every day, beating in rebellious waves against the thin boundary of her skin.

"Don't go to Montréal, Sophie," he said. "If you go, I think I will lose you. You will never come back." Feeling the heat of his body, the weight of his arm around her, remembering the kisses with which he had greeted her, Montréal seemed pale and far away. And yet, she *would* go. She whispered to him, "I *will* come back. I *will* come back to you." Then more kisses, Pierre handling her sweetly, tenderly, her waist, her neck, her forehead, lifting his hands to her torso and resting them just below her breasts. She knew she ought to object, but she did not. Were they not now promised to each other?

"Chouinard has come, eh?" he whispered. She froze. But in this village everyone knew everything, nothing escaped the town's eyes. He had come with his parents and they and Sophie and her grandparents had sat in the *salon* drinking tea and making halting, boring conversation while Sophie ignored André as if he were more than merely invisible, an absence in the room. From the corner of her eye she had seen him more than once glancing at her quickly before he lowered his eyes. She would never marry André Chouinard. Never.

"They will make me marry one of those men," she warned him. "I will get only to help choose which one."

"Who?" She named them.

"I hear that Mathieu Grandmaison has taken ill."

"What? How ill?"

"Very ill, they say. They say he grows thin." He shrugged.

She hoped it was true, then felt ashamed. And anyway, one less suitor made no difference to the outcome.

"You want me to ask too?" Pierre inquired angrily. "You know they will send me away." For the first time he pulled his hands back from her.

"We could run away," she dared to say. He turned back to her, spoke angrily.

"No one would marry us, or if we found someone, they would only have it annulled."

"We could live somewhere else, not come back here."

"Merde!" he said. She could feel her cheeks heat at the careless expletive. "I want to live here. I don't want to leave everything behind!" That sudden rise to rage: how it both startled and excited her. She thought, what? Are we talking about marriage already? We have only just… But, she thought, we have always known this, and she thought of that orange yolk of the duck's egg oozing down her skirt. It seemed a thousand, no ten thousand years ago.

"I must go soon," he whispered. "Come to *la fête de la St.-Jean-Baptiste*, will you?"

"I can go with grandfather," she whispered, a flicker of fear or puzzlement at what had happened to her the first time she had been allowed to stay for the bonfire struck her and involuntarily she shivered.

"I'll see you there." It was only two days away.

They kissed, and kissed again, and then again, while something rose in her that both frightened and thrilled her. It was only his pulling away from her that stopped her from – from what? She knew only she had given over her entire being to be close to him, closer even than this. "Enough," he whispered. He murmured to her, much of it so softly she couldn't hear, but didn't need to ask. Then he stood, moved backward, and disappeared soundlessly into the dark shadows of foliage. She waited. A slight sound, a muted creak, and he was gone.

Safely back in her bed, she lay in the darkness and went over and over again in her mind every move, touch, caress, kiss, each word each had spoken. Now she thought, *He will marry me.* The word evoked nothing, instead, a wall, a darkness that she dared not probe. Her mind raced hither and thither, searching. What came to her then was his passion when he came out of the darkness and seized her, when he encompassed her with more than just his body. What else did she need or desire? His protection of her from the world. Their becoming one person.

Daylight was coming faintly through the white muslin curtains. Soon she would have to get out of bed and begin her *toilette.* She thought of the moment when she had paused to listen as she stepped outside into the night and the garden, how she had discovered her impatience, her simmering rage had gone, leaving behind that crystalline sense, everything at once precise, perfect.

Now, as morning approached she felt the familiar but nameless *pushing* rising again, this at the thought of yet another day following grandmother about, down all the familiar paths of the village, seeing all the familiar faces, hearing sounds she had been hearing every day since she could remember. How the days dragged on! Only the thought of going to Montréal, or the thought of Pierre brought her relief.

Pierre's father was a poor farmer, some of the land he farmed belonged to grandfather. Pierre had begun to work in the fields and with the animals when he was a small child. He had barely gone to school. Yet what choice had she, in the end, but to marry? She thought of finally being allowed to leave the village for Montréal and the homes of her brothers, Guillaume in particular who was a solicitor, as Hector, a banker, did not write himself, but let his wife, Isobelle do his duty to his grandparents, and that rarely. Anyway, she didn't want to go to Hector's. There was some trouble, between her grandparents and Hector, she didn't care for him herself, and whenever she thought of him, felt funny and uncomfortable. Yet, he was her brother, wasn't he? Sophie did not like his wife Isobelle who was stiff and kept her distance, although she loved Guillaume's pretty wife, Claire, who despite their age difference treated Sophie as if they were sisters.

Her door opened widely, quickly, at the same time as there was a knock. "Hurry, Sophie, hurry," Antoinette said, whisking into the room, pushing back the curtains and lowering the window.

"Leave it, Antoinette!" Sophie cried, angry. "Leave my window alone!" Antoinette was so surprised she stood with her mouth hanging open. Immediately Sophie felt guilty.

"I am sorry, Antoinette, forgive me," she said.

"You didn't sleep well?" Sophie couldn't help but smile.

"I slept terribly," she told the maid, in a solemn tone, and then laughed aloud.

NEAR MIDNIGHT AS SHE waited in her room, fully dressed, no candle lit, for it to be time to meet Pierre in the garden again, she heard a short, anguish-laden cry coming from her grandparents' bedroom two doors down from her own. So odd was the sound, so burdened with the helpless shock of extreme pain and perhaps also with sudden understanding, and horror at the understanding, that she couldn't tell whose voice it was. The sound lifted her to her feet, while goose bumps sprang up on her arms and legs; she stood stock still, straining to hear. No further sound broke the night's hush.

The cry her grandfather had made all those years ago in his study when *le curé* Deschambeault had been locked for hours in it with him came back to her as clearly as if she were just now hearing it again, that time – that time when – ah yes, it was when Uncle Henri had died and *M. le curé* had told him… That must have been what happened: the priest telling him that he must accept that his brother wouldn't be buried in the village cemetery. This insight came to her out of nowhere, or out of shock, at the same moment she heard her grandparents' door open, the rapid thudding of slippered feet on the hall floor, her own door handle turning, the door swinging open so that it banged against the wall.

"Wake Antoinette! Send her at once for the doctor!" It took Sophie an instant before she said, as rapidly as her grandmother had spoken,

"I will go myself," and ran from the room. She was almost at the bottom of the stairs when she realized that, planning on meeting Pierre, she hadn't undressed, and surely grandmother would have seen that and wondered. But she rushed through the house, bumping into furniture, catching her skirt and freeing it, to Antoinette's door downstairs by the kitchen, banged on it with the side of her closed fist – Antoinette was notoriously hard to wake – then opened it and called, "Go to grandmother, quickly, I am going for the doctor."

Antoinette thrashed about in her sheets, cried, "What? What?" in a thick voice, but Sophie was already gone leaving the door wide open, although she hadn't taken the time to light a candle, and hoped that the kitchen's cool air would flow into Antoinette's stuffy bedroom to keep her awake. To further this end, on her way out of the house she deliberately banged the front door hard. Then she was rushing down the flagstone path, the moonlight bathing the whitewashed village houses so that they gleamed, and out the gate and down the street to the house of *M. le docteur*. Dogs had wakened at her door slam and were barking. She ran up the path to the doctor's house, onto the open verandah that ran across its front and pounded on his door as she had done on Antoinette's.

"Monsieur! Monsieur!" she called. After a moment she could hear someone coming down the hall, the door opened, a lighted lamp thrust in her face, and the doctor's male servant, Denis, his voice loud and angry, demanded, "What is it?"

"My grandfather!" she cried. "We need the doctor at once. Is he here?" The man, attired in his night clothes, held the door open so she could enter and as she did so, a new light appeared at the top of the stairs, this one a candle held by Doctor Belanger. If he isn't careful, Sophie thought, he will light his beard, and then was shocked at such an idea overtaking her in so dire a moment, as if she were still a child or an *idiote*. The doctor said, "Yes, yes, yes, who is it? Who is it?" as if he were not at all used to being wakened in the middle of the night by frantic people. He too was wearing his night clothes and was trying to fasten with one hand, his dressing gown.

"Mon grand-père," she called up to him, too loudly, so that he took one hand from his candle and patted the air downward with it, to calm her. She swallowed hard. "I know nothing else, nothing else, I came because *grand-mère…*"

"Yes, yes, yes," the doctor said. He was at the bottom of the stairs now, not bothering to go back and throw on trousers, and Denis was helping him on with his coat, handing him his bag that evidently was kept by the front door for such emergencies, and at the same time taking his candle from him. The doctor did not look at his servant, nor at Sophie, cleared his throat loudly, twice, Denis opened the door behind Sophie, brushing against her as he did so, so that she had to move out of the way, and then they were back outside in the night, dogs barking, moonshine lighting the way.

When they arrived at the house, the doctor carrying his bag, Sophie still out of breath from shock and from her run to the doctor's, and hurried up the stairs to her grandparents' bedroom, they saw at once that grandfather had expired. He lay on the clean pine boards of the floor, his limbs straightened and a quilt pulled from his bed neatly covering him as if he might feel chilled. Grandmother and Antoinette, still in their nightclothes, were seated, each on one of the two chairs in the room, Antoinette sobbing, but grandmother who had lighted a lamp and set it on the stand by the bed at her husband's head, sat with her rosary in her fingers, staring straight ahead, not moving or turning her head even when Sophie and the doctor entered.

"We have lost him," Antoinette wailed as if it were her husband who had died, and grandmother hissed, not turning her head toward her servant, "Calm yourself."

The doctor was kneeling by the body, and when, after closing the old man's eyelids and pulling the quilt up over his face, he stood back, crossing himself, his lips moving in a silent benediction, Sophie knelt by his body. She dared to lift the quilt back so that she might kiss his cheeks one last time, and saw, in the slackness of his facial muscles, the thinness of flesh against his strong cheekbones, his eyes sunken into his skull, how very old he was, how inevitable this moment had been all along only she had never even thought of it, had thought that grandfather would live forever as would grandmother, she would herself, and now she saw that this was not so, had never been so, and she was only a foolish young girl who knew nothing at all. She was too stunned even to cry.

Downstairs someone was knocking on the front door, insistently, loudly, but carefully. The doctor put his arm under Sophie's upper arm and with a series of gentle tugs, caused her to rise to her feet. She became aware that Antoinette was still snuffling in her chair. Grandmother said, "Antoinette, go and dress yourself at once," sharply, as if her husband was merely being annoying as he so often was, lying there on the floor in the middle of the night. But in the harsh command Sophie heard some other, new sound, the meaning of which she couldn't decipher. The knocking downstairs continued, and grandmother said, less angrily, "Sophie, go and answer the door. Doctor, I must dress." Dr. Belanger answered, "I will find some men to lift him back onto the bed; we will come in when you are ready," and Sophie said, "I will tell someone to go for *M. l'abbé*."

She had just put her hand on the door handle when someone tapped gently on it from the other side. Startled, all eyes turned toward it which now opened slowly to reveal the curé Deschambeault, breviary and cross in hand, a frightened-looking small boy, just visible to one side of him.

"Alphonse Charron has gone to Our Lord," the doctor said softly. Antoinette, at this, still crossing herself, squeezed past the men in the door and could be heard going clumsily down the stairs.

"I heard the *tintamarre*," the *abbé* said. "I came at once." He turned to the child. "Jean-Pierre, go to the house of *le notaire*. Tell him he must come. Tell him to bring another man or two of them. Go now, quickly." The child could be heard at once scrambling down the stairs. At some point, probably while Sophie had gone for the doctor,

Antoinette had lit lamps downstairs and a lamp cast its light from the stand in the hallway outside the death chamber. Grandmother was standing now, had cleared a small table that usually stood by the wardrobe and began to move it beside the body. The priest was opening his small bag, preparing to say the proper words over her grandfather who had died so quickly and unexpectedly there had been no confession, no extreme unction. *L'abbé* would do what ever needed to be done to assure her grandfather of his quick place in heaven. And yet, still, she thought, even grandfather would suffer in purgatory first, and was angered at herself for this thought at such a moment. She couldn't understand her own mind. What was wrong with her that she had such thoughts?

It was then she remembered that Pierre was to wait for her in the garden, would be there now, no doubt. But no, she thought, when all the commotion had started, the dogs barking, the door slamming, the lamps being lit, he would surely have gone away so as not to be found out.

It was at this that she began to cry, at first silently, tears streaming down her cheeks and falling onto her dress, soaking into her bodice, and then, gasping for breath, she began to sob out loud uncontrollably, her chest heaving as great lumps of air rattled it. Grandmother hissed at her, "Silence yourself!" but Sophie couldn't get her breath, couldn't stop the heaving of her chest or the tears that poured out of her eyes. In the midst of this bodily paroxysm, she felt her head would burst with the pressure of the water, an ocean of water pushing to get out that she had no idea lived inside her very body; she would flood the room, all of them, grandmother, the doctor, even Antoinette downstairs in the kitchen would dissolve in Sophie's sea of unstoppable tears.

But now the doctor came to her, holding her gently, then moving to her side, his arm around her, pushing her head gently so that it rested against his upper arm, guiding her very slowly out of the room, murmuring to her as she gasped and shook, her chest cracking in its quest for air, "It is only the shock, my dear. It will pass, Antoinette!"

"Monsieur?" Antoinette called from the bottom of the stairs, more knocking on the door, a "mon Dieu, what now," from her as she was about to open the door, still listening for what the doctor would tell her, when it opened again of its own volition, but no, two men stood on the other side, and the doctor repeated, "Brandy, bring brandy at once. Is there any in the house?" as men came up the stairs and Sophie, released by the doctor, letting the wall support her, bent from the waist, still crying, though less noisily. The doctor pointed to the bedroom where grandfather lay, dead, then turned to Sophie and asked, "Your room?" but she couldn't speak and guessing it to be hers, he ushered her in and set her in the one, straight-backed chair at the foot of the bed, as Antoinette entered carrying brandy and a small glass on a tray.

She would have wished never to remember one thing about that night. She would have wished all of it to have been washed away in her tears, but no, she remembered drinking the brandy that the doctor had told Antoinette she must give to her, and that Antoinette must not leave the room until she saw Sophie had emptied the small glass. She remembered the ringing of the church bells, waking the village. She remembered how grandmother had slowly melted over the night with exhaustion, how worn her face, how dulled those frightening eyes, how slow her usual brusque movements. Could it be she had been grieving? And yet, she said nothing aloud, while her lips moved in constant prayer.

Women had come, the wives of neighbours, and *la sœur Marie-Joseph* to take charge, and they had relieved Sophie and grandmother of the necessity of washing the body. She remembered she had been surprised that grandmother had not insisted, how instead, seemed to have felt it a reprieve not to have to do a task that seemed, ever so faintly to Sophie, to revile her. For herself, she felt only fear at the idea of washing grandfather's cold, stiff limbs. But she wondered then if grandmother and grandfather had ever loved each other as she and Pierre did, tried to picture them as a newly-married couple. She thought, if I were to marry that Chouinard, this too, is how it would end. Her rebellion, for that brief moment, seemed fully justified.

When morning came, the house began to fill with grandfather's business acquaintances and his friends as well as all their many relatives, people whom they rarely saw otherwise, as well as the store clerks, and the leading citizens. Food appeared on the doorstep and through the backdoor into the kitchen. If grandmother noticed, she said nothing, not even her usual curse, *We are not peasants!* Every now and then *M. le curé* led all of them in prayer. She would remember after how it was that she had moved about like an old woman, her every step hurting her, as if she were recovering from a hard fall. At last, toward evening, the Hippolyte family arrived, Pierre included. By then the room upstairs where grandfather's body lay was crowded with people, grandmother in a fresh black gown sitting in silence beside him, and people went up and down the stairs speaking, pausing only to cross themselves, as they did so. Madame and Monsieur Hippolyte had gone up the stairs and the girls had gone to help with the food in the kitchen, the three other brothers were outside on the grass where *habitants* were smoking their pipes and speaking soberly to one another.

"What will happen now?" Pierre asked her, having found her alone in the sitting room across from the *salon* where the senior relatives were perched on the hard furniture in stiff silence, as Antoinette served them tea, the women dabbing at their eyes now and then with thin hands holding lace handkerchiefs. "How pale you are. How cold your hands..."

"The funeral..." she said, aware how high and thin her voice sounded, not her own voice at all. "He will go into the graveyard..." She almost began to cry again at this, but managed to stop herself. The brandy, hours ago, had flushed her body with an unwelcome, cloying heat, then she had grown sleepy and for half an hour, as surely the doctor had meant her to do, had drifted in and out of consciousness, then had wakened again and ever since had felt dry-mouthed, her brain bathed by a faint, steady ache.

It was then that it struck her how hard it would be to live in this house without grandfather, even though it occurred to her now that she didn't think that what she felt for him was exactly love – when had he ever been close enough to her for her to feel anything but his authority, his innately gentle but wholly interior nature – he who had controlled grandmother's worst instincts whenever he noticed them at work, he who provided an anchor for them all. And the business, who now would run it? It struck her then that grandmother would not let her go to Montréal, that she would have to stay all the long winter, alone with her.

Pierre held her hand, he gazed into her eyes, she could see how he wanted to hold her and kiss her as he kissed her in the garden in the middle of the night when there was no one to know or to see. She was filled with distaste for this in him, wondered how he could even feel such emotions for her in her presence at such a moment, when she had just lost her grandfather who had been a part of her life ever since she could remember, whether there had been love or not on either side. What seared inside her and would not go away or stop was the suddenness of it, the relentlessness of it, the world thrown utterly into disarray. Pierre's kisses would bring no comfort, belonged in some other part of life, were at such a moment blasphemous. What was it she needed now? It was to have things, as unsatisfactory as they were, to go back to that way.

But he did not speak of their plan to marry, nor mention his rival, *that Chouinard*, spoken by both of them with such disdain as if the actually worthy suitor was no better than a hardened criminal. In years to come Sophie would laugh uncomfortably about this. Pierre went away with his family finally, not seeking her out again, nor trying to speak alone with her. Later, remembering her anger at his wanting to kiss her, and then how well he had behaved at the end – although that too had angered her – she could only press her lips together and shake her head at her own young girl's confusion at this sudden death and all that it threw into doubt.

Guillaume came from Montréal as soon as he could, not waiting for the train that did not run until a day later, mud-splattered, exhausted, and without his young wife Claire who was too near giving birth to make so rough and fast a trip. Hector would follow later, he told them, but by the way grandmother had turned away, Sophie knew that Hector would not come at all, although she didn't know why not. At this, she wanted to hold her head in her hands: Secrets! No more secrets, please God.

The funeral, the burial in the stone-walled graveyard far from his younger brother's grave in the field, the reading of the will, the hastiness about the store which, grandfather had written must now be sold, Guillaume and *le notaire* in constant, steady conversation, Guillaume's anxiety to return to his wife and the child who might even now be born, Sophie herself thrust into the job of managing the household with the help of Antoinette and Mme Gauthier, waiting patiently for the moment to ask Guillaume to take her home with him immediately. Pierre was always on her mind, but they had made an agreement: she would go to Montréal for the winter, he would go into the woods to earn money. In the spring they would be married, the thought bringing now no glee, no emotion at all. He didn't come for three days, and she oscillated between dying for the sight of him, for the sound of his voice, and being glad he wasn't there as one more thing she would have to manage when she was already managing so much, and filled with grief, and anger, and sorrow, underneath which ran in cold silence, an undercurrent of sheer terror.

At last only two days were left before Guillaume was to leave, the notary had departed to draw up documents, to advertise for the sale of *Charron frères*, the doctor off to care for other patients, the relatives gone away to tend to their farms and businesses wherever they might be, or in one or two surprising cases, to collect the rent from *les habitants* who occupied what had once been their *seigneury*. Grandmother now spent hours in the bedroom she had for fifty years shared with grandfather, emerging only for daily mass and to visit the kitchen where she seemed about to give orders, but never did, save to demand tea. She didn't speak to Sophie, nor look at her, communicating only with a gesture, her eyes turned to some distant, hard place. Sometimes, it seemed to Sophie, her eyes took on a confused look, they would move about the room slowly, as if she were trying to orient herself, before, gradually, they returned to that new darkness.

Sophie had been waiting on the stairs for over an hour, when Guillaume, who had been gone nearly all day, where she didn't know, opened the front door. It took him a second, in the gloom, to notice her on the stairs, and he appeared at first startled before he made out that it was his younger sister.

"What are you doing sitting there in the dark?" he said, as if he had spoken reflexively, his mind elsewhere. He was taking off his hat, resting his gloves inside it, setting the hat on the bench by the door. His movements were slow and deliberate as if thoughts fully occupied him so that he hardly noticed what he was doing. He was now the head of the family, only he could override grandmother's wishes.

"You are too thin," he said, as if much had been going through his mind concerning her and this emerged first.

"Take me with you. Please." He put his arm around her shoulder, guiding her gently across the hall, into the parlour where he sat on the sofa, patting the spot beside him to indicate she should sit there too. She did as he asked, but as if in warning, told him in a rush, "I am going to marry Pierre Hippolyte in the spring. I will not marry M. Chouinard." He raised an eyebrow, thoughtfully searched her face with his eyes, then looked away, across the room, holding still for a moment while she, in turn, held her breath. He breathed deeply in through his nostrils, turned back to her, this time resting his eyes on the sofa and not on her at all.

"Spring is too soon after grandfather's death," but he muttered, didn't seem insistent, sighing instead. *"Ma chère petite sœur*, he is a poor choice."

"Why?" she cried, loudly enough that he put a hand over her hand where it rested on her knee. She knew very well why he was a bad choice – he had no money, he had no land, she would have to learn to work. Anything better than this non-life, she thought, and then that she wouldn't be alone anymore. "I *will* marry him; he loves me. "

"Yet you want to come to Montréal on Wednesday." He seemed genuinely perplexed.

"We have plans, Guillaume," she faltered. She told him how Pierre would earn money all winter in the woods, and not exactly meaning to, she told him also how she dreaded being alone with grandmother, how she didn't want to marry without ever seeing Montréal. He smiled gently at her as if she were only six years old, "You, in the city," he said, shaking his head. "But everyone knows country life is far better than city life." Hadn't she been hearing this since she was a child? The joys of the country; the cleanness of it; cities dirty and vice-ridden, full of the poor, of typhus and cholera and small pox...

"I don't care!"

"You're too young, too inexperienced in the world to know what is best," he said, and now he was firm, frightening her just a little. "There is nothing for a young girl like you in the city. It isn't safe."

"But I have heard of girls from the farms who go to the city and do very well!" He shook his head, his mouth grim.

"You cannot imagine," he said.

"They are free!" she cried, and was surprised at what had come out of her mouth. He stared at her, some small light dawning in his eyes, as if he was coming to understand something about her that hadn't before occurred to him. But then he dropped his eyes and said, grimly, "Free to be abused, to take up drink, to..."

"I would never do that!"

"You do not know what you would do, or what might happen to you there." But his voice had dropped, his words slowed at this last, as if he felt perhaps he had been arguing on the wrong tack, or that argument at all was useless.

Responding to his change in mood, she said, "But you and Claire would take me ...about...wouldn't you?" She faltered now, was trying not to let her tears fall. "I cannot stay here," she told him, her voice low. "I would work," she offered. "I would care for Claire and the baby –" He shook his head, no, speaking gently.

"You will have a better life here. And grandfather has left you a few *louis*. Not much, but a little money of your own so that you won't be utterly dependent on our grandmother. Look about for a better husband. Don't marry someone only to escape. You should consider André Chouinard. He is a pleasant young man, and he does very much want you."

"But, it is Pierre whom I love!"

"Sophie, don't marry that Pierre, no matter how handsome he is." He smiled at that. "He is penniless and too fond of having a good time. I wouldn't trust him with you." Before she could speak, he went on in a more gentle tone. "There is land with Chouinard, his father has made some good investments, and André has some education. Is Pierre even able to read and write?"

"He is!" She declared, angry, although she had never seen this in practice.

"You have all this winter to think about things," he said. "Don't do anything hasty, Sophie, promise me." She knew he was afraid she might run away with Pierre.

"Without grandfather I will be dead by spring if I stay in this house," she said, petulant, so that he laughed. "I will not marry before spring," she told him. Both of them knew very well that *l'abbé* Deschambeault would refuse to marry Sophie and Pierre, especially if Guillaume told him of his disapproval. She didn't know what grandmother would do. Disinherit her, of course, but pooh on that.

"Sophie..." He paused again, before going on. "Dear to me though you are, I will not consent to your marriage to Pierre Hippolyte." He paused. "Never, Sophie. I mean it. And if you are foolish enough to run away, I will see to it that you are brought back and the marriage annulled. Such a man will destroy your life. Believe me."

She couldn't catch her breath. She couldn't believe what her beloved brother had just said to her. He went on, “I will speak to Pierre Hippolyte myself, before I leave. There will be no marriage.”

But only days later, when the funeral was over, and grandfather lay in his grave in the cemetery, Sophie torn between continuing sorrow at his loss and happiness because tonight she would finally, once again, meet Pierre in the garden of her grandmother’s house, she was walking slowly on an errand for her grandmother to the store that had been theirs when she saw coming toward her, André Chouinard. Startled, she almost stopped and looked across the street in hope of rushing there before he saw her, but no, even as she considered an escape she realized that he had noticed her, that she wouldn’t be able to avoid him.

“Mademoiselle,” he said. “Good morning,” gravely. Even though she replied politely, “Good morning, Monsieur,” he didn’t move on.

“Forgive me,” he said, looking down at his polished brown boots, then lifting his eyes back to hers. At last he said, swallowing, in a choked voice, “Is there no hope for me at all?” He had fixed his eyes on hers, and she was disconcerted to see the sadness in his eyes, she had never thought when she had rejected him so vehemently, that she might hurt him. She said, pressing her reticule nervously against her skirt, “I have told my brother so.” When he lowered his eyes again, she said, hastily, “I am sorry, Monsieur, I am sorry,” her words rushed.

“I craved to hear it from your own lips,” he told her. When she said nothing more, he took a step back from her. “I am sorry if I have upset you.”

“I am not upset,” she told him hotly, although she was upset, and clutched her reticule tightly with both hands.

“I…you know that my prospects are…good?” Now he was unable to meet her eyes, apparently embarrassed at having said this. She was seeing him up close in the bright morning light, she realized that he wasn’t a plain man, as she had thought, but that his mouth was full and beautifully shaped, his nose straight and just the right length, his eyes, a light blue, held a clarity she had not seen in Pierre’s, where there was only that occasional, sudden flash of light that she so loved. He moved one foot back and forth an inch or two, his boot scraping the dirt, not seeming to notice he was doing this.

"I hope…I pray that you will forgive me," she said.

"If you should change your mind –" but she was already shaking her head, no. He sighed, looked off into the distance over her head, he was a foot taller than she. "I will have to find a bride soon," he remarked. "Father says I must give them grandchildren. As does *maman*." He smiled for an instant, gazing out over her head, then he lowered his eyes to hers, and repeated, gravely, softly, "If you should change your mind…"

"I will not," she said quickly, stepping back from him. *"Pardon, Monsieur,"* and stepped around him, her skirt brushing his trousers, to rush on toward the store, having to stop herself from breaking into a run. And yet, it was as if the cloth of her skirt were her own flesh, her leg under it tingling as if, naked, it had touched his.

CHAPTER TWELVE

Work

RISING THE NEXT MORNING in darkness she had forgotten, but as she stood before the mirror, memory came back – *today she might be with Harry again* – she had to grasp the washstand to steady herself. At the same instant she was touched by shame, wanted to turn back, to give him up, but just as quickly her need rose again. "We are both free," she muttered aloud, staring at her reflection floating in the stained, silvered glass. All she could make out in the lamp light turned low so as not to wake Charles was a mass of dark hair falling over the white shoulders of her nightdress, and two black eyes burning back at her. *I am still young; I am young;* had she spoken aloud, it would have been a cry. But surely he wanted only – he would desert her too, he would tell everyone – he could destroy her.

She grasped her hair into a thick plait, twisted it on her hand, pushed it back into a *chignon*, slid in hair pins, then rapidly tucked in the loose strands around her cheeks and ears, not taking her eyes off the mirror. Seeing how pale she was and fearing a comment from Mrs. Emery whose astuteness couldn't be discounted, she patted her cheeks to bring colour into her face.

Mrs. Emery was, unusually for her, already in the kitchen, the cook stove radiating heat and the kettle beginning to steam, when Sophie hurried in.

"You slept poorly?"

"Backache," Mrs. Emery replied. "The heat from the stove feels good. Tea will feel even better." Sophie was tying on her long apron, hurrying to check the pot of porridge, then gathering the cutlery for the table.

"When you have your tea why don't you lie down a while longer? I will take care of breakfast," Sophie suggested. Mrs. Emery murmured assent, peering glumly out the window into the darkness, surely able to see only the reflection of herself and the kitchen behind her.

After a moment, Sophie said, carefully not looking at her, reaching for the stack of plates, "I have something I wish to talk with you about." Mrs. Emery said quickly, "You been thinking about my proposition?"

"Oh, yes," Sophie said, "But this is something different."

"Then tell me now," Mrs. Emery said, her tone heavy. "I'll just sit down here." She pulled a chair from beside the work table and sat down with an audible thud. "Wouldn't rest a minute worrying about it." Sophie set the stack of plates onto the table.

"I want to – I wish to – start my own business." Seeing dismay followed at once by a kind of calculating interest appear in Mrs. Emery's face, she rushed on. "It isn't that I don't appreciate your offer to stay on here –" She hesitated. "But I need your help – I mean, your advice." She stopped again, looking imploringly at Mrs. Emery. "I – Mr. Adamson –"

"I knew it," Mrs. Emery said. "You are going off with him."

"No! Why would you think such a thing?" She could feel her face heating.

"He's a bachelor," Mrs. Emery said, unperturbed. "You're a pretty woman – a young one. They all want wives – they know they can't hardly manage out there without one," tossing her head to indicate the vast, empty prairie spread out around them. In her agitation, Sophie saw it suddenly as a gesture all the homesteaders made, that toss of the head toward the enemy, containing hate, as well as yearning. Mrs. Emery was scrutinizing Sophie's face without sympathy.

"I am not free to be anyone's wife; I cannot marry – we barely know each other –"

"Don't mind me," Mrs. Emery said. "It's only that – people –," she sighed, "People are watching."

What did that mean? Had someone seen them together the night they made love? But how could anyone have – it was pitch dark – or was it only that conversation on the street last evening? Mrs. Emery had probably already guessed the rest. And yet, she was not chastising Sophie, not trying to send her away, nor calling her an immoral woman. Sophie went on, struggling to sound calm.

"Mr. Adamson is going away for the winter months. He has offered me the use of his house and his furniture. My idea is this: I want to start a small café. A sort of resting place for ladies." Mrs. Emery sat without speaking, looking up at Sophie's face, her expression altering as she listened to one of disappointment, then to a kind of resignation that twisted Sophie's heart. But she had to think of herself first, just as Mrs. Emery was surely doing when she had taken on Sophie and Charles, as much as it was because she wanted to help them in their need.

"Maybe I should've grabbed that Lily when I had the chance. But I didn't like her looks – some of 'em, they get mistreated too much, they turn bad," she said. "Then there's no rescuing 'em."

"What do you mean?" Sophie asked, deflected from her aim.

"Didn't you hear? That Lily's gone over to Adelaide Smith's house." Sophie stared, speechless. "That's right," Mrs. Emery said, satisfaction mixed in with her indignation. "Mrs. Kaufmann told me. Had enough of being a servant, I reckon, and that Smith woman, she was just waiting to pounce. Mrs. Fancy Archibald is fit to be tied. Wants to see Adelaide thrown out of town."

She had seen Adelaide Smith and Lily only a few days ago in the Kaufmann's general store but intent on her own concerns, the fact of the two of them being together hadn't quite registered. They were off to the far side, well into the shadows where the Kaufmann's kept the dry goods. They had taken a bolt of fabric from the shelf and having unrolled enough of it to see the pattern, had carried it to the one window on that side of the store and were examining it there. They didn't look up at the jangle of the bell announcing Sophie's entrance. Sophie saw them from the corner of her eye and then didn't look in that direction again. She had seen Mrs. Kaufmann glance over at them, occasionally, as if to decide whether the two women were ready to make a purchase or not. Or perhaps she was looking to see if they were stealing.

It occurred to Sophie that had she been the one examining the dry goods, Mrs. Kaufmann would have stayed by her side discussing this fabric and that, and pulling down bolt after bolt from the shelves for her to imagine how her new dress would look, how the fabric would hang, whether the colour of the flowers sprinkled across it would look well with the colour of her hair and eyes. I might be wrong, Sophie thought, but it seemed unkind to her that Mrs. Kaufmann would offer the women no help. Women? Lily was perhaps sixteen. Unwelcome, the thought that Marguerite wasn't much older, came and went as quickly. Why could she not pity Marguerite? She remembered now that Mrs. Emery had said that what had happened to Lily was probably worse than beatings. Suddenly, she knew what that meant and a flush of revulsion, or perhaps it was something much deeper than that, passed over her, leaving her feeling shaky and uncertain.

"But – Lily is a free person. Surely she can go wherever she wants?" Mrs. Emery shrugged, then muttered, as if to herself, "No woman's a free person, the way I see it. Leastways, not a poor one, not one who is pretty much still a baby." Their eyes met, one seated, the other standing; simultaneously, both looked away, Sophie still puzzled, not understanding why she felt as ashamed as if she had been the one abused by a father. She felt ill, would have pulled out a chair and sat down too, but Mrs. Emery, not looking at her, said in a dull voice, "What do you need me for?"

Sophie succeeded in making her voice sound normal, toward the end, even brisk. "To come with me today to see his house. You are experienced in cooking for people. Come and see it and tell me if you think this idea could work. And what I would need, what problems I might run into." She lowered her gaze, "It wouldn't be proper for me to be in his house without another woman present. You know that," pleading now, even as she pushed aside the deepest reason for wanting Mrs. Emery to be with her. No, she insisted to herself. She needed her support; she was afraid to take this leap without at least talking it over with her.

"I'll come with you," Mrs. Emery said, spreading out her hands as if to show she had nothing to hide, and also, nothing to offer. "Don't know about your idea, though. And where does that leave me?"

"You can still sell your house. Or find another woman in the situation I was in when you took me in with such kindness. I will never stop being grateful to you for that. You saved me, Charlotte."

"Can't blame you for wanting to better yourself, I guess. And if you don't want this, here –" she gazed around her kitchen, "I'll just have to muddle along for a while more." She sighed, and as was her habit, gazed at the floor or the wall as she spoke, not at Sophie. "I think I knew from the start you wouldn't stay long. I always figured, if you got enough gumption –" She broke off. "Did he tell you when to come?"

Before she could answer, she heard Charles coming down the stairs, calling for her. She said over her shoulder as she hurried from the room, "He said he would be there all day today and we should drop in whenever it suited us."

Mrs. Emery said. "About two?" Sophie called back her agreement, lifting a protesting Charles who promptly pushed against her shoulder with both strong little hands and arms, wiggling in an effort to get back down again. The bigger he got, the stronger he became and the more unwilling to accept her constraints. How did women manage with five or seven or more of these little ones around? She knew the answer. Slapping, sometimes much worse, and just as bad, in Sophie's opinion, the big ones, the girls in particular, were the real mothers to the smaller ones. If Pierre should ever return and they had more children, there would not be more than she could manage. If Pierre ever returned. Hah!

HARRY ADAMSON WAS A TALL MAN, and to more comfortably accommodate his long arms and legs he had built his house slightly larger than most two-roomed bachelor shacks. A worn rag rug covered most of the floor in the main room that would be her dining room, extending under the rough wooden table with its four chairs with their pressed back designs, none of the designs matching any of the others, and all pulled close to the cook stove to keep the seated person warm in bad weather, or else to save him having to get up to reach the coffee pot or frying pan. A large kerosene lamp hung from a hook in the ceiling above. A tall cupboard, roughly made, stood against the same wall as the stove, its shelves containing a few cups and plates. On the opposite wall from the cupboard and stove, Harry had attached a long shelf on which a few books sat beside a stack of official-looking papers and a small sheaf of opened letters still in their torn envelopes. On either side of the shelf sat a threadbare armchair, and in the centre, under the shelf, and between the two chairs, was a backless, iron-framed couch, a second bed, covered with a neatly smoothed Hudson Bay blanket with its multi-coloured stripes. The one window, to the left of the outside door, faced east, which meant the morning light would keep the kitchen bright. The stove had been polished, the nickel trim shone and, judging by its lack of smudges, Harry had used stove black recently on the iron. The effect was surprisingly homey, she thought, and was already mentally trying to rearrange the furniture this way or that to make it work better for her purposes.

"Thanks very much for letting us come to see your house," she said, looking at his shoulder rather than his face.

"Room for one more table in here," Mrs. Emery announced. "Another four chairs if you move things around."

"Come and see the bed – the other room," Sophie thought he had flushed slightly, although it was hard to tell in the poor light.

"Your house is very comfortable," she told him primly, as if seeing it for the first time.

"For a bachelor shack," he said, laughing easily, standing by the bedroom door to usher them in. She wondered at his ease: Was he used to such subterfuge? An ugly, tan-coloured curtain rather than a door separated the kitchen area from the back room and this he had pulled back and hung onto a long nail pounded into the wall at, what was for Sophie, shoulder height. This room was smaller by perhaps a third than the first room, the single bed to the left of the door neatly made, a handmade quilt stretched tightly over it, and another, smaller rag rug spread in front of it. The floorboards around the rugs were still damp from washing and gave off the musty, wet odour that Sophie was all too familiar with from the floor of her homestead cabin, and that, stupidly, gave her a pang of homesickness she overcame almost as quickly as it struck. The single window directly across from the open doorway was curtained with the same material as the one in the kitchen, pulled across it, making it hard to see the room's detail. She wondered who had made the curtains for him, something she hadn't thought of when she had been coming each day to care for him during his illness.

"Here," he said. "I'll take the boy from you so you can have a good look." Surprisingly, Charles made no objection to being handed over to this stranger, immediately beginning to fiddle with the top button of Harry's shirt. Sophie thought that maybe Charles was wondering if this man was his missing father, or if it was only that he had gotten used to strange men at the boarding house, who, except for Sam Wetherell who seemed not to like children any better than he liked women, made a fuss over him as a handsome little man.

To her right, by the doorway, over a washstand with blue granite basin and pitcher sitting on it, a mirror hung, set too high for either Mrs. Emery or Sophie, both small women, to see into. A large cupboard, newly-made and still unpainted, stood against the wall opposite the bed, and a single wooden chair sat between the bed and the one window, where it served as the nightstand. The chair where weeks ago she had set his glass of water and their eyes had met with so disconcerting an effect.

"It seems very nice, Mr. Adamson," Sophie said, smiling at him and reaching to take Charles who had begun rubbing at his eyes with his fists and whimpered pitifully so that she had to laugh.

"He is missing his nap."

"Give him to me," Mrs. Emery said, "I'll just set down here and rest while you talk." She went into the front room and sat in the dubiously better of the two armchairs. Sophie handed Charles to her, and he settled himself into her lap, his head on her shoulder. Over the weeks of having him around Mrs. Emery – Charlotte – had overcome her faint distaste for the child, and now mothered him readily. It warmed Sophie's heart to see them sit that way, or it would have, were she not so intent on the real purpose of her visit, and on disguising it.

Adamson had followed Sophie back into the main room. He brought forward the kettle that already steamed quietly at the back of the stove, reached for his teapot and put in a handful of loose leaves taken from a tin on the shelves. Sophie sat at the table.

"There's enough room, " Mrs. Emery repeated. She held Charles, jiggling him gently, hardly seeming to notice she was. Harry was pouring the hot water into the teapot, then setting three cups on their saucers on the table.

"Boy's asleep," Mrs. Emery remarked. The adults halted in their motions to look at the child, marvelling in silence at the way small children could sleep. Sophie rose quickly and lifted the boy from Charlotte's arms and set him gently onto the couch in between the two armchairs. Mrs. Emery rose with her usual difficulty and sat down with them, remarking, "There's an extra table in the upstairs hall, been in the way up there since I bought the place. I don't mind lending it."

"I don't have many dishes," Adamson said. "But use what I have."

"I still have my porcelain," Sophie said, tentatively.

"Tsk! You mustn't use that, Mrs. Hippolyte," Mrs. Emery declared, aghast. "It will only get broken, or the gold will wear off from so much use. Don't even think of such a thing." Sophie had one day unpacked a plate to show her friend, whose eyes had widened, her mouth making an O. They had gazed in silence at the plate until Sophie reverently re-packed it. They both had sighed, turning away, the better to erase the reminder of such dreams as they once had.

"Then I will sell it," Sophie declared. Mrs. Emery set her teacup with a decisive click onto its saucer.

"I've got some old pots too," she said. "I'd be glad to get them out of the way." She pushed back her chair. "Now I have to get back." She turned to look at Charles who hadn't moved since Sophie had put him down. "Let the little one sleep. He'll be awake soon enough and you can come back then." Sophie had begun to rise, flustered, and Adamson said, his voice convincingly casual, "If you pick him up he's just going to wake up. I don't mind if you wait a bit. We'll just leave the door open and maybe sit outside until he stirs."

Mrs. Emery already had her hand on the doorknob. She opened it now, ostentatiously pulling it back and leaving it that way so that anyone passing by could easily see inside through the screen door. Sophie thought, she knows very well I could just pick up Charles and come with her, yet she is allowing me this. She couldn't bring herself to look at Charlotte.

"You come along as soon as you can. There's pudding to make." She stepped outside, closing the screen door carefully, and disappeared from view.

Sophie and Adamson sat listening to her retreating footsteps, not looking at each other. Now the only sound was the far off cry of an exultant hawk, his scream a dying fall. There was not a breath of wind, but flies still buzzed against the screen, it not having been cold enough yet to kill all of them. Harry went to the door, opened it a couple of inches to peer down the boardwalk, then quickly stepped back, reaching for the main door and pulling it shut too.

He said, "The street's deserted." Sophie had gotten uncertainly to her feet. He was at her side in two strides.

"The other room," he breathed, putting one heavy arm across her shoulders and turning her, pushing her gently before him into the back room, pausing only to pull the separating curtain off its nail. It dropped into place, swishing slightly. His mouth was on hers, already he was lifting her skirt, pushing her backward to the bed and falling onto it beside her. But he paused, sat up again, and when, puzzled, she raised her head, she saw that he was putting on a sheath. Then his mouth was on hers again, and she was lifting her hips to help him pull down her underwear. They clung to one another, scruples, niceties, even tenderness, all lost to their long-repressed desire.

It was over too quickly, Sophie didn't want to let him go, clinging to him until the waves of pleasure passed, their mutual grip slowly lessening, and he lay beside her panting as she too gasped for breath, one of his large hands resting, fingers spread and hot, on her abdomen. After a moment, she put both her own hands on his, gently lifting it aside, then pulled herself to a sitting position, struggling to re-button her bodice, to find her discarded clothing, to pull her twisted skirt around into place. But he pulled her back again, kissing her face and neck and shoulders so that she felt her resistance melting, and she kissed him back with such hunger that, far back of the overwhelming desire, she was faintly afraid of what he had roused in her, that it would be possible to lose all control. Out of that, she foresaw only ruin. There was no sound from the other room, no sound at all from outside the cabin. It was so quiet as to be eerie, but rather than relaxing her, she grew anxious, and then more so. He was still kissing her, his hands holding her breasts, one pushing away cloth to slide down between her legs again, but now she pushed him away, whispering, *"Non, non,"* rolled from under him, managed to stand although shakily, then rushed to the washstand, and without thinking, using his towel to wipe between her legs, splashing water onto her face, scrubbing her hands, then sniffing at them. Tremors still ran through her body and she nearly gave up her efforts to tidy herself, but then, fear spurred her.

"It's all right, here, it's fine." While she was cleaning herself, he had stepped out through the curtain, pushing it back, and hanging it on the nail again. "The boy hasn't stirred. The road is just as empty as it was five minutes ago." In her panic she hadn't heard him get up or leave the room. She fitted pins into her hair with fingers gone clumsy, then followed him into the kitchen.

"Only five?" she said, able to laugh a little now that her apparel and hair had been returned to respectability. He said, "More like ten, or fifteen, I reckon, hmmm?" He was moving slowly now, his voice had taken on a velvet, as if their encounter had reminded him that he was a man first, something that in his long bachelorhood he had nearly forgotten.

"Is my hair in place?" He studied her, smiling.

"Nobody would ever know. You look pretty." He was moving toward her again. She allowed him to kiss her, then stepped back.

"I have to hurry now, or Mrs. Emery will be suspicious."

"The boy is still asleep," he said, reaching for her again; she saw that he wanted to lead her back into his bedroom.

"No, Harry," stepping away."I don't dare risk it," although all she wanted was to throw herself again into his arms, to lie again with him in his stuffy little bedroom. "No husband would let his wife come into my tea room if he thought that I was an immoral woman." He let his arms drop to his sides, wordlessly acknowledging this, and she felt such regret, even as she stiffened her resolve, telling him, "Nor would any woman come in. Except perhaps Madame Beausoleil – and Mrs. Emery."

He said, "And Mrs. Smith," wryly, and Sophie breathed in sharply. "No, no," he said, seeing her dismay. "She wouldn't ever come in." He moved closer to her again, touching her face, her neck, her breasts, as if he hadn't just acknowledged that they mustn't. Once more she stepped back from him as he moved away from her, pushing at a soiled tea cup on the table as if he meant to knock it over. Seeing this, she felt a pang at his sadness or bitterness or whatever it was, and nearly succumbed again to his need, yearning to touch and soothe him, but forcing herself to turn away instead.

"I'll be leaving in another week, I think." His voice had returned to normal. "Let me know when you want to bring the table over, and the extra dishes. I'll help you. And I'll show you how to use the stove – you got to get the dampers just right. You can move in the minute I leave, if you want to." As he spoke, she had gone to the couch where Charles lay motionless.

"I can't abandon Mrs. Emery. I'll have to help her at least part of the time until I begin to earn a little money here. Then I'll move in." She was gathering her sleeping son into her arms, and she turned with him toward Harry again, and said, her lips barely touching her child's damp forehead, "Oh, Harry, how will we…?" She felt hot all over, and her breath was coming in short gasps, it was all she could do not to drop her child back on the sofa and run into Harry's arms again: A chance at a new life, destroying her link to Pierre as viciously as he had destroyed his to her. This thinking alone halted her; it seemed to her ugly, unkind, and anyway, surely, not true. Surely she was not so vile? She cared for Harry, she wanted to be close to him, she wanted…

"I'll try to think of a way," he said. "But if not, then next spring when I come back." His words sobered her, the heat sweeping through her dwindling, dying. How had she thought this would end? Mentally, she drew back a little from him: Did he think she was to be his easy woman for as long as he might want her? Wasn't this, after Campion's offer, just what she had struggled so hard to avoid? Nausea rose, and she swallowed it down, trying not to let him see how he had upset her. Charles stirred; tightening her arms around him, as if to secure him as the barrier between herself and Harry and all he stood for, she walked quickly to the door.

"I will let you know when I need help to bring the table over," she said, pushing open the screen with her shoulder and the arm that held Charles, turning only her head toward him. "Thank you again." And then, embarrassed, added, "I mean, for the use of your house. I cannot ever thank you enough." He laughed.

"You've already thanked me enough." She stopped smiling. "I didn't mean that. You know I didn't." She stepped out through the open door, letting it bang shut behind her, and marched around the corner and across the hoof-pitted street as Charles lifted his heavy little head and gazed around wonderingly. Let him not think that I'll be available to him whenever he wants me. *Let him not think that,* and she walked faster, her heels thudding onto the boardwalk, as if she were a much heavier woman than her appearance suggested.

But in the days that followed she forgot her pique, wondered if perhaps being angry at him was easier than admitting that, in her need, she had given herself too easily. A mortal sin, and hers, not his. Without Confession, childhood teachings rearing up to overwhelm her, how could she go on? But to be married forever to a man who had deserted her and his child! It was too much to bear, and she thought of the murmurs she had heard around town about this woman and man who weren't really married, though they lived together and claimed to be and even had children and God had not treated them any worse, as far as she could tell, than anyone else. Out here it seemed that people got along fairly well without churches and priests to rant, painting terrifying pictures of eternal hellfire, screaming of damnation. The memory of *Père Deschambeault* and his endless sermons, the pictures he repeated of flames burning forever struck her with the old childish terror. But didn't the church also say that even small children were sinners, a teaching that she felt defied all reason, and for the first time she thought, but it doesn't matter what the priest says: He is only a man after all. The perception made her snort out loud. *And so is the Pope,* in her anger, half-expecting to be struck down on the spot.

Her ruminations were blotted out by the memory of the intense pleasure they had shared, the joy of it, and the – she knew no other word for it – the feel of the *rightness* of it. When Harry had helped her move the table from Mrs. Emery's to his house, and then some of the pots and dishes she had managed to get together for her kitchen, they had walked briskly, not speaking or looking at each other, hadn't touched hands or bumped shoulders, or made any attempt to steal so much as a kiss. She couldn't have said why. Maybe it was only that now people were, indeed, watching, and both of them knew that to show the slightest sign of real interest in each other would confirm to the townspeople what was now only a suspicion.

She was scrubbing the floor when Mrs. Emery came into the kitchen. "Harry Adamson's out front. Come to say good-bye." Sophie dried her hands on her apron, untied it, threw it over a chairback, nervously patting her hair, and followed Mrs. Emery out to the street. Harry was seated on the wagon holding the reins but with both hands as if he meant to depart at once, but when he saw Sophie emerging from the house he tied them loosely and climbed down. She thought he seemed tense, there was a tamped-down eagerness in his eyes, as if he couldn't wait to be off. It reminded her of Pierre; she had often seen that look in Pierre's eyes, and had always glanced away from it.

"I'm dropping off my team and wagon at Williamson's," he told them. "They'll look after 'em in return for using them now and then. I'll catch the train at Swift Current."

"How far you going?" Mrs. Emery asked.

"I hear there's lots of work for a carpenter in Winnipeg. If I can't find anything there, I'll keep moving east."

"I didn't know you are a carpenter,"Sophie said, not quite meeting his eyes, although, perhaps she had known.

"A rough one," he replied. "I knocked up a bar on the inside of the door of my house. Gives you a little protection. Woman alone..." He shrugged.

Sophie said, "But surely –"

"Too much drunkenness in town, Mrs. Hippolyte. I don't like to say it, but there is, and with that house..." He tossed his head toward the end of town where the livery barn sat next to the new house with the askew windows. Mrs. Emery interrupted, "Now, don't you worry none, Sophie. You can sleep nights with the door barred."

"Thank you," Sophie said, staring down at the boardwalk, her hands at her waist, primly clasped.

"There's elements about these days. Social evils that seem to find us even out here."

Sophie wondered what she was referring to, and where that expression 'social evils' had come from, but decided against asking. Drunkenness, she supposed. And 'social evils' from the preacher, Oswald. She didn't know why exactly she'd taken a dislike to the preacher, wondered if it was only her Catholic sense of superiority to all such misguided upstarts who "invented their own religions," as grandfather had once said, meaning that the Roman Catholic Church was the first and only true church. For the first time ever she found herself wondering if that was true. Of course it was true.

"I put my old hammer and some big nails on that shelf. You hear any trouble, you bar the door, then you pound those nails down into the window frame so the windows won't open. You can pull 'em out later."

He stood there, staring down at her, until Mrs. Emery said, "Well, Godspeed, Mr. Adamson. I must get back to my work." She bustled back down her sidewalk and into her house. Neither Sophie nor Harry watched her go.

"If Hippolyte comes back..."

"I would not be afraid of him," she said, surprised.

"You don't know," he told her. "Maybe he'd want money, or –"

"Have you heard something?"

"Not a word, but if I do on my travels, I'll send a letter to Mrs. Emery."

"Thank you," she said. "And even if you don't, please send us a letter so we'll know you are all right. We'll worry, otherwise." She thought she detected a faint flush in his cheeks, and wanted to move close to him, to press her body against his, to have again what they had shared. She thought, too, she could feel his desire.

They stood looking into each other's faces, until he murmured, "People are watching," holding his head low so that she could barely hear him. Still, they stood.

"I will look after your house," she said, barely above a whisper.

"I know you will." Silence. "I have to get on my way or I won't make it to Williamson's before dark." They both looked up at the sky, and then to the western horizon. A long, smoothly-rounded bank of pale grey cloud had settled there, motionless. "Snow coming," he said.

"Au revoir, Harry," she whispered. "Until spring."

"Until spring," he said, climbing back onto his wagon. "Better get somebody to fix up the dirt banked around the house. I forgot about it. Floor will be too cold for the boy if you don't." She nodded, waited until he said, "Giddup," and the team began to move away before she too, turned and went slowly back inside.

And yet, his departure failed to cause her much pain, because she began at once to plan establishing her business, a task that occupied her mind so fully that for long stretches of time she didn't think of him at all. Evenings, after Charles was asleep, and as it grew too cold and the arrival of snow made walking on the prairie difficult, she would go to Harry's house and scrub and clean, just as she had been doing all day, and try the furniture this way and dissatisfied, move it back again. She arranged the pots and pans, she played with Harry's cook stove so she would know exactly how to work it, and despite the expense, kept a fire burning in it at all times so that the house didn't freeze so badly that it would take it several days to get warm again.

She discussed with Mr. Kaufmann, the storekeeper, where she might get supplies, swearing him to secrecy even as she knew that probably everyone in town knew exactly what she was up to. He ordered flour, sugar, coffee, tea and other staples for her, small quantities to get her started, since she hadn't the money – until her business was actually running – for more than for the first couple of weeks. With the names he suggested to her in hand, she went to this neighbour and that, offering to buy home-canned foods – vegetables, canned beef and chicken – enough to get her started, and to hire small boys to take care of chopping her firewood and bringing in a regular supply of water. She made arrangements with the butcher for meat from a frozen beef carcass, and if there had been a baker, would have made arrangements there for bread, pies and cake. There being none, she added that task to her own load. Some day, I will be in a town where there is a baker and the baker will do the bread, buns, pies, cakes, puddings, and cookies for me, she vowed. Night after night she counted her pennies, figured ahead to costs she saw no way to meet unless her business actually began to bring in money, the business she couldn't seem to get herself to start. When she wasn't adding and subtracting, she was muttering over how she would price things, what was too much, what was not enough, what people could afford to pay.

The day came in mid-November, when the house was more than ready, and every item she owned except her and Charles' night clothes were neatly stored in Harry's bedroom. She had only to walk from Mrs. Emery's house with Charles at her side, go inside, and close the door behind her. And yet she hesitated, and held off, and said to Mrs. Emery that she would move in the next day, it being such a cold night and besides, tomorrow was a bread-baking day and Mrs. Emery needed her. At last Mrs. Emery grasped her by the shoulders – they were facing each other in the kitchen, both of them still wearing their aprons, their day's work finished – and forced a surprised Sophie into a chair.

"Now you listen to me," she said. "I been watching you day by day for weeks now. You done everything to get that house right and ready, you got food, water, fuel, and I don't know what all else and there ain't nothing – nothing! – to keep you here in this house any longer. Tomorrow you go!" Sophie began to laugh and cry at the same time, digging in her apron pocket for a handkerchief, her nose running.

"I'm afraid," she gasped, finally.

"Don't you think I know it? That's why I'm after you," Mrs. Emery said, her tone exasperated, but with something less harsh under it. "After breakfast tomorrow I am walking you over there, and then I'm going down to the Kaufmann's and every other store on main street and I'm telling them your business is open. You hear me? By noon tomorrow you'll be cooking for ten."

Mrs. Emery made two more trips over to Adamson's house the following morning, once carrying two loaves of bread she insisted Sophie take, and the second time, two pies. After she was gone the last time Sophie found five dollars on the counter as well and would have run after Charlotte, but thinking, surely I have earned five dollars above room and board for Charles and myself, stopped herself. As she gathered the coins though, she remembered taking money from Frank Archibald and from Harry that first day in town, how she had suffered over it, and thought of giving it back – giving it back! – when she was desperate and penniless and with a hungry child! Grimly she pocketed Mrs. Emery's gift – What gift? *I have earned this a thousand times over*, and was only faintly ashamed at how hard she had become, knowing it was money Charlotte could barely afford.

By the time she had finished cooking, serving, and cleaning up after the noon meal for, not the predicted ten, but four curious townspeople and one stranger, she had to face the fact that she couldn't keep Charles underfoot. She had spent the several hours stepping carefully past him as he sat on the floor playing with the wooden horses Monsieur Roche, long returned to Québec, had given him, and of which he never seemed to tire, especially since Sophie had made him a half-dozen paper men to ride them, while she rushed back and forth from stove to table or into the back room which she also used as storage. He would be stepped on, or fallen on, she would spill boiling water or hot grease on him when she was in a hurry, she would be too busy to notice when he got too close to the stove and he would be burned.

There was a Mrs. Wozny who, some weeks earlier, had come to the boarding house looking for work, and been turned away by Mrs. Emery who couldn't afford to hire somebody for a wage. The woman's husband had died, she'd left the homestead to her grown sons and moved into a shack hastily thrown up by them, and had at least six younger children with her who prevented her from moving into the boarding house as Sophie had, to be paid in room and board. Now she was taking in laundry and doing housework for Mrs. Archibald – whatever might bring in a few coins each day. She wasn't an ideal caregiver for Charles: barely speaking English, uneducated, and staggering already under the burden of so many children. But it would be only over the noon hour, surely Sophie could counteract any bad influences during the much longer time she had with him, and when the weather was bad, her café would be empty, she could keep Charles with her and would save the day's cost.

Mrs. Wozny had shown no sign of surprise when she opened the door to Sophie and when Sophie had made her inquiry, answered, "Fifteen cents a day."

"Ten cents," Sophie said, to which Mrs. Wozny replied, "Them older girls do it."

"If the children care for him then it is worth only eight cents." Mrs. Wozny was stirring a kettle on the stove, cabbage soup, judging by the smell, and at this she turned her head to look over her shoulder at Sophie. Sophie stared back, trying not to blink.

"We do it. Eight cents," Mrs. Wozny agreed. "Start tomorrow. My girls help Mrs. Archibald today." For a long second Sophie looked at the other woman, across the gulf that separated them, of background, of birth, of education, of customs.

"No," she said, "I'm sorry. I will pay you ten cents a day."

The winter began in earnest, snow piling up outside the door, and Sophie had to add a new expense, this one to pay her boys who brought her water and coal and chopped her wood, to shovel the walk and steps into the café. In the days since she had served her first noon meal for five, she had eight at the noon meal until everyone in town had satisfied his or her curiosity, after which attendance had dwindled enough that she had been terrified that she'd made a mistake. The spectre of moving back into Mrs. Emery's stared at her, this time without the twenty-five dollars. Then, slowly, the business began to grow again as more people from elsewhere heard about it. Since then she had never had fewer than two, and had finally instituted two sittings at noon because she couldn't accommodate more than eight at a time and often had ten looking for a meal then.

Even as she smiled, and dropped the occasional remark into the conversation, she was calculating. Noons, charging forty cents a plate including coffee, she averaged around four dollars. Morning tea or coffee, and cake or pie, sometimes brought in as much as two dollars and afternoon tea did better. She served an evening meal only for those who had nowhere else to go. On her best days, she brought in ten to twelve dollars. Even with all the worrisome expenses involved, she calculated that by spring if all continued to go well, she would have perhaps a hundred dollars put away, if she was lucky, a little more. But wait, out of that she had to pay Harry Adamson rent, surely not more than five dollars a month. It was a shack, after all, not a proper house. When she thought that Mrs. Emery had practically to push her out the door before she could find the courage to take this step, she had to laugh. Never again, she told herself, as she lay exhausted in Harry's bed at night, would she be so unsure of her own judgement. Then, thinking of Pierre, who was never far from her mind, she qualified: at least, not when it comes to business.

She was wakened one night from the shallow sleep of the truly exhausted by the noise of pounding on her door. Without pausing to light a lamp, she stumbled from her bed into the other room, where the few cracks in the cook stove let flickers of light into the room, lifted the curtain, and peered out to see a bulky male figure swathed in a buffalo coat and hat with lowered earflaps, raising his fist to pound again, then falling into one of the snowbanks piled at each side of the door. She could hear his curses clearly through the thin wall as he fell, then struggled to push himself back onto his feet, and raised his fist to pound again. She had dropped the bar Harry had built for her before she went to bed, and now she wondered if she should get his hammer and nails to secure the window, then realized that he had only to raise his fist to break the frost-covered glass if he really wanted in.

But even as she debated, not really afraid, the drunk gave up and crunched and squeaked his way, falling and pushing himself up again, back down the icy sidewalk in the general direction of the other end of town. She supposed he wanted a meal – she hoped that was all he wanted – and hoped also that someone would let him in before he froze to death. Then it occurred to her that he was almost certainly going to Adelaide Smith's house, where he had probably gotten drunk in the first place. Maybe he had gone outside to relieve himself, and his drunken condition confused his directions, and had been pounding on her door thinking it was Mrs. Smith's.

Other than the drunk, no one else had bothered her, and with her business's success, she soon began sleeping well at night, rising only to add a lump of coal or more wood to the fire, and at once falling back into sleep.

SHE WAS JUST EMERGING from the back room carrying potatoes in her apron, when the door opened, letting in a wash of freezing air that swept through the main room and penetrated even into the bedroom. A male voice, which Sophie recognized at once as Constable Lewis's, boomed, "Any grub in here? I'm a starving man." Her other guests offered greetings, and one of the men, too loudly for the small space, said, "Shut the door, Constable. You're freezing us." Another said, "It's so cold out there I do believe hell has frozen over," causing everyone to laugh, as if the sally had never before been dreamt of, much less offered. Having been one herself, she was sympathetic to these homesteaders, who alone so much, when they met in groups, were infected with a giddiness that made the slightest attempt at humour seem hilarious to them. Or was it that their lives were so hard that they grasped at relief as a drowning man clutches a straw? She had seen a female homesteader break into tears when it was time to leave this tiny café to start the long, cold journey back into solitude.

"Yes, indeed, Constable," she said, referring to his request for grub, and putting a lilt into her voice."Today it is roast beef – for a change!" Everyone laughed again, because it was always roast beef, unless it was stew, or except on the rare occasion when someone would sell her either a pair of live chickens, or a jar or two of home-canned chicken.

She didn't like that look that passed between Mrs. Hartshorne and Mrs. Murphy, when the Constable entered. It was because the Constable, who had only recently replaced the bad-tempered Constable McMann, was single, handsome, and a known ladies' man. She felt a small, unpleasant shock, that even in her own house she couldn't behave as she chose without people watching her and telling others what they had seen. This was followed by a twinge of anger, quickly suppressed.

Her seven customers had turned back to their heaped dinner plates and the Mountie sat at the one with only three people. The conversation fell back to a normal level as Sophie served his plate and set it in front of him from across the table, thus avoiding getting too close to him, giving him a quick, impersonal smile as he lifted his head to thank her, turning back to the stove at once. She concentrated on her work, re-filling the kettle, pulling it forward where the heat was the most intense. In that small space it wasn't easy to avoid passing by him too closely, but she did her best, wanting to avoid the rush of feeling that came over her if she caught his tobacco smell, or the pomade he put in his hair, or whatever it was that emanated from him as a male that was less easily named. Sometimes in the night she twisted in her bed, and groaned aloud with longing, and was shamed by this. Always, Pierre came first into her mind at such moments, and then Harry Adamson.

Lewis was probably looking for a bride, but surely he knew she couldn't marry, so there could be only the one reason for his so far fairly inoffensive pursuit of her. She felt no attraction to him beyond that not so nebulous desire, and so avoided him even as she smiled at him, and used that lilt in her voice that seemed to charm all the men so that they would come back, a lilt that spoke of femininity without complexity, of angelic good nature, of a desire to please. *I have to survive*, she told herself, and if *le bon Dieu* gave her a pretty face, she would make good use of it. She knew there was a place where she was ashamed of this, but she did her best never to look at it.

It was her few women customers who brightened her days, people she could talk to rather than listen only, who understood how hard she worked, and what she suffered. But there was no denying that the men had the more interesting conversations, and it was from them that she began to learn something about the very world in which she had lived with Pierre for four years in isolation on the homestead. The men who passed through the town even during the worst months of the winter came to consider whether Bone Pile would be a good place to start a business, but went away again quickly when they discovered that no one expected the railway to reach the town for another year or two. Most of them, though, were looking for land to buy, in order to sell it again for profit when the time was ripe. She had even heard that a few were intent on getting together blocks of land so as to be able to drive up the price of any quarter. She supposed that Walter Campion would be one of those. She had heard too that they were all of the opinion that the railway and the Hudson Bay Company both owned far too much land and were setting too high a price on it, unimproved as it was, and that no matter what scheme they tried, the sections set aside for schools, whether used or not, were untouchable. It hadn't occurred to her that one might complain about government decisions. But who was government, she asked herself, but men – and men who had never been West themselves, although there was the Territorial Council, she now knew, but had no clear idea of what they did, beyond what she overheard in her café.

And yet, she would remember how it was on the prairie, the distinctive, faintly peppery smell of it, how the long grasses whispered and rustled in the steady wind, and then the perfect stillness of the early morning and the evenings when the only sound was the birds calling so sweetly to one another, as if it was their work to pull down the curtain on the day. How often she and Pierre paused to search the infinite layers of sky, looking there for what they did not know, how it vaulted over them, without beginning or end, yet reassuring in its constancy. They lived their lives only from sun up to sunset and from one day of work to the next, most day-night cycles punctuated by the indelible passion of their bed, yet their eyes always fixed on their goal of some day being the sole owners of a profitable farm. More than once when no one was around, she had wept and wailed aloud for all that she had lost, even as another part of her scolded that such emotion, left over from her childish years in the French village she'd come from, was a luxury she couldn't allow herself.

Now she listened carefully, trying to understand the ways in which the things she heard from the men in her café might be applied to enhance her own situation. She began to feel in some obscure way that she had an entire part of herself – of her mind, and maybe even her heart – that had never been opened and that she was slowly, carefully prying open that closed door, affording her a glimpse of a wider world beyond even the bold act of coming West, or of some other dimension that was also filled with possibilities.

Glancing over her shoulder as she poured hot water into the empty roasting pan, she saw that her customers were ready for their dessert. Hurriedly she gathered their soiled plates, stacking them in the small space under the cabinet to the left of the sink, and rushed into the back room to bring back Saskatoon pies. She cut them rapidly, put the slices on plates, and began handing them around.

"You need a bigger place, Mrs. Hippolyte," Mrs. Hartshorne declared, frowning when Sophie bumped the arm of one of the bulkier of the men, who had to bend to retrieve a fork that had fallen from the last plate she was now lifting.

"Or some help," Mrs. Murphy offered comfortably, as if didn't they all need more help and wasn't such a thing never available?

The itinerant farrier and the silent woman who travelled with him who looked to Sophie to be Indian, were pushing back their chairs.

She dried her hands on her apron, and went to her cash box in the bedroom, into which she dropped the coins the farrier had left. Every afternoon she took any profit to Frank Archibald who kept it for her in his safe, the best she could do until a bank came to town. Next, Jake Ambrose rose, the livery barn owner, the scent of horse wafting from him, borne to her on the freezing draught from the departure of the farrier and his woman. Then two men, strangers to her, speculators, she guessed, rose to go.

As she squeezed back again, the space not so tight now that five places had been emptied, she glanced quickly at Constable Lewis's plate. Was she mistaken or was he eating unusually slowly? But then the two farmers' wives began to stir as if they were getting ready to leave. Hastily, not wanting to be left alone with the Constable, she said, "Ladies! Allow me to offer you another pot of tea." The two women, flustered by the unexpected suggestion, looked at each other, smiled, and awkwardly reseated themselves. As Sophie brought the teapot to the stove to refill it, she noticed the Constable's moustache twitching. He began to wield his fork with more speed. "Do have more pie," she said sweetly to the women, at which point Constable Lewis stood noisily, threw coins onto the table by his plate, and went to the door.

"Constable, no tea?" she asked.

"I have no time for tea today," he said, clamping his hat onto his smooth black hair, and went out without another word, closing the door unnecessarily loudly, causing the two female customers to stare at it.

"Why Mrs. Hippolyte," Mrs. Hartshorne said daringly, "I do believe the Constable wanted you all to himself!"

"He will have to try harder than that," she told them gayly, rushing to set the pie on the table along with a serving tool.

"At least he ain't a married man," Mrs. Murphy said, waiting her turn for the pie.

"I hear he has other vices," Sophie said. "They say he –" she twisted her torso away from the dish pan to whisper the word over her shoulder, "gambles."

"No!" Mrs. Hartshorne declared. "Such a terrible vice that one be. You are better off without him, my dear," she added, popping a forkful of pie into her mouth.

"Better off without a husband at all," Mrs. Murphy said. "Baby followin' after baby." Even from the other side of the table Sophie could feel Mrs. Hartshorne's disapproval of this comment.

Mrs. Hartshorne inquired, "Have you seen the woman yet?"

"Which woman?" Sophie asked.

"Calls herself Mrs. Smith."

"I passed her on the street once," Sophie said. "She's not very friendly."

"Hah," Mrs. Hartshorne declared. "She is too friendly for anyone's good." Mrs. Murphy put her hand over her mouth to hide her laugh. She said, "Talk is that that Reverend Mr. Oswald that comes through now and again? Gives a service in Mrs. Archibald's parlour until he raises enough money to get a church built? Talk is he will drive the hussy out of town." The only sound was Mrs. Hartshorne sipping her tea. "Of course, he is a Methodist," Mrs. Murphy added. "I am Presbyterian myself."

"Well, you must know, Mrs. Hippolyte," said Mrs. Hartshorne, "about the girl Lily." Sophie nodded. "That woman promised her fancy dresses, some money of her own in her pocket, a little fun. What kind of fun do most girls get out here? It's just work and more work."

"She's ruined," Mrs. Murphy said, comfortably. "No decent man would have her now."

"I heard," Mrs. Hartshorne told them, lowering her voice, "That Mrs. Oswald and Mrs. Archibald went over to see Mrs. Smith."

"Whatever for?" Mrs. Murphy asked.

"Hard to say, but I think maybe to try to get Lily back?"

"You'd think all that would be Constable Lewis's job."

"If you ask me," Mrs. Murphy said, colour rising in her cheeks,

"That Constable Lewis is a little too friendly with that Adelaide Smith himself." Mrs. Hartshorne gasped.

"They should of taken Mr. Oswald," she said firmly. "He'd of set them two straight."

Sophie couldn't stop herself from asking, "So what happened?"

"All I know is that they came back out again in a hurry, and they didn't look none too happy." Mrs. Murphy laughed out loud at this and Sophie, picturing it, would have too, except that she kept thinking about what Mrs. Emery had said might have happened to Lily, and found herself shuddering.

"They will find a way to remove her, I have no doubt," Mrs. Murphy said. "This can't go on. There are children here."

"Tsk, tsk, tsk," Mrs. Hartshorne agreed. "But what can they do?"

"Just take her to another town, I reckon," Mrs. Murphy said. "The Mountie says he can't get rid of her until somebody gives him some evidence she's breaking the law." Mrs. Hartshorne snorted yet again.

"All he has to do is sit there after midnight and count 'em comin' and goin'." Sophie wondered how Mrs. Hartshorne knew that. Despite her business, or maybe it was because of it, she knew herself to be isolated from the everyday life of the town, and uncomfortably knew that she had somehow chosen this. "It's as if –" Mrs. Hartshorne paused, then went on, a plaintive note in her voice, "as if somehow they don't want her to go –"

"Oh, now," Mrs. Murphy interrupted. "I have heard with my own ears the men saying she must go. We all know she must go."

More disturbed by all of this than she could understand, Sophie said, "I must run down the street and get Charles. Mrs. Wozny will have had quite enough of him by now." She hurried into the bedroom for her mantle, and before either woman could speak again, went to the door. "Will you look after the place for me for ten minutes while I get my baby?"

"Sure and we will," Mrs. Murphy declared and Mrs. Hartshorne murmured assent through a mouthful of pie, grateful, Sophie thought, to have reason to stay in the warmth and comfort of her room for a little longer, where they didn't have to worry about making tea or pies or straightening up the room. What luxury it was to them. No one knew that better than she did, Sophie thought.

As she hurried down the path, snow banked up on either side, she was thinking, where had all that talk about faithfulness, about sacrifice, about prayer, gotten her? The most prosperous woman in town was Adelaide Smith. And had she not, one sleepless night when she had stepped out of the house to get a little fresh air, seen Frank Archibald hurrying across the street to his own house as if he were coming from Mrs. Smith's? And yet she had heard him with her own ears sitting in her café, saying that something would have to be done. She wondered what went on between Mrs Archibald and her husband when they were in bed together every single night. Or maybe they slept in separate rooms now.

Before she quite realized it, Adelaide Smith and what she did for a living came into her mind, thoughts of how such acts might play themselves out in real life – the strange man undressing in her boudoir – no, not boudoir, a homely room with a hard, narrow bed, no decorations, no silks, no perfumes, probably freezing cold too, in this weather – herself stripping off her clothing – Here Sophie came back to herself. But the moment between the anonymous man, the voluptuous Adelaide with her hard face and frizzled, too-red hair insisted itself into her mind's eye. It – the act itself, then the money coming from the man's pocket and Adelaide's taking it in a hardened boredom as she threw a wrapper over her nakedness. She gave the man a beard, then took it away in favour of a poorly-trimmed moustache. Made him fat, gave him an appalling odour of dried sweat, saw his unlovely elbows and knees, scarred and rough, and then allowed herself a glimpse of his genitals.

Inadvertently, her hand came to her forehead, she had been about to cross herself. But the picture of the man's body made ugly by work, accidents and hardship, the woman's falling breasts and protruding stomach without her stays, her fiercely-died hair, and that air of clamped-down emotion that she had observed on every occasion Sophie had seen her, made her drop her hand to her side. They were, surely, no different than she was, only that she was younger and still had a pretty body, despite her baby. But Lily looked as if she hadn't had a good meal in her life, as if she'd been born with the bruises on her arms, as if they were her natural state. She was filled with pity for the girl, even as distaste rose. She scurried, slipping and nearly falling, on the hard-packed snow that formed a path to Mrs. Wozny's where she knocked, too loudly, on the door.

NOT LONG AFTER she had put Charles to bed, she heard again the tell-tale creak of footsteps on the snow outside her cabin, judged them to be a woman's, followed by a firm knock on her door. She had been sitting quietly mending Charles's small trousers by the light of the kerosene lamp, tired out from her long day, yet not really wishing for her bed. She set aside her mending, crossed the room, lifted the curtain, then, seeing that it was Mrs. Emery at her door, she kicked aside the folded blanket she used to stop the draught coming from under it, lifted the bar, and pulled the door open. Mrs. Emery hurried in, red-cheeked and puffing, riding on a freezing blast.

"Is something wrong?" Sophie began.

"Well, yes and no," Mrs. Emery responded, beginning to unwind the shawl she had thrown over her head and shoulders, even as she stamped her feet on the rag rug to throw off the snow on her boots. "Mrs. Tremblay is in my parlour. Poor thing, she couldn't bring herself to come here, so she came to me instead. I told her I'd see if you'd talk to her." Sophie stood, frozen. "Now, Sophie," Charlotte went on. "You just put on your things and go over. Poor woman is in a state." She had begun to take off her mantle. "I'll stay here with the boy. Now off you go." Sophie could only think that now that the moment finally had come upon her, her chief thought was that Mrs. Tremblay would know what had become of Pierre.

When Sophie was dressed in her warm outerwear, her hand on the latch, Mrs. Emery said, as if she had just remembered meaning to say this, "She is so ashamed, torn between her daughter who has ruined herself, and her grandchild that she wants so badly, and you. She knows you're a decent woman. She says she is so sorry –" Sophie pulled open the door and stepped outside, shutting the door on Mrs. Emery's voice, hardly noticing she had.

Grandchild! It was as she had feared – so much so, that she had been unable to think in any rational way about the possibility. Marguerite was expecting a child, a half-sibling to her own beloved Charles: Pierre would never come back now. She knew it, she wanted to fall full-length on the hard–crusted snow and beat her fists against it. Pierre, in his desperation to escape their life, had fallen low; now he had dragged her down with him. It was all she could do not to scream aloud. All his protestations of his great, unending love for her; his ecstatic praise of her body, his near worship of it. And this, this it had come to! Rage, too, propelled her, stomping across the snow-packed street.

Already the cold was seeping through her mantel, her toes were curling in protest against it; she was wracked with shivering, as she hurried, the deep cold rendering the path icier even than usual, slipping and catching herself. Off balance, staggering like a drunk, she reached Mrs. Emery's verandah, where she paused with one hand on the railing, the other lifting the mantel's trim at her shoulders to press the fabric over her mouth and nose, against the air so frigid it couldn't be breathed except through cloth lest it freeze her throat and lungs.

She was through the door, was in the hallway removing her hat, mitts, her heavy coat and boots, and then opening the door into the parlour where a fire burned and Mrs. Tremblay sat perched on the edge of the horsehide sofa, much as Sophie had only a few months before asking for refuge, and as though she expected momentarily to be sent away. The woman's eyes were red and swollen, she held a cotton handkerchief in one hand and passed it to the other, then passed it back again, crumpling and straightening it only to crumple it again. At this sight, Sophie's rage deserted her, replaced by a colder anger.

"Let us speak *en français, n'est–ce pas?"* She was not unaware of the irony of choosing to return to her native tongue at a moment of extremity when so often she seemed to have repudiated it. Mrs. Tremblay, a small woman grown even smaller by her life of unrelenting work, had the largest, darkest eyes Sophie had ever seen – they were like holes in her bony face. She nodded, never removing them from Sophie's. "Madame Tremblay, I do not hold you responsible for your daughter's transgression." Sophie, in view of Mrs. Tremblay's alarm, thought it best to make this clear. Tears poured down Mrs. Tremblay's cheeks.

"I thought she was ruined," she said, her voice so soft Sophie had to listen closely to hear it. "But she says that *he* is getting your marriage annulled, that the priest has told him it can be done, and that before their baby is born, they will be married."

Sophie found herself sitting.

"Annulment?" she whispered. Mrs. Tremblay lowered her eyes, wiping them with the handkerchief, and the sight of her tears angered Sophie so that she demanded, "Where is he? Is he here?" She was not too upset to notice she had left Marguerite out of the question.

"They are travelling to Québec for the annulment." Now she stared at Sophie, while her hands crumpled and straightened the piece of cloth.

Sophie said, "He will seek an *annulment?"* She paused. "An annulment of our marriage?" her voice rising. "We were married by a priest; it was a legal marriage. We have a child, a son, he cannot…"

"I know nothing about that," Mrs. Tremblay said hurriedly, raising one hand as if to protect herself from the onslaught of Sophie's emotion. Such a frightened little woman she was, Sophie thought, contemptuously.

"The priest said that they are very hard to get. That is why *he* wants to go back to Québec – to see a priest there."

"He is still my child's father. How does he plan to annul that?" Sophie demanded. Then, trying to get command of her thoughts,

What was it she had waited all these months to hear? "Did he send a message for me?" She hated herself for asking. Mrs. Tremblay blinked and lowered her eyes again.

"He told Marguerite that he was sure you would have taken the boy and gone back to Québec."

"From where was I to get money to go back?" Her rage had returned and she sat rigid, trying to contain it.

Mrs. Tremblay said, "I had to tell you how sorry I am. Marguerite is a child, she made the mistake a child makes, even now she can't see what harm she has done you. But I am a woman too; I suffer too; I know what she has done to you." She produced this torrent of words in a low voice. "Jean, her father, Monsieur Tremblay, he says he won't take her back, she can't come back, she has to stay with *him*. I want only to see her, and to hold my little grandchild –" She buried her face, sobbing, into her handkerchief.

What use was there to be angry with this woman, who, even as Sophie pitied her, she also wanted to shake by the shoulders until she gained some backbone. She drew in a deep breath through her nose, mouth closed, straightening her back, placing her feet together neatly.

"I pity you Madame," she told the other woman in a voice that was as cold as an Englishwoman's. "What's done is done. But I do not wish to meet Marguerite – or Pierre –" her voice rising on the last word, "And I will never – never – *jamais* – see their child. That child will never know my child. Tell them that." She got up from the sofa, rushed from the room, replaced her mantle over her shoulders, pulled on her boots and went outside.

She would concentrate all her energies on escaping from Bone Pile so that she would not have to be reminded of this every single day, for now she saw at last that Pierre's action was deliberate; she saw now that his sale of the farm went beyond mere impulsiveness. He had done it so that he would be forever free of her and of their marriage, so that he could never go back. He had repudiated his own son. As for his talk of annulment – she had no idea what if anything she should do and for an instant wished she could find a priest to talk to, then squashed the thought. *Le bon Dieu* knows I no longer want to be married to that blackguard. Let him do what he wants. *But he will never see Charles again.*

As she walked through the freezing darkness, not even feeling the cold this time, she thought how strange it was that a life could begin in such a normal way as hers had, and go on so easily, until suddenly, one day, God struck out and in one crushing blow erased all those happy years, and she, never knowing what it was she had done to lose His favour. She lifted her eyes to the star-ridden sky above her, all those little eyes, she thought, shining in the darkness, watching us all. *Do your worst*, she told them aloud. *I will never beg; I will only carry on.*

CHAPTER THIRTEEN

Fire

SHE OPENED HER DOOR one cold morning on her return from taking Charles to Mrs. Wozny's house, to find a man sitting at the table, his back to her, warming his hands over the cook stove. She was startled, but already he was rising, turning back to her, smiling in a not-quite friendly way.

"Mrs. Hippolyte," he said. She saw that it was Walter Campion, and a jolt of fear passed through her, some fleeting thought that having taken the farm, he might now be after her café, but then, she reminded herself, what she didn't own, he couldn't take. He shifted the chair around to face her and sat down again.

"Mr. Campion," she said, withholding warmth from her voice. She closed the door firmly, pushing against it, shaking out her shawl as she crossed the room to hang it on its hook just inside the bedroom, doing the same with her mantle while he watched her in silence.

"I helped myself to some coffee," he said. "I hope you don't mind."

"Certainly not, Monsieur," she said, but stiffly, her back on him as she moved kettle and coffee pot around in order to check the fire.

"I put another stick of wood in," he said. "Didn't want it to go out on you. It's a bad cold day, it is."

"You are here for breakfast?" she asked.

"Didn't know you served breakfast."

"I do not," she answered, "But of course I will make an exception for you." Now she sounded simply angry, and smiled quickly, to mask it. She could see that he wasn't fooled, nor did he mind much her anger. "I have salt pork, I have fresh bread, but the chickens are not laying in this weather. There is porridge."

"Some of that fresh bread would be just the thing," he said. She went to the narrow counter under the shelves that held the dishes and began to cut the bread. She put two fresh slices onto a plate, carried it back to the table, not even bothering to toast it on the stove, and set the plate down in front of him. She had already placed a pat of her dwindling supply of butter on a saucer before he had come, and now, pulling his chair into the table so that there was room for her to stand at her customary place by the stove, he reached for it.

"You are here on business?" she asked. He chewed, swallowed, sighed, leaned back in his chair making it groan as he tipped it back. Seeing her disapproval, he quickly dropped the front legs and put his heavy arms in their wool tweed on either side of the plate of bread. There was a good fire in the cook stove, but the heat it gave battled the cold seeping in from outside. Even then, or maybe because of it, a curlicue of steam rose an inch or two above the rim of his thick cup. She fixed her eyes on the steam, and waited in the posture of every homesteader, back as close to the stove as she could place herself without scorching her dress. The smell of the burning wood, its crackle and sometime thud occupied her; she nearly forgot Campion sitting so close to her that her skirt brushed the back of his chair. He moved, about to speak, and she stepped quickly away from the stove.

"I come here to take you away," he said, amiably, and with his foot pushed out the chair across from him for her to sit on. Reluctantly, she did, his words having made her unsteady, even as she loathed his rudeness.

"What do you mean?"

"Word of this business of yours has spread. Ran into somebody in Regina who just came through Bone Pile. Said your prices are low, you make fresh bread, cakes, pies, roast beef every day, pots of thick soup, lots of taste to it, fresh biscuits with it, place always clean, friendly as can be. Said people like coming here." He wasn't smiling as he spoke these words, but was instead studying her, his eyelids partly lowered so that she couldn't see into his eyes and had only the impression of cunning, and something else – a shrewdness in his judgement of her that she felt, possibly, flattered her. Although she did not want his flattery.

"I do my best," she told him, "But it's hard to get supplies, my space is small, and I should really have help. And when I began a few months ago, I had very few customers. For a while I was afraid I might have made a mistake." She laughed, prettily, aware of the falseness of the sound, not knowing what to do or say to him, and not able to get control of her uneasiness.

"I can put you in a better place," he said, as if she hadn't spoken.

Again, she said, "What do you mean?" And after a moment, trying to clarify, "There are no other available buildings in this town. I don't want to go into debt to build." He lowered his eyes to the thinly-steaming coffee, lifted a spoon, turning it in his fingers, then set it down decisively. "You'll never make any real money this way. You can break even, you can even put some aside, but I'll wager that if you can't handle more customers, you're going to be stuck here in this place forever." She had thought this herself, but did not like hearing it, especially not from him. "Has Mr. Hippolyte returned?" he asked, his eyes on the table.

"Surely you know he has not." Then, her composure slipping a little, "Have you seen him?"

"I haven't seen him since the day last summer when we went to the lawyer together." She stared at him, but he was still not looking at her. "Makes it hard for you," he said. "The church not allowing you to marry again."

"As it happens, Mr. Campion," she said, her voice tight, "it seems I don't need a husband to survive."

He glanced at her, chuckling as if her spiritedness amused and pleased him. Ahh, here it comes, she thought.

"I am here to persuade you to start a new business in a bigger town, over by the Cypress Hills."

"Garden City?" He nodded, yes. "Why?" she asked. "Why do you want to help me?" He said nothing, and she wished she hadn't asked, realizing that his goal would never be to help her, but to find another way to help himself. She was to benefit enough to persuade her to help him do so. "What are you proposing?" Other questions crowded in, but she held her tongue, counselling herself: *Wait.*

"Garden City is growing by leaps and bounds – good business opportunities there for somebody. Every single train through leaves behind settlers and speculators looking for land, others looking to buy cattle and horses, big lots of 'em." He paused, picked up the spoon again, then set it down. "The Truesdale brothers are building a hotel there. It's going to be a quality hotel – none of your boarding house bedbugs or crowding and filth. With a proper lounge and facilities. Big chairs in the lobby for people to wait and visit together. Indoor plumbing," he said. "Electricity." He paused to glance at her as if to assess how this news was affecting her. "They want a dining room for it. I'm doing a bit of business with the brothers and I said I'd find somebody good, clean, reliable, to run the dining room. Good dining room – people will choose the hotel just for that service.

She sat, looking away from him, thinking. A larger town, more people, a bigger room for her café, maybe a hired girl would even be possible so that she could get some rest now and then. And if she worked less hard, she would be able to serve breakfast too. Maybe there would be a laundry, a butcher, a bakery, so she wouldn't have to do all the work herself. A bigger town meant a real school for Charles. She turned to Campion, to find him watching her, but the instant she looked at him, he dropped his eyes back to his coffee.

When she had left Mrs. Emery she had said to herself, in her private accounting, that she had made her first, longed-for, step forward. She knew she had to make another one, and not a day passed when she did not consider how she might do so. Could it be that Campion would be the instrument of that next step? As he had once been the instrument of her disaster? They sat silently, she waiting to hear what more he would propose, he silent for what reason she didn't know. Maybe it was only to give her time to consider what he had already said to her.

"You are in business with these Truesdale brothers."

"I am," he said. "Just a small part. An incentive, to get them to build faster. Garden City needs that hotel. I need it. It's a cattle town, I'm in it often on business. I'm tired of crowded boarding houses or having to sleep at the livery barn because there's no room. The Territories are moving forward," he told her. "They are getting modern."

"I like the idea in principle," she said. "But I foresee many complications."

"No business is without complications. I like complications," His shoulders raised and lowered as he chuckled in a secretive, pleased way. She could imagine him doing that when he was alone and a deal had gone his way, or he had succeeded in fooling someone to his own advantage. In that instant she found him disgusting. But wait. He was offering something she might be able to use.

"I need to be able to trust you, Monsieur," she said, her heart pounding at her own audacity. "How do I know I wouldn't be joining the enemy?" He lifted his head, his eyes glinting.

"That farm of yours? Hell – pardon me – that was just business. Business is all it was. And look – you came out all right, didn't you?" She could feel her lips pursing tightly, her cheeks growing hot, and breathed through her nostrils.

"I do not have you to thank for that," she told him. But what use was it now to show her anger?

"The boys hauled in the lumber for the hotel a week or two ago from that sawmill in the Hills. Soon as it warms and melts they'll be building. Once they get started that hotel will be up and running in no time. Say, four months from now. And the dining room needs to open with it. I can't wait long for an answer." Footsteps could be heard coming down the narrow trail shovelled in the deep snow outside the cafe's door.

"Are you staying in town overnight?"

"I can," he replied. For an instant, she wondered where he would stay, then thought that he had to be sleeping maybe in her old bed at

Mrs. Emery's, or perhaps the Archibalds would put him up. Mrs. Smith's house crossed her mind, but the thought that a respectable man of business might simply go there for a place to spend the night scandalized her, even as she wondered if in this too, she was being naive. Men, she was learning, did not view the world in the same way women did, paying lip service to the women's view, but going about in secrecy in a different, less moral world. To join Campion, would she be joining that world too?

The door was creaking open now, the usual cloud of freezing air filling the room.

"I'll need an answer tomorrow morning."

"My answer," she said, ponderously, "Will depend on how you answer the questions I put to you." She stood, turning to the newcomers, a Galician farmer and his towering son, their clothing frozen stiff, creaking as they moved, and radiating cold, both of them, she knew, speaking only a few words of English. It would be a struggle to find out what they wanted and to tell them how much it would cost. They pounded their heavy mitts together, trying to put life back into their frozen fingers.

"Good morning to you," she sang, her practiced smile already on her face. "Come in, come in. It is so cold out there today – another blast of winter," she said, using exaggerated gestures to invite them into chairs. "Sit down here, warm your hands at my fire," miming her hands out to the fire, fingers spread, palms down. When she turned back to the first table in order to go around it to the stove, she saw the door closing on Campion's back.

After the farmer and his son had gone she cleaned, washed dishes and put them away, baked a cake and put it away too, and then, having decided that no one else would be coming in – the day was getting colder and now the wind was up; it was too cold even for the hardiest – she pulled on her boots and heavy wool coat, wrapped her wool shawl around her head, thrust her hands into her fur-lined mittens, and went down the street to retrieve Charlie from Mrs. Wozny's clan.

She carried him back through the frozen grey day, occasional gusts of wind blowing snow into her face so she couldn't see where she was going for moments at a time, cloud banks, low and grey, were moving closer and shutting out the wide glow of the sky. A storm was coming. Charles had grown heavier and taller in the few months since they'd come to Bone Pile, was almost too big for her to carry now, and she tried not to let him overbalance her and tip them both into a snowbank as she hurried back to Adamson's house which she realized she had, over the months, begun to think of as her own. It was not often she had enough time for Charles, or what felt to her like enough time, although she was well aware that the other women who were farm wives or worked at doing laundry and ironing, or sewing, or cleaning to support their children, would consider five minutes spent giving a child full attention too much and would spoil him. In the privacy of her rented home though, whenever she could, she played with him, talked to him and sang to him for an hour or even two.

"I'm hungry, *mama*," he sang into her ear now.

"You are always hungry, my sweet," she sang back to him, so that he giggled.

"What did you do today?" she asked, as she moved along the narrow trail of hard-packed snow.

"Played horsies," he said, the question seeming to bore him. "Played wedding." She started at this, wondering what he meant, but then Mrs. Wozny had only daughters who would play at being married, and of course Charles would be the bridegroom, this without his having the faintest idea what that meant. She would have to explain it to him, she supposed.

Whenever she could find a book, she read stories to him, for the first time in her life studying the bible, one given her by the minister, Mr. Oswald, having come from a world where ordinary people did not read the bible – unless they were Protestants who, she had heard, read it themselves. He had come into her café one afternoon when she was between the noon meal and the evening one, had quizzed her politely about her faith: "You are a Roman Catholic, I believe?" watching her solemnly.

"I was, of course, raised as one. Where I come from everyone is Catholic," she said, "Although there was a whole English, Protestant world right in our midst and we just pretended they didn't exist, as they pretended we didn't." For the first time, she understood that this had been a strange way to live, especially now that it occurred to her that here in the West Galician, Scottish, French and others worked and built and entertained themselves together. "We laughed at them, as they laughed at us, instead of trying to live together." She was frowning, the lessons of the nuns spinning in her head about war and being overwhelmed and...whatever else.

He said, "There is no priest here, no church." She nodded, nervously, not liking that he seemed to be standing too close to her, that he was keeping her from her work, not liking the gaze he fixed on her from his too-piercing brown-gold eyes, strange eyes, unpleasant eyes. "I come every third Sunday to conduct a service in the Archibald's parlour. We are looking for a house, maybe even here, but in the meantime, sometimes the Olsons and sometimes the Archibalds put us up. I hope you will join us next Sunday. We are here for the week." She swallowed, grasped a chair back as if planning to sit down, lifting a foot and putting it down again. *Never, in a million years.*

"I am not a Protestant," she said, lifting her voice into prettiness. "But thank you for thinking of me."

"I think of your eternal salvation," he said, although mildly, and she felt a twinge of revulsion in her chest that she subdued quickly.

"I cannot," she told him firmly. "It is the church's teaching. I am sure you know that."

He had been carrying a cloth bag, like a woman, and at this, he reached into it and pulled out the bible, a cheaply printed one, but new, and had handed it to her. If a Catholic priest came to her door, she had wondered when Oswald was gone, what would I say to him?

She read the bible in wonder combined with a horrified semi-reverence and with the deepest interest, selecting only certain passages to read aloud to Charles for their beautiful sound, so that he might learn to love poetry. That Mr. Oswald had been thinking of converting her to Protestantism she found ridiculous. As with most Catholics, she felt sure, it would be Catholicism or nothing. It shocked her to realize she was leaning toward nothing. Maybe, she thought, it wouldn't be possible to extricate herself fully from the church she was raised in. Such an all-encompassing world it was, touching everything, a belief system without which she would find herself emptied of all richness in life. Yet, all around her, people survived very well without it. She didn't know what to make of this, but kept on reading parts here and there from the bible to her son, not sure why she was doing so. As a substitute, perhaps, for the lack of religious training or even church going, a lack she felt strongly, but made no move to change.

Once in a while when her day's work was done, she would drop in to visit Charlotte Emery. They would settle into her parlour where Charlotte would stretch out on the sofa, Charles would seat himself on the floor with his toys, and two women would chat about the weather, about their housekeeping difficulties, and any gossip either of them might have come across. Sophie enjoyed these visits, they were a welcome break from her own company and from the tiny house in which she lived and worked. Charles too, slept better after he'd spent an hour or two in a different house.

Not long ago a box of worn, homemade toys and ragged books had arrived from the Hippolytes. She was able to receive mail as she always had, here at the post office in Bone Pile where it had always been held for them until they could get into town to pick it up. Thus, she didn't know if anyone back home knew that Pierre had left her. If they did know, although nobody gave any indication of it, Pierre would have told them, which she doubted. But on his travels with the new woman he might have run into someone else from their home district, had told that person, who then relayed the story back to the village and their families. Nevertheless, whether they knew or not, how grateful she had been for the books and toys. There was never anything from Guillaume and Claire, nor from Hector and Isabelle, not that she had expected to hear from them.

Still, it hurt, made her both angry and glum, and she was glad that Charles didn't know them and so didn't miss letters or gifts from them. Sometimes when both the books and the toys failed to amuse him, Sophie would make up stories and tell them to him. In their spare hours she had even begun to teach him to read, tracing the letters of the alphabet in flour that she scattered onto a table, asking him to repeat the names of the letters after her, or to identify them and name them to her. She was filled with pride at how quickly he learned. In her plans for the future she now included a good school – not a homesteader's anything-will-do school, but a really good school for him.

Then she would mentally count the money that Mr. Archibald kept in his safe for her, hoping against hope to get enough together to start a fund for Charles' education. All the time, in the back of her mind, praying that Frank Archibald was, at least in this matter, an honest man who wouldn't steal her money from her, or worse, that a fire would not consume the entire frame building, burning up her savings with it. She would cross herself, then shake her fingers as if she had burned them. What to do, when you can't pray? Before she realized she had, though, she would pray, *Please God, don't let anything happen to my savings.* The irony of this made her laugh, but grimly.

No one came by all afternoon and she spent the time playing with her son, who had recently taken a great interest in two rag dolls that were in the box. He christened them Boar and Bimmy, Sophie had no idea where the names had come from, and he always chose to play with Bimmy. She said, "We could call him Alfred!" He had looked at her angrily.

"No!" he said. "Bimmy, bimmy, bimmy, bimmy," and went on singing the word while he waggled Bimmy's long ears. Bimmy was a rabbit.

"What is Boar?" she asked him, as they sat together on the lumpy sofa, a blanket over their legs against the cold. He tipped his face up to search hers, as if the answer might be found there.

"He has a horse," he decided at last.

"Oh, so he is a man," Sophie suggested.

"No, he not a man," Charles said. "He a boy. He has a big horse. He gallops..." He raised one arm to move it back and forth. "He gallops everywhere!" this last a shout.

"What fun!" Sophie cried. "Gallop, gallop, gallop!"

"No, *maman!"* he declared, pushing at her hand that she had lifted in imitation of his movement. "He gallops – you don't gallop."

She wanted to laugh, rarely understanding how his mind worked, but delighting in trying little things with him to see how he would react, pushing him, just a little, in the interests both of better understanding him and in teaching him about possibilities. "Does he like cake?" she asked, making Charles laugh out loud as if she had said the silliest thing possible.

Soon he grew tired, and for a little while, napped, while she worked on some heavy trousers she was sewing for him; he was growing so fast that nothing fit him anymore. Evening came, she fed him supper and put him to bed, then fed the fire, and sat in the warmth of the room by herself, her feet up off the freezing floor, a blanket tucked around them, resolving to at last cut herself some new cloths for dish washing and drying and to get at least one of them hemmed before she went to bed. If she couldn't embroider to satisfy a nun or her grandmother, she could at least stitch well enough to make what she needed. The long, bitterly frigid day had given her time, for once, to think, and she put her mind, as she had promised him, to Campion's proposition.

Come spring, everyone said, the current trickle of settlers would swell to a flood. Opportunities would abound, people said; the frontier was the place to make a fortune. Her own experience had her doubting such a thing because most people she saw had come West for the free land, to have land of their own was, in many families, a dream that was generations old. What the countryside abounded with, she knew now, was shysters and confidence men, and the ever-present land speculators, of which Campion, it turned out, was one of the biggest and most successful. Yet nobody seemed to know where his real home was, or if he had a wife or children, or how he had gotten the money to start his buying and selling. Everyone knew him and had done business with him at one time or another, however small the venture. If they feared him, or mistrusted him, they kept silent about it.

Still, many were the stories of small kindnesses he had done: taking meat and potatoes to a starving Galician family, lending money to someone who hadn't a cent and charging no interest. She thought, privately, that it was more likely he had done them to get on the good side of people, reasoning that the better his reputation, the easier it would be to make deals. But she had no proof of this, based this only on the look she had seen in his eyes, cold, assessing, that belied the ready smile and the good cheer that came from his mouth. *Cast thy bread upon the waters*, came to mind. And yet, he had taken away her farm, even knowing what that would do to her. Trust him? Never.

She worked alone in the warm silence for half an hour or so, falling into a deep reverie, as she cut and stitched. Pierre was in her mind, how they had loved one another, how they had worked together in those early days on the homestead, how they had come together to love the prairie as others loved their gardens or their children. Loneliness overcame her, and with it, longing; she dropped her sewing into her lap, her hands falling idle onto it, while misery crept in, and tears she hardly noticed were there ran silently down her cheeks. She sat, while the fire slowly began to run out of fuel, burning lower and lower, the room growing colder and colder.

Charles stirred in the bedroom, let out a sharp cry as if someone had poked him, which drew her upright in Harry Adamson's armchair from which she could still smell his tobacco, sometimes thought she could feel the length of his warm body. She waited, but there was no more sound from Charles. Now she longed for Harry's warmth and kindness, for his overwhelming desire. Her body had begun to ache, not in any one place, but all of it, as if her pain were another self that was her too, inhabiting her in the way that love once had, and she rose to her feet with difficulty, to fix the fire, to take refuge, if she could, in sleep.

The motion helped, the pain lifted a little, enough that she could remind herself as she always did at such moments, that others suffered too, some more than she did: all the dead children in the West, all the hungry ones, all the failure and despair, all the Mrs. Woznys, all the Lilys. Had she not her beloved Charles still? Had she not a home? Was she not succeeding, however low the standard? Were they not all succeeding in their way? Mrs. Emery, Mrs. Archibald, Mrs. Kaufmann. Even Mrs. Smith?

She knew then that she would go with Mr. Campion, despite the risk that he would try again to destroy her when it suited him, when it was to his advantage. She would start anew in Garden City, and Campion or no Campion, she would succeed there too. She thought, some days, that if you kept your wits about you, if you had wits to begin with, it was hard to fail. And yet, all around her, she saw what she knew to be failure: slave labour, hunger and despair. Was it only what you called your life that made the difference between success and failure?

She thought again of Pierre, but he was remote now. Pierre's good looks, that white-toothed smile, his outgoingness and unfailing charm, would carry him wherever he went. She, Sophie, would rely on her brains and her resolution. And caution would be her byword. No longer would she be that reckless, foolish girl she had been when she came West. In that instant, understanding this, she felt a hundred years old.

She thought of Campion's tight control of himself. I need that too, she told herself. But he is not a mother; I think he does not know anything about love. And she wondered, not for the first time, if perhaps there was something wrong with men that their affections seemed to count for so little in their lives, that everything else seemed to matter more. Or was it only that she had found herself with that kind of man?

She thought too, of Harry Adamson, whom she would be leaving behind. There had been one letter from him, sent as he said it would be, to Mrs. Emery. In it he had said that he had come to rest in Winnipeg where he had found ready work as a carpenter and a boarding house in which to live, "This town is booming," he wrote, "and we are crowded together six men to a room. I can't wait for spring to get back to my shack and my land." He had also written, "I hope Mrs. Hippolyte is doing well and that her café is working out for her. How is her boy? He seems a smart little fellow." She had hoped he might put a note inside for her eyes only, but he hadn't. She wondered if this was to save her reputation, or if it was only because in the city there was so much to see and do that it was easy to forget the small pleasures of the country. Easy to forget her, Sophie. She felt regret that he too, seemed to care so little, and then remembered that he had said that he was not proposing marriage, only – *Pah!* She told herself. Forget him as he has forgotten you. He hadn't the power to make her suffer as Pierre had, and she took comfort in that, and thought further, that she would curb her passions in the future, would not give herself to a man again in her, so far, no-holds-barred way. She would learn from her past.

The great, snow-covered pile of buffalo bones came into her mind's eye; under the glare of the pale sun, they seemed to give off white light, and for an instant she thought she could hear the sound that came from them, a deep thrumming noise, as if far below the piles' chaotic surface, a great heart beat still. It was the heart of the prairie, beating away; it was the earth itself. In her near-despair she remembered that first day when she and Pierre had found their homestead, when so exhausted she had tried to climb from the buggy and her legs gave way and she fell, face down on the ground; instead of only dry earth and grass she had been surrounded by, filled with the precious scent of prairie roses whose fragrances saturated the air, and would forever after seem to her the true fragrance of the prairie. She could not reconcile the two: the great grief of the bones, the precious beauty of the roses, one as real as the other.

SHE WAS DREAMING of fire, of a conflagration in a town she didn't know, the entire place flaming upward toward a black sky. The flames were spreading, coming closer to where she watched and she screamed, waking, half rising before she understood she had been dreaming and had only groaned aloud. She fell back onto her pillow, pulling up the quilt against the cold, seeing that Charles hadn't moved, her heart still pumping hard until she had managed to quiet herself. Then she thought, as she was awake anyway, she would build up the fire in the stove, so that the house would be warm when she had to get up.

As she was putting on her mantle against the cold, finding it by feel rather than bothering to light the lamp on the bed table, she became aware of an odd smell. She went into the kitchen, still sniffing, realizing with a shudder of incipient terror that it was smoke – no wonder she'd been dreaming of fire. But the stove was barely warm, the fire needing stirring to get the coals glowing again so that she could add wood, and perhaps one more lump of her precious coal supply. She did this, still puzzled, and wondering if she had perhaps only imagined the smell. It was while she waited to be sure the wood would catch fire, changing the dampers to allow in more air, that she thought she heard a shout. A quick glance out the window told her only that there was no one outside her door, so, reluctantly, she lifted the bar, slid back the ragged blanket that kept out the draft, the frozen hinges creaking loudly, managed to pull it open far enough to see outside.

Now she heard them, voices, somewhere down the road at the other end of town. The smell was strong and when she went out onto her step she saw a savage orange light in the sky to the north. Something was on fire: the livery barn, someone's house, a business, perhaps. Freezing in her nightclothes, she stepped hastily back in, closing the door hard, kicking the blanket back into place. She lit the bedroom lamp and set it on the floor in the doorway between the two rooms so she could find her clothing without waking Charles who lay under a mound of blankets, his small form motionless, his face turned to the wall.

She pulled on her warmest clothes, her new warm boots, the leather gauntlets that had been Pierre's that had been in the bottom of the portmanteau she had carried with her all that long day in August when she had come to this town, penniless and frightened, with the omnipresent land speculator, Campion. The very fact of the gauntlets' presence was evidence of how confused she had been, that she had not even seen them, not noticed that they took up a good part of the bag, forming a cushion, though, for all the other items she had placed in them, especially the jar of drinking water. Then she thought, her hand on the door latch, the other pulling tight the shawl around her head and over her chin and mouth, but I did remember, I think I might even have put them there for just that purpose, and both amused and aghast at what might have been going through her head when she did that, she stepped outside and pulled the door shut behind her.

She hadn't paused to try to see the clock, but as she turned her face toward the north and began walking, guessed that it was perhaps three in the morning. She was strangely disoriented by the billowing orange, red and yellow against the blackness at the far end of the street, the entire building in flames and far beyond saving, she could see, but was still not sure which of them it was. She began to run, although she wasn't sure why she was running, could hear shouts now, saw small black figures low against the violent colour streaming upward, of people standing as if mesmerized, others rushing to throw water onto the side of the livery barn to keep it from going up too.

Then she was standing beside Candace Archibald of all people, who so seldom went out, preferred that others come to her, who found the town and its society beneath her, had even, in some years, been known to go east for the winter months. Next to her stood Mrs. Oswald, the preacher's wife, tears starting down her face to be scrubbed away before they froze to her cheeks. Beyond them she saw Charlotte Emery, and even Mrs. Tremblay. To her right, knowing her by her height, she saw Mrs. Kaufmann striding down the narrowly shovelled path toward the group of women where Sophie had halted.

She had known for some incalculable minutes that the building on fire was Adelaide Smith's, but somehow this fact had not reached a conscious level. Now she stepped forward, Mrs. Archibald clutching at the decorative cape over the shoulders of Sophie's mantle, saying urgently to her, "Go no closer, no closer!"

But Sophie was looking for Adelaide, taking a few steps this way, then that, snow crunching underfoot, the men shouting incomprehensibly, water hissing viciously as it struck the hot wood of the barn, and one man, Ambrose she supposed, led rearing, twisting horses outside, while the other women called her to stay, stay where she was, and finally Mrs. Emery stepping in front of her, her round glasses shining orange in the firelight, her mouth moving frantically, no sound audible over the cacophony.

"Sophie, Sophie, stop, stop right here, now!" She put both hands on Sophie's upper arms and held her – how strong she was for all her years and her short stature – and Sophie stilled for an instant, her heart pounding so loudly that she could hardly hear over it, knew only the confusion, the shouting, the flames raging skyward, the black smoke billowing around them, choking them.

"Mrs. Smith, where is she? Where is Mrs. Smith? The girl – Lily – where is she?" Sophie wailed, struggling to pull away from Mrs. Emery.

"Calm yourself!" Mrs. Emery shouted, and Mrs. Oswald, in her role as preacher's wife, came and put her arms around Sophie too, from one side and Sophie caught the awful scent of soured cologne and old face powder, even through the choking smoke, and wrenched herself away from both women, screaming, "Adelaide, Adelaide!" The flames roared skyward behind her and burning rafters showered in perfect silence, orange and red, through the blackened remains.

Then Mr. Oswald came, stinking of smoke, and stronger than the women. He held her tightly while the women watched, their cloaks, scarves and faces black in the darkness as the flames, having consumed the house to its last lace curtain, began to die.

Calmed then, when there was barely a bonfire left, the livery barn wall smouldering, and people were drifting away to their houses and their warm beds, Sophie allowed herself to be turned toward home too, and said, in reply to Mrs. Oswald's cooing into her ear, "I am fine now, thank you, thank you," and kept moving, not looking back, even though she knew that the women would be following her with their eyes until she disappeared through the outer rim of the red glow into the darkness.

She had made no attempt to lock Harry's house when she left in such a hurry, but apparently she had shut the door tightly because she had to shove hard to get it, frozen as it was, to creak open. Not too disoriented now not to be puzzled, she hesitated to take that first step inside, wondering, but then the cold forced her and in the end she rushed, shutting the door hard behind her, kicking the blanket into place and then turning.

"Shshsh," a voice hissed at her. Her heart leaped again into her throat, her hand reached back for the latch, but then she thought of Charles and froze, waiting for her eyes to adjust so that she could see who crouched in the blackness beyond the gold glowing through the cracks in the iron heater. The sound of fabric: a woman then. A figure came into the faintly red-gold light, tall, her skirt too full for a homesteader. "It's me," she said, her voice so low that over the crackling in the stove, Sophie could barely make out the words. She shuddered, her back straightening of its own volition. Adelaide.

It was as if a wind raced through the room, creating a din, chilling her despite the newly-built up fire. Relief was her strongest response, a thing that surprised even Sophie.

"You are all right," she said, a statement, not a question. There was a rustling in the bedroom, the curtain separating the rooms that at night she always left hooked on a high nail so that every bit of warmth from the stove would go into the unheated room, had been dropped and now it lifted and a slimmer, shorter figure took a soft step into the front room where Sophie stood, still wearing her shawl and heavy coat, looking into the hazy darkness. She saw at once that it was Lily, but said nothing, nor did the girl speak. Adelaide moved suddenly, purposefully, as if she had just thought of something to be done at once. Before Sophie had a chance to react Adelaide had pushed her aside and was slamming the bar down on the door so that nobody could enter.

"Don't light the lamp," she said, in a normal voice. "Pretend you're in bed." Lily gave a nervous snicker, then went silent again.

Her shock diminishing, Sophie moved to take charge. Was she not in her own house? She began to take off her shawl and coat, hanging them on the hook that she found by feel that was by the door for her customers' outer garments, although it was seldom used, the winter being so harsh that most people preferred to keep their warmest garments near them. Turning, her eyes now adjusted to the shadowed light, she saw that Lily had stretched out on the one sofa on which she often stretched herself once Charles was in bed and she was alone. Adelaide had returned to the stove and was warming her hands in the radiant heat. It must have been she who had further built up the fire that Sophie had stoked before she had so abruptly left.

"I am glad to provide you with warmth," she said, then was embarrassed because this wasn't quite what she meant to say, though she'd no idea what she had meant to say.

"I guessed you would," Adelaide said, not turning to Sophie. "Ain't nobody else would."

"Oh, I'm sure..." Sophie began, then halted, thinking, surely – surely no one would send these women out to freeze to death. And yet...

"We wuz burned out," Adelaide remarked, as if it were not of much interest. In that brief sentence Sophie had heard a tone that reminded her of something else, although she couldn't quite find what it was, some voice in her memory?

"Do I know you?" she asked slowly. Adelaide laughed, a harsh sound, not bothering to look in Sophie's direction. Sophie came forward then, stood on the opposite side of the heater from Adelaide, tried to peer into her face. The woman's face powder had come off in patches, her lipstick was either missing or smeared, and the fierce red hair was, in this light, dulled, but with yellow highlights from the firelight. "Ahh," she said, and Adelaide gave a wry, unpleasant snort.

"That's right. We met on that train."

"You were with your sister," Sophie said, causing Adelaide to snort again. "Where is she?" Sophie asked more out of confusion than curiosity about a woman whose face she couldn't even remember. Before Adelaide could speak, she knew: The woman, Mary Ann – if that was even her name – was not a sister to Adelaide.

"She weren't my sister, as you guessed," Adelaide said, a peculiar dignity entering her tone. "She wuz just my – friend. We decided to team up for the trip. Help each other, doncha know."

Lily rose from the sofa and wearing the blanket she'd found on it as a shawl moved slowly across the room to join the other two women at the stove.

"It's cold," she said, in a high, thin voice, as if to complain of other, bigger things, but not knowing the words for them.

"What happened, I mean, tonight?" Sophie asked finally.

"I said," Adelaide pointed out. "Somebody burned us out." Sophie was silent for a long second, thinking. Hadn't the women all said this would happen? Did one of them set the fire?

"How do you know it wasn't your own heater or your cook stove or somebody knocking over a lamp?"

"Don't you think I keep a good eye on things?" Adelaide demanded. "Somebody did it on purpose. It ain't the first time one of us got burned out. Won't be the last." Again, Sophie was silent, but beside her Lily's frail body shuddered, both hands went up to her face, and then down again.

"All my dresses," she said, in that same thin voice.

"Never mind them dresses," Adelaide told her. "I'll get you more. Go lie down. Go to sleep. We'll be gone tomorrow." Lily did as she was told without so much as a whisper, surprising Sophie. The two women watched the girl move like a ghost across the room, stretch out on the threadbare sofa, throw the blanket around her body, turn her face away from the light, dim as it was, to the sofa's back. "That's right," Adelaide said so softly that Lily couldn't have heard.

"How did you get out?" Sophie whispered. "Didn't anybody see you? Did you see anybody?"

"I seen a shadow, nobody seen me and Lily though. We went round to the east, creeping, you know, and then we come in here. Harry, he would have taken us if he'd been here. But I knew you would. I could tell."

"But..." She tried to think. "Who was it? Where did the fire start? Why didn't you try to put it out?" She remembered the roar now, how sometimes it had been too loud, overwhelming, and sometimes she couldn't hear it at all. She started to raise her hands to her face, but put them down before they had done more than appear to jerk involuntarily.

"Started at the back, o'course," Adelaide said. "I keep out a good eye, you can bet on that." She paused. "No water. Can't save a fire without water, right? So," she shrugged, "me and Lily got out. That's all."

"So," Sophie began trying to think, "Nobody knows you're here, and you don't want them to know?" Adelaide didn't answer, just cast a sneering glance in Sophie's direction. It was so laden with bitterness, that Sophie almost took a step backward. "But, tomorrow..." thinking of her customers.

"Somebody'll come for us. We'll be outta here by afternoon. If you don't tell no one we're here."

Surely she could claim illness, or Charles's illness, or some problem and tell anybody who came – if anybody did – that she would be open for supper.

"Yes, all right," she said. Then, "But who will come? Who will even know?" Adelaide laughed again, a snort of derision.

"You wait," she said. "He'll come." Sophie wanted to ask who 'he' was, but refrained. It was all too much for her, she felt as exhausted as if she had been throwing pails of water on the fire, or leading around half-mad horses.

"I'll just sleep over here," Adelaide announced, and began pushing the two armchairs so that they faced each other. Seeing this, Sophie went into the bedroom and took one blanket from her bed and brought it back for Adelaide, who accepted it in silence, throwing it out over her extended legs, letting her head loll back, and closing her eyes. Sophie stood looking at the two guests, first one, then the other, but for only a second, then went into the bedroom, checked on Charles who appeared not to have moved, and went to bed herself.

For a long time she didn't sleep, puzzling over the relative calm of Adelaide and Lily, who seemed only mildly perturbed, nor surprised by what had happened to them. She wondered too what had happened to her that she had been the only one of the women of the town to be overcome by a mere house fire. She did not think she knew why she had been so wholly out of control, why the sight of it leaping high into the night sky had so overwhelmed her. Yet she couldn't find it in herself to be embarrassed by her emotion; it puzzled her too much. Vaguely she remembered the great fire the town had built every June to celebrate *la fête* and how when she was still a child it had so frightened her. But then, she told herself, after all, she was ill that time. It was a fever she had. She even wondered, for a brief moment, if maybe she was the only one there who had reacted in the reasonable way, if all the others, by the hardness of their lives, the suffering they had endured, had been blighted, were no longer able to be fully human. Or was it only because they so hated the prostitutes?

Then she thought for the first time, in astonishment at herself that she hadn't to this second even consciously been aware of this, that if anyone found out she was or had been sheltering two prostitutes, she would be shunned by everyone. Worse, her reputation that she had struggled so hard to preserve would be utterly ruined and that, for Charles's sake, she would probably be forced – just as the prostitutes were – to leave Bone Pile for a place where no one would know her. She would be tainted forever.

Morning came, hard and cold. It was difficult to remember that last night a fire had raged yards from where she lay on Harry's bed. Her small son who had stirred earlier and she had brought him into her bed, was still deeply asleep nestled against her body. She had been reluctantly about to extricate herself from Charles to stir the stove and add wood, but the room seemed unusually warm. She remembered then that she had guests, that doubtless one of them had roused herself when the cold grew too much, to build up the fire. She lay still even longer, thinking how she could stay abed this morning at least until Charles woke, but the presence of the two women in the other room troubled her; she didn't know how to behave or what to do to keep their presence a secret. Or if she really needed to.

They had come to her because they did not believe anyone else in the town would give them sanctuary; they must have believed that worse insult than fire would happen to them if they gave themselves over to the villagers. She tried to grasp this: What would that be, for the women would hardly take to them with pitchforks, surely? Having the fallen women in their power at last they would scold, berate, insult, demean them directly or indirectly. They would hold them for the police to come and take them away. They would say that Lily must have set fire to the house because she was angry with Adelaide, or deluded or mad or simple and vicious. Anyway, Sophie thought, they would go to the men for help, not the women. She did not want to think what the men might do. But surely the men would not hate them as the women did? All the power in the town lay with the men, except for Adelaide herself, who frightened the women, although she wouldn't, in the end, frighten the men. There was nowhere to hide in the town, nowhere where they would not freeze to death, nowhere where they wouldn't soon be discovered. She lifted her arm carefully from under Charles's head and slowly began to push the covers back from her side of the bed, trying not to wake him.

"No one will come round before noon," she whispered to Adelaide when she woke as Sophie lit the lamp she had placed on the centre of the table. "But that is when I start serving dinners, and it would be unusual if nobody came then." Now she was pouring water from the pail by the stove into the coffee pot. Thanks to Adelaide's tending the fire during the night, Sophie hadn't had to break through the usual layer of thick ice on the top. She whispered so as not to wake Lily with whom she did not quite know how to deal. Now she measured coffee into the pot of water, closed the lid, set it on the cook stove, turned back to her guest who was extricating herself slowly, with some effort, from the blanket she was tangled in. The odour of stale sweat rolled across the room and engulfed Sophie before dissipating. Some other sour smell rode on it and she thought, the woman has her menses, was revolted, then ashamed.

"You could go outside now," she suggested. "It is still dark; no one will be about." Adelaide gave no reply. "Or you can use my chamber pot, in the other room." Adelaide was straightening her clothing, pushing at her hair. She muttered a reply Sophie couldn't make out. She began to spoon raw oatmeal into a pot she had filled with water and set on the stove. Before too long there would be porridge. How hungry the women must be and ever since the day she had come into Bone Pile with Charles in Campion's buggy she had vowed she would never let anyone be hungry if she had the strength to lift a finger or a crust of bread to give away. Yet how she dreaded, for reasons she didn't try to understand, the moment when the girl Lily would wake, sit up, begin asking for things, or… She shook herself; she was still a child, children needed care and generosity. She would at least try, and set her shoulders firmly, unaware that her mouth had gone into a tight line until she felt the prickling in her lips and loosened them.

Lily stirred, though there was still not a sound from Charles.

"You awake then," Adelaide said, and Sophie thought that despite the willed harshness of the tone, she detected a note of – something – some warmth, she thought, and was faintly surprised. Lily merely grunted. "Say good morning to our mistress," Adelaide went on, as if making a joke, and Lily said to Sophie's back, "Good morning, Mrs."

Her voice was high and soft, a little girl's voice, and Sophie, struggling with the coffee, the oatmeal, the cook stove's heat, the horror of the night, at the sound had to catch herself hard not to cry. She turned rapidly, smiling.

"Good morning, Lily. I hope you were able to get some sleep my dear." That 'my dear' surprised even her. Ah, so I choose to be the mother, she thought, amused. In the richly spreading lamplight she was touched to see the guileless smile that had settled on the girl's face. Adelaide went to her, sat beside her as a mother would do, touched her cheek gently, then fingered Lily's lank hair, tsk, tsking softly.

"Can't do nothing with it," she remarked, as if she were telling the girl she loved her. So much so that Sophie turned her back to them and began to take bowls and cups from the shelves and place them on the table. She could hear the two of them stirring about behind her, the floorboards creaking, fabric slithering and brushing against the furniture. At last she glanced over and saw they were about to go outside. A snuffle followed by a chirping noise came from the bedroom. Charles. When she returned with him to the kitchen, the women were outside. She was helping Charles use the chamber pot when they came back in shivering, blowing on their hands, taking off their cloaks and hurrying to the stove to warm themselves.

"Who dat?" Charles inquired, pointing, then lifting his face up to his mother's.

"They are friends," Sophie told him cheerily. He was, after all, quite used to strangers being in the house with them, although not so early in the morning.

"Oh," he said. "I'm done now, *maman*." She lifted him, began to clean him, then dress him in warm clothing to counter the freezing air in the room.

At breakfast Adelaide said, "We thank you for not sending us out. For not rushing off to get the preacher or somebody to take us off your hands." Sophie didn't know what to say. She lowered her head in embarrassment, thought of replying *anybody would*, but knew that was not true. Could it be that I am a good person, she wondered, then laughed at herself. Circumstances was all it had been. Had she not done things with Harry – and she a married woman.

"You said someone would come for you today?" Adelaide nodded, not speaking.

"Who will come? How would anyone know to come for you?" She felt she had earned the right to ask such questions, but immediately regretted this because she could feel sudden anger coming off Adelaide, low, maybe always there, just a little released now. She wanted to say she was sorry for asking, but would not. Lily was eating her porridge loudly, as if she hadn't had food in a year, and yet, how thin she was.

"Slow yourself down," Adelaide growled to her, and she subsided at once, and began to eat daintily so that Sophie had to repress laughter.

"Look," Adelaide said finally and Sophie did not doubt who she was speaking to. She was careful not to meet Adelaide's eyes, it not occurring to her until now that such women might be dangerous – *could* be dangerous. "Look. I run a business. You see? A business. It takes money to get started in a business. Did I look like I had money on that train?" She was silent then, in what seemed to Sophie to be a final way, as if all had been explained. She wanted to ask more, but didn't dare. She thought as she sipped her coffee, ate a little porridge, attended to Charles's needs. Adelaide was telling her, she finally divined, that someone, a man of course, had given her the money to build her brothel and furnish it; it would seem that that man would now come and take her and Lily away to another place where, she supposed, he would set her up in business again. But who was the man? Well, she sighed, I will soon know. And what kind of man would it be? Clearly, a villain, someone so evil that he would make his money off destitute women's despair. She shuddered.

"I'm still chilled from last night," she said, by way of explanation when she felt Adelaide going alert at that shudder.

"Funny that," Adelaide said. "Coulda sworn it was hot." Sophie laughed as the safest thing to do.

At her usual hour she dressed her little boy warmly, bundled up herself, and left to take Charles to Mrs. Wozny as she always did. She heard one of the women put the inside door bar down as she walked down the icy path, and the thought that perhaps they wouldn't let her back in again crossed her mind before she dismissed it. At least I could go to any house and would be taken in, she muttered angrily.

"I am not well today, Mrs. Wozny," she said, holding her scarf over the lower half of her face so that the woman couldn't get a good look at it and be suspicious. "I am not going to open my café until five or so, if I feel better by then. But you know how much attention Charles needs and I think I should rest for a few more hours."

ONE OF THEM MUST have been looking out the window because before she even knocked she heard the bar going up and the door creaked open slowly. She slipped in quickly, pushing it shut behind her using her back, reaching to pull down the scarf and unwind it from her head. But someone sat staring at her from across her own table. A man. For one second, before her eyes adjusted to the poorer light after the brilliance of the sun on snow outside, she thought it was Pierre, and gasped and froze. He moved. It was not Pierre after all, it was Walter Campion.

"Mr. Campion," she said, about to say she wouldn't be cooking, then realizing the futility of this for was he not already in the room? Was he not staring across it at Lily sitting quietly on the sofa and did not Adelaide sit across from him, both of them with steaming cups of coffee?

It took a minute for her to adjust to the idea that Campion was the owner of the burned-down brothel. Fury swept through her, she could feel her face getting hot despite the cold sweat that broke out on her brow, before she could think a single clear thought. She remembered him proposing to her that she could run his house – her own house – and what he might have hoped to get from her. She had begun to shake and trying to hide it, turned her back as she took off her outdoor clothes and hung them up. How she had teetered on the edge of the abyss and knew it only dimly, or hardly at all. Under control now, she turned again.

"You have had a business reversal," she said, tightly, her voice clear, not even trying to hide her contempt. The hotel in Garden City he wanted her to run. Was she to go unwittingly into a brothel? Provide the clients and prostitutes with good food? What a desperate fool she was.

"That there is business," he said, either not perturbed in the least by her tone, or hiding it well. She was, after all, just another woman. "I thank you for taking in my lady friends last night. I appreciate that. I suppose you could say we all owe you a debt." He seemed amused, she was surprised he didn't guffaw at his own words.

"You owe me nothing," she told him, then refrained from saying more. *I was happy to do it. No Christian would refuse; they would have frozen; I am happy to have been of service?* In fact, she didn't know what she thought about it, only that she was not happy. "I didn't see a rig out front."

"Left it at the livery barn. It'll come soon. Then we'll all be going. I'll take some of that porridge, by the way," he told her. She debated for a fraction of a second, then got a bowl, took it down, filled it with porridge, put a spoon beside it, and set it in front of him, then sat down herself. Adelaide was on her left with her back to Lily who sat motionless on the couch, and Campion on her right.

"You were in town last night?" she asked.

"I was not," he said.

"How did you find out about the fire?"

"Ask a lot of questions, don't you," he grunted, although he didn't seem annoyed. Adelaide was grinning into her coffee. Sophie wanted to reach out and bat the top of her head. Ridiculous hair piled there like a giant cow pie.

"One of the men rode for you," she said. "A cold night for riding anywhere."

"It was indeed." She wondered how the man, whoever he was:

Archibald? Ambrose? Kaufmann? Tremblay? had known how to find him, but chose to ask no more questions. "Just lucky I wasn't that far away." He had finished his porridge and pushed the bowl away as if it bored him, as if he had to instantly organize himself and get on to the next thing, whatever that might be. "All right then," he said. Lily rose and Adelaide pushed away from the table, both of them moving about, reaching for their outdoor gear. She watched them for a second, then let her glance finally rest on Campion. He had stood too. She saw that he wasn't in the least ashamed; *Now I know his worst secret*, she told herself, and was both elated and frightened.

There was something here she had to understand, some dark well of knowledge about the world; she did not want to think of it, to ponder it, to throw herself head first into that abyss where such things as she did not want to know lived. She thought of the peace and protection of her little room in her grandparent's home so far away in what seemed now another country, one where flowers bloomed, soft rains fell, on snowy mornings voices muffled yet carrying across the roads and yards. A flash of yearning, that was all. I have chosen life, she told herself. *This is life: I must not look away.*

Seeing her gaze on him, he said, "When will you be coming to Garden City?" There was a soberness in his voice she did not think she had heard before, as if he could glimpse her thoughts, knew something more than she did about where they might lead. As if he saw what she had just seen. She drew her hands back from the table top, putting them to rest on her lap.

"I will not be coming," she said, and was angry at herself because her voice was low, as if she were speaking to a husband, rather than clear and firm, as if she were in control. She stood now too as he went toward the door, where he turned toward her.

"This is a mistake," he said. "I know people; you can go far; I am giving you the chance."

"You would turn me into your…" she couldn't think of the words. "Your prize cow." She did not know how angry she was. How rage consumed her in the face of this...this... She was seeing the future if she went with him: One step at a time, she would end his mistress until he tired of her, or in charge of a brothel, step by step, she would descend, pretending she wasn't, into the dark world where he and the prostitutes lived. In the barest flash she saw herself wielding her charm with men so they would choose to buy her services, and stepped back, away from him. But he appeared more interested in her reaction than upset by it.

"You don't know things yet," he told her, as if Lily and Adelaide were not dressed and standing by the door, as if they were alone in this suddenly vast room. "You will find out that it's every man for himself in this world. You will find out that if you don't do people first, they will do you." His face had reddened, his heavy moustache moved about as he chewed on his words and did not spit them out. Then, "You will find out." She put a hand to her throat, feeling he had cursed her.

All she could think to say was, "I have a child." Pleading. She threw out a hand at which he gazed at first with something that seemed to be contempt, then weary resignation.

"All right then," and Lily began to pull on the door to open it, Adelaide pulled her shawl up over her face and then reached out to do the same for Lily. Sophie saw this as trying to keep warm, as something they all did in winter, then understood that it was to hide their faces.

In the passion of the moment she had heard nothing but his voice. Now she recollected that she had heard a rig driving up and stopping, the ringing of the bridle, the creak and snap of cold buggy wood, the hissing of sleigh runners on hard-packed snow. She did not need to look to know that Ambrose or his helper had been ordered to bring the Campion rig down to her house, that Campion, Adelaide and Lily would make a fast exit, probably no one even having time to notice them going, or seeing only their backs as they raced out of town, would not know who they were, although, she thought, some will know, others will have their suspicions. She was not free and clear.

CHAPTER FOURTEEN

Winter

THE WINTER STRETCHED ON without any lifting of the intense cold, while Sophie cooked for her customers and looked after Charles. Blizzards blew up and stayed overnight, or a day or even three days, when she was trapped with her child in the thin-walled shack, hoping not to run out of wood before it was safe to go out and get more, hoarding her coal supply, wondering when more would come into the town. Then no one came for meals, or cups of coffee and conversation, and the days seemed endless and empty, and her sadness, both from her situation and from what she had seen with Campion, grew from the occasional few hours to a near-constant state.

She found it harder and harder to keep cheerful. Once indoors, she could not even look outside as the inside of every window in Bone Pile was etched with opaque wild frost jungles: ferns, exotic flower-like tracery, curlicues that might be seen as faces, or animals, or plants of the rarest varieties. Or so she told Charles when he too grew restless, wanting to run about and play, when outside there was only screaming, snow-laden wind and cold so severe that it was a risk to step out the door. Then they would stay at the window, Charles standing on a chair she had put there for him, and Sophie with her arm around him, tracing designs with her finger and saying, "What is that, do you think?"

"Fower," Charles would say, delighted, and then, "Fern! Tree! A kitty!" and she would hug him and try not to let him see that tears were sliding down her cheeks, tears she had neither willed nor whose source she fully understood.

She wished for a woman friend. Even as a child, although she had

had school friends, she had to steal away from home to play with them, was never allowed to go to their houses, or they to come to hers. There had been Violette Hippolyte, but after she had gone to the convent, Sophie had never seen her again. And here, who was there? Only Séraphine Beausoleil, a true friend, though more like a mother, and the same was true of Mrs. Emery. Often she drank tea with Mrs. Wozny, but they had in common only that they had both been abandoned by their husbands, and had to make their own way for themselves and their children. That, their imperfect command of English, and their unwelcome but unrelenting sense of themselves as being not quite the right thing in this village, in this West, because they were not from the British Isles and were not Protestants, their Catholicism, whether renounced or not, seeming to be something the others could smell on them, and wondered, is this why people marry? So as not to be alone?

But she couldn't allow herself to think about marriage, her chest contracting with pain as if an iron bar had been thrust in there that could never be taken out, so that she raised her head, stretching her neck, trying to open her heart and lungs so it would be dislodged, and when this didn't work, turned to her little boy to caress him and murmur to him, fixing on his needs because only her love for Charles was strong enough to make her forget her sadness. Sometimes she caught herself moving as if she were an old woman, her limbs and every joint aching, or else a lethargy invading them so that they were hard to lift. Then she would long to be away, anywhere that wasn't this collection of shabby huts, the peaked roofs all that could be seen in the field of snow, the shoveled banks rising even higher, while day after wintry day thin plumes of smoke streamed upward into the distant blue of the sky.

On the stillest of winter days she dressed Charles in so many clothes he could hardly walk, and herself in layers of wool under her heavy coat and boots, and they would go outside. Sophie waiting, huddled, or else using the time to move snow from around her entrance and steps, the shovel's iron ringing in the crisp air, its noise carried across the village as she could hear the shovels of others on the other side of town scraping and pinging, while Charles threw himself in the snow, talking away to himself. He would make angels with his widespread arms and legs, or with the small shovel she used for coal would work away at building a snow fort – it was invariably too cold to make snowmen as Sophie had done as a child in Québec, the snow would not stick together, although it broke readily out of the hard-packed snowbanks as large flat chunks ideal for building snow forts.

Sometimes Mrs. Wozny's little girls, seeing them outside, would stuff themselves into their shabby outdoor clothes and come to help Charles. He was happy then, and Sophie could walk away to the end of the narrowly-shovelled road that opened out to a trail that led into the countryside, to the farm where she and Pierre had labored fruitlessly for three and more years, to where the Beausoleils lived, and on, down to the American border, or through town to the other end of the road that ran north to Swift Current and the railway, or curved west to Garden City, then Calgary, then Banff, then the mountains that formed the western boundary of her known world. Beyond that, her mind opening out to the great sea that she had never seen, and beyond even that to an Orient that appeared to her as only formless colour and movement.

She was stunned by the beauty she saw as she paused from her shoveling to rest, her viscera wide open to the land, to her sorrow she always battled to keep away, and to the great mystery that she was learning in her loneliness and pain, was human life. Often there was such a sunbright sheen stretching out to the horizon that the snow-covered land was too bright to look at; even shading her eyes with a hand she could catch only glimpses of the wide spans of glistening blue-white and had to close them against the streaks of radiant silver so bright her eyes would run with tears; she would be stunned by the heartlessness of such beauty, a frozen paradise, fit for no human. When she looked back to where the children played in the snow, noses running, cheeks red, puffing out billows of frozen breath, she would be nearly blinded by what she had seen. She dreamed of something then; what it was she wasn't sure. Not to have lost Pierre, and in such an ignominious way, not to be alone and scrabbling like any peasant to stay alive. Not to be alone.

And still, no more word from Harry beyond that one letter he had sent to Mrs. Emery. She was aware that he could send her no private letters because the mail was laid out in the shack used for it as well as for the Mountie's business, and everyone could see if they wanted to who had sent her a letter. He had been gone months now and she was beginning to wonder if he had forgotten her, or if maybe he had met a woman in Winnipeg and was living with her, or even had promised himself to her. Maybe in the spring he would come back with his team and wagon, the woman on the seat beside him. She covered her face with both hands when she thought this, the two figures on the wagon seat melting into Pierre and Marguerite. When he returned, however he returned, what would she expect from him? She asked herself do I love him, but couldn't answer. She would not allow herself to say yes, because if she did, the fact of her still being Pierre's wife in the eyes of the church would intrude and she would have to deal with that. And anyway, she sometimes thought she cared as much as she did for him only because he had wanted her when Pierre had cast her aside and she was wounded to her very soul and no longer sure of her own worth. In wanting her he had also given her hope. In the end, she couldn't answer her own question.

She remembered then what over the course of this long winter she had half-forgotten, that she was occupying his house, that when he returned she would have to leave. In fact, she thought one night as she lay in bed trying to fall asleep, while two steps across the small room Charles slept deeply in his cot, and blew tiny bubbles through his lips on each exhalation, that she would have to be gone before he returned. But how? There was still no empty house to be had and she didn't want to spend what little money she had managed to hoard on building another small shack. If I do that, she told herself, shuddering, I would be well and truly trapped in Bone Pile. I'd have no money left to go anywhere else. No. Her best hope was to get out of Bone Pile as soon as she could; there was still time; maybe something would come up.

On the third day of a blizzard, during a short lull in the wind that slammed against the town, plastering snow against the west side of all the buildings, banking it six feet high across the town's streets while leaving other stretches bare down to the iron-hard frozen ground, there was a thumping at her door. She opened it as fast as she could, not caring who might be there. Frank Archibald stood on her step, nearly vanished behind a huge bundle of chopped wood so that she had to peer around it to see who it was.

"Well, now, before you go thanking me," he said, pushing past her to drop his load partly on her clean floor and partly into the woodbox by the stove, "It was the Mountie, Constable Lewis who reminded me you might be needing supplies." He straightened, grinning, brushing bark, wood chips and slivers, and small chunks of snow and ice off his coat. Flustered, she still didn't know what to say other than, "Thank you. I was running out, I was starting to worry…" Then, struggling to regain her composure at this unexpected kindness, went into the bedroom, calling over her shoulder, "Sit down. I'll make you coffee. How is Mrs. Archibald?" Returning, she carried her metal cash box out of which she made change for her customers.

"No, no," he said, pushing the proffered coins away with his palm. "This is a gift. Tomorrow, if the weather clears, Carmody is bringing a load of wood for us down from the hills. He couldn't get it out for the snowbanks, and anyway, all the trails were impassable. As soon as he can he'll be bringing loads down and I've told him you'll be wanting some. Of course, you will pay him," he added, looking down.

"I am so grateful to you," she told him, full of relief. She had made arrangements herself in the fall for a regular supply of wood from Carmody, but when it didn't come and didn't come, had begun to suspect he was satisfying his male customers first, that she was far down his list. "And of course, I run a business, however small, and must pay my own way as everyone else in business does." She said this smartly, echoing what Campion had said to her weeks ago.

"Mrs. Archibald would have sent baking but she said it would be like carrying coals to Newcastle." They laughed together, Sophie finally understanding that the saying must mean that there is a lot of coal in that English city. He was sitting across from her at her table now and she was surprised at how pleasurable it was to have so good looking a man near her, one whose attention was all on her, even if it was entirely proper.

"She is very kind," Sophie told him, although she didn't for a second believe this, thinking instead that Mrs. Archibald was selfish and proud. Or else simply alien, not comprehensible to someone like herself: a Québecoise, a Catholic, a woman who couldn't keep her husband.

Charles, who had been playing on Harry's couch with his now smudged and torn paper men and their horses, climbed down, went to the chair between Archibald and Sophie's and with the Archibald's help, got up onto it, and sat, gazing directly into Archibald's face as if wondering once again if perhaps this was *papa*. Archibald let his large hand rest lightly on Charles's head for just a second, then turned back to Sophie, clearing his throat gently. She saw at once that he had come for some reason that had nothing to do with wood, that the wood was an afterthought. She was at once frightened, and a small, quick pulse had begun to flutter in the base of her throat and she touched it with her fingertips to quiet it.

"Have you heard anything from your husband?" He was careful not to look at her as he asked this. She shook her head, no, not speaking, her eyes fixed on his face. He went on. "We – Mrs. Archibald and I – were in Garden City for a few days last week. Would have gone on to Calgary but the rail line was so blocked with snow it'll be spring before they dig it out."

"Yes?"

"Now Candace – Mrs. Archibald – thought I should tell you that we saw –" another long hesitation, "Monsieur Hippolyte there."

"Who?" her voice coming out too high, pitiful-sounding so that it was her turn to clear her throat. She started to smile, then stopped.

"Your husband."

"What..." *What was he doing there?* would have been her question, but she felt it was a foolish one. "So close?" She had imagined him south in St. Paul, or maybe in Fort Benton, or on his way to Montréal, never only a day's ride from where she sat with their son.

"I think he was looking for work," Archibald told her, adopting a light, conversational tone. "We saw him first go into a hotel, but then, a half hour later when we were walking back to the stables he was walking there too, going fast, as if on business." Again, she didn't speak, her eyes still fixed on his face. "He was alone," Archibald told her, gently. "He didn't see us. At least, I don't think he did." She wondered what had happened to his quest for an annulment, if he had given it up, or was waiting until spring after all.

Sophie turned her body away from him, reaching out to lift Charles off the chair he was bouncing on, pulling him to sit on her lap where she held him tightly, the child acquiescing, letting his head rest against her shoulder, humming softly to himself. No matter what, he was a happy child; he would always know he was loved.

"I suppose she will soon give birth," she said, dully, then realizing to whom she was speaking, gasping, and pressing her lips together.

"I don't know," he said, his voice still gentle, but turning his face away, flushing. Of course, everyone would know too, that Marguerite was pregnant. She shuddered.

"I must go now," Archibald said. He rose at once, and not having taken off his coat, went straight to the door and put his hand on the latch. "I am sorry to bring you this news." Now he was business-like and the certainty that Candace had sent him filled Sophie with shame and revulsion. Candace would demand to know how Sophie had looked, what she had said at the news. No, she told herself: Wasn't Candace a woman too?

"I wish they had stayed away," she admitted to him, still holding

Charles tightly to her. "But thank you for telling me." She saw only that she was not through with Pierre, that she would never be through with him. "I am so grateful to you for the firewood. Thank you so much for thinking of me" blinking back tears.

"It's only an armful of wood," he muttered, smiling. Sobering, gazing into her face briefly and then looking away, he said, "I can help you with a divorce if..." Sophie drew in her breath quickly, too confused for a moment to reply. "I know you are a Roman Catholic," he said, pausing as if he had more to say, then deciding against it.

As Archibald opened the door, two farmers were about to mount the two steps in search of a hot meal, and such were her circumstances that she had to greet them with a smile, welcome them, comment on their courage to be out in such cold, and hurry to get their food ready.

OVER AND OVER AGAIN she went through the memories of her years with Pierre, twisting in shame in her bed at her own declarations to him of eternal love. She remembered again and again the morning he had left her, she barely paying attention, having no idea she would not see him again. She puzzled over his betrayal, wondering how he could want a mere seventeen-year-old, no matter how pretty, over her and their child, wondering why, what was it exactly, that would make him give up what he had for so uncertain a future with someone he barely knew. Why? Unless... She gasped aloud, half sitting up, then falling back, her realization draining her of even the strength to pound her pillow, her body hurting as if she were wracked with rheumatism, the pain passing as rapidly as it had come. He had left because Marguerite had told him she was pregnant. Maybe he was even reluctant to go, but weighing the alternatives – two families to feed, maybe the Mounties getting involved at his making a young, unmarried girl pregnant, Marguerite's family certainly... Would that explain why she had thought he had been angry when he left that morning? Angry at having to make the choice? Or had he been as enchanted with Marguerite as he had once been with her? How hard it was to think the latter was probably true. She saw now, when it was far too late, that Pierre didn't have the nature of one who stuck with things.

He would have got her pregnant in spring, she thought. By August he would know, August was when they had run away. How could he have had relations with a girl Sophie hardly noticed? How could that happen? Because he chose for it to happen that way, she thought. More than once he was in town when I wasn't with him. Once I stayed for two days with Séraphine Beausoleil rather than wait in town with him. I gave him the opportunity to see her. I did. Maybe they had gone out onto the prairie as she had done with Harry. But was marriage only for keeping watch on each other? Wasn't it made of trust, besides love?

On one of her evening visits to Mrs. Emery, Sophie herself came into the parlour carrying Charlotte's silver-plated, elaborately engraved 'company' tray, not even having to ask whether to use it or not, or where to find it, with two cups of coffee, the cream pitcher and the sugar bowl on it, and a cookie for Charles.

"I don't think I could have heaved myself up to get that there if my life depended on it," Charlotte told her.

Once seated, the coffee dispensed, Sophie asked, "Charlotte, are you well?" There was nothing to see outwardly of illness, other than how much she had aged this winter, and how pale her skin, and then, a wince that periodically came and went from her features suggested fleeting, but unignorable pain.

"I can't work no more," her friend said, then clamped her lips together, her eyes on the wall at the foot of the sofa, not on Sophie.

"What?" Sophie faltered. *I can't work no more?* This was a death sentence. The West, as far as Sophie had seen, and she thought now how long and bitter her learning had been though she was not many years past twenty, was only about work. Those who could not work were thrown on the scrap heap of Western society. It was true in the towns, for all she knew in the cities too, and as she knew all too well, out on the land. The fate of those who couldn't work anymore was to lie abed, scorned and forsaken, until they died, that was the fate of those who could not or would not work. Or if a woman, to lie abed as Adelaide Smith, the prostitute did. Or to have no bed on which to lie, to beg in the streets. To wander into that frozen land, like any heathen Eskimo, and be found in the spring. To ride south, or north, chasing gold or work, poorer each passing day. To end like Sam Wetherell, in a single room in a boarding house, your mind fixed on the glorious past.

"What is it?" she asked, reaching tentatively to cover Charlotte's hand that lay loose by her side on the sofa. Charlotte didn't pull her hand away, nor did she move it to grasp Sophie's, but let it lie, under Sophie's, inert.

"I got…something, neuralgia, sciatica, the rheumatism, I don't know. All I know is I can't work no more. It hurts me too much and if I force it, it hurts me more. I get tirer-der and tirer-der 'till I don't never feel good no more."

"The doctor?" Sophie asked, leaning toward Mrs. Emery as if her hearing had gone bad.

"Potions and lotions and grease and pills. Hah! Nothing helps. I need to just lie down and die." Sophie was astonished, and drew back just a little. Was self-pity the other side of the extreme toughness that was the way of the people she had met out here? She stopped herself, ashamed. "I need to sell my place. Now," spoken angrily. "You want to buy it? You got to get outta his place soon, before Harry gets back, where you gonna go? I'll make you a deal so you can pay me by bits. I'd want to stay on and live here." She had finally looked at Sophie as she said this last and for the first time, her eyes behind those small frameless circles of thick glass were large and watery, her bottom lip trembling for a scintilla of a second before drawing tight again. "You could turn it into a hotel, make more money that way…"

"More work!" Sophie interrupted, then wished she had kept silent. "But, Charlotte, until the railway comes I couldn't even keep the rooms full, unless your men stay on. There's nothing to say the railway will come, either. I've heard people say that it will pass us by, we're too far off the main line." She had stopped looking at Charlotte, turned her head away, saying. "And if I take it, I will be trapped here as you have been." She had softened her voice to say this last so that it came out gentle, wavering toward ruefulness.

Charlotte sighed. "So I was," she admitted. "But," querulous now, "my only girl was buried out there," that toss of the head again to indicate the enemy, "and to tell the truth, I had no place else to go. So I stayed. And stayed. And now I am old and can't work no more."

"Surely you could find another buyer?" Outside a team and wagon went by at a trot, they could tell it was a wagon by the noise it made, the wood creaking, iron ringing with the cold. Surely, Sophie thought idly, it is too cold for horses?

"Who?" Mrs. Emery asked, belligerent again. "Who that would pay me and keep to a bargain? There's nobody." What she said was true. Again Charlotte looked away from Sophie, the bleakness in her eyes, that trembling mouth, stirring such pity in her, yet how could she agree to accept Mrs. Emery's burden when she had her own to carry?

"Campion came by," Charlotte said.

"He would." This exchange coming fast so that the phrases were on top of each other.

"He said he'd buy. Give me a good price."

Sophie opened her mouth but could think of nothing to say. Outside, the wagon was gone by up to the livery barn. Somebody taking advantage of a clear day to head out to his land maybe, to make sure everything was all right, that no matter what, the land was still there.

"Well, you know Campion. First, he ain't gonna give me a good price, although he will say he is and try to get me to believe it. And second, do you know what he would use my house for?" She swung her head rapidly to face Sophie, who simply stared, before what the boarding house would become came to her, now that the other had been burned to the ground. They sat in silence together, drinking their coffee.

Charlotte said, after a while, "If nobody else comes along I might not have a choice." Sophie met her eyes, then looked away, nodding reluctantly.

A moment later she stood, dressed Charlie in his snowsuit and then herself in her winter gear, and with muted and short good-byes, went back to her own house.

She had thought, as Mrs. Emery talked, that she had to find a place to go to, and soon, or she would wind up staying in Harry's tiny house with him and her reputation would be ruined. Unless Harry married her, and here he hadn't even written to her all winter. Clearly marriage wasn't on his mind. If he did propose, would she accept him? At this thought a fine perspiration popped out at her hairline. Marry so as to live? Wasn't that the very thing she would not do? And in any case, having forgotten this herself, and was amazed and baffled that all her past in her Catholic village, all her years at the convent, all those rosaries said and Masses attended had brought her to the moment when she could not even remember a basic teaching: that she was married to Pierre forever, that only death could release her from her vows. Or the annulment Mrs. Tremblay had said Pierre was after.

She did not know what to make of it. So hard a taskmaster, the church she was born into, full of the greatest of gifts, at the same time the harshest and most implacable of tyrants. Her great-uncle Henri's grave all alone under the beech tree in a farmer's field, forever denied the glory of the church to which, as far as she knew, he had been faithful. *It was a forced marriage*, she told herself angrily, then blew air out through her nose, because she had so wanted it and had acquiesced in it. Was she not now bound by it? And yet, all around her were people who lived as she did, no differently, no more sorrow than she had, who had never set foot inside a Roman Catholic Church. What was to be made of that? That all she had been taught was a lie? Foolishness?

But this line of thought frightened her so she forced it away to fix her mind on the immediate problem: Find a place to move to before Harry returned. But another, even more unwelcome thought intruded: that she had betrayed Charlotte. Her friend, in her true extremity of need had begged her for help, and she had refused. The woman who had taken her in when she was destitute, had no one to help her, and she with a small child. And yet Charlotte hadn't said this to her, hadn't accused her of hard-heartedness. Now she wondered why not: Because of course, nobody understood better than Charlotte Emery how hard it was for a woman in the West, and how if she were to survive without a man, she must harden her heart, set her eyes and her mind on her own survival.

But wait, she thought. Couldn't there be some sort of compromise? She and Charles could move back into the boarding house and do the work for a while, just until Mrs. Emery found a buyer. She considered, dreading this solution with all her being. To fall backward into slavery: no, she couldn't. She would bank on fortune saving her, that something would come along, quickly. If it didn't, she could still change her mind.

But to refuse to help a friend in need! We even spent Christmas there at her house with the boarders who also had nowhere else to go. She gave Charles and me mittens she had knitted herself. With those fingers knotted with rheumatism. Then she thought, but I slaved from morning until night there for months, for no pay, just room and board. She took me in, yes, but she needed me as much as I needed her. Surely I owe her nothing. But she couldn't convince herself of this, any more than she could convince herself to help Mrs. Emery by taking over her business.

A week passed in the same way as always, people coming and going, she cooking, taking Charles to Mrs. Wozny's and bringing him back again, the extreme cold finally beginning to lift a little, people growing cheerier knowing winter would, after all, end. But with it came the worry again that soon Harry would be back and she still had no place to go. There was no help for it; she would have to take Mrs. Emery's offer. With that realization, her stomach dropped, she had to sit down, a wave sweeping through her of such despair as she hadn't known since the day she realized that Pierre had gone for good. She sat this way for a while, there being a lull between customers, and faced the fact that she had no alternative, none that she could live with, combined with her fear that once there, she would be unable to leave again, she would grow old in the service of that misbegotten house. She had a vision then, that one day the countryside, still largely empty, would be dotted with such monstrosities, the product of lies, vanity, and foolish dreams.

ONE AFTERNOON she was wakened from her usual short nap between cleaning her place from the lunch service and beginning preparations for the supper service by a steady rapping on her door. Rousing herself, she called, "Who is it?" and without waiting for an answer, "I'm coming." When she opened the door a woman she knew only by name stood there wrapped in a heavy dark red mantel that she had pulled over her hair as well.

"May I come in?" She was shivering.

Sophie opened the door wide and stepped back. "By all means," she said, puzzled. "I know you are Mrs. Roberts," Sophie said.

"Yes, yes," the woman said, as she unwrapped herself and stamped snow off her boots. "We have never been properly introduced, and I'm sorry to say I've never taken advantage of your hospitality."

"Please, sit down," Sophie said, pulling back a chair. "I'll make us tea."

"No, no, please don't bother," Mrs. Roberts said. "I know I've interrupted your rest period and I hope you'll forgive me, but I've only a few minutes. I have a proposition." Sophie simply stared at her. Mrs. Roberts laughed, embarrassed. "I am sorry to sound so mysterious. It is only that I have a house to rent and I would like a reliable, decent tenant..."

Sophie gasped, raising a hand to her throat, then quickly lowering it. "I've heard nothing of this," she said, surprised. "What...house?"

"My father's," Mrs. Roberts replied. "Humphrey Gowland. Do you know of him?"

Everyone knew of him, in fact, although few any longer paid any attention at the mention of his name. He had been one of the first of North-West Mounted Police who had come West in 1874 and when he had mustered out, had taken his land grant and started a ranch. In no time at all he lost it through gambling and from then on had gone from one scandal to another, adding drinking and womanizing to his gambling addiction, until in his old age, ill and an alcoholic, he was reduced to bare existence in a shack in Bone Pile, with his widowed daughter living next door and bringing his meals to him.

"Oh, no," Sophie said.

"Yes, indeed," Mrs. Roberts replied. "He has died, and I want to rent his house while I decide what I must do next – after we bury him properly of course. Which can't be until spring." No explanation of this was required; Sophie knew the ground was frozen too hard for any burials until the spring thaw. "The Mountie has taken his... corpse...and stored it with another until then; in spring he will be buried in the Mounted Police cemetery at Garden City, and in the meantime, I have been cleaning and cleaning..." She swallowed, halting, as if she had at last run out of her admirable clarity and was overcome by all that had happened.

Sophie said, haltingly, "How very hard for you. I am so sorry. But..." She wasn't sure how to carry on. Surely it was crass of her to simply declare she would rent the house when he had just died? And yet...

Mrs. Roberts appeared to have regained control. "Yes," she said, crisply. "It is too bad. It is very sad. But" – here she paused, drew air in through her nostrils loudly, and went on. "But the house can't be left empty. If mice and rats don't move in, then some scallywag will and I'll have to locate the Mountie to get him out again. I would be grateful if you and I could make a bargain – about rental, I mean. I need someone reliable and decent."

"How did you know I was looking for a place?" Sophie asked.

"Mrs. Kaufmann told me."

There was a brief silence, then Sophie said, "I would need to see it, I suppose."

"We can see it right now if you wish," Mrs. Roberts said.

She supposed that Mrs. Roberts would have made an effort to keep the shack from disintegrating, washing sheets with her own wash, she supposed, carrying over food on her own dishes and bringing them back to clean them. What was to be done with such men: Heroes in their day, losing it all as soon as their strength and prowess began to weaken, as if they had nothing else to live on but their daring, their fearlessness. She wanted to feel contempt, but what she really felt was instead a kind of wonder, that men could be so different from women, at least, she thought, not knowing whether she should laugh or not, Western men. It must be, she considered, that the men who came West are of a certain type, remembering old Sam Wetherell. Even Pierre... But look at Harry Adamson. But she would not. She would get to work with the moving, having already known that no matter how bad the Gowland shack was, she would take it. A little dirt did not frighten her. Mrs. Emery's situation touched her, but *I must save myself, as she saved herself,* and tried to push out of her mind what she saw as her own selfishness.

Nevertheless, having inspected the Gowland shack and agreed to rent it, she went that evening with Charles to the Emery house, knocking loudly, but then entering without waiting for Charlotte to come to the door. She found her friend lying on the settee in her shabby *salon* that was also a common room for all her boarders, none of whom, thank heaven, were there this evening. Charles sat down on the rug and began to play with his wooden trains. Mrs. Emery's eyes flew open when she realized she had a visitor, and widened when she perceived it was Sophie.

"Don't move," Sophie said, hastily. "I just thought I would drop by." She realized then, by the alert expression on Charlotte's features, Sophie thought that Charlotte was hoping she had come to say that she had decided to take her offer.

But Mrs. Emery made no comment about it, and said instead, "I've been hearing that your husband is in Garden City."

"Where did you hear that? Sophie asked, drawing back, although of course she had heard it too, although it seemed to her that she had not, or that she had dreamt she had heard it.

"Light that lamp, will you?" Charlotte asked, pointing to her parlour kerosene lamp, its base painted with pink flowers that sat on the round oak table in the corner. Sophie did as she was asked and the three of them were bathed in its warm gold light, shadows seeming to grow from it in the corners of the room. It looked to Sophie as if all of it – the plain pump organ in the corner that nobody played, the faded, dark-framed pictures on the wall of no one she recognized, nor she supposed did Charlotte know them either they being relics of the rancher Quinn's family, the porcelain knick-knacks crowding the dust-laden surfaces – all had been coated in aspic, that she was back in eastern Canada, about to sit with her grandmother to do the hated needlework.

Carefully, Charlotte worked herself to a sitting position. Charles made roaring noises on the threadbare carpet with his train, thumping it down once or twice. She thought how he had never seen a train; was there one in one of his picture books? She sat in an armchair, awkward because the springs were gone and she sank farther than she had expected. Recovering herself, she remarked, "The days are lengthening at last."

"Can't come soon enough," Charlotte grunted.

"Have you found anybody to buy your house?" A red-streaked sky could be made out through the sheer curtains, a last reflection of the sunset behind the house.

"I did what I had to do," Charlotte answered. For a long moment Sophie was silent.

"What was that?" she asked, finally. Charlotte raised her head, appeared to be staring at Sophie although Sophie couldn't see her eyes behind her glasses that had become opaque shields.

"I have sold to Campion." Sophie drew in her breath, at once shocked, while well aware that this was because of her refusal to help her friend. Shame flooded her. Charlotte went on. "All of it, lock stock and barrel. Everything."

"What will you do?" Sophie asked, stunned into whispering. Mrs. Emery shrugged, spread out her hands, palms up, set them down on her lap again.

"He'll give me enough money so I can go someplace else. Don't have to watch what he'll do with it. No houses here," she added. "Except old Gowland's shack and I'm not cleaning up no old fella's mess. Go to Garden City, maybe. I have to decide soon." Sophie wanted to say something to acknowledge the other woman's fate, if that is what it was, but what else would it be? But she couldn't think of anything that wouldn't sound false, and her pity – she was afraid of her own pity, what it might make her do, that she did not want to do, that she knew would be the worst possible thing for herself and Charles. So she hesitated, moving her fingers nervously on her lap, glancing over to Charles as he played on the carpet, then back at Charlotte.

"I have taken Gowland's shack. I'm moving there as soon as we can get it ready. It isn't very clean, but it has enough furniture that Charles and I will manage."

"Harry'll be back soon."

"I have to move before he comes."

Mrs. Emery studied her. "Why? Ain't you on the lookout for a new husband?" She laughed a little as if she knew she was being offensive, trying to cover this in a joke.

"Husband," Sophie echoed, as if she'd never thought of such a thing. Charles was blowing air loudly through his lips, then made a high-pitched "Woooo," sound, imitating a train's whistle. He must have learned it from the Wozny girls. "I think I would like to marry again, but nobody has asked me, and having made a mess of things once, I am going to be very careful before I make such a decision again." She was faintly surprised by her own answer, having refused ever to allow herself to consciously think about marrying again because of her belief that as long as Pierre was alive, she could not. She thought again of Campion's offer to her on that day that she could barely bring herself to think of, when she had first come to Bone Pile without money or friends or anyone to help her. *I was strong then*, she told herself. *I can be strong now, too*, but she swallowed with difficulty to keep down the lump that was rising in her throat, then stood quickly, going to Charles so Mrs. Emery wouldn't see her emotion.

"You knew when you refused me I would have to go to Campion." Sophie's back was to her and although she had halted, she kept her back to Charlotte.

"Yes," she said, lifting her head as if high above the house there was a noise only she could hear, and she was listening hard for it. "Yes, I knew it." She wanted to say, *I refused Campion and survived; couldn't you?* But knew she was being unfair, Charlotte was old and ill, as she felt Mrs. Emery was being to her, even though she was young and strong. She wanted to say good-bye, she wanted to maintain all civilities as she had been taught to do, but emotion overcame her, and she couldn't speak for fear of crying, and Mrs. Emery had turned her face away from Sophie.

She went on out of the house, Charles trundling behind, beginning to whine for her to pick him up. It was clear to her then that her friendship with Mrs. Emery had just ended, and it seemed that her heart was beating hard enough that it pulsed against her coat making the fabric quiver in rhythm. She thought of how far she had come from the day she had left her convent in Québec, an innocent, filled with excitement about what the world would bring her.

It would bring her this. She knew this now. And yet, she had to save herself and her child, she had to take opportunities when they came; she would not stay behind forever in Bone Pile, stuck in her little café until she ended like Charlotte Emery, reduced once again to nothing, and with no place to go. She wanted to berate herself; she *was* berating herself for being such a foul human being as against all the teachings she had ever heard, she was walking away from need: Worse, she was acquiescing in evil – Charlotte's house would be a brothel; Campion making money off abused, destitute women who with him could only fall further into alcoholism and disease, no matter how pretty their dresses or how much fun they might have for a while – she was entangling herself in it. She could not, by this action of turning her back on Charlotte Emery, keep her skirts clean. She would have wailed aloud, all the years of her teachings at the hands of priests and nuns flooding over her – the fires of hell, damnation – but hugging Charles to her, she moaned only so that he pulled his head back from her ear to look into her face inquiringly, his *maman* frightening him.

"Yes, my Charles," half-whisper, half-groan to him, kissing his round little cheek, pushing his head back against her own. "This is what the world is. Sometimes one has no choice," but Charles had nothing to say to this.

ONCE SHE HAD MADE up her mind, in just under a week she and Charles were living in the Gowland shack, her business having moved with her, most of their belongings piled onto Charles's sled, that she had used making trip after trip. The shack itself, roughly the same size as Harry's but with a shallow earth cellar, wasn't really in as bad a shape as she had expected it to be, and although she also felt that major cleaning was required, she knew very well that it was more because Gowland had been a reprobate, a character who had lost all respect of anyone, what with his drinking and gambling when he should by now have parlayed his land grant into a sizeable ranch, but instead had died in grimy poverty. She had felt no need to clean quite so ferociously with Harry's house; it was Old Gowland's shame she needed to remove with her scrubbing. Or was it her own? Ridiculous, she told herself, and scrubbed harder.

CHAPTER FIFTEEN

Return

ONE MORNING, it being such a bright, hopeful day with the sound of water dripping off rooftops and running in the distant coulees, on her return from dropping off Charles at Mrs. Wozny's house, instead of going straight back to her house, she stopped in at the Kaufmann's store to buy some yeast. Ever since her move she had been experiencing a kind of freeing of her spirit not only because spring was finally arriving, but also because she now owed Harry nothing, that is, but the rent, and because she felt that now they could be clear and honest with each other. The two feelings vied with each other, first her uneasiness at her own ambition – or whatever it was – and then her lightness of spirit that she was free of everyone who might, whether well-meaning or not, oppress her, prevent her from finding and fulfilling her destiny, whatever that might be. But it swelled inside her, every day telling her there would be more, much more, if she kept strong.

"How is the new house?" Mrs. Kaufmann asked at once. She was nearly a full foot taller than Sophie, and carrying her height as if it embarrassed her, had taken to standing in odd positions so as to look less tall. When she could, she sat behind the counter. Seated, she and Sophie could look face to face.

"It will do," Sophie said, it not being the way in this village to wax eloquent about anything, and ever trying to fit in, subdued her tendency to gush. "Mrs. Roberts kept it clean, I'm happy to say." Mrs. Kaufmann's eyebrows went up, just a little.

"Not easy with that old man," Mrs. Kaufmann said. On Sophie's left Mr. Kaufmann was busy moving the barrel of pickles so as to make a better path to the shelves behind them.

Sophie said, "I've come for some yeast." Mrs. Kaufmann reached behind her. It being her duty to attend to the orders of the women of the town, she had lightened her work by keeping the in-demand items easily within her reach. "Soon it will be real spring," Sophie offered.

"And mud everywhere," Mrs. Kaufmann replied, the exchange purely ritual. Could there be no real conversation in this village? Not that Sophie had experienced 'real' conversation with anyone but Pierre, his sister Violette, and lately, with Séraphine Beausoleil. The package of yeast sat between them on the counter. Sophie kept an account with the Kaufmanns which she paid promptly every two weeks. No need to dig in her reticule. There was a silence, Sophie having run out of the standard conversational bits, and Mrs. Kaufmann seeming to have an air of expectancy about her.

"I can't say I'm looking forward to the mud," Sophie ventured, trying to keep up her end.

"Have you heard?" Mrs. Kaufmann said suddenly, in a rush coming in over Sophie's lame remark. She knew that she was about to hear bad news by the look on the storekeeper's face, and drew air in through her nose, nervously, trying to steady herself.

"That woman, the Tremblay woman, is back in town." Her voice fell away at this last, as if she had just realized what she was doing by telling this to Sophie. Sophie didn't reply, trying not to give away her emotion.

"Oh?" was all she could come up with, this after a second too long, although the air in the badly-lit store had grown nauseatingly rank with the smells of leather, oil, fish, coffee, pickling brine, and too-strong cheese. Heartened by so innocuous a reply, Mrs. Kaufmann took it as license to go on, her tone shifting to self-righteous.

"Oh, yes, indeedy, she has come back," lowering her voice to a whisper although only her husband and Sophie were in the store besides herself, "She is going to give birth any day now by the look of her." The woman pulled her hands back from the countertop where she had been leaning forward, her weight on them. She sat straight, moving her shoulders self-importantly, as if to set them in a proper position. "Wanted her mother, she did, I hear. Fine time to want your mother after what she did to you. And no sign of *him*." Behaving as though her indignation were on Sophie's behalf. If Sophie could have fainted, she would have; she wished to sprout wings and fly away, or to dissolve into invisibility in front of the storekeeper.

It seemed to her now that all the goods on the shelves, stacked along the walls, sitting in barrels and boxes, and hanging – halters, bridles, small-animal traps – from the ceiling, were listening attentively, that the wave of listening would engulf her, and the smell – she would be ill with the smell. She picked up the yeast cakes, took a step back from the counter, gave a small, speechless nod, and forcing herself to a normal pace, not looking back, went out of the store. Outside, she walked straight to her new home, went inside and shut the door. She would leave Bone Pile this very day, if only she could. She wished also to sob and cry, but the pain in her chest was so great that it squeezed out all possibility of tears. She made a fist and held it against her forehead, not breathing until she had to, then took in three, four long, deep breaths, subduing her own tumultuous feelings, pressing them down, down, to where they could – she thought – do no harm. When she was calm again, she began to set her bread. Before too long, her hands stopped their trembling, although it was hours before her stomach felt normal. Already her business had gone back to normal, and cooking and dish-washing with it.

A few days later she was sitting on her steps to enjoy the early afternoon sun on her face, shading her eyes against the brilliance of the melt water and the diminishing piles of snow all down the street. Stream after stream, some short, some very long, of wild geese passed through the clear air over the town, sounding their plangent calls as they beat their wings in their unhurried, purposeful way. Some flew so high that when she tilted her head upward she had to shield her eyes with her hand and even then they were only a black v-shape of dots passing between earth and sun, while others flew so low it looked as if she might reach up and pluck one out of the sky for her dinner. How noisy they were, she thought idly, and yet their very cries, like organ notes, celebrated spring. Ducks too, fluttered by, quacking; she even saw a flock of white birds that she recognized as swans, or thought she did. They might have been snow geese, flying in a clump, blazing white against the cloudless blue. All over the prairie there was water, puddles, ponds, whole shallow lakes of it, plenty for the birds. Their cries stirred something in her reaching up into her throat, so that she blinked, and puzzled over what it might be. The desire to leave this place forever, to go somewhere better, more exciting. To find love as she had once had love with Pierre. But she turned away such thoughts, resolutely, as beneath her now that she had learned what she had learned about life. The sun shone warm on her face, and for once she basked gratefully in its heat.

From between the houses before her and to her right she caught glimpses of a wagon pulled by a team of horses coming into the town from the south. She watched idly, thinking how she must rise and get Charles and not be so lazy, enjoying a brief respite between the noon and supper customers. When the team didn't reappear as it passed the next house when she expected it to, she assumed that it had stopped in front of Harry's house. She gave a start: Surely it was Harry, returned from his winter's labour. She found herself standing, hurrying inside, closing the door, leaning with her back against it while she tried to calm her unexpected confusion.

What was this reaction? She wasn't sure. All winter long he had not sent her a single note, not a word, not even by someone else, except for that early note to Mrs. Emery. When she moved to the Gowland house, she had left a note for him on his table saying where he could find her and telling him to come and collect his rent from her that she hadn't thought it wise to leave there on the table with the door not even locked. That he would soon come by she had no doubt, perhaps not today, but tomorrow. But then, she thought, if he hadn't brought supplies with him, he would have no food in the house and would have to come to her for his evening meal. But then, didn't everyone in town know him, and knowing his situation, wouldn't they all offer him supper? People loved to have company, were especially starved when the winter had been so long.

Unable to stand her own unsettled feelings any longer, she put on her shawl to pick up Charles at Mrs. Wozny's whose house sat midway, although back a street, between Harry's house and Sophie's new residence. But she fixed her hair with some care, or began to, before she grew annoyed with herself and stopped, put on her winter boots without thinking about it though rubber boots would have been better what with all the standing water around, and left her house.

She chose not to go down the main street, although that was where there were a few stretches of rough wooden sidewalks, because she didn't want anyone to think that she was out because Harry had returned, knowing very well that if she had seen him return, so had everybody else. She was going carefully, her head down, skirting puddles or jumping over them, nearly falling and putting out a hand to steady herself against a melting snowbank when she became aware of a movement to her right. She glanced in that direction, was in time to see a woman pulling back the outer door to enter a house, was horrified at herself that in the tumult of feelings at Harry's return – if it was Harry, she suddenly thought – she was passing Tremblay's house. It was not that she saw the woman's face, but knew at once by the awkwardness of her movements, of the kind only pregnant women make, and the curve in her back from carrying the load of the child at her front, that it was Marguerite Tremblay.

The door had already shut, no curtains moved in the two front windows. She kept walking, beginning to speed up, thinking there had been no sign of Pierre, no saddle horse tied to the fence, or a wagon or buggy pulled up by the house. Perhaps he had left Marguerite too, she thought, before she dismissed it as merely her own desire not to be the only one humiliated. She felt sure that Pierre was not in Bone

Pile, this mostly, she had to admit, because she couldn't bear the thought of his being there, with her, this girl-woman who had stolen him. And their baby. She had been leaning forward from the waist, her feet moving in short steps, clutching her shawl to her chest, and now, thinking of the baby they would have – her husband – she straightened, stiff and as tall as she could make herself, lifted her head, slowed, tied her shawl over her chest, and dropping her arms to her sides. At Mrs. Wozny's house, when the door opened at her knock, she did not know where she was, or why she was there, but went confusedly inside, blinking, struggling to adjust her eyes to the gloom. It was not until the woman spoke that she began to collect herself.

"They play out there," Mrs. Wozny said, tossing her head to indicate the back of the house. Now that she thought of it, she had heard the faint shouts of children in play out behind the houses, on the low knoll nearby that would be dry, and had ignored the sound as normal, not thinking that Charles might be one of them. Sometimes she still thought of him as a baby, had forgotten he was four years old. "I will get Olga to bring him home to you when they…stop." Her English had improved, but she still had to search for words, as indeed, Sophie still did. But every day her French receded farther from her. Still confused, Sophie could think of nothing apt to say, although she was thinking, he will be soaked, his clothes will be sopping wet. I'll have to… "Sit," Mrs. Wozny said, turning a chair with one hand. "I need to rest. Coffee," waving her hand as Antoinette might have done. At this Sophie nearly sobbed aloud, but held the wretched noise in, gulping and pretending a cough. She did not want to sit, but she did, still trying to get her mind to settle on the moment and the place.

"I'm always glad to see that Charles is having fun," she said. "Your little girls are so good with him."

"He good boy," Mrs. Wozny said, not seeming to pay attention to her own words. "Now," she said, breathing out heavily through her nose, her voice louder, engaged. "I think you go away soon."

"Me?" Sophie stared at Mrs. Wozny. The woman stared back at her, unflinching. She tossed her head meaningfully in the direction of the Tremblay house up the street beyond where they sat together. Sophie blinked again, then said, angrily, briskly, "I have always meant to go. Opportunities here are too limited."

Mrs. Wozny nodded slowly. "In summer they will build here a school."

Sophie stood, no coffee having yet appeared, so that she felt it safe to leave. "I must go. If Olga would bring Charles back when they are finished playing, I would be very glad." As she opened the door, she thought to add, her voice softening, "And never forget how grateful I am for the good care you have taken of my boy."

Mrs. Wozny nodded as if this were only to be expected.

Sophie suddenly wanted to kiss her on her broad forehead, but instead, went out, shutting the door quietly behind her.

HARRY CAME IN THE MORNING, while Charles was still eating his breakfast porridge and she had only just finished her *toilette*, dressed, but not yet fastened her hair that lay thick and glossy on her shoulders. It was no use not to answer the door; whoever was there would soon push it open and call in through the crack as if no privacy were required in such a world as theirs. What was there to hide anyway? But when she called, "Come in," pretending blitheness, and saw Harry's face, one hand went up to her chest, and the other touched Charles' shoulder as if to reassure him, when it was she who needed reassurance.

"I'm back," he said, his tone light. "But I bet you knew that."

"Indeed I did," she said, turning to Charles who had asked for nothing, to hide her pleasure. Then, recovering herself, she walked gracefully, like the convent-bred girl she was, the four steps to where he stood just inside the door, putting out her hand to him, but he used it to pull her to him, close enough to brush her forehead with his lips, that was all, then raised one hand to touch a lock of her hair lying on her shoulder, pulling it back quickly as if he hadn't meant to do that. "I am happy to see you," she told him. "Is your house in satisfactory condition? Have you come for your rent? Do sit, and I will make you breakfast."

"Had breakfast," he told her, although he sat down. "Just for a minute," he said. "I'm thinking of getting out to my land, see how the shack is and all that. Not sure if I can make it with a loaded wagon. Too much mud." She saw the prairie, bright, blue and green, sparkling with minute white daisies and yellow golden beans. It seemed she could smell it, and for a second thought her heart would break, that its cracking would be audible to him. "I'll have to take you out there one of these days," he added. "I'm guessing you miss it."

"Especially in the spring," she said, swallowing, touching her throat. She didn't dare sit too close to him and chose the far end of the table with Charles between them.

"Hello, little man," he said. "Did you miss your Uncle Harry?" She felt his awkwardness, the falseness of his tone and words to her son. So he was uncomfortable too. She had poured them both coffee and lifted her cup to sip from it.

"You didn't write," she said, her tone low, not looking at him. She was fingering the envelope in which she had been keeping his rent and pushed it across the table to him. He pushed it back to her, without remark.

"I couldn't," he said. "We worked long hours, we were stuffed into a boarding house attic, six men in one room. There wasn't any time. I'm sorry." She nodded. "Didn't know what to say anyway."

Now it felt safe to look at him. He seemed to her pale, but then he had been working indoors all winter, it was said to be too cold in Winnipeg to work outside much then, and his shirt was one she recognized, faded though, and torn on one sleeve where the cuff buttoned.

"I think you need some sprucing up," she said. He laughed and ducked his head. "How was it?" she asked, and at last in his reply he sounded like the old Harry.

"Tough," he said. "No denying it, but it was work and I made good money, all in all. Nobody to spend it on. And I'm no drinker. That's why I'm not taking your money. You kept my place clean and looked after. I just moved right back in." She chose to ignore this, but didn't touch the envelope that now sat between them.

"I was...I thought you might have found a bride."

"No such luck," he answered. "Mrs. Emery is the only one who'll have me." She was angry with him for saying that, and kept silent. "Look, I've come for a reason. I'm taking a buggy up to Garden City and thought you might like to come along – catch a ride with me, I mean," he said. "I don't suppose you've been out of this place all winter." She was silent, trying to think at so unexpected and welcome a suggestion. And a chance to see if she could fit into Garden City, a town she didn't know. She hesitated.

"Would I take Charles?"

"Up to you. We'd be gone three days or so, it takes a day or more just to get there. Maybe four days we'd be gone." She thought, too long to leave Charles, he would be frightened, he's never been without me. As she thought about it, her breath began to come quickly, she could see the prairie opening out before them, the trail leading on toward civilization, a big town, houses, stores. Churches. Excitement filled her that she tried to dampen down. People would think she and Harry were up to no good.

"I'm taking Richard Sloan with me too. He's visiting the Oswalds and needs a lift back." She didn't know who Richard Sloan was. Harry said, "He came here looking for spring work. Got some with the Johnsons, has to go back for his gear. It's way too soon to get on the land." Whoever Richard Sloan was, his presence would stop the gossip, or at least, some of it. She considered, or pretended to, trying her best to suppress the bubble of happiness forming in her chest. She lowered her head, remarked thoughtfully, "I'd have to close my business – unless Mrs. Wozny would take it over for me when I'm gone. When would we leave?"

"A couple of days," he said. "I've got to organize a few things first."

"Oh, Lord," she said, "the gossip."

"Here we go again," he said, but he was smiling. "Everybody knows you've got nobody to look out for you. And anyway, if they think we're a couple, so what?" She thought to herself, that 'so what' was not so small a thing, but her desire to get away, to get back out into the world was so strong that even she couldn't care enough to stop her from going. She was grateful to him for not mentioning Marguerite, or maybe he hadn't heard about her return.

Then a wave of longing came over her, amazing her, as if all the endless winter she had suppressed it, denied it, not allowed it near her, and now her lover sat before her, and all she wanted was his mouth on hers, to have him inside her again, to feel her skin against his. She lifted a hand and put it over her mouth, its coolness surprising her when she was so hot, so very hot all over, and put it down again.

"Yes," she said. "Yes, Charlie and I will go with you." She had never before called her baby 'Charlie,' although everyone else did, and she was taken aback by this, too.

IT WAS EVEN SAID that the weather was better in Garden City, despite the fact that it was further north than Bone Pile. But it lay in the lee of a range of high hills that protected the town from the worst and when the warm snow-eating winds blew in from the mountains a couple of hundred miles to the west they reached all the way to Garden City and warmed it enough to melt the snow even in the dead of winter, where Bone Pile was frigid from November into April and sometimes May usually without a single break. She thought of Garden City and a new life there; she thought, once, of Calgary having heard how it was booming, lots of business to be done there, all kinds of people about. Strangers, who wouldn't know her history. No Marguerite just a few doors down from where she sat, and the thought of this, even in this context, sickening her. She wouldn't allow herself to think of Mrs. Emery, except now and then when she would find herself remembering how they had worked together and been friends. Her shoulders would stiffen, she would lower her head, and put all her energy into kneading her bread or sweeping her floor, or would suddenly be over-attentive to Charles and his game so that he would cast her an exasperated glance and push away her hand that touched one of his paper horses.

Tomorrow she must see if Mrs. Wozny would run her business for her while she went to Garden City, she told herself as, Charles long asleep in his cot, she in her dressing gown, she pulled the pins from her hair. There was a soft, quick knock on the door. Startled, she spun about, trying to think if she had remembered to wedge the table knife into the door frame so that no one could push it open, there being no bar for the door here as there had been at Harry's house.

"It's me, Sophie." She recognized at once that it was Harry, and rushed to let him in before he was seen. As soon as she slid out the knife he pushed his way in, closing the door carefully, silently behind him. She wanted to, but couldn't speak, stood before him, one hand still raised shoulder high with the dull knife in it. He took it from her, and set it behind her on the table. As if the gesture had wakened her from her dream, she spun quickly, picked it up, and while he waited, thrust it back where it had been. He lifted his hand and brushed it gently under her hair where it lay loose down her back.

He would have taken her into the bedroom, but she refused, "Not with Charlie there," she whispered, and so they lay together on the horsehair sofa, prickly, lumpy and hard. She had thought she would refuse him when he came – had she really thought that? – but once he touched her, she was as eager as he, could give no thought to what the town would think, or to whether by this acquiescing she was implicitly agreeing to more than she meant to. It was all skin against skin, sensation after sensation, their mutual eagerness ending the act in moments. She felt for an instant in the aftermath that she loved him, then frightened by this, not sure why, not caring why, shut off such a feeling as one she dare not allow herself. How could she know what was real and what was not when it came to love?

She lay, though, with her head on his arm and their bodies pressed against each other on the narrow sofa, and asked, "When are we going?" He was silent for a moment longer than she thought he should be, and in that too-long instant her heart sank. When he finally answered her she was not surprised.

"I went to see Mrs. Emery today. She needs some help moving. Campion knew of a small house in Garden City. I said I'd help her move. Those sons of hers –"

"I can help too," Sophie said, not adding, if she will let me.

"No, but you see," he said, and hesitated. "I mean that I will take what furniture she is bringing with her in my wagon to Garden City. Sloan will help me, in return for the ride. And Charlotte is coming too, although I don't know how she'll manage on such a long trip. But, she's determined."

Sophie began to struggle to a sitting position although he tried half-heartedly to hold her back.

"You mean that there will be no room for Sloan, Charlotte, you, Charles and me."

"I'm sorry," he said. "Maybe we could go together later on." She was surprised to find herself blinking, holding back tears, was grateful that in this dark room he couldn't see this.

"I was so looking forward to it," she said.

"As soon as I get back I'll take you and the boy out to my land for the day if you like. We could start setting things to right there for seeding." But Sophie didn't reply, already wondering if she could rent her own buggy and horse from the livery barn and drive herself and Charles to Garden City, the notion of getting away for a few days having been implanted, had taken such a hold on her. But she didn't know the way, she was thinking, and, how safe would it be for her alone? Maybe she could find somebody to go with her. If only the railroad would give the village a branch line, but everyone says they wouldn't come down here, or at least, not for years. But if it did she could go so easily.

"When we do go out to my place we can have more time together," he said, buttoning his shirt, pulling on his pants. "Nobody watching us." He paused in his dressing to look at her as she half-lay, half-sat on the couch, her feet against his back. When he turned his head toward her moonlight coming in from the single window lit his face and she saw a gentleness in it that moved her, so that she could speak again, and put out a hand to touch his arm.

"I think I would like that." Although it crossed her mind to wonder how long they could go on this way with the secrecy, the constant danger of being found out, and the shame that, for her, would surely follow. What would be next? He would ask her to marry him, she supposed, but he was standing, reaching for his boots, pulling a chair out at the table so he could sit to pull them on.

When he had gone, she couldn't sleep, her chest heavy with disappointment, her desire to leave Bone Pile and never see it again growing stronger by the minute. If she could have gotten the buggy and the horse that moment she would have left then and there, not even bothering to pack, leaving behind everything but Charles. She saw the town waking in the morning to find her gone, her cabin door wide open to the elements and the animals. When she was nineteen, she thought, that is what she would have done. No matter what hardship such a leaving would have cost her it would have seemed worth it to her, she would never even have looked back, and she couldn't help but remember how she and Pierre had left their village forever, she impatient and upset not from the leaving, but only because it hadn't been fast enough. Now, she didn't even seriously consider such an action. When the time came, she would go, and in the proper way, with dignity, she told herself. *When the time comes?* When would that be? When she got together enough money, and groaned again because lying in the dark with Harry gone she could only think that it would be years before she managed to save as much as she needed to move them to Garden City without putting herself or her child at risk.

Then she remembered that Harry hadn't said a word about a future with her, only that brief mention of a day on his land, and was indignant and for a second, suspicious. But when she thought about how Harry might simply have used her tonight, she found herself too tired to dwell on it, saying to herself only, *and I him*, and surprised as she was by this errant thought, almost at once fell into a restless, dream-laden sleep.

She woke late the next morning, Charles had gotten himself up and was tugging gently at her hair so that when she opened her eyes the first face she saw was his peering into her own with a look somewhere between mystification at the fact of this sleeping woman who was his mother, and mischievousness that she didn't see him and would not tell him to stop. She began to laugh, gathered him in her arms and swung him onto the bed beside her.

"Are we going today?" he asked her. She remembered then that the promised trip had been taken from them, and grimness descended over her spirit. But she said, "Today we go to see Mrs. Emery! We will help her put her things in the wagon!" Quite satisfied, the boy climbed down from the bed and went into the other room to find his toy box that they had left on the floor beside the sofa, while Sophie cooked his breakfast.

But an hour later when she walked with her son to the Emery house, it was to discover that no one answered her knock, and when she opened the door to peer in to see if Mrs. Emery was perhaps upstairs – but come to think of it, she told herself, Harry isn't even here yet with his wagon – no one answered her call. She stepped inside, Charles following her, and called again, "Charlotte, are you here?"

From the back of the house she heard a latch click and then a door open; she hurried down the hall to the kitchen and was just in time to see a bulky figure in dark clothes entering through the back door. He was as surprised to see her as she was to see him, although it took her a second to realize that it was Walter Campion.

"They have left," he told her, and let air out through his nose, heavily, as if he regretted their going. In her sudden fright she had placed a hand over her heart, and Charles, sensing this, had leaned against her skirt, hugging her leg as if for protection. "She didn't take much, didn't take long to load what there was. And it is a long way with a loaded wagon to Garden City. Need an early start." Sophie wondered what had become of the boarders, but didn't ask. Moved on, she supposed, dispersed through the village.

"I wanted to say good-bye," she said, beginning to back away, out of the kitchen, to go down the hall, out onto the muddy, rutted street back to her own house. He stepped forward, arresting her movement.

"How are you doing, Mrs. Hippolyte?" he asked. "Nearly a year or so has passed since you came here with me." He paused, made a short guttural sound that might have been a laugh. "And refused me, too." He repeated that odd grunt again. Sophie stiffened.

"I am a decent woman," she told him. "You had no right to speak to me in such a dishonourable way." Now his laugh sounded more like that of a normal person, as if she had made a witticism and he was laughing politely to acknowledge it. The sun was moving around, though slowly, and the shadows in the room seemed to lift so that she could see him more clearly, or maybe it was only her own vision that cleared.

"It is the West," he told her, conversationally. "No rules apply."

"They do!" burst out of her before she had time to think. She almost turned and ran out of the house at this, but stifled her impulse, trying to gather together some feeling, some emotion, some wisdom that hovered around her that she waited to coalesce so that she might say it to him. About herself. About him. About such a life as he proposed.

How bulky and large he seemed although he was not a tall man, how much space he occupied. How dark he appeared, his garments heavy, creased and folded with age. It would not have surprised her, in that moment, to see seaweed or grey rags of dust hanging from his forearms and shoulders. Her forehead prickled with what she apprehended.

"There will be no railroad," she told him. "You will lose the money you have put into this venture."

"There *will* be a branch line," he answered. "It will be built this coming fall. Business will boom. Those kind of mistakes I don't make." He cleared his throat, gave a bark of a laugh as if at those who *did* make such foolish mistakes, then going on in a less harsh tone. "I won't be here to see it."

"Where will you be?" She was uncertain, thinking that he meant more than he was saying, or that he was giving her some message too mysterious for her to understand.

"I'm moving on," he said. "I have done what I can here. Calgary is waiting, people pouring in, limestone mansions, store after store down the main street. I will try my hand there." He was complacent, dismissive of her as part of what he would leave behind.

"Somewhere, sometime, you will go too far. You will be caught."

"Caught?" His voice was loud, the tone harsh. "Caught?" She stopped herself from backing away as he stepped forward.

"You make your way over the bodies of others," she told him. "The women...the homesteaders...especially the women." She was thinking of Adelaide Smith, that hungry woman on the train West, and of her pride as she marched down the street in her near-garish finery, and at the memory of that pride, or contempt, wavered for a fraction of a second. No, view it as you may, she knew it, the woman was used. Her life was no one's first choice, unless out of despair. He let air out his nose again, as if Sophie were a hopeless case, then turned away and went back to the outside door.

"And *you* are minutes away from starvation – you and that boy of yours. Minutes! Don't you see that? One thing goes wrong and you are finished! In the gutter!" This she knew well, although she rarely allowed herself to think of it, the notion of it being too terrifying. He was calming himself, she could see the effort it took. Neither spoke nor moved, staring through the gloom at each other. She saw his small, dark eyes begin to take on a glitter that she had seen before, when he had found her alone on the homestead, expecting no one, and Pierre gone for good.

He had brought her her downfall, had not wavered a jot at doing it.

"Work for me and together we will conquer this place." His hand was on the doorknob, he was turned sideways to her, looking at her slyly over his shoulder. "You're a pretty woman. I like pretty women. I might even marry you. Imagine that. You riding in the buggy beside me in the finest garments money will buy. Blue silk, ermine, a diamond necklace for that pretty neck of yours. The great ladies would bow to you."

She saw it herself. Dark red, not blue, a matching ruby necklace. But it was as a fairy tale. Thoughts flashed through her mind so quickly she could barely catch them. Not a fairy tale; it might well be real. Her cheeks burned at the realization of how real it was.

"And how the great ladies would hate and revile me," she said, as if she were the sophisticated one, and not he, and swallowed hard, her breath coming quickly. "I think you are evil," she said, surprised at the lightness of her own voice, its purity in the dusky air. It seemed to her there was a whisper in the air behind her head, the movement of cool air, shivers went down her back. At this, he turned the doorknob and went out, not so much with footsteps or the movement of his legs, as a kind of slipping away of a shadow. The door closed behind him.

"Mommy!" Charles declared, pulling at her sleeve, startling her, she had forgotten him entirely. "I want to go. I want to play with Sonja." Had not the air in the room taken on a texture and become visible? She shivered, chilled, waves of something more emotional than physical were passing from her lower abdomen up to her chest and back down again. She thought she might be sick, but Charles went on. "Mieka wants me to play horses today. Come on, Mommy," tugging at her sleeve again.

It took her a long time, the entire day, to rid herself of the smell of Charlotte's kitchen, and the feeling of the air while she had stood there. Every time she thought of it shivers ran down her back again. With descending softness of the early evening air, she began to think she had been imagining things, because she did not like Campion, because she thought of him as a malign influence on the town and the countryside, with his graspingness, and his willingness to do whatever would bring him money, no matter what the cost to others. She wondered at the dress she had seen herself in, rich and colourful, the matching necklace, while he had offered the Blessed Virgin's colour, and the white flash of diamonds. It seemed so odd to her, how they both saw her, and she couldn't think what this meant if it meant anything, and yet, some part of her insisted that it meant something profound. But if presented with the situation again, she knew she would not change her choice. *I wish to be a grown-up, a woman, not a girl,* came into her mind, surprising her. Before, it seemed to her, she had only wanted to *seem* a woman, to *seem* to others in control of her own actions and her world. Why would Campion wish to clothe her as a virgin? It frightened her, to think of this. Or was she being a fool to think of it at all. Of course she was.

THE NEXT DAY was mail day, an event for which the whole town waited anxiously, she supposed for a variety of reasons from the arrival of important bank documents, to advertising about farm machinery, to newsy letters from the longed-for home in Ontario or England or North Dakota. She expected letters from no one, although she received bills in every mail, and seldom received one except from her old friend Hélène, perhaps once a year since she had arrived in the West, and once from Violette Hippolyte, when Violette had taken her final vows. And the Hippolytes had sent that box of books and toys for Charles. Still, she waited as eagerly as anyone else in the town for the mail coach to come racing in, the mail bags dumped onto the sorting table, and late in the day, finally, to be able to go to the shack called 'the post office,' to pick up one's letters. She supposed everyone had noticed that there were rarely letters for her, and it embarrassed her a little, although never enough to keep her away from the crush. She was hardly the only one in town who never gets letters, she told herself.

In mid-afternoon she went out to pick up Charles, who as usual these warm spring days, was out galloping around with Mrs. Wozny's smallest daughters on the dry hillside behind her house. Charles apparently hadn't seen her approach for he kept on running and calling, waving a stick about in the air, disappearing down the far side of the hill out of her sight. It was then that she saw, for what seemed to her the first time in a very long time, the long high pile of buffalo bones still waiting in the sun to be carried away and sold. It astonished her anew to see how many bones there were. The sun was warm enough this afternoon that the pile seemed to waver, rising and falling, growing bigger, then smaller in the heat waves coming off the prairie. Why did it always seem to her to be calling or beckoning? A long time ago she had thought they were about power; now, she no longer knew. Maybe it was only grief.

Then Charles returned from the far side of the hill to its crest above her, still brandishing his crooked stick, still calling and running, a black figure against the whiteness of the bones, taller even than the bones far behind him.

Rather than taking Charles straight home, they went together to the post office, walking among their neighbours. She was about to look around for Mrs. Emery when she remembered that Mrs. Emery was gone; it registered as a blow to the heart, her mind racing through the months she had spent with her, her kindness, her toughness, how Sophie had wronged her. Or not. It was then, for the first time, that she wondered what had become of Mrs. Emery's boarders, of Old Sam Wetherell in particular, who had kept her awake nights pacing around overhead. She thought to ask Mr. Reed, who lived alone and knew everyone; he shrugged. "They took him over to the hospital in Garden City. They'll keep him as long as he lasts."

"Some illness?" Sophie asked.

"Naw, just old. Just wore out," the farmer told her. Something that might have been regret went through her, and the pictures renewed themselves, him racing on horseback through the moonlight, his rifle across his saddle, his bowie knife strapped to his leg, danger all around him. His wildness, his recklessness, his lack of sensible fear. Although, she thought, how she hated what she knew of him, as if they were born enemies.

She always held back a little at the post office, letting others more certain of letters enter before her. She and two or three others trickled in finally as the rest of the village walked away, clutching unopened letters to their sides, hurrying home so as to read them in private, or not able to wait, tearing them open right there in front of everyone and beginning to devour them, laughing aloud at their contents, snorting, or gasping. And she thought, *why are they here? In this wilderness, so far away from the real world? Why do they stay?* She knew the answer in a sort of way, that they were poor people and the West represented hope in the form of their own land. If they survived the hardship, grew old on that land, left it for their children to live on and work, would they die in satisfaction? Or would they die in profound regret for the mothers left behind they had never seen again, the sisters and brothers, the green villages and forests, the burbling streams, the cloud-filled skies, the narrow, homey vistas? Who could love the wide, empty, grass-covered plains in the same way?

But she had a letter, one she saw when she looked hard, was stamped with the name of her village in Québec. Her fingers began to tremble, but she opened it slowly enough, as if it were nothing, and seeing the handwriting inside, not recognizing it, began to walk home without pulling it out of its envelope, Charles trotting ahead of her, racing in circles, on his imaginary horse. She walked quickly, unable to stop herself, and once inside the house, the screen door open to the warmth of the day, took out the letter, spread it flat on the table top, and looked at the signature first. It was from André Chouinard, her would-be suitor from a thousand years ago. Tall, gangly, fair-haired André. She began to read.

My father is sending me West on a business venture, or rather, to search out business ventures; I am hoping to visit you if you are anywhere near Calgary, and if you will see me.

He made no mention of Pierre but in her surprise she knew at once that what had happened to her was no secret back in her own village; the knowledge made her gasp, she sat straight, for an instant forgetting the letter, shame flooding her, horror that she had no privacy in the entire world, that nothing was her own, but shame.

I leave the first of May, he wrote. *You may write to me at this address in Calgary.*

She drew back, surprised again. "You may write to me?" But then, she thought, he has his pride too, and also, he didn't want to offend her by being too forward. She wondered if he still loved her; it has been five years. She thought he would have married someone else by now, that his father *le notaire* – how long it had been since she had thought in French – would force him into marriage.

The screen door creaked open, a man and his wife, people she didn't know, looking for supper before they headed back onto the prairie, there now being no place in town for strangers to stay overnight.

"I am – I am – not prepared," she said, laughing, embarrassed, and hastily folded the letter and slipped it back into its envelope. "Can you give me half an hour and then return? I do apologize. I..." tucking her hair in place carefully, reaching for her apron. "It has just been one of those days," she said, switching on her carefully nurtured charm so that they might forgive her and not refuse to return, laughing gracefully at her own fecklessness.

The wife said, faintly injured, "We were told you prepare good meals, and quickly." And the husband said, "Of course, Mrs. Hippolyte. I have one more errand and then we'll come back," touching his wife's shoulder perhaps a little heavily, so that she stepped aside so he could open the door and they could exit. Men, she thought, both in faint surprise and something like despair, she could always charm men.

It was spring, people were on the move, farmers coming into the village to look for supplies and machinery parts, or wagon repairs, or new horses, or men to work for them during seeding. How business would flourish, how hard she would work for the next few weeks, how she would have to rush about and sleep only a few hours each night so as to keep up with the baking, cooking, dishwashing and cleaning. It was said that when the land dried enough the village would begin building a school. She tried to imagine staying on in Bone Pile and watching while it grew, building by building, as she suspected it would once the branch line was a reality. Yes, if Campion said there would be a branch line, there would be one. Yes, she thought, and then she would be old, having spent her life, raising Charlie here so that he would never achieve what she dreamed of for him. Or she would marry Harry and go back to the land, spend her life there in poverty, working like a slave.

THE DAYS WERE BECOMING LONGER this time of year, it sometimes seemed to her that the light never really left. At the end of this long day, hours after Charles had been asleep, her work at last done and things ready for the next day's onslaught of work, she went outside to sit on her step and feel the cool night air on her face before she went to bed. Tired to the point of exhaustion, she leaned back against the door, then let her head rest against the frame. Presently she heard the jingle of harness to her left up at the livery barn, saw a light inside, a lantern had been lit, and thought, someone coming in late. How would he ever keep to the trail in the dark? Although it wasn't really dark, not pitch dark as it sometimes was on the prairie on rainy nights when the stars and moon were blotted out by clouds. She leaned forward to see who was still up in the village, but all along the street as far as she could see there was only silence, the shops and houses closed, the windows dark. But wait, her eyes, sweeping the village, paused at one house down the street to her right, between her and Mrs. Wozny's house. There a light blinked on and swelled, someone lighting a single lamp. She wondered when the village might get electricity, everyone not afraid of it said it was as good as a miracle, and supposed that if the train really came to Bone Pile, there would be electricity in town soon enough.

Then she realized the house with the new light in the window was the Tremblay's and in a second she knew, *Margueurite is in labour*. That must have been a doctor from elsewhere, or more likely the midwife who lived out on a nearby homestead come to help. Is she perhaps in trouble? But that seemed unlikely. It was odd how she felt so removed from this knowledge, how little at this moment she could make herself care that her rival was only a few houses down from where she sat in the cool shadows waiting in her exhaustion for the desire to sleep to come to her, while Margueurite Tremblay labored to deliver the child of Sophie's own husband. Whatever it was she felt – anger, shame, disgust, contempt – it was distant, and she wondered at that, but distantly, too. I am too tired, she told herself. I will feel all of it when I am not so tired. She let her head fall back into the shadows again, resting against the slivered door frame, closing her eyes. There were rapid footfalls coming down the road past her. The villager's curiosity overcoming her, she opened her eyes, just as he passed so that she caught a glimpse of his profile and then his shoulder, and his back.

It was Pierre, come to be with his woman while she gave birth to their baby.

CHAPTER SIXTEEN

Le village

IN THE DAYS THAT FOLLOWED Guillaume's departure for his family in Montréal Sophie walked about the house quietly, tidying rooms that didn't need to be tidied, going into the kitchen to work silently beside Mme Gauthier without asking if she might and strangely, the woman making no protest, or even helping Antoinette, who found stooping difficult now, gather flowers in the garden to be taken to the church. She did not know what to do with herself: Guillaume would not take her to the city with him; she had not seen Pierre since Guillaume had refused to allow their marriage. Had Guillaume gone to M. Hippolyte and told him that Pierre was to stay away from his sister? She thought that probably he had not; his anxiety to get back to his wife and baby was too strong; he wouldn't have taken the time to ride out to the Hippolyte farm. But might he have seen M. Hippolyte or Pierre in town and spoken to them there? And they had listened and that was why she heard nothing more from Pierre since their agreement that she would spend the winter in the city and he would go to work in the bush to earn money for their marriage in the spring?

The more the days passed and she heard nothing from Pierre, the more anxious she grew, and the more restless. More than once she caught Antoinette straightening from where she was tucking in a bed-sheet at the far side of the bed, staring at her, her lips pursed and eyes at once thoughtful and hard. She felt she would burst if something didn't happen, she thought of Uncle Henri's suicide and wondered if she had the courage for such a gesture because if Pierre had forsaken her and she had no choice but to marry *that Chouinard* she would kill herself. She would.

Grandmother appeared at the table at mealtimes, though she ate nothing, and didn't speak. She had grown thinner, and her pale skin had taken on a bluish tinge that worried Sophie, or would have worried her, she thought, had she cared for the old woman.

She couldn't quite get a grip on her own feelings, couldn't pin them down with names, except irritation, impatience, an unruly desire that had no end other than Pierre, who had disappeared. She spent most nights lying awake, or leaning against her window frame, gazing out over the shadowy village through tree branches, their leaves quivering in whatever breeze might come up. The night is never merely darkness, she thought; it has life, it lives itself; it is a transformation of waking things. What? Had she just thought that? Was she losing her mind with this...this...her life was as vast and as uncertain as this night. How would she survive? During the day she had begun to move about the house as if she were dead too, or a ghost, and Antoinette kept giving her more of those strange looks. She wondered if there were some way that she could go to the Hippolyte farm herself, without anyone knowing. She knew she could walk with no trouble, but wasn't sure what she would find there, and felt keenly the possibility of humiliation. And there was no way she could pretend to have dropped in when she was passing by. Where was he? For what was he waiting? That he might have stopped loving her crossed her mind, but she dismissed it at once, certain of his love. She was sure too, that Guillaume's disapproval wouldn't stop him from wanting her. She took that thought no further.

Three nights of this and she fell asleep and then didn't know if she had wakened or was still sleeping. It seemed that the door into her room had opened; someone stood in her doorway, a figure made of shadow, faceless, but with the shoulders of a male. She didn't know she had, but at this vision she had cried out, a mewling whimper, not the scream she thought she had made. The figure came toward her, climbed onto the bed with her, she a child again, not the woman she had become since Pierre had declared his love for her and grandfather had died. And yet, was she not both at the same time? She was sweating, hot sweat soaked her flannel nightdress that was drawn up into a lump at the small of her back, that she was lying on, that hurt her so that she was trying hard to move and could not. Why could she not move? What was this weight she felt on her? What this pain? The roaring in her ears?

She came fully awake, her heart pounding like the hooves of a galloping horse, drowning out all other sounds, sweat pouring down her temples and neck, trickling from under her breasts, a lake of sweat on her belly and between her legs. She couldn't catch her breath, and terrified, forced herself up off the bed to stand in the darkness beside it while the night that she had been seeing in multi-coloured streaks began to grey and darken again to a deep blue. Her chest rose and fell rapidly against the muggy dampness of her nightdress and she shucked it off and pulled a shawl around to cover herself.

At last her heart began to slow, she swallowed and swallowed again, licking her dry lips and teeth with her tongue, wiping her face with the shawl, the night air drying the sweat on her body so that her skin tightened and cooled. Such images as swelled in her brain, and changed and swelled again. Her brother Hector. She sat down hard on her bed. Hector. Why Hector? What is this? She sat that way for a long time until, thoroughly chilled, she lit the lamp, went to her bureau, pulled out a fresh nightdress, slipped it on, and climbed back into the bed, pulling the quilt up to her chin. She trembled still, but on the inside, not visibly, as if she were now made of something so fragile that she hardly dared move for fear of breaking.

Why Hector? Whom she had not seen for many years, except perhaps that time so long ago when she had been ill and nearly died. Nor heard from. Had her grandparents heard from him? She thought not. No one ever said. And why was she so frightened at the thought of his name? She tried to remember what he looked like but could not bring back a face. Not like Guillaume, she remembered that he was fair where Guillaume was dark. And why a nightmare about him? A nightmare that didn't feel that it was a nightmare, but felt that it was a reenactment of something that had happened?

At this, she caught a flash, that was all, a flash, and in an overwhelming fraction of a second, so powerful she would have fallen had she been standing, she remembered, remembered how he had come into her room, not for the first time, had gotten into her bed with her, she pleased at first, how then – and the door had opened and grandmother screamed – yes, grandmother had screamed – had something like this happened to grandmother when she was a girl? She had screamed and the lamp went sideways, the chimney crashing to the floor, as the flame guttered and sucked the air and bloomed wide, then suddenly died, and grandfather had come and dragged Hector from her room, grandmother following, slamming her door behind him so that she couldn't see anything more, and she was alone, listening to thumps against the wall and then the crashes of someone falling down the stairs. The heavy, brooding thud of the door into grandfather's study. The long silence while grandmother stood listening and praying – Sophie remembered hearing the slight brush of the beads against grandmother's nightdress, the delicate tinkle of the silver links hitting each other – in the hall outside her door, Sophie in some exalted state of what could she say? Boundarylessness, or as if she were floating above herself and could hear and see everything. Grandmother not reentering her room, at last, after a very long time, padding down the hall back to the bedroom she shared with grandfather, opening the door, shutting it so softly behind her, the latch clicking with finality.

After this, she fell into a deep sleep. She must have, because the next thing she knew it was morning as if she had used that sleep to know fully the things she couldn't, waking, bear to know. Now she lay watching the light and shadows play on her ceiling as she had been doing as long as she could remember. Waiting for Antoinette, or grandmother to come. *Hector was gone when I came down to breakfast the next morning,* she informed herself as if reading from a schoolbook, *and I never saw him again.* When she asked for him, they said, Gone away to school. Never mind. Then no one even spoke of him. And once, when she had tried to ask about that dream she had had, her grandmother had glared at her so fiercely that Sophie, truly, for one instant, had felt a mortal fear, so that she too never again mentioned his name.

She got out of bed, and stood as if cramped and in pain, rising slowly to her full height.

She had had, during all of this waking time, even, she thought, when she had slept, an unshakeable sense of grandfather being in the room. It was overpowering although she couldn't quite have said what it was: a memory, perhaps, of his physical presence made palpable, but as if he could be everywhere at once, his essence diffused through the air of her room. Although she wanted the comfort of his presence, still, she tried to shake the feeling away, telling herself that he was dead, that this could not be happening. It refused to go; she couldn't make it, and it seemed to her that if she couldn't control it, it was not caused by her, but came from elsewhere. She thought, grandfather has given her this remembrance; it was his gift. But *why?* When she so didn't want it, wanted never to have to think of Hector or his visits to her room so long ago as long as she lived. She bent over, her chest a knot of pain, her mouth in a wide grimace, a soundless cry from the deepest well of her being. How would she live knowing this? Better if it remained forgotten.

She thought of Pierre then, and was baffled because Pierre's caresses were to her so delicious, as if she had waited all her life for that meeting between herself and such a lover. As if Hector and his sin against her and Pierre's touch were entirely different things. They *were* different things. She would cling to that thought; it would keep her alive.

Antoinette knocked sharply on her door.

"You must run an errand," she said. "Sophie?"

"Yes," Sophie said. "Yes, I'm coming." Antoinette would know she wasn't dressed, because her pitcher of hot water was still sitting outside her room. She could hear Antoinette going heavily down the stairs. She thought then, there is still Pierre. And the thought of him caused a rushing of lightness like a warm wind up from between her legs, through her chest, opening it, and upward into her mouth and brain. There was Pierre; she would cling to Pierre who would cherish her and protect her. Pierre would come; she had only to wait, and a calm settled through her surprising in its perfection.

After that, each night she waited. One night, two nights, three nights, and at midnight she went to the garden to see him, but he wasn't there, not the first night, nor the second, nor the third. Her faith that he would come did not waver as she made the silent return trip to her room. On the fourth night, still no Pierre, and his continued absence made her waver in her belief, made her remember that she was only a child who didn't understand the world, who could be disappointed or elated at the turning of the world.

But on the fifth night he was there, leaning against one of the fruit trees that flanked the bench where they had sat and held each other. When he saw her coming down the path, he rushed toward her, put his arms around her, and kissed her face, and then her mouth, drawing her into the shadows so they couldn't be seen from any of the windows, although the only occupied room at the back of the house was Antoinette's by the back door.

In the garden that night, when she had seen Pierre's shadow against the tree she had called, "Pierre," before she remembered to be silent, and he came forward, laughing, his finger to his lips.

"Sophie, Sophie," he said, as he always did, while he kissed her face, her hair and then at last her mouth, and she held him as tightly as she could, pressing her body against his, until he lowered one hand from her waist to hold it firmly against her hip pushing against him, then lifting his other hand to touch her breast. Always, then she pulled back, and made him sit on the bench with her where once again they held tightly to each other and kissed and kissed, and such heat rose in her she thought she would burn, no melt – melt into him. He had begun to unbutton the long row of tiny buttons that started below her chin and went all the way down the dress to the place where her legs cleaved. She thought to stop him, but then asked herself why? When they would soon be married, one way or another. She longed for his hands on her breasts.

"Pierre, Pierre." He took his mouth from hers, panting, one hand reaching down for the hem of her skirt, pulling the fullness of dress and petticoats up toward her waist. She held his hand still.

"What is it?"

"We will be married?" He drew back an inch or two.

"Married? How?" he asked. She was puzzled by this and pulled back too, one hand on the opened buttons of her dress, holding the bodice together.

"Married," she said, hesitantly, as if to explain the term to him.

"We are forbidden," he said. *"L'abbé* Deschameault will never marry us if your grandmother and your brother forbid it." He seemed surprised. Her hands fell away from her dress, that he had unbuttoned to the place where her breasts, plump and full, began to separate.

"We must run away." But she had grown uncertain. "Don't you want to marry me?"

"Of course, I want to marry you," he said, and reached toward her buttons and the skirt hem again.

"I love you so," she whispered, leaning toward him, wishing she could see his face, but they were under the trees and the leaves made shadows on him so that she caught only glimpses of his skin, or a glimmer of light on his coal black hair.

"I love you too," he whispered, putting his mouth back on hers. Then, although neither of them saw it, a light was coming down the path, and when Pierre began to push her down so that she would be lying on the bench, the two of them were suddenly bathed in yellow light. Pierre leaped to his feet, causing Sophie to fall backward and then to scramble up, one arm shading her eyes from the light that spilled over them. A hiss.

"Traître, putain."

She had expected Antoinette, but it was grandmother.

They scrambled to their feet, side by side facing grandmother, Sophie fumbling for Pierre's hand, not able to find it. Grandmother had moved the lamp so that it no longer blinded them and they could see her face. She seemed, Sophie saw, to have grown in size until she was larger than the two of them together; her shawl was black, her gown black, her small widow's silk cap also black, and by it Sophie knew then that grandmother had been waiting for Pierre to come, had known that Sophie went out each night to wait for him. Her body stiffened with fear, she tried to speak but could make no sound. Pierre cleared his throat, put out a hand as if to ask pardon or for calm, but *grandmère* drew back as if it were the head of a viper.

"Inside." Beside her Sophie felt Pierre twitch, as if all the remaining boyishness in him wanted to run, as if he had been caught stealing apples. Such a relief that he stayed.

"Grandmère," she began, a whisper.

"Vite," the woman said, and there was such icy rage in the sound that Sophie could do nothing but turn and start up the path toward the kitchen door. She hoped that Pierre was following, but in her mixed fear and confusion couldn't tell. They went, not into grandfather's study as she had somehow expected, but into the small sitting room across from the *salon* where, before grandfather's death she had spent so many long evenings doing needlework beside her grandmother. Chills ran up and down her back and she too, wanted to run away, but forced herself to stay. Or else she stayed because she was too afraid to do anything else. They stood again side by side in the small room, their backs to the unlit fireplace, Pierre still not having taken Sophie's hand so that she moved closer to him, wanting his protection. At this, he stirred and put his arm around her shoulders, she seeing then that her buttons were still undone, and beginning to fumble to do them up.

"Arrêt!" grandmère demanded and Sophie found her hand stilling

before falling to her side. The door behind her that grandmother had closed as she followed them in opened now. Antoinette. But no, it was the *le curé*, it was Deschambeault. He had been waiting too. Sweat broke out on her brow and she looked up to Pierre's face and saw only puzzlement mixed with alarm on it. Would they send her to join Violette in the convent in Montréal? Would they send her to a workhouse? She gasped aloud at the thought.

Grandmother began to speak. She used full sentences as if she had rehearsed what she would say, her voice low, coming tightly from her chest, as if it hurt her to speak. "You have violated every rule you have been taught. You have shamed yourself, your mother, your father. You have shamed your grandfather and me. You are no better than the worst village whore." If Sophie hadn't been clinging so hard to Pierre, she would have covered her ears with her hands. That she should have to hear such things.

"I love him," she began, "he loves me. We *will* be married one day. You cannot stop us," although of course, they could.

"Be silent," grandmother said to her. "You are a child." Why didn't Pierre say something? Why didn't Pierre speak? Behind grandmother *le curé* Deschambeault stood quietly, a soldier in the Lord, waiting, for what Sophie couldn't imagine. "I would send you away to the nuns to keep you, you could serve them to learn humility, but now –" she turned to the priest. "Speak to them," she demanded, and went past him out of the room, shutting the door behind her. Deschambeault stepped forward, his movements slow, his expression stern.

"I am here to question you," he said. He turned his face to Pierre, the two men's eyes meeting in a lock that was broken by the priest after what seemed to Sophie an eternity.

"Madame," he said, causing Sophie to draw her breath in sharply. Why now, Madame? But she was afraid that she knew only too well what was meant by this. She waited as his eyes went over her face as if he had never seen her before, then down past the opened buttons to her waist, before sweeping up again, up, beyond her head or Pierre's.

She lifted her hands and began awkwardly to engage the tiny buttons in their fabric loops.

"Êtes-vous enceinte?"

She gasped, wanting to protest, putting her hand over her mouth and dropping it again, lowering her eyes to the floor while she struggled to find a language in which to answer such a charge. She understood only that this was not a question, that he believed he knew the answer even though he looked harshly from one face to the other, seeming to collect information, and understanding, he thought, his visage hardening with his own determination.

She said, pleading, "We wish to marry."

"Your family forbids this marriage," he told her, "Your brother has told me not to allow it." Why didn't Pierre speak? He should speak, and she turned her head to look at him.

He said, as if she had prodded him, "We decide ourselves," but he sounded feeble to Sophie, she hadn't thought he would be so afraid of a mere priest. But he cleared his throat and said, "We want to marry."

The priest shouted, or perhaps he didn't shout so much as change his tone to something that even though Sophie had known him all her life and heard him say Mass a thousand times and deliver his messages to the congregation every Sunday in the churchyard, she had not heard before. Implacable, hard as iron. She understood it to be the same voice that would have, all those years, before, told grandfather that his brother could not be buried with the rest of the family in the churchyard.

"Silence," he shouted, and paused, his mouth working as if to control himself. "Under the circumstances I have no choice but to marry you. Now."

It took her a second, but Sophie understood in a rush that the priest was convinced that they had been intimate together, had had "relations" as men and women did, further, that by her lowering her eyes to the floor, or to her reaction to his question about being pregnant, he had understood her to admit that this was so. And she was amazed, at the same time as she opened her mouth to protest that she still had her innocence, her virginity, that she had not sinned in that way, that in her struggling to think of a way to be allowed to marry Pierre, she had never once thought of letting herself become pregnant by him, so that marriage would be certain. It hadn't once occurred to her. She felt the air go out of her, and willed her mouth closed. Beside her, Pierre had grasped her hand too tightly, so that she had to twist it a little to get him to loosen his grip.

He said, weakly, as if in protest, "Now?" The priest didn't answer, but went to the door and let grandmother back into the room with them. She looked questioningly into the priest's face, who gave a brief nod, and her face contorted into revulsion, then smoothed again into the same implacability as the priest's.

The idea was growing in her that they would be married if she would let them think she was a sinner. A small exuberance was growing in her as well; what did she care about what they thought if she and Pierre could this very night be one?

Pierre started to speak.

"Silence," the priest said again, and Pierre, to her amazement also closed his mouth.

"I will get Antoinette to be the other witness," grandmother said, and went out into the hall and called her by name. She came at once, fully dressed, and Sophie saw that she had known too that grandmother was setting a trap. And she hadn't once warned Sophie. But then, Sophie thought rapidly looking at the woman who refused to look at her and who just might be crying, maybe she was only told tonight to be ready. The priest had gone to the table on one side of the room and was placing his silken scarf around his neck, lifting his missal, returning to them and making the sign of the cross over them with the edge of his long, pale hand.

When the brief ceremony was over, grandmother said, "Now you will leave this house. Do not return, ever." Sophie said, trembling a little, "May I get my things." Grandmother nodded once.

Sophie ran from the room, up the stairs, propelled by glee. It was only when she was in the room that she realized how little she had that was her own: her missal, her rosary, some toiletries, several books that she would leave behind, a few dresses, undergarments, and shoes. Even the one suitcase in the back of the closet wasn't hers, but belonged to someone else in the family and had been there as long as she could remember. But she had a large cloth laundry bag and into this she rapidly stuffed the few things she was taking with her.

She hadn't been gone ten minutes and hurried back down the stairs to find her husband –think of that! My husband! – still standing by the fireplace, Antoinette sitting on the edge of the settee – and no one else in the room. In the doorway, she stopped, looking across the room at him, as he looked back at her. All her life she would remember that mutual gaze, that moment when they had recognized that they were now linked together, now and forever. She had gazed with love at him, near adoration, she would recall, but he had been tentative, appraising, then his native cheerfulness returning, he had broken into a grin, and come across to where she stood, lowered his head to hers and kissed her hard and long with Antoinette sitting right there. Soon, she thought, they would be laughing over how they had fooled the old priest into giving them what they wanted, had wanted all along, and been forbidden.

"When I left my house tonight," he told her, "I didn't think I would come back a married man." How she had laughed at this as he helped her onto the back of the plow horse he had ridden into town, he getting on in front of her and she shoving the stuffed laundry bag between them so as not to frighten the horse with it bobbing and slapping against its side. When the heavy front door of the old house had closed behind them for the last time, Sophie felt such relief and happiness, even as they were encompassed by darkness, and then by the chill of the night in those coldest hours before the dawn.

"Where will we go?" she whispered, pushing herself against him.

"Home," he said. "To the farm. There is nowhere else."

"Will they take us?" This hadn't occurred to her before. If not, what would they do?

"Of course they will take us," he said, scorn in his voice, and she was aware that he had been humiliated by what had happened just now, and further, not only by the priest. That he was only the dirt beneath her grandmother's once aristocratic feet, and he knew it, and hated grandmother for it.

All the way to the Hippolyte farm she clung to Pierre, leaning against his back as well as the laundry bag would allow, and thought of how she loved him and how happy they would be. Or maybe she thought only of Pierre and the warmth of his body against hers.

At the farm Pierre wakened everyone shouting that he was now a married man. His father and mother leaped out of bed, she still in her nightclothes, his father having paused to pull on trousers and to put felt boots on his feet before he followed his wife from their bedroom. His older brothers, both bigger and taller than Pierre, came thudding slowly down from the attic where they slept, looking sleepy-eyed at their ebullient brother and assessingly at Sophie before giving her copies of Pierre's grin and coming forward to take her hands and give her brotherly kisses on both cheeks. His sisters came out pulling wraps around themselves and kissed her too, although Marie-Ange was of course not there, nor Violette who was missed most of all by Sophie.

Madame Hippolyte said, surprisingly, "There is no help for it. My dear, you will be my daughter too," and cried, although Sophie wasn't sure why she was crying, perhaps for the loss of Pierre? Or for some secret dream she had for him? But her mother-in-law said briskly to the sisters, "Both of you, into one bed now, give your new sister-in-law a bed, and Pierre, you…" Here she hesitated, "Go up with your brothers. Take a quilt." When he looked askance and his brothers looked at each other and chortled, she said, angrily, "For tonight, that's all. We will sort that out later."

But Monsieur Hippolyte brought out a bottle of his homemade brandy and was setting out glasses and calling for everyone to come around and drink a toast to the newlyweds, and everyone did, and there was much laughter and muttered good wishes, and Sophie drank some too and was surprised at how hot she suddenly felt, and gay. The girls went to bed then, and Sophie would have too, but Pierre said, "No, stay. We have to talk a little." She pulled up a chair and sat next to Mme Hippolyte whose head had begun to nod.

"Now," M. Hippolyte declared, "We don't want to hear the story now," as Pierre opened his mouth to tell his parents what had happened.

"I can guess all too well," Mme Hippolyte said, and crossed herself and muttered a prayer.

"We must decide what is to become of you. Have you any plans?" he asked his son, and Pierre, laughed a little, looking at his hands cupping the small glass as he pushed it back and forth between his palms. M. Hippolyte reached out and filled it again. The room was quiet, only the fire crackling in the stove, and Mme Hippolyte's heavy breathing as she fell asleep at the table, her head falling forward causing her to wake again. In her exhaustion Sophie was beginning to think that perhaps they had made a mistake by allowing the priest to marry them so quickly. Could she have refused? She wondered if perhaps Pierre had been going to refuse and leave her there alone, but he had not, and now they were husband and wife and nothing could undo that. A thrill of happiness went through her.

"I made no plans to be married so quickly," Pierre admitted. "So I don't know..."

"You know there is no land for you," his father said. "I can maybe help you get a little. Plamondon is thinking of selling that bit over by Harris's. We could go see him in the morning." The Hippolytes, Sophie knew from her grandfather, had had this bit of land for seventy or so years, but year after year seemed not to better themselves by buying more. So many children, her grandfather had said, sighing, four sons, shaking his head.

"It is so little," Pierre pointed out. "We couldn't feed ourselves on it, and there is no house, we'd have to build one." The two men were silent, Pierre staring into the distance as if calculating, his father gazing into the blackened, unlit hearth.

He stirred at last and said, smiling, "But we had nothing," speaking to his wife, "when we married." She shrugged, not smiling. "Not a sou or a louis," she said, "Only the muscles in our backs."

Sophie sat up straight. "We could go West!" her excitement bubbling up so that she spoke louder than she had intended. Both the men looked at her. Mme Hippolyte cried, "No!"

Pierre and his father turned from Sophie to gaze at each other, a man's look it was, assessing, evaluating, considering together in silence.

"We could," Pierre said. "We could have free land if we went West." His father spread his arms, hands open toward them as if to show they were empty, that he knew nothing about the West.

"You need tools, machines, animals, you need money to go…" Mme Hippolyte said, "On this place there are how many bits and pieces of this and that that we don't use anymore, or that are broken but could be fixed. My old butter churn that leaks…"

"I have some money," Sophie said, thinking of grandfather's few louis or sous Guillaume had said grandfather had left her in his will.

"You will need to go soon if you go," M. Hippolyte said. "You have to plow, get a crop in or you will starve all winter and they say the winters are bad, very bad," shaking his head slowly. Better you wait until next spring, non? Spend the winter getting some money in the woods, and you," he turned to Sophie, "can stay here with us."

Sophie could feel blood rushing to her face, it was all she could do to suppress a loud *no!* She turned to Pierre whose eyes were fixed on the table, as if he were deep in thought. She ventured a timid, "I would like to go now?" Pierre lifted his head and gazed thoughtfully at her. She suspected he wasn't seeing her at all.

"I think now, too," he said slowly. "I have saved some money from working for Fournier. I can make a little more before we go."

"Relatives will help when they know," Mme Hippolyte said. She kept looking at Sophie out of the corner of her eye. She thinks I have money Sophie thought. She thinks…that I cannot do this; that I am too weak and foolishly brought up to go West and be a pioneer. She wonders if I know enough – how to make butter, how to sew, how to grow things.

The West loomed large over the scarred and chipped kitchen table. How many years had the table sat there for generation after generation of Hippolytes? Someone had made it, some clever *habitant*. It was not grandmother's heavy carved and polished table that had come all the way from France a hundred years earlier.

Could she do it? Everyone said it would be hard, although she suspected that she had no idea how hard it would be. She found she didn't care. To have a new life in a new place; this was what she had dreamt of.

"Show me how to make bread and pies," she said to her new mother-in-law.

"You don't know? But there is no time!" the woman said, throwing out her hands as her husband had done.

"How long?" Pierre asked his father.

"Fast," he replied. "Very fast. Two weeks?" Pierre looked taken aback, for an instant regret or something more profound Sophie couldn't name swept across his features before it vanished.

"Yes," Sophie said. All eyes had turned to her. "Two weeks and we are gone from here."

That was how it went, to everyone's surprise. A brother went to the town and ascertained how one went West, by what train, how long, how much money would be required. Pierre and his father and uncles and cousins went about the farm and the countryside gathering the essential tools and making repairs, while Sophie worked from morning until night in the kitchen, and out in the barn learning how to milk a cow, how to separate the milk so she could make butter, a few basic skills at sewing, the one craft about which she knew a little.

"Quand les enfants…" Mme Hippolyte began, then shook her head and went on punching down the bread dough. "She doesn't even know

how to make pickles," she wailed to the kitchen wall one afternoon, went to the stove and stood over it holding her head in both hands. Sophie glanced over her shoulder, and said, grimly, "I will learn." She wanted to add, if everyone can do it, she certainly could, but felt it unwise to say so.

During all of this she and Pierre slept apart. There was barely time to speak to each other and no place to do so in private. But more than once at night they had crept out together to the barn where they climbed into the hay loft, and where she had once been told by his sister that her great uncle was a suicide, there in the straw Pierre initiated his bride in lovemaking, leaving her speechless and sore and filled yet, with mixed wonder and delight.

And then, the Hippolytes and the neighbourhood having done what they could to prepare the young couple for their adventure, it was time to go.

THE NEXT MORNING when Sophie rose the sun was already shining on Bone Pile and she realized that both she and Charles had slept in, and she with so much work to do. She decided to let her child sleep as long as he needed to, but got out of bed herself, washed, and dressed. She found herself thinking about the letter from André, and was surprised at how very warmly she felt toward him this morning. I'll wait until he is settled in Calgary, she decided, brushing her hair, and then I'll write to him, just a simple letter, and began mentally to compose it.

Cher André,

I was so happy to hear from you. For five years I have seen no one from home, nor heard much from anyone, not even from my brother Guillaume. Your letter was like a drink of cool water on a hot day. And to think you are here, in the West.

She thought that perhaps she was being too forward, mentally erased that line, then put it back: She would be truthful; she would find and tell the truth about her own feelings.

You will know of my disaster; I am sure everyone back home knows. How one pays for the folly of one's youth! But here I am, and there you are, or soon will be, and perhaps we will meet in person one of these days before too long. I hope so.

What else should she say? That she would perhaps be in Calgary in a few months and would call on him? But she had no idea if that was true or not, and perhaps it would be too forward in any case. Then she considered how to end the letter finally settling on,

Your friend,
Sophie Charron Hippolyte

Satisfied, she smiled to herself, deciding to write the letter while it was fresh in her mind, and perhaps even mail it to the address he had given her so that it would be waiting for him on his arrival. She didn't allow herself to think beyond the moment when he opened it and read it, and knew she no longer spurned his advances. Perhaps she should add, *As you might expect, I have grown up since those days in my grandparents' parlour.*

Then she remembered that, while she stood brushing her hair, watching over her sleeping child, thinking of her long-ago scorned suitor, Pierre was down the street, only a few houses from her. Once again it seemed that she had spent the brief hours of sleep absorbing this knowledge because now when she thought of him she felt none of the panic she had felt the night before, nor any of the desire for him that had so plagued her since his departure. She felt nothing at all, until she remembered that he had surely come to oversee the birth of his child, and stopped brushing, pulled her hair back quickly and tucked it into its usual chignon, deftly pushing in the hair pins without bothering again to consult the mirror.

She went into the kitchen, stirred the stove, added a bit of coal, and pulled the coffee pot forward, filling it with water and grounds. Then she pushed the table aside and lifted the door in the floor to the cellar below, holding her skirt up, going down the two steps and reaching for the pot of soup she had placed there to keep it cool until she needed it. *I should be thinking about Pierre*, she told herself, but her thoughts were slippery as eels and wouldn't be caught. Maybe, she told herself, after the child was born, no doubt towards morning he had left again, to return when mother and child were ready to travel. She couldn't believe how calm she was, and wondered if there was a crack forming somewhere in this stoicism that was widening, that she would suddenly break apart with her shame. Unless the realization of Harry's desire for her had strengthened her, that she wasn't merely a discarded woman any more, but one that another man wanted. Thinking about Harry was fruitless, she decided, not knowing where that was going. She was surprised that surrounding all thoughts of André she felt a warmth that hadn't been there all those years ago in her home village. How she had despised him then, she was so blinded by Pierre's good looks, and laughed aloud in embarrassment at what a ridiculous girl she had been. She vowed again that as soon as she had taken Charles to Mrs. Wozny's she would write that letter, and mail it at once.

Then bitterness at Pierre's treatment of her returned. How the town must be gossiping about her now, with Marguerite in labour, or the child born, and her husband and his lover only three doors down the street. For a second she didn't think that she could bear the humiliation, and hated Pierre with a profound hatred that made her clench her jaw, her whole body going rigid.

Lost in her reverie she hadn't heard Charlie get out of bed until now the sound of his urinating into the chamber pot that she had left out for him – if she didn't, he tended to spill it trying to pull it out from under the bed – could be heard clearly. She wondered then if Pierre would try to see his son.

"Mama?" Charles called, and she answered quickly, "Hello, my sweet, good morning." He came from the bedroom into the kitchen where he climbed up onto a chair as he did every morning and waited for his breakfast. "Did you sleep well?" she asked him, just to let him know she was thinking about him.

"Mmmmm," he said. "Can I go outside to play today?"

"But of course," she said. "We'll go down to Mrs. Wozny's soon and the girls will play with you."

Outside their dwelling there was the sound of men's voices as they called across or down the street to each other, and the welcome jangle and creak of a dray going by pulled by a team of heavy horses. The general store would be open, Mrs. Kaufmann sweeping dirt out onto the short section of boardwalk outside, and Mr. Kaufmann bustling around inside without appearing ever to accomplish much. Before too long her first customers would come wanting soup and sandwiches made of her homemade bread and whatever was left of the sliced beef. And pie after. Was it for this that she had braved the West? Her resolve failed, and if Charlie hadn't said, "What is that noise, Mommie. Is that oxen out there? I want to see," beginning to climb down so that she had to tell him that it was, as usual, only someone's team going by and that he must sit back down and wait for his breakfast.

"Did you wash your hands?" Without replying he climbed down from his chair and went back into the bedroom where she could hear the loud splashing of water that meant he wanted her to think that he was washing his hands, whether he actually was or not.

When she took Charlie down to Wozny's house she was careful to go down the main street so as to avoid the Tremblay house. But, still, she found herself listening for a newborn's cry. She had heard there was a French community in or near Calgary. It was called Mission, and Father Lacombe, she had been told, had gone all the way to Ottawa to procure the land for it. Would she wish to live again among the French, her own people? Yes. Then she remembered how stifled she had felt among them, how she had yearned for freedom, and what had freedom brought her but this?

She took the same way back, hurrying, but no neighbours were on the street, and when she thought to look back over her shoulder to Harry's house she saw the team was out front, now hitched to his wagon. So he would go back onto his land today. He wouldn't even know that Pierre was back; maybe no one but the Tremblays knew of Pierre's return. He may be gone by now, she reminded herself, and couldn't tell if she wanted this to be so, or not.

Hearing a shout up the street from where she was hurrying along, Sophie lifted her head, thinking someone was calling her, but no, in fact there was no one about, the call must have come from the stable, a horse acting up perhaps. Mr. Kaufmann was leaning against the wall of his store smoking a pipe and two farmers Sophie recognized were standing with him chatting, paying her no attention. The shouts of small children came from the Wozny's house behind her and over one street. She saw no one else, and moved more quickly, anxious to get back into her house before she'd been seen. *As if I have committed a crime*, she thought indignantly. She was reminded of the day a year ago or so when she had perambulated the town's main street with Charles, looking for a place to sell her wedding ring and her brooch and had met Adelaide Smith in her finery and had failed to recognize her as the poor, thin woman who had sat across from her on the train a few years before on the trip West. When she reached her café, she hurried in and shut both the outer screen door and then the inner one, pausing to give her eyes time to adjust to the now shadowed room before she began work.

"Sophie." She thought for an instant that it was Harry, and felt annoyed as she had a great deal of work to do and little time in which to get it done. But it was Pierre. He was standing at the stove, facing her.

For an instant her breath caught and dizziness struck, retreating as rapidly as it had come. At last she said, "What do you want?" emphasizing the 'you,' to remind him he had no rights with her.

"Nothing," he said, mildly enough.

"Has…the woman…had your child?" She wanted to hurt him as badly as he had hurt her.

"Yes, a girl," he said, before she could ask.

"Why did you come here?" It was a cry, she wished never to have to see him again.

"I came to say…I wanted to see you again…"

"For what?" The rage in her voice astonished even her. He came toward her and she took a step backward, it seemed as if he would use his old tricks with her: touch her, kiss her gently, and she would be lost, still, after all that had passed between them.

"To say good-bye," he said. There was some note in his voice she didn't recall having heard before, her ears perked at it. Even in her anguish she wondered if he had at last grown up and recognized her worth and her womanhood, that she had to admit he had helped her to create.

"It is late for that," she said, finally, and found herself sitting down at the table. He hesitated, then sat down across from her.

"You didn't need to come," she told him. "I wish you hadn't come."

"Where is Charles?" he asked. "I hoped I might see him one more time." At this it was all she could do not to cry.

"He is at the Woznys'," no use to refuse to tell him; everyone knew where Charles spent his days. "I don't want you to see him, he needs a father." She was ashamed at the illogic of her statements, but her mind was too confused. He did not want to come back, he did not want her back, he wanted only to see his son.

"I will see him before I go," he told her. Now there was emotion in his voice.

"You won't take him?" she asked, her voice shaky. He could, he could do that: How frightened she suddenly was.

"No," he said, his voice having gone gentle. "I will not take him. Maybe later, when we are settled, you might send him to visit me?" She was about to declare, never, but thought better of it, nodded as if she agreed.

"I am sorry to have left you," he said. "It… I…am sorry." No suggestion of it having been a mistake, or dishonourable. No true apology to her, although, of what good would an apology be now?

"You left me with nothing."

"I knew you would manage," he said. "I knew what you are made of."

"And in the end, did not like it," she said. "How did you get from such perfect love," sneering the last two words, "to leaving me with nothing? Not even telling me you were going, much less why?"

He said, "What do you mean, perfect love?" He raised his voice now, although not to a shout. "I was forced into marrying you. I thought, I will need a wife soon, why not this one? I like her well enough, and I have to live in this place. Might just as well do the right thing." And he laughed. She could have killed him because he laughed. "And the old priest, he was ready to kill me, so I thought…"

"You said that you loved me," her tone shamingly querulous, how disgustingly pathetic she sounded, but hadn't he just taken away her last support that explained how she had come West, that explained how she sat in this worn shack, poor as a church mouse, and alone with her fatherless child? Curses rose in her, words she didn't know she knew, but not one passed her lips. How one learns in the West, she told herself. How one learns.

"I despise you," she said. "You deserve to be despised by all."

She put her head in one hand, her elbow resting on the table. She was panting, remembering the night they married, remembering the excitement of the preparations and the parting and the long trip West with him by her side. Suddenly she knew that he was lying to her, for what purpose she could not divine.

"It was the work, wasn't it," she said. "It was the loneliness. You missed the village and the farm, and all your family. You came finally, to blame me. You forgot that you once loved me. Why did you think that Marguerite could bring you more than I did?"

The silence in the room was a presence in itself, the anguish she felt filling up the space.

He said, "I missed the forest, the two wide rivers, the great silver lake shining against the sky." Another long silence while she tried to absorb this, trying to hold back the sobs that roiled in her chest and throat. "When she is fit to travel, we will go back. We will get an annulment. People will forget in time."

"And me?" He was moving past her now, toward the door, but now he paused, lifted his hand, touched her hair gently, and went by. At the door, he said, his back to her, "You wanted the West, didn't you? Now you *are* the West."

AT LAST IT WAS TRULY SPRING, all the snow gone, the land dried enough for seeding crops, animals put out to pasture where there were fences, flocks of ducks and geese and wild swans long returned. Two more families had moved into Bone Pile, none of them looking any different from those who were already there, and both speaking English and of Protestant faiths. One of them, a Mrs. Cunningham said to Sophie as she drank tea in her café, "I think you are French!" as if this were the most astonishing thing.

"I am," Sophie replied, perhaps a little too crisply.

"Why didn't you go to where the French people live? I hear there are French towns all over."

She said, "We came where we wanted to be."

But for a long time after that she couldn't help but wonder if maybe the source of the failure of her marriage to Pierre had been, not their failure to tell the truth that night so long ago, but that first, early error, for which she was to blame. She was the one who rejected going north to Prince Albert or further West and north to the communities near Fort Edmonton. She thought of her youthful dream of freedom, and wondered if such a thing were even possible, anywhere. Where had she gotten the idea to start with? She supposed she had heard the men talking of it in the churchyard, at the summer festivals each year, and at her grandparents' table.

She knew the women didn't speak of freedom, and she wondered what it was they did speak of: marriages, children, houses, gardens, not even of education. But she had wanted more than the things the women spoke of, only she had no way of knowing what it was she wanted and using the language of the men, who seemed to have more than the women, she had grasped onto the word, 'freedom,' and taken it as her own. The West meant freedom; so why was it that she was in the West now, and of it, Pierre had claimed, and she felt only marginally more free than she had felt as the unwanted child in her grandmother's home?

When, a few weeks earlier, Pierre had walked from her door and she knew she would never see him again and had no sense of true apology or shame from him, she had thought, *I am free now*. Should I go to Prince Albert? Should I go to this new "Rouleauville" at Calgary? But always she was brought back to the sorry fact that she hadn't yet enough money to go anywhere. Another year, she told herself grimly, and I will have enough to go. No one, she thought with some glumness, is free who does not have enough money. She wondered too, if perhaps André Chouinard had gone back to Québec. If perhaps he and Pierre were meeting on the streets of the Québec village from which they had both come, and were friends now, because neither of them possessed Sophie Charron. She doubted it.

She remembered too, now, having been too angry to think of what she knew, that no child born in wedlock became a bastard because his parent's marriage was annulled. That was a teaching of the church she would cling to, and tell Charles when he was old enough to wonder. And she thought further too, that she would be glad of an annulment, that if she had married in the church, she could be un-married by its own rules.

Pierre's claim that he had never loved her came back to her, and she remembered that she had felt when he said it that he was lying so as to free himself of her, she supposed. Now she wondered if she had chosen to believe that this was a lie because she couldn't bear to think that her dream of love was just that, a dream of her own, and never of his. She thought about their early days together, their lovemaking, the things he said to her, how he held her, and kissed her and said there could be no life without her. How could she disbelieve what she had known with every cell in her body to be true? Or had she been only a prize he had captured and the thrill of that had worn off? But if he had once loved her as she believed he had, how could such love go away? Yet, it had. Such sadness as she felt, as if the world were made of sadness.

She began to understand then that there were not always answers for the deepest questions, that some things, no matter how important, were things that a person would never know, and that all the thinking in the world wouldn't give an answer. Then she thought, *but I am different now: something must have happened when I thought and thought and thought and thought and never knew what to believe.* She supposed that what was different was that she was now drained of passion that had been the only way she could think of him: with hatred, rage, or love, all of which clouded her vision and prevented her from thinking clearly. Now, she told herself, she could think clearly.

The men of the town had at last begun building a school. And none too soon, because by the time it was finished and a teacher had been found, Charles would be ready for it. But then, she thought, I want better for Charles, a better life than this, a better place than this. Only one year, she promised herself. Then I'll be gone to a bigger place where there will be more opportunities for him, and much better schooling. But thinking of her tiny hoard of cash waiting in Frank Archibald's safe, she was daunted, knowing of the poverty that would await them in Calgary, and how hard it would be to get ahead.

Always, in the back of her mind was the notion of the benefits of marrying again. But Harry offered only his farm and she had had enough of that, or so she thought, and there was perhaps André? But when she had finally written to him, and he had promptly answered her, his reply had made no offer other than the suggestion that if she should come to Calgary she should visit him. What that meant, she couldn't tell. She had begun to think that he would have gone back east by the time she made it there, and sighed.

She was reminded that today was mail day and with the weather so good and the trails dry, the stagecoach carrying mail would soon reach the town, or perhaps, already had. She untied her apron, touched her hair with her palms, and went out onto the street, pausing to look up and down and, saw a faintly greenish tinge across the land that encouraged her.

Beyond the town the pile of bones still sat gleaming in the sun white as snow, brighter even than the snow, as if it was some precious mountain set there to mark what had been. Still, though, when she went near it, she was chilled and saw the cracks, jagged broken edges, and chips in each individual bone and the dirt embedded in those long cracks, and the stains on them from birds and small animals, and from blowing earth. And on days when the sky was low and purple and indigo, the light blue, and the vast pile black, it seemed to her that its very presence cast a pall on the town, was perhaps the source of its ill luck, its cruelty to its own inhabitants, to each other, and its poverty and failure. As if, perhaps, the bones were cursed. Or the bones themselves cursed the town for what had gone before she had even heard of the West.

People came and went as she waited for her turn at the table where some of the mail was still being sorted. She said hello, and yes, what a beautiful day, and how soon the crops would be in, and people could travel again without worrying about storms, and had she heard that surely this year the railroad would come to Bone Pile? She hardly noticed when the husband of the family that carried the mail handed her a couple of envelopes, one she saw at once a bill for coal. She would wait until she returned to her own house to open the other, a plain envelope, unfamiliar handwriting. Although she barely glanced at it, she thought, pleased, that it would be from André.

When she finally took the time to sit down and look at it, she noted that it had come from a bank in Montréal, had been forwarded from a bank branch in Calgary to Garden City, that had sent it on to her in Bone Pile. Puzzled, she used a knife to carefully open it, then spread the thick paper out on the table. The letter was written in the formal language of bankers and lawyers and said that it concerned the estate of her grandmother. She was shocked: How could it be that grandmother had died and she hadn't even been told? She felt no grief, nor any pity, not for her grandmother, nor for herself, but knew in a new way that hadn't been there before that in her own time emotion would come.

The letter went on to say that she had been left nothing, which was, hardly a surprise, yet deep in her chest a hard knot formed that threatened to rise and cause her to vomit. She swallowed hard, keeping it down. Grandmother had left nearly all her money and her land to the church, also, not a surprise. A small amount had gone to each of Sophie's brothers. That grandmother had left money for Hector amazed her and she took it as a blow directed at her.

But wait, there was a smaller envelope inside the large one. Now with fingers that trembled, not even bothering to use the knife, she tore it open. Inside was a bank draft attached to a note in Guillaume's hand.

I send you some of the money that our grandmother left for me. My business is very slowly improving and money is less hard to come by these days. As well, I blame myself in part for the situation in which you find yourself. As Claire has told me many times, I was wrong not to have let you come to us in Montréal. Therefore, I am sending you a small portion and hope that it will help you in your life.

He had signed it merely, *Guillame Charron.*

The draft was for five hundred dollars. It was to her a fortune; with what she had managed to save she now had nearly a thousand dollars, enough to move to Calgary this very day if she chose, and imagined herself packing a suitcase for herself and one for Charles and walking out. She wouldn't even shut the door behind her.

She began to cry; the tears she had for so long forbidden herself pouring down her cheeks. Her tears were of relief, they were of sorrow of such depths that she was astounded herself: her loneliness, the sadness of her childhood, the abandonment that had nearly broken her in two, only her dear Charles saving her. Leaving at once consumed her, but as soon as she began to rise to begin packing regret came: Regret because she would leave this village even though she had hated it and never been part of it, but in which she had had friends of a sort, and had made her own way. Memories of her village in Québec swept through her next; in this moment she missed profoundly the vast forest that surrounded it, missed running on the hills with her friends, screaming until her throat hurt, missed the yellowness of the sun there, and the damp air, missed the balsam and sycamores, the wild columbine and honeysuckle, missed the two rivers and the silver lake shining under the sky, and thought, remembering grandmother's unkindness and that of the nuns, remembering how the priest ruled as a king: *Where we came from becomes a myth in our minds.* This thought, surprising as it was, dried her tears. Calm once again descended on her.

I can go from here, she reminded herself, and began at once to make her plans for their departure. She thought now of Pierre, because now it was safe to think of him; now she was a woman of some means and could leave him behind.

Ever since she had talked to him she had doubted herself, thinking first that she wasn't wrong and he had loved her, then thinking she had been a fool and the love was all on her side, and girlish nonsense as well. She had thought that she had done well once he had left her, that she had made her own way, and that with a small child, was something of which she should be proud. But ever since he had stood in her kitchen and offered her not a crumb, she had seen how poor she was, how hard she had to work for the little she did have, and how she remained alone, and had no one who could save her. No one who even wanted to save her, except perhaps Harry, although she suspected that he really thought, even if he didn't realize it, that she would save him: With her hard work, and her good sense, with her mere presence, no matter what any of it cost her. And now André Chouinard had reappeared in her life. But she mustn't think of him; from now on she must depend on no one but herself.

She had, too, her precious Charles on whom to lavish love, so he would never know what it is to grow up without a mother, seeing for the first time that she would never stop grieving for her own mother, that it would be her pain to bear long after she had gotten over the deaths and betrayals of others.

Now she could leave Bone Pile this very day. She knew it would not be as she left her childhood home, lost in a dream of passion and glory, believing she could shuck off all her past without a trace of regret or even remembrance. Nor as she left the homestead, in terror, ill with shame and her loss, unable to understand what had happened to her, or why. She and her son would go away from this place of wonder – for it was a place of wonder after all – would move on to the city where there were women with hearts and minds like her own, maybe even French women, and warmed at the thought of speaking French again. She knew a little of herself now, and that knowledge would be the rock on which she would build the rest of her life.

She stood in the doorway of the shabby rented house she called home and gazed out over the town that stood gleaming in the spring sun. She had not loved this village, nor the way people lived in it. The way they would not admit to their own errors, or to their hardship that they would never escape although they said they would, they believed they would, and saw for once a glimpse of the nobility, well-hidden by the daily pettiness and venality, that their Western venture invested their lives, the suffering that was inextricably part of it.

Out beyond the village was the vast prairie broken only by a narrow trail wandering south and west through the limitless expanse of grass, another going north, another heading east. How happy she had been when she had first seen this place from the windows of the train. How in love with it she had been when she had lived all that long summer on it, in a tent batted by the steady wind, its constant soughing in the grass, the scent of sage, wild onion, gumbo primroses, cinquefoils, wolf willow, strange grasses, and many, to her, nameless plants, some odour that was *prairie* and nothing else. She remembered the day so long ago when she had fallen from the wagon and landed by a patch of wild roses so that her first real memory of prairie was of their bright pinks and reds, the air around her drenched with their delicate, musky perfume, for all their beauty, the plants themselves as tough as any weed. No, tougher. Wild animals always nearby, though unseen, and when the pitiless sun sank below the distant horizon, the constellations, old as the world, and the white-faced moon their only light, the sky then so vast and boundless that her soul had come loose and drifted out among the stars.

ACKNOWLEDGEMENTS

I wrote this book, or a version of it, during the most tumultuous and possibly most difficult time of my life; I wrote it in Perth, in Sydney, and in Tasmania, in Ireland and in the Czech Republic, in the Saskatchewan countryside where I lived for something like thirty-five years, and then, eventually, I wrote it here in Calgary. Then I wrote it again to create this version. For this I thank especially David Margoshes, who is an incisive and supportive editor. Along the way I had help from Jennifer Glossop, and before that from Charlene Dobmeier and from Phyllis Bruce, and from other writers – in particular Dianne Warren who fixed an astute prairie eye on it – also from my sisters, and friends too numerous to name. Thanks very much to Gerald Schmitz for his careful editing of any French text. My agent Jackie Kaiser helped me find my way through all advice and my own conflicting notions and desires concerning this book, and to say the right thing as the joy of writing came to me, and went away, and came again. In the end, it turned out that nobody could write my book but me (although lord knows I tried to escape that), and all its shortcomings are my own. My deepest thanks to the people named above, and those not named who know who they are, as do I. Blessings to my deceased husband Peter, wherever he might now be.

To those prairie historians who object that in the early 1880s there were virtually no settlers in the area in question, I can only answer: This is a novel. I give the same answer to the assertion that most French settlers, either from France, Belgium or Québec, chose to settle in groups. Indeed they did, including my own Québecois grandparents (from the Eastern Townships) who settled near St. Isidore de Bellevue around 1911 and who, around 1940 went to Ste. Rose du Lac in Manitoba and finally spent the remainder of their lives in St. Boniface, and my own generation who scattered from one end of the West to the other.

ABOUT THE AUTHOR

Photograph by Teri Posyniak

SHARON BUTALA is the acclaimed author of sixteen books of fiction and non-fiction. Her first book, *Country of the Heart,* was published in 1984 and was shortlisted for the Books in Canada First Novel Award. Since then, her work has been shortlisted for the Commonwealth Prize in the Canadian-Carribean section, as well as for the Governor General's Award. Sharon has also been the recipient of the Marian Engel Award, the Saskatchewan Order of Merit, and the Cheryl and Henry Kloppenburg Award for Literary Excellence, among others. Butala's work has been published in newspapers, magazines, and literary magazines across Canada, and she has given readings around the world. She is an Officer of the Order of Canada.

Butala was born in an outpost hospital in Nipawin, Saskatchewan. After graduating from the University of Saskatchewan, she taught English in Saskatchewan and British Columbia and also taught in Halifax, Nova Scotia. She eventually returned to Saskatoon, before moving to Eastend, Saskatchewan, with her husband Peter Butala in 1976. She currently resides in Calgary, Alberta.

FSC
www.fsc.org
MIX
Paper from
responsible sources
FSC® C016245